The Colsonburg Chronicles

Book 1

When Pathways Cross . . .

By Thomas P. Wright

"Do not be afraid or discouraged,
for the Lord your God is the one who
goes before you. He will be with you;
he will neither fail you nor forsake you."
　　　　　　　　　　–Deuteronomy 31:8 (NLT)

WESTBOW
P R E S S
A DIVISION OF THOMAS NELSON

WestBow Press books may be ordered through booksellers or by contacting:

WestBow Press
A Division of Thomas Nelson
1663 Liberty Drive
Bloomington, IN 47403
www.westbowpress.com
1-(866) 928-1240

Because of the dynamic nature of the Internet, any web addresses or links contained in this book may have changed since publication and may no longer be valid. The views expressed in this work are solely those of the author and do not necessarily reflect the views of the publisher, and the publisher hereby disclaims any responsibility for them.

Any people depicted in stock imagery provided by Thinkstock are models, and such images are being used for illustrative purposes only.

Certain stock imagery © Thinkstock.

ISBN: 978-1-4497-4071-9 (sc)
ISBN: 978-1-4497-4070-2 (e)

Library of Congress Control Number: 2012902642

Printed in the United States of America

WestBow Press rev. date: 03/07/2012

All the characters and events (with the exception of the Superstorm and the
Central Pennsylvania Fourth Fest) in this book are *fictitious*; *any* resemblance
to actual persons is absolutely coincidental and unintentional. The key
places, and the entities associated with them, in which the story takes place,
are *fictitious*; these include, but are not necessarily limited to: Colsonburg,
Laingeville Center, Faith Bible Chapel, Compact, and Blueberry Haven. In
order to give it a realistic feeling, some places are *real*; these include, but
are not limited to: Elmira, Williamsport, Mansfield, Presque Isle, Cortland,
Guilford, Mingoville, Paintersville, Centre Hall, Lewistown, Cumberland
and Centre, Mifflin, and Garrett Counties; Pete fictitiously attended a real
university and Beth a real nursing school. No serious effort has been made (yet)
to connect the story of the Colsonburg Chronicles to the major current events
of the time (for example: 9/11), but it has not been ruled out for future volumes.

This book is dedicated to the memory of my grandparents:

Leslie & Mary Wright
and
George & Helen Slocum

These two couples, though just as human and imperfect as me, still exemplified the values and teamwork that surrounded the main characters in this story and helped make them who they became. My grandparents have done the same for me and many others.

It is in like manner dedicated to memory of
My wife's grandmother

Ernestine Marie Miller

* * * * * * *

Countless thanks are due as well to my parents (James & Judy), my wife (Angie), my children (Brittany, Dominic, Caleb, and Lydia), the churches I have served in (Stevens Point, Antioch [in Ohio], Faith & Stairville, Nittany Valley, and Paintersville), the other churches in my life (Delphi Falls, New Woodstock, Guilford, Wilmore, Huber Heights, Greenwood and especially Smeltzer Road, now Cornerstone), the pastors in my life (Ron Onder, Jim Cooney, Ron Wenzinger, Everett Aldstadt, Ken Nesselroade, Jim Nelson, and the late Jim Caister, and others as well.), Thiel Kauffman of the Friendship Bookstore in Lewistown, the fire companies I have "run" with (#19 Guilford, #16 Walker Township, and #5 Decatur Volunteer), Kay Hamilton CEO of Lewistown Hospital and the Lewistown Hospital School of Nursing, my editor Debby Yoder, and my test readers including Dad, Brittany, and several from Paintersville CMA, to my hometown of Guilford, my teachers (see, I *finally* wrote a book!), and so many, many more (yeah, that probably includes you if you couldn't find yourself in the list above).

* * * * * * *

But the greatest thanks of all go to God the Father, Son, and Holy Spirit, for all He is and has done for me and innumerable others who have been willing to give Him a *serious* chance. I firmly believe this book was His calling; it is my humble privilege simply to offer it to you, the reader, from a pastor's heart, as a help, an encouragement and a thought provoker.

Contents

Preface

When I was initially asked to describe this book to someone, I called it first of all, *contemporary.* I believe myself called to write neither about the past nor about a culture or sect that is safely distant to me and probably to you. Let's face it (with all due respect, and much is due) there are plenty of books about the Amish and the nineteenth century; I will leave it to those authors to handle those things; they do it very well; I could not. So what follows is what I have predictably dubbed as "right here, right now."

It is *fiction*, that is, a story, not a manual or a lecture or a biography or autobiography.

It is also *Christian*, evangelical even. I hope that won't stop you from reading it. I am not proselytizing with this book; I am not attempting to argue with anyone, nor am I minimizing the faith that is so very dear to me. If you share my convictions, you will certainly enjoy reading this and saying "amen." If you do not, or suspect you do not, I hope you will read with the intention of simply enjoying the story and understanding, from an inside perspective, an important part of our American society. From there you can take it or leave it but at least try to appreciate it, even respect it. If it changes you, so be it.

It is also *realistic.* Many have been brainwashed into thinking that people, especially young people like the ones in this story, simply do not exist today. Some have even suggested they never existed, even in the "old days." I could not disagree enough. These are *real* folks in the sense that there is a healthy, strong part of our contemporary society that has actually lived by the same convictions that the heroes of this book lived by. This is true of young people (ages sixteen to twenty, in particular) as well as their parents and grandparents. I know this because I have met them, lived among them, ministered to them, and dare say I have been one of them, though I am older than I used to be (go figure!). I fear this group of evangelical Christians may not truly be a majority in America today (admittedly, I have a very narrow view of what an evangelical is), but they are a segment that must be acknowledged and taken into account, even learned from.

What is also realistic about it is the set of problems that the characters encounter; life includes both joy and heartbreak. It includes the fact that people go astray and make poor, even stupid, choices. People often hurt one another, though they shouldn't. Christians struggle with temptation and sometimes fail in the struggle but victory and restoration *is* possible. Our expectations are usually not met; our dreams usually do not come true just the way we dreamed them. But, thankfully, God is bigger than our expectations and our dreams; often He gives us different, better dreams than we ever had for ourselves. Even when disappointment devastates us, He can pick up the pieces and show the way forward from that point. God heals broken hearts, broken relationships, and warped minds. This book is an extended "case study" in all of these things, and more.

Since it is realistic it is also poignant, actually downright blunt at a couple of points. Fear not. Everything is appropriate but some of the themes are serious ones and sometimes not dealt with as much as they ought to be. I made a commitment *not* to back down from the hard subjects (see *Lessons at Camp, Pete's Big Day, The Finish Line,* and *Capturing the High Ground*). These things are not written about for their shock value; it is because they are real and important issues that I feel strongly about and have a huge impact on our society—more than what most will ever admit. I have made sure that it is all approached from a tasteful, Christian/ Biblical direction. This is not written as a children's book (for those under about twelve) though your children could certainly read it if you judge them ready for it. But if you are reading only for the warm fuzzies of it or in order to escape reality, then please buy a different book. But it is not an opera, either—it ends well (and there *are* many warm fuzzies, by the way). Remember: in the end, the good guys *always* win!

My heart in this story is especially, though not exclusively, for the teens and young adults of our society. The choices made today *will* inevitably affect the future. Some will be good choices that will be helpful. Some will be poor choices. Some will bring ruin to self, and possibly others too, forever, if they are not rethought and reversed. But this book is also a reminder that God is real and is always there, even when we do not at first perceive Him, even after we have messed everything up. The choices we make will work to either include His loving presence and His generous help or exclude both.

This book is only a start. The dream God has given me is for a *series* of books—*The Colsonburg Chronicles.* The second book is already developing. Because it is a series of books, you will find some "loose ends" that would otherwise represent just poor writing on my part (see the ending of the chapter *Christmas, Wilmor Style* for an example. There is a loose end in *Back on Call,* too). If you wonder why a person, place, or thing has been mentioned but not further developed it is because this represents only a preliminary introduction of someone or something that will be dealt with later.

Also, in terms of *style,* I have been intentional about using a *variety* of writing styles. These styles include dialogue, description, and narration as seems to best fit the present need in the story. The chapters (or as I often characterize them, episodes) are organized as basically chronological but also topical therefore the reader will often experience a phenomenon I call "telescoping." Telescoping is when one episode overlaps, in terms of time, with the one before it. What separates the two is that the topic or focus of the episodes is what differs. This will happen first thing in the relationship between *South Meets North* and *58 Elm Street*; both episodes take place in the same two-plus year time frame but each one focuses on a different set of characters. This also happens in groups of chapters. As an example the episodes *The P.K.* through *Rhonda* overlap in terms of time with *Up on the Farm* through *Geoff.* So now when you see that you will know that "I meant to do that."

Finally, *When Pathways Cross...* is written in two parts. I almost wrote it as two separate books; the second one would have been *From Bitter to Sweet*. But I could not find a compelling reason for you to read the first one, except that you might trust me that it would all make sense in the second one. So I went with a two-parter preceded by a hopefully "teasing" prologue. If it seems too slow for your taste, then simply express to the second part; I don't think you'll get far before you feel compelled to go back to finish the first one.

I have had the time of my life writing this book. I hope you enjoy reading it, even a little bit.

> --Thomas P. ("P.T.") Wright
> December, 2011
> Lewistown, Pennsylvania

Prologue

January 1, 2010, 12:01 AM
The New Year Party
At the home of Fred & Meredith Holt
On North Main Street

Pete stood next to her; he looked down at her and watched her for a moment. She was laughing with the rest, her smile wide and glowing. She looked up at him as she laughed and he smiled down at her. It was good to see her again and to see her so full of joy, despite everything she had been through. In his mind he journeyed back to that horrid March day in Lewistown when she was so broken and lost; the contrast, what God had done, was so evident.

The experience of seeing her that way also reminded him of just how far he had come since that life-altering August afternoon almost four and a half years ago. He had never been the same since.

...He simply looked at her and smiled as he said, "Happy New Year!"

"Happy New Year to you, Pete," she reciprocated, smiling up at him."

--from *The New Year*

Over twenty years earlier...

Mother's Day, 1989
At Faith Bible Chapel
In Western Kentucky (near the Tennessee line)

The young family stood at the front of the church where the middle aisle reached the altar rail. The husband, Pastor Dan Morton, stood with his wife, Virginia (everyone called her "Ginny"), their oldest daughter, Patty, and their son, Billy. Patty was five and Billy, clinging bashfully to his mother's skirt, was just two years old. Their newest addition, Elizabeth, now only a month old, was in her mother's arms as they faced Pastor Dan's District Superintendent, visiting all the way from Cincinnati in order to conduct this infant dedication service. Dan was called to Faith Bible almost six years ago and was dearly loved and appreciated by the church.

Dan and Ginny had grown up together in Garret County, Maryland. After high school Ginny went to work to raise money for her college tuition; her parents were good people but not well-endowed or skilled financially so she would have to pay her own way. Dan grew up in a large but well-to-do family with five other siblings; unlike Ginny, though, he was raised without church or faith but embraced Christianity at a youth rally a friend had invited him to when he was just sixteen.

Dan went to college in northern Georgia to begin preparing for the ministry; his parents paying the costs, though they did not share his faith or understand his dreams. He and Ginny fell in love during the course of his breaks from school. They were married the summer after his college graduation and then were off to New York State for seminary. Ginny worked fulltime to pay their way as the Morton support had been discontinued. In the end she never went to college; Patty was born nine months after Dan's seminary graduation.

Dan was a somewhat stocky looking man, built a little like a wrestler, not overly tall but strong. He was clean shaven and already growing bald in the middle of his dark brown hair. Ginny was the same height as her husband, relatively thin and very attractive, with long straight red hair. Patty shared her dad's brown hair, though hers was long and Billy had his mother's red hair, though his was short. Elizabeth was virtually bald but had the beginnings of red hair, too.

Having read several relevant Scripture passages, the Superintendent began reading from his handbook, "Throughout the ages, godly parents have presented their children to the Lord in dedication. You follow a noble heritage."[1] A few moments later, after several other important words, he took Elizabeth and held her in his arms as she watched him with wide, alarmed eyes. He began the conclusion to the service with the prayer, "Elizabeth Virginia Morton, I dedicate you to God in the Name of the Father, and of the Son, and of the Holy Spirit...May your young life be nurtured and matured under the gracious influence of the Holy Spirit [and the Word of God]. May God protect you physically and deliver you from temptation. May He early call you into His kingdom and ultimately into His service, using you to advance His glory and to hasten the coming of our Lord Jesus Christ. Amen."[2]

Ginny's parents wanted to be there, but her mother was too sick from the chemotherapy and could not make the long trip across West Virginia and most of Kentucky. At least the news was encouraging for her as the tumors were definitely shrinking. Dan's parents informed him that they had already attended two of "those things" and did not see the necessity in doing so again, especially on Mother's Day. Come June, though, they wanted to know (again) if Dan and his family were coming to Maryland for Father's Day.

But one relative was there, Dan's Aunt Cynthia. Ever since he had been a teenager Cynthia had been a rock of moral support for him and then also for Ginny. Cynthia had come to spend the whole weekend. She took Dan and the family to a nearby buffet for lunch—on her. While Dan and Ginny did not normally eat out on Sundays, they also did not want to make Cynthia feel bad either. If it had not been for Cynthia the whole day would have been very much just the usual routine again—just the four, now five, of them.

Also on Mothers Day, 1989
At the Colsonburg Community Church
In Pennsylvania's "Northern Tier"

The young couple had nervously brought their first child, a son named Peter James Archer, to the front of the church to stand facing their pastor, Ron Zeckman. The father, John Archer, Jr. grew up eight miles west of Colsonburg in a little crossroads village of three-hundred fifty folks called Laingeville Center. His father, Jack, (John Sr.) was a dairy farmer there, but John did not share his father's passion for farming and was making his mark as a carpenter. He met his wife, Joanie Wilmor, while working for a contractor doing renovation work on her home church near Cortland, New York. Joanie was the church's part time secretary and John was a frequent liaison to the church office on behalf of his boss.

He became interested in her over the course of the long project and, though she liked him, she would not have anything to do with him unless he professed to be a born-again Christian, as she was. He made that choice at the conclusion of the rededication service for that same church and they were married there within a year. Until that year was over, it seemed John would wear a set of ruts in the roads between his home and hers. She returned to Laingeville Center with him after the wedding and honeymoon to help him start a contractor's business of his own.

In the meantime, John left his mainline church roots in the Laingeville Center First United Church and he and his new wife began attending what Jack sarcastically called "that holy roller church" on the south side of nearby Colsonburg. But they were actually relatively calm; the real "holy rollers" were at the new Grace Celebration Center along the highway well *north* of town.

John grew spiritually strong under the passionate Biblical teaching at 3C, the nickname for the Colsonburg Community Church, quickly catching up to his wife's level of spiritual maturity, with both continuing to grow year on year.

It troubled Jack that neither of his sons, nor even his daughter, loved the family farm enough to make it their dream, too. His younger son, Jim, had taken a job in State College and was living there now as he pursued a university education. His daughter, Judy, would soon marry a heating and cooling technician from the Wellsboro area.

John was tall, trim, and strong. His hair was brown and he donned a matching mustache. Joanie was shorter but typical in height for a woman. She had medium-length wavy light brown hair. Both had brown eyes. They had bought the dilapidated old Merchant home on Elm Street—one of only two side streets in LC, short for Laingeville Center. The house was next door to the Lainge Township Volunteer Fire Company. John was renovating the house, making it a showcase of his abilities, as well as a comfortable home. In the meantime he and Joanie rented a small apartment over Holmes' Country Market at the center of tiny LC.

Reverend Zeckman read serious words from the same handbook being used by the Superintendent down in Kentucky that very same morning, "...While dedication is a worthy act," he read, "you must understand that it offers no saving virtue. Dedication does not guarantee your child's salvation, for this requires a personal commitment that each one must make on his own...Salvation is obtained by grace through faith in Jesus Christ as personal Savior and upon repentance...."[3] He later offered a spontaneous and heartfelt prayer for the new baby and his young parents.

Jack sat on the front pew with his arms crossed over his chest. His face was likewise "cross." He thought about what a disgrace this was; it was no kind of a baptism at all. There was no water, no liturgy, only "made up" prayers, the pastor wore nothing but a three-piece suit, and *NO* Communion! His wife, Dorothy, however, sat next to him in another world, as it were. She was glowing at just the very idea of her *first* grandchild. That's all that mattered to her! On the other side of the aisle sat Joanie's parents also glowing with approval and excitement.

A family gathering followed on the side lawn of the farmhouse, almost a mile north of LC on Slocum Road, one of the two roads that made the main intersection near the middle of the village. The other road was simply called State Road. Everyone was there, as usual, including Joanie's parents, Jim up from State College, and Judy's fiancé, Jerald Smith.

The Archer family was very close and gathered together at every opportunity. Almost every event, though, took place at the farm. As a dairy farmer, Jack worked long unrelenting hours every single day without any variation at all. He had to be there to milk his cows at the same exact times. Jack and Dorothy had not even been on a vacation since their honeymoon. Without John or Jim to help, his predicament only deepened as he aged but he secretly hoped he saw a future for the farm now in young Peter.

Part 1

The Years Before
Lunch in Lewistown

Prologue to the section
The first Saturday of August, 2008

"Look at them," Ginny said to Joanie, indicating the table where Beth, Pat, and Pete were seated, "They're so grown up."

"Where is the time going?" Joanie wondered in response....

Before leaving, Dan and Pete walked together along the beach for a while.

--from *Presque Isle*

South Meets North

Moving Day

It was a Friday morning in late June and even though the sun had not yet risen, it was hot. It had been hot all night. The evening before, the Mortons had eaten take-out pizza from paper plates so there would be no dishes to wash.

The moving truck had been packed the day before under the hot, blazing sun and crushing humidity. Only the mattresses and a change of clothes for each one had been left out. All the good-byes had been said on Thursday night. Now Dan and Ginny loaded the mattresses into the last open spot in the back of the truck while Patty, Billy, and Elizabeth said good-bye to their rooms—the only rooms they had ever known. There were many tears shed as they drove away in the pre-dawn darkness. Dan drove the truck, towing the car behind, and Ginny drove the van, the children and the dog riding with her. It would become a familiar arrangement over the years.

Soon the orange-red sun began to appear above the horizon and burn through the thick haze of summer. The highway was steadily filling up with morning commuters with cars speeding up every on-ramp to join the Mortons and the rest of traffic. These were the days before cell phones were common so Dan and Ginny worked hard to stay within sight of each other at all times, using signals from their headlights, taillights, and turn signals to communicate with one another, based on a predetermined set of codes.

Breakfast was in Elizabethtown. It was so hot already that one's skin seemed to burn just on the short walk from the air-conditioned vehicles to the fast-food restaurant. The breakfast was short as the drive would be long and the dog could not stay in the parked van for long without a walk or the air conditioning back on again. Elizabeth informed the rest of the family that this town belonged to her and they all had to do what she said while they were there. Everyone laughed and played along as much as they dared.

The family drove all day. It was quiet for Dan in the truck but torturous for Ginny in the van. If she heard "are we there yet?" or "how much longer?" or "is this Pennsylvania?" just *one... more... time...*.

North and east they trekked to a place seen only once before—through Louisville, Cincinnati, Columbus, Akron, Youngstown, and, well, the forests and mountains of Pennsylvania.

Darkness was setting in again as Dan followed the signs to Williamsport from Interstate 80. Then it was north from there. The signs told of places called Mansfield and Corning, N.Y. It was completely dark when the headlights caught a simple Department of Transportation sign, along a rural highway that read "Borough of Colsonburg."

"We're in Colsonburg, kids," Ginny cheered over her shoulder, exhausted but relieved. The children had, ironically, all fallen asleep.

Almost immediately a large white sign to the left read "Colsonburg Community Church." It already had "Pastor: Dan Morton" on the bottom line. Almost a block later, Dan turned left onto West Luzerne Avenue where the parsonage was located on the left side about five hundred feet up from South Main Street.

Dan and Ginny had planned to simply unload the mattresses and wait for help in the morning. But two surprises awaited them. First, the lights were on in the parsonage, cars parked all around it, and the house was full of men and women and some teenagers waiting for them so they could help them unload the truck. The second surprise was the chill in the air; someone said it was in the forties; no insects chirped or called in the cold Pennsylvania night like they did back in Kentucky the night before.

Re-introductions accompanied by smiles and handshakes were shared all around the empty living room that smelled of relatively fresh paint and carpet shampoo. One of the women set out a tray of cookies and crackers and pitchers of red punch. A man handed Dan a check as Dan handed him the receipt for the moving truck. Then the man, smiling, gave Dan a gift certificate to the local IGA so the family could get some groceries the next day. (It had closed at nine o'clock.) He also gave Dan a set of several keys. The men then moved the boxes and furniture to the various rooms and the women helped to unpack whatever Ginny asked them to. Two teenaged girls showed the children around the house and kept them from being in the way of the men.

It was very late. Everyone was exhausted and the children were nervous about their new surroundings. So, at Ginny's suggestion, Dan moved all the mattresses back to the living room floor and the five had another "camp out" together. Everyone slept late on Saturday morning.

First Day

The morning air was filled with the non-stop chorus of singing birds. The bright, gentle sun filled the house, the yard and the neighborhood, which was marked by tree-lined streets and modest but well-kept homes. Somewhere a gas-powered weed trimmer was running. Back in Kentucky the lawn had already yielded to the summer heat and turned a dead-looking brown but here the grass was rich, lush, and very green.

Dan left in the car to find the market, gift certificate in hand. Ginny unpacked a few boxes. The children, under eight-year-old Patty's watchful eye, explored the new yard. The chill was gone and the air was light, pleasant and smelled like honeysuckle.

The children first surveyed their new domain from the patio. The church and parsonage shared a large sloping lawn of about four acres at the southern edge of town. There was also a picnic pavilion and a small playground. Straight ahead, across the wide lawn, woods began at the edge of a steep hill. A school, the children had been told it would be their school, was visible behind the house and well to the right. The church was visible behind, to the left and slightly downhill, opposite from the school. A stone path went from the parsonage to the back door of the church. In the distance beyond the church, large, forest-covered hills rose up to meet the blue sky. There were neighbors on either side of the parsonage, and up and down West Luzerne Avenue.

As they ventured onto the grounds, the children remembered the church as they walked around it. It was a generous-sized building covered in white vinyl siding and a charcoal-grey shingled roof that was high and steep. This church had no spire or bell tower, like the one in Kentucky did. The section with the classrooms and fellowship hall was parallel to South Main Street and set well away from the road. The sanctuary section was perpendicular to the first, making it an "L" shaped structure. A paved parking lot filled the open area of the "L." Clear glass windows looked into the classrooms and fellowship hall; the sanctuary windows were not quite clear but instead frosted, making them translucent.

Across South Main Street from the church, a plain-looking but large garage had written above the several doors in large characters: "Colsonburg Ladder & Hose Company." Below that line it said in smaller characters: "Station 16." Upon her sister's request, Patty read the words. Elizabeth commented that it was funny that they made both ladders *and* hoses in the same factory. Billy tried to correct her, letting her know that it was a fire station not a factory. Elizabeth argued back and forth with him but later Dan settled the matter once and for all; it was a fire station.

They walked the long path back to the low ranch-style parsonage. It looked small but had a finished basement, making it surprisingly spacious.

Inside the decisions had been made: As the oldest, Patty would have a downstairs room in the basement and the rest would sleep in the three bedrooms on the main floor.

The kitchen was on the back wall and opened directly into the dining room. A long living room took up the space in front of the kitchen and dining area. A hall led to the bedrooms and bathroom. Downstairs was Patty's room, a guest room, all-purpose room, study, and utility room. There was no front porch like the one on the rented farmhouse in Kentucky but there was a large patio off the dining room looking over the spacious open lawn. Shrubs and trees dotted the front and side lawns.

Several visitors stopped throughout the day. One church deaconess brought a tray of hoagies from the Colsonburg Deli in downtown Colsonburg. Another deaconess brought a crock pot of homemade chili made with venison and some cornbread for supper. Whenever possible something was removed from a box and set up somewhere in the home on an at least trial basis.

First Sunday

Though still surrounded by boxes, some opened but others still taped shut, there was now a table and chairs plus a refrigerator with food on Sunday morning. Dan was in the church office also full of boxes (mostly of books) by six o'clock; this was his customary practice for each Sunday morning. By seven-thirty the children and Ginny were eating cereal together. Two of them were showered with two more to go.

Billy and Elizabeth would be in the same Sunday School class until fall when Billy would be promoted to the next older class. Though a little shy and reserved toward the "new kids," each child in the class politely said "hi" to Billy and Elizabeth. The two felt strange and out of place trying to imagine these new kids as their friends from now on. One boy, Peter Archer, kept watching them, especially Elizabeth, since she did most of the talking.

Finally Peter could hold it back no longer and finally blurted out the question that was stuck in his mind.

"How come you talk funny?"

Little Peter Archer had never heard a southern accent before. Mrs. Schumacher was horrified but before she could scold Peter, Elizabeth wrinkled up her face and said sarcastically *and* with the most pronounced southern "drawl" heard in Colsonburg in years, "I don't talk funny, *you* do!"

The southern accent would wear off long before Elizabeth's disdain for Peter. Over time her feelings about him were only made stronger by his practice of calling her "Ketchup Head," referring to her red hair, and "Spot," referring to her numerous freckles. Elizabeth, however, was no delicate flower and Peter had bitten off more than he could chew when he started into her. Billy did nothing to defend her. Instead he became Peter's friend.

The worship was robust and uplifting. For his first Sunday sermon at 3C Dan gave his testimony of how he became a Christian even after growing up in a home where they never went to church or even mentioned religion. He included how a friend's invitation was key to that choice, how he came to see God wanted him to be a pastor, how God directed him and Ginny (a childhood friend and neighbor) to fall in love and be married, and decide first to go to seminary, then to Kentucky and now to Colsonburg. The people listened attentively, frequently nodding or occasionally responding with a gentle "amen" or "praise the Lord" to something he had said.

The congregation had a potluck dinner under the pavilion afterward. In the evening service Ginny gave her testimony. She told of coming to her own personal relationship with God, how being from a Christian family was no substitute for her own commitment to Christ. A sundae and floats social followed in the fellowship hall as it was too cool to eat ice cream outside.

The Seasons

The hot weather eventually found them again even in northern Pennsylvania but it would last only a couple of days at a time and then subside. Fall came earlier in Pennsylvania and then the children experienced their first white Christmas. The snows were frequent instead of only once or twice all winter long and the snow stayed on the ground for weeks at a time instead of days or even only hours. In February it snowed over one foot deep in one storm. The children had never tried to stand or walk in snow that deep before. They tried to make a snowman but the snow was too powdery to pack so instead they went sledding with the other neighborhood children on the steep open hill behind the middle school as they did many times each winter. But the days were generally cloudy and cold. Everyone missed the chilly but comparatively bright winter days of Kentucky.

Strangely, they never missed more than one day or even just one *half* day of school because of snow. Every time it snowed, even an inch in Kentucky, Patty missed days' worth of school as they waited for the ice and snow on the side roads to melt, sometimes with the help of salt. But then in March something called the "Superstorm" came through Pennsylvania and dumped about three feet of snow with mountainous drifts that left everyone digging out for days and school closed for a week. It happened on a weekend and it was the only time 3C did not have a Sunday morning service because of snow. Colsonburg Borough workers faithfully plowed and salted the streets all the way to the curbs after every snowfall instead of waiting for it to melt, which could have taken weeks or even all winter long to happen.

Spring came slowly and was marked by mud, dirt and overflowing creeks and rivers. Then all of a sudden the lawn needed mowing.

VBS

For the next two years Vacation Bible School was held in late July. Meredith Holt and Holly Corbin took turns as Directors. That particular year Meredith, another former southerner with just a *slight* hint of an accent now, was the director.

All went well until Wednesday. Peter and Elizabeth's battles had also gone on now for those two whole years. Peter would tease or even insult Elizabeth. She would yell at him or even try to hit him. Both would tell on each other and both got in a lot of trouble at home for it all.

All the children were seated in a circle on the lawn beside the church as eighteen-year-old Mitchell Holt, college-bound in the fall, supervised them. Elizabeth was "it" and walked around the circle touching each head saying "duck" as she did so. Everyone thought she would never finally say "goose;" it seemed she had circled them a *thousand* times.

At last she said "goose" as she intentionally pushed on Peter's head so forcefully he almost tipped over but he was ready and on his feet in a flash. As he reached out to tag her, though, he tripped and fell forward. Somehow one of those red braids ended up in his fist as he tumbled, yanking Elizabeth's head back and pulling her down on her backside.

Elizabeth could take it no more. As her scalp throbbed, she sprang up and screamed in blood-curdling tones, "You did that on purpose, Peter Archer!" Before Mitchell could reach her, she kicked Peter in the shin—hard. Even as Mitchell reached for her, she kicked Peter's other shin. Peter lay holding his legs and crying as Mitchell lifted Elizabeth up and away from him, lest something even worse happen next.

That noon in a corner of the parking lot two sets of parents and two five-year-olds, one with bruised legs, had a very serious and very uncomfortable talk about getting along, apologizing, forgiving, and *not* taking revenge. Each child mumbled something to the other about being sorry and forgiving the other one. All four parents were agreed in their dealings with the children, putting up a united front.

The next day in the closing assembly Meredith explained again about being "saved": admitting you've done bad things, asking Jesus to forgive all those sins, and deciding to live differently afterward. She asked, as the children's heads were bowed, if anyone wanted to make that decision. Everyone's eyes were supposed to be closed so Peter lifted his head and looked all around. He saw a hand raised up high; it was attached to a red-haired, befreckled girl with her eyes pinched closed and her feet alternately sweeping forward and back, not quite touching the floor. Looking up, he noticed Meredith glaring at him so he quickly put his head back down but kept his eyes open.

The next day Peter congratulated Elizabeth on her decision declaring, "You sure needed saving!" Elizabeth limited her reaction to simply sticking her tongue out at him. Peter, however, would wait years to make that same choice; he later envied Elizabeth for settling that matter so early on in her life.

Elizabeth's more measured responses diminished Peter's interest in teasing her and the outward contention mostly subsided. Elizabeth and Peter avoided each other as much as possible; this was not easy as Peter and Billy often hung out together after church. When the two rivals were near each other, they simply ignored one another. Fortunately they went to different elementary schools.

58 Elm Street

The Visit

"Hi Pastor, John Archer here, Joanie said you guys needed directions to our place for lunch on Friday."

Dan had been making a sweep of visits through the church families during his first year to try to fully acquaint himself with as many of them as possible. It was September and he was only halfway finished with the project. Billy and Patty would be in school when he, Ginny, and Elizabeth joined John, Joanie, Peter, and baby Patrick at the Archer home.

"Yeah....Let me get a pen....Okay, go ahead."

"You'll want to go right from West Luzerne onto South Main. As soon as you leave the borough, take the first right. That will take you up the Narrows. Remember, it's steep and curving, so be careful. Follow that road for about two miles to the "T" and turn left onto East State Road. In about six miles you'll see the Lainge Township Municipal Building on the right; that is at the edge of the village. The next right turn will be Elm Street. Follow it back and when it turns ninety degrees to the left, *you* go ninety degrees to the right—right into our driveway, Fifty-eight Elm Street. The fire house will be straight ahead of you as you turn into the driveway. See you at noon."

It was a pleasant day for a drive. The road up the Narrows, as they called it, swayed back and forth as it climbed the gorge and ultimately up the ridge that was the backdrop for the borough. Lainge's Creek tumbled down through the rocks to the Morton's right on its way to join Colson Creek, and a thick canopy of oaks, maples and other leafy trees darkened the houseless stretch for about a mile. At the top of the Narrows, the road burst out into the mostly open farmland dotted with houses, barns, silos, and herds of black and white Holstein cows.

Along State Road the woods came down the rolling hills to meet the road from time to time. Otherwise it was alfalfa, corn, soybeans, pastures, and more Holsteins. Lainge's Creek meandered through the countryside well to the right, snaking its way through the fields and woods.

Twice the family had to follow a slow moving tractor. One pulled a wagon full of fresh bales of hay but it soon turned in to a farm. But the second one was pulling a hay mower. The mower was offset from the tractor causing the two pieces of equipment to take up all of one lane and what tiny shoulder there was along the already narrow road *plus* part of the oncoming lane; they followed it *all the way* to Elm Street at a staggering fifteen miles per hour.

The Archers' home was a relatively long two-story house, over a hundred years old. It sat parallel to Lainge's Creek which then ran diagonally under the turn in Elm Street. A gravel driveway separated the house and the creek. The gable end faced the street but was partially shrouded by two great maple trees. The wood trim around the windows, doors, roof, and corners was bulky but ornate and painted white; the siding was painted a very light blue. A porch with white round pillar-like posts and a railing ran all the way across the front. A bay window on the right side went up both stories and looked out over a generous level side lawn. A high-pitched slate-shingled roof covered the whole structure. A garage and shop in an old barn-like building was to the rear and ripening soybean fields stretched out beyond the back yard.

Joanie answered the front door, little bald Patrick on her arm watching the guests suspiciously. She led them back through the house. The front door entered into a hall with an open stairway and banister on the left. To the right, through a set of French doors, was the living room with its floor-to-ceiling bay window. Straight back they went through the dining room with a great picture window also looking to the right (which was also to the south), a stripe of stained glass gracing the top twelve inches of the window. An office was to the left and a spacious eat-in kitchen was directly behind the dining room with a serving window between the two.

The trim inside was as fine as the outside and painted a glossy white. Wallpaper covered every room and shiny hardwood floors stretched from wall to wall reflecting the bright light from the tall windows. In the dining room two photographs told the tale. One was of a dilapidated, messy house with weeds all around it; it was labeled "July 4, 1987." The other one was the same home, this home in its present state, with the label "July 4, 1992."

Joanie noticed Ginny's interest in the photographs; looking at the pictures she explained, "John was twenty-five and living at home when we got married so he had a lot of money saved. We bought this house at auction and he restored it. It took almost every weeknight and Saturday but it was worth it. It sharpened his skills, gave him an example of his abilities, and we got a charming home out of it all. The upstairs isn't finished yet—just our room and the boys' room—but he's still working away at it."

The kitchen was spacious and modern with two full walls of counters and cabinets. The appliances carefully segmented the oak cabinetry and laminated countertops. A door to the left led to a back porch, facing the driveway and the creek, and another on the back wall led to a laundry and pantry area. Going into the laundry they immediately were taken out a side door and onto the open south lawn where John was grilling some chicken strips.

At the picnic table under the shade of a black locust tree, the adults shared back and forth about their lives, past and present, the church, and all the "important" things adults talk about over food. Joanie helped Patrick with his meal and then put him down to play in a portable crib. Peter and Elizabeth finished eating and were off to play on the swing set and in the sandbox but they could not agree on the rules and continually returned to the "supreme court" of their parents for decisions on their disputes.

"Dad wanted my brother and/or I to take over the farm," John began to explain about his chosen vocation, "but it just isn't for me, or my brother. Dad works literally *all the time*. I had never been on a vacation until our honeymoon. Dad's livelihood is completely controlled by the price of milk and what you pay in the store is not necessarily tied to what he gets paid for *his* product. On the other hand, I work four ten-hour days a week, set my own rates, have weekends off and can take a week of vacation when I want to. I do my estimating on Fridays and if I don't have too much to do I take the rest of the day off. For me, this is ideal, compared to what I grew up with. I know Dad's disappointed and afraid for the farm's future but it's just not the way it used to be."

Dan and Ginny listened with interest to John's description of his work and his testimony of finding a life with Christ in just a moment of time in a place called Cortland, New York, not to mention finding Joanie there, too—the "icing on the cake" he called her, smiling her direction. She smiled back. Joanie, John bragged, was his receptionist, secretary, and treasurer in the business—the "brains" behind it all.

Joanie and Ginny were almost instantly as sisters. Though Ginny was actually several years older than Joanie, they had much in common, including a love of cooking and baking. They traded several tips and ideas across the table before going inside to look at some of Joanie's favorite recipes and gadgets.

But Dan and Ginny needed to be home before Patty and Billy returned from school. So the extended lunch was concluded with plans to "do it again sometime."

The Children
Two years later John and Joanie added a girl, Amy, to their family. Having added a girl now they would stop having more children. John could no longer afford to buy evermore expensive health insurance for himself and his family, so three would already be more than they could

technically afford. They literally prayed for everyone to stay healthy and kept putting savings back to pay for visits to the doctor, medicine, and unplanned emergencies.

Over the years Peter and his siblings walked to the Lainge Township Elementary school together. They walked down Elm Street, then right onto State Road, past the small park and soldiers' memorial, then left onto School Street. At the corner with State Road, Peter would meet up with his pal Bryan who lived next door to the Township Municipal Building. Starting with sixth grade the kids would meet a bus at the elementary school and travel into Colsonburg to attend the middle school and then, later, the high school.

Changes

One winter's evening as the family finished supper around the kitchen table, the phone rang. Ginny called from another room for John to please answer it.

As he listened to the caller, John's face became very serious and he spoke in somber tones, so low the children could not hear. He hung up the phone and went the direction his wife had gone a few moments ago. Nothing could be heard of their conversation. John returned to the table where eight-year-old Peter, six-year-old Patrick, and three-year-old Amy had just finished eating.

"That was Uncle Roy from up near Delphi Falls. You kids know how Grandpa Wilmor has been sick for a while and even been in the hospital a couple days?"

They all nodded in acknowledgment. John's voice and lip were quivering uncontrollably. With breaking words he finally found a way to say what had to be said.

"Grandpa couldn't get better so he went to be with Jesus today," John explained.

There were plenty of tears. John was hurting too but he had to be strong for his wife and kids. The next day he called his current clients and explained the need for a couple of days away from their projects. Everyone understood, which was a relief. Joanie left with Amy in the morning and the rest joined her the next day for the viewing and then the funeral in Cortland.

Things were normal again for a couple years. Then one day when the children returned home from school their Dad was sitting on the front porch—an unusual sight that early on a weekday.

"Come up and sit down, guys," John instructed them. Again he was the bearer of bad news.

"Grandma Wilmor was taken ill today and they took her to the hospital," he started very seriously, even quietly, "but it was too late to help her and she's with the Lord now." All the children were crying. John lifted Amy to his lap. "Mom left a couple hours ago to help her brothers get things ready."

The next day he and the children left for Cortland and yet another funeral.

Grandpa and Grandma Wilmor were quite a bit older than Grandpa and Grandma Archer, as Joanie was the youngest and John was the oldest among their siblings. Grandma Wilmor's passing changed a lot of things in the extended family as each branch of the Wilmor clan became more independent of the rest, now only seeing each other a couple of times a year. But little changed for the Archer family, except that the kids kept growing and becoming more individual and independent with each passing year.

The holidays were all spent with Grandpa and Grandma Archer now. There was the annual family trip to someplace like Niagara Falls, Washington, D.C., or the beach on Maryland's coast.

After a terrific overnight thunderstorm all five of the Archers might be found stacked up on the queen-sized bed in the master bedroom along with the two cats. But one by one the kids outgrew this need.

Early every morning John left for his work, Joanie got the kids ready for school and every evening all five gathered around the kitchen table for a homemade supper. In between Joanie answered the phone, often taking requests for estimates for John, she did the bookkeeping for the business, and kept up with the cleaning and cooking. There was plenty of talking and laughter over those suppers. Sundays and Wednesday nights were church down in Colsonburg without fail—sun, rain, or snow—every time the doors were open.

Errands

It was not uncommon for the Archer family to spend the latter part of Saturday morning in Colsonburg. They would make the rounds to the bank, the post office, other stores as needed and the market. Often they would finish with a lunch at the silver and neon-clad Colsonburg Diner—a favorite spot for them and countless others, if not there, then the Pancake Palace or the Log Cabin Buffet. It was normally their only meal out all week long.

After turning left onto South Main Street at the end of the Narrows, the borough of Colsonburg began to take shape quickly. Two-lane Main Street went straight through from one end to the other, the various side streets (most called avenues) joining at mostly four-way intersections.

The buildings went from scattered to plentiful—mostly houses—older the closer they were to downtown. Then businesses began to mix in and a church of one denomination or another was never far from sight. The center of town was at the intersection of Main and Susquehanna Streets.

As one approached this intersection, the only corner with a traffic signal, the Square, bordered by Main Street, Susquehanna Street, the Presbyterian Church, and the Episcopal Church, was situated to the right. It was dotted with trees, shrubs, a soldiers' memorial, and a Victorian-style gazebo right in the center, pathways leading to it from each corner of the Square, crossing, as it were, in the center of that gazebo. The lawn was perfectly manicured and decorated with annual flowers. At Christmastime the gazebo and the trees were draped with strings of simple petite white lights and a Nativity was set at the corner of the two streets (the square was not public—it was owned by the Episcopalians). From Memorial Day to Independence Day, flags flew throughout the tiny park. A single lane, one-way street came around the square past the two churches' front doors.

The block past the square was the business block with three and four-storied buildings constructed directly against each other on either side of now North Main Street. On the left the buildings were of wood construction but on the right they were all brick; that was due to the 1909 Colsonburg Block Fire that wiped out all the wood frame buildings on the right. As a result, the Colsonburg Ladder and Hose Company, a volunteer fire department, was founded in 1910. The Colsonburg Diner was right after this block on the right side with the Colsonburg IGA next door.

If one turned right onto Susquehanna Street and traveled just a little over two blocks, he would cross Colson Creek after which Susquehanna Street quickly disappeared into a set of winding rural roads on the so-called "East Side." If, on the other hand, one turned *left* onto Susquehanna Street, he would find that the street began to go up a gentle hill and end at a "T" intersection with School Street, the historic red brick Colsonburg Area High School straight ahead of him overlooking the borough. The Colsonburg Area Middle School was next door, to the left, and the Colson Township Elementary School was four blocks to the left at the end of School Street where it intersected West Luzerne Avenue, not far from the Colsonburg Community Church's parsonage.

Life in Laingeville Center, Colsonburg and the surrounding county, was, like the two locales, simple and plain but also surprisingly satisfying and full of activity. It seemed like a throw-back to a bygone era but it was actually a right-here, right-now life, still very much a reality in most of rural America in the 1990's. Larger towns like Elmira and Williamsport offered malls, theatres, shopping, and other excitement. But the big cities of New York, Philadelphia, and Pittsburgh were a multiple hours' drive away. There were no interstates but rumor had it that U.S. Route Fifteen, the closest major north-south route, would one day become Interstate 99, connecting Corning, New York and Bedford, Pennsylvania.

The P.K.

(written with help from Brittany & Caleb Wright)

Peter and Elizabeth were both eight years old that Sunday morning in June. Church seemed just like any other time; nothing unusual had happened that week or that day. But the Mortons, Ginny and the children especially, were quiet and subdued compared to normal. Elizabeth had tears in her eyes once during Sunday School but no one knew why and she would not give a reason.

The worship service proceeded as usual—until the very end. Pastor Dan said, right after the sermon was over, that he had something else to share. Ginny drew the girls, one on either side of her, close.

"I have come to the conclusion, after much prayer, thought, and discernment, that the Lord is leading me and my family to accept a call to pastor a church in central Maryland," he told everyone.

There was a collective gasp from the hundred-plus parishioners. A few sniffles and even whimpers followed. Dan's voice cracked several times as he explained the transition.

"Please don't think that we are unhappy at 3C. Quite the opposite is true. As you know, the passing of Ginny's mother a year ago combined with both her and my father's poor health has challenged us greatly. As an only child, Ginny has no siblings to help her father and the frequent trips back and forth to Maryland are just not sustainable for very long. You have been very patient with our absences from time to time but you need better and we cannot keep up the pace. It is not good for our children either."

At that time the roads across central Pennsylvania were not as good as they would be in the future. The trip back to Garrett County was time-consuming and the highways notoriously dangerous.

"As we prayed for a resolution we also investigated openings in that district and the Lord seems to have opened a door for us to be within an hour or so from our families *and* serve in a church that is looking for my gifts and experience. We will start in Maryland before the beginning of the school year. I am very confident that the Lord will send a man to pastor and teach here at 3C who will be exactly what you need."

Pastor Dan was treasured by the church and the ministry had gone very well. But he still secretly struggled with not being able to identify why he was at 3C. No particularly great work had been accomplished in five years' time. The attendance and membership were stable but not growing very much. He had no special talent that seemed to set him apart for this church.

"Someday maybe we'll be allowed to know more about why God brought us here and what difference it really made," he confided to Ginny that night.

Joanie Archer and Ginny were close friends and the news was hard for either one to bear. But the whole church mourned the moving of Pastor Dan and his family.

The send-off in August was filled with memories, gifts, compliments, prayers, and tears. When the send-off social ended, the Mortons all stood at the door as the congregation filed by one at a time. Peter simply said "bye" to Patty who was now thirteen.

"Take care bro'," he said to ten-year-old Billy.

"You, too," Billy answered.

Peter and Elizabeth were not close. The rivalry of their early years had subsided but left them distant from one another.

"See ya," he said to her, pretending to punch her in the arm.

"See ya," was all Elizabeth could or would say in reply.

* * * * * * *

The church in Maryland was, like 3C, a "town church." But instead of the sprawling grounds of both 3C and the neighboring school, the church and parsonage were tightly packed into one small block. The parking lot took up most of the rest of that block. Fortunately there was a nice park only a couple minutes' walk away.

The parsonage was a huge old house with spacious rooms, high ceilings, and large windows. The Mortons' furniture looked out of place in size and style. People walked right past the windows as they followed the sidewalk toward downtown.

The congregation was warm and friendly enough. Dan had no major problems in that church.

But the plan of being closer to Dan and Ginny's families was not at all what they had anticipated. In fact, it was literally "backfiring" in comparison to their plans. They were close enough that the expectation they would be a regular help was becoming overwhelming and overutilized. They were constantly asked to drop whatever they were doing and come help with even some small task. Doing so would tear up most of a day which only put more pressure on them. Dan, Ginny, and the kids were more tired than ever.

Ginny's father, though, died a little over a year after the move. Both her parents had no life insurance and the estate had been liquidated to pay for their care. This forced the Mortons to bear the cost of the funerals, cemetery lot, stone, and burials. Dan's family expected more than his fair share from him. His father died three years after the move. But Dan had no plans to leave Maryland right away. The family finally calmed down again.

Billy loved that church. He had a lot of friends there. Patty seemed to quickly adapt to, and fit into, any setting. Elizabeth came to be known at that church as Beth since there was already another Elizabeth there who simultaneously agreed to take the nickname Liz. Every one, including Elizabeth, liked the new version of her name so it stayed with her from that point onward. But Beth was the most deeply affected by the transition and the loss of her grandparents, especially Ginny's parents.

Dan became more and more involved in speaking and ministering to teens and even conducted two local youth conferences. This new and developing ability did not go unnoticed.

One day a district superintendent from New York State called Dan's office after first speaking with the superintendent in Maryland. He wanted Dan to consider an opening in his district in upstate New York. The church he spoke of had a desire to do a large-scale youth ministry but could not afford to call both a senior pastor *and* a youth pastor. Since some other area churches also wanted to do a better job of reaching out to the teens, a regional youth ministry was established, but they needed a dedicated, gifted director who would also serve as a nearly fulltime pastor.

Dan and Ginny prayed about it and it seemed that the notion was still strong in his heart and mind. Dan made an overnight trip to meet the superintendent, the local leaders, and "case out" the place. He felt that he should candidate and see what the response was. The candidating weekend was in May and it went extremely well. The Board's call to Dan was unanimous and the Youth Council was solid in their support as well.

Patty, Billy, and Beth could see what was coming. Patty was fine with the change. Billy was anything but fine with it. He had friends in Maryland and he was getting involved, and advancing in, sports at school. Beth had become inward and shy and did not react strongly; she just accepted the change with a quiet resignation.

So the announcement was made and in July the family moved again, this time to Compact, New York—so named in honor of the document signed by the Pilgrims at Cape Cod.

Compact was a busy village not far from the Adirondack Mountains. But the church and parsonage were again at the edge of town with a nice yard and a spacious front porch where the Mortons spent most of their summers. Dan was busier than ever but enjoying his work more than ever.

Patty enjoyed Compact. For Beth the years in New York State brought a necessary turning point in her bruised life. But Billy was angry about the move—especially about starting all over again in sports after advancing so well at his last school. He blamed his father for his unhappiness and his mother for not resisting Dan's leadership in the decision. Dan and Billy were at odds most of the time and it only grew worse.

All the Morton children graduated from Compact Central High School. Patty went to college in Binghamton, meeting and falling in love with a Broome County man by the first name of Daryl. Billy left home with a friend a few months after his high school graduation and moved to Albany. Billy was going to finally have things his way with no one to tell him what to do. He viewed moving away from his parents as a "good riddance" and a way of punishing them for not giving him his way back when he was just fifteen years old. Everything would go his way now, or so he thought. Beth remained at home for the five years at Compact opting to move after graduation in a way similar to what her sister Patty had done—by leaving, on good terms, to attend school.

* * * * * * *

While there were trials in their life, as in everyone's, the Mortons were a happy and close family. Even after Billy began to rebel, the other four remained a tight-knit unit. Ginny remained a stay-at-home mom all those years and assisted her husband in the ministry even despite their difficult financial condition. Dan worked long and sometimes unpredictable hours but always took his days off very seriously and faithfully used every bit of vacation each year.

Patty and Beth did not mind being PK's (Preacher's Kids) but their lives were very different from their friends' lives. Dan only had four Sundays a year he could be away from the church so when friends were visiting grandparents or taking weekend getaways, the Mortons stayed home almost every weekend. When Dan had his day off (Monday), the kids had school. The family seldom went anywhere on Saturday afternoon or evening because Dan was finishing his Sunday sermon preparations. The few times they did go out left him either feeling unprepared or he was very tense the whole time. On Sundays Dan was at the church early then, after worship, home for dinner and a quick nap, then back in the study until the start of the evening service. The family saw little more of him on a Sunday that almost any other parishioners. He came home every Sunday night exhausted. The other evenings were very often filled by meetings, appointments with parishioners, and, of course, the Wednesday evening service. Holidays were usually spent at the parsonage due to church obligations at those times and only rarely did Dan's family come—the exception being during the Maryland years.

But the worst part for the kids was moving so often. Beth, especially, saw friends whose fathers changed jobs but they did not always move as a result. Each time Dan changed churches, the family automatically moved. Moving meant leaving friends and surroundings and never quite becoming settled anywhere for long. Making new friends was a long process fraught with potential problems; some new friends were not all they claimed to be and sometimes Beth was rejected or even betrayed by other girls. Just when she thought she knew who her friends were, it would be time to move again. None of the children had serious love interests until well after high school.

When Beth started junior high and then senior high school, it seemed that being a PK distinguished her in some unwelcome ways. Many classmates, but even more so *teachers*, expected her to have advice and answers about everything religious or even psychological. A teacher might look to her and say "what do Catholics believe about that, Beth?" How was she to know? She wasn't Catholic. She might be asked what she believed about drinking alcohol or premarital sex only to be openly mocked by her classmates as a result or the teacher might debate the point with her. Some of the more cynical classmates openly accused her of not drinking, smoking, or having sex *only* because her father was a pastor. Many had already concluded that if her father was not a pastor, she definitely would not go to church so faithfully. But she enjoyed church, and thought it was helpful and important to her. For her it was her relationship to her *heavenly* Father that really made all these things important to her. And if Beth ever did make a bad choice (and she did sometimes) she was doubly scolded by all involved because she was a pastor's kid and she should know better.

But it was far from all negative. The church was a kind of huge extended family. Over the years Beth had accumulated several sets of surrogate grandparents in the form of older church members who took a shine to her and her siblings. The family was often the recipient of gifts, some quite generous, of cash or new or used items. They were often invited to homes for dinner, a picnic, or to swim in a parishioner's pond or pool.

As a family, the Mortons may have been closer than average, despite the issues with Billy. Most people understood about him and were supportive but there were exceptions and some of those exceptions even dared pass judgment on the Mortons seeking to blame Dan and/or Ginny, not Billy, for his own rebellion. That did not help and only made the pain of his choices even more searing.

Dan loved being a pastor, especially teaching from the pulpit and he enjoyed working with teens. He could easily have been a *fulltime* youth pastor. There was never a doubt that he had been called to this work. The only doubts that ever arose were those he struggled with in his own mind. They came when he felt especially inadequate or hurt by someone in the church. But the hardest part for him was repeatedly dealing with the deaths and the grief of church members. Every death was like losing yet another family member; it was especially hard when it was someone close to his own age. Dan performed more funerals in a year than many people attended in their lifetime. His own grief was sometimes overwhelming but he wept privately, prayed for strength to get through it and God always granted that request.

Ginny worked hard keeping the home life organized and helping her husband. She answered the phone and took messages for Dan, helped him counsel women, and hosted church families, visitors, and guest speakers at the parsonage. She kept the house and laundry clean, hot meals on the table, the kids' homework corrected, and fevers under control. She and Dan were co-laborers, best friends, and, yes, lovers too.

This is not to say Dan and Ginny never had their differences; they did and some of them were sharp. But somehow, even after the disagreement, they would come to some compromise that met each one's need or expectation to some degree—each giving something but also receiving something. One time Dan might get more of his way and another time Ginny would, but in the end it all averaged out. One thing was certain and that was that Dan was the head of the home, but he tried to be a loving leader, ultimately (even if in the long run) putting his family ahead of himself. The other certain thing was Jesus was Lord of their family so every difference had to be resolved in a way that kept Him in that first place.

Almost without fail the family gathered for supper at five o'clock. During the New York years, though, it went from five seated at the table, to four, and eventually three. Dan's supper was always rushed as he needed to soon be somewhere else. In the earlier years Ginny always got the kids ready for bed and they were all sound asleep when Dan arrived home at nine or even ten o'clock. Later, as the children observed more adult bedtimes he was actually able to see them and talk with them for a while.

* * * * * * *

No one bothered to notice where the time was going. One day, it seemed, Dan and Ginny realized they were fifty years old and it would soon be just the two of them again. But unlike those first four-plus years before children, now they would have perhaps decades together, just the two of them, but with grown children and hopefully grandchildren to go visit and have visit them as they worked away at fulfilling God's purpose in their lives. They were excited about the future that would soon stretch out before them.

A Talk with "Aunt" Tillie

At the church in Compact, Missions Conference took place in the spring, generally between Mother's Day and Memorial Day. In May of 2005 Beth had only recently turned sixteen years old. The woman had mostly arrived, even as the girl had almost entirely faded. Patty had just arrived home from college for the summer.

Beth loved Missions Conference. Somewhere in life she had latched onto the notion of becoming a missionary. She dreamt of being one of those guest missionary speakers, telling the tales of conversions and lives changed in the heart of Africa, Southeast Asia or even secular Europe. It was a good dream but more than just time and credentials separated her from attaining it. She needed two more elements: a clear call from God and a courageous heart.

The missionary for that year's conference was a single woman by the first name of Matilda. Beth wanted to be like her with the exception that she did not desire to be single all her life; she wanted, longed, to marry, have a family, *and* serve God. Matilda was in her mid fifties but had been a missionary for only about ten years. There was indeed a story behind why she never entered the mission field before her forties.

* * * * * * *

Missions Conference started on Sunday morning. In Sunday School Matilda introduced herself to the children and teens as either "Miss Tillie" or "Aunt Tillie," whichever they preferred. Tillie spoke again in the Sunday morning service then returned home with the Mortons where she would stay during the four-day conference.

Sunday evening Tillie shared her personal testimony of coming to faith in Jesus Christ and how He called her to be a missionary. Tillie was called to be a missionary when she was still a teenager; she had no doubt about that.

"So why did it take thirty years for me to get out to the field?" she asked partway through the message. "Well, the answer lies in a four letter word: F-E-A-R. As a child, teenager, and young adult my life was controlled, not by God, but by fear, doubt, and uncertainty. I was afraid of everything: failure, leaving home, inadequacy, you name it, I was afraid of it. I wouldn't drive a car, go on a date, go to college, leave my parents' sides, anything. I call those years 'the lost years.' I almost lost a lot more than just *those* years. If God had not broken through to me in a very powerful way at the age of thirty-four I would probably still be tucked safely away at home."

Ginny did not say a word. As she kept her eyes on Tillie she reached over with her hand and patted Beth on her leg just above the knee. Beth got Ginny's silent message: "Pay attention, kiddo."

Tillie had lost to fear everything that had not been taken by the natural course of time or tragedy. Eventually her siblings had left home to start families of their own. Tillie lived at home, never going away for college, taking only occasional and part-time work, and remained largely in the house. She and her parents were in a terrible car wreck when she was thirty-three and she alone survived. It was as a result of that tragedy that God at last got through to her.

Late that evening Ginny and Tillie talked in the living room of the parsonage. Finally Ginny broke the ice: "I am glad you were so open and honest tonight. That story really needed to be heard."

"Beth?" Tillie asked to confirm what she already suspected.

"Yeah," Ginny answered, her voice breaking some.

Dan came into the room and sat on the sofa next to his wife.

"I started to tell Tillie about Beth," she caught him up.

Dan let out a long exasperated sigh with a distant look in his eyes.

"I can see it in her," Tillie told them.

"Oh it shows, I know," Dan admitted. He continued, "We've done everything: prayer, encouragement, Scripture, counseling, you name it—everything but medication—and we're almost desperate enough to try that."

"When did it begin?" Tillie inquired.

Dan and Ginny looked each other in the eye. "Oh about three or four years ago, maybe sooner," Ginny said, Dan nodding back at her. "We didn't really notice it though. It started slowly, subtly. By the time we figured out what a problem she was getting into it was fairly severe and she was gripped by it."

Dan added, "Neither of us has ever experienced that, personally, or in our families. I've seen some of it in a few people but when I saw it in them it was already full blown so we never saw it coming. I suppose that losing three grandparents, moving twice, plus all the turmoil of adolescence—all within five years' time—just finally took a toll."

Tillie asked, "What controls her?"

"How long do you have?" Dan asked.

Ginny spoke up, "It is a mixture of crippling worry *and* fears. We almost drag her kicking and screaming into things; she doesn't want to go anywhere, especially anything unfamiliar. She frets over everything and has it all figured out that anything and everything *is* going to go wrong or end in failure."

Dan joined back in, "If it wasn't mandatory by law she wouldn't even go to school. Homeschooling, which is what she wants, would only cement the problem. She's constantly worried that she is sick and/or dying of something. She has had every test, scan, and x-ray to disprove that but she still believes something, multiple things, are wrong with her. According to her, *no one* likes her. All of that, coupled with Billy's rebellious attitudes are almost too much for *us* to bear some days."

"Let me talk with her," Tillie offered nodding thoughtfully, "There's sometimes truth in the statement, 'takes one to know one.' One reason we share testimonies in the church is because we never know when our experiences converge with someone else's, giving a chance to encourage or even help another."

"Please do," Dan embraced the idea, "she's headed for a long, lonely life if she remains on this course."

"She's a lovely girl. We can't let that happen," Tillie observed with a twinkle in her eye.

* * * * * * *

Monday was beautiful and unusually warm for upstate New York in May. Ginny and Tillie sat at a small table and chairs on the porch talking and enjoying iced tea together when Beth and Billy arrived home from school. Beth sheepishly started to walk past the women toward the door, hoping to escape any attention or questions.

"Come join us girls, Beth," Tillie called out.

Fearing she would offend the treasured and respected guest, Beth accepted the invitation and quietly, shyly joined the two grown women. She didn't say much at all but acted as polite as possible, looking only at her mom and never directly at Tillie. The phone rang inside so Ginny got up to answer it. Beth looked panicked as Ginny arose and walked away leaving her alone with the virtual stranger. Ginny deliberately failed to return to the porch. Beth was filled with alarm but did not feel she could escape either.

"I already told your parents," Tillie started, "that it takes one to know one."

Beth looked at her briefly and curiously.

Tillie looked her in the eye, and filled with empathy, said, "I can see the fear, Beth. I can sense it, feel it, 'smell' it. I know it all too well."

Beth did not answer. She just tucked her chin down toward her chest and looked blankly at the tabletop.

"Take it from someone who yielded literally decades of her life to it. I know what I'm talking about. Do you think it's true?"

"I suppose," Beth almost whispered.

"What are you troubled by?" Tillie asked, trying to make eye contact.

Quietly Beth replied, "Mom says I'm a hypochondriac, and a hermit, a worry wart...that I think no one likes me."

"Is that what *you* say?"

"I suppose so."

"Were you always that way, Beth?"

"No." Beth almost blushed a little, perhaps somewhat embarrassed. "I used to be outgoing and pretty feisty—Mom talks about me 'getting my red up'," referring to her red hair and the legendary proverbial temperament that supposedly goes with it.

"Do you know how or when or why it started?" Tillie continued to mine for leads.

"No, not really," Beth answered in shaking, nervous words, looking down at the table.

"What do you want to do with your life, Beth?" Tillie's questions seemed meandering but she was actually following a strategy.

Beth looked up and lit up. "I hope I can be a nurse—a missionary nurse."

"That's great," Tillie cheered, "We missionaries need all the help we can get. But do you think you could do that with the way things are now? A missionary has to be very brave, fearless even. How are you going to face the issues of the mission field?"

"I don't know," Beth resigned, looking back down.

"You know, Beth, God has great plans for your life. But those plans don't include living like this. He loves you too much for that. You know a lot about the Bible, don't you? It says many wonderful things about your problem. It says, for instance, that 'You did not receive the spirit of bondage again to fear.' (Romans 8:15a) But that's where you are—in bondage." She looked down a little to try to let her eyes plead with Beth's. "Take it from someone who has been on both sides of it—there is no comparison between bondage to fear and freedom in Christ."

"But I've tried and I just can't help it," Beth explained.

"You may be right about that," Tillie surprised Beth with the unexpected answer. "The Bible also says '...God has not given us a spirit of fear, but of power and of love and of a sound mind (2nd Timothy 1:7). The power comes from God, not you."

Beth knew the verse; she had read it and heard it many times. Her father had preached from that passage. But for some reason certain familiar things take on new power and meaning at a particular point in time. The Bible might call it the "fullness of time." Some would label it a "divine appointment" or a "chosen time." But whatever it is called, God was moving in on Beth's situation in a decisive way and, if she would cooperate with Him, a transforming way, and Tillie was His unexpected but appointed messenger to her that day.

"You're a Christian, right?" Tillie asked Beth.

"Yeah."

"When did you make that decision?"

"During vacation Bible school when we were still in Colsonburg. Mrs. Holt gave the invitation after the closing one day and I responded," Beth smiled and blushed a little as she added, "not long after I beat up Peter Archer."

"Oh my," Tillie lit up, "at least you beat that boy up *before* that decision, not after! Okay, so you're a believer. The Bible also says, 'Repent and let every one of you be baptized in the Name of Jesus for the remission of sins; and you shall receive the gift of the Holy Spirit.' (Acts 2:38) You have the Spirit spoken of in that verse; so what is the key? And there is one."

Beth looked at her blankly but she knew the answer.

"The Apostles received the Holy Spirit in John 20:22. Jesus breathed on them and said 'Receive the Holy Spirit.' Some call that John's version of Pentecost but that's not really true, is it? We know something changed dramatically in Acts chapter 2 where it says they were all *filled* with the Holy Spirit; that was Pentecost. Jesus had promised they would 'receive power' when they were 'baptized with the Holy Spirit.' (Acts 1:8, 5) The difference is that by Acts chapter 2 they were completely yielded and in anticipation of the Spirit's power. What I suspect about you is that you have yielded yourself instead to fear and therefore given the Devil a foothold in your life. You cannot allow the Devil, or self, or fleshly desires to control any part of you but you must yield *all* of yourself to the Holy Spirit's control and once you do, you'll never want to go back. He gives us power and a sound mind in place of bondage to fear or anything else that can grip us. Does that sound like something you want?"

"Yeah. I really don't like feeling this way or what it's doing to my family, especially my parents," Beth said apologetically, "I don't mean to hurt them."

Tillie made one more point: "Sound mind," she explained, "literally means a 'disciplined mind.' You see, with the power of the Holy Spirit, you can discipline your mind, subdue the fears, and victoriously live above them."

Beth was crying but only quietly. Tillie took Beth's hand in hers. "I'm living proof that the Word of God is true. My only regret is that my parents have not yet seen what God did in me—but they will in Heaven, won't they? I'm going to give you some Bible study guides on fear and the Spirit-filled life; I wrote them up myself and they should be a help to you."

"Okay."

"Let's pray," Tillie invited, "Dear Heavenly Father, thank you so much for this dear young woman. She loves You and wants to follow You fully, even be one of Your ambassadors. Pour Your power out on her, help her to make a full surrender and experience power, love, and a sound mind. Replace her fear with courage. Set her free from the bondage she is in today and let her soar and sing for You!" Tillie suggested, "Why don't you pray too, Beth?"

So Beth quietly started, "Father, I know that this isn't what You want for me and I don't want it either. I wish I knew how I ever got in this mess," she choked back the tears. "I *do* want the fullness of the Holy Spirit's power so I can overcome these things. Give me what Aunt Tillie talked about and let me become like her. Thank you for sending her, for her sharing her testimony, for what you did in her life. Just please help me, too, God. Amen."

Tillie patted Beth on the hand, "Have faith, dear, He will do it. There will be trials and doubts but don't give up. He will do it."

The two sat and talked a while longer. Beth asked several questions. Tillie answered every one as best as she could. She shared many tips and hints for handling fear and worry using a mind disciplined by the Holy Spirit and the Word of God.

Finally Tillie said, "Well, I've given you a lot to think about. Now I think I'll go see if your mom needs any help in the kitchen."

When Beth finally went inside too, Ginny gave her a hug from the side and a smile indicating she knew about the conversation on the front porch but also that she wasn't going to push or pry but let Beth just absorb it all and share as much as she was willing, when she was willing.

That evening at the conclusion of the service, Beth went forward to kneel at the rail. The decision had already been made; she was only publicly declaring it and thereby sealing it not only in herself but before God and the whole church. Tillie prayed with her, though only briefly there at the rail, and promised to give her those study guides after the service was over. After church Beth asked Dan if she could get her driver's permit "next week."

It would be a falsehood to say that all of Beth's problems simply disappeared instantaneously on that day. But it *would* be true to say that it was a turning point. In the days, weeks, and months that followed, Beth's life was truly changed as she entered different phases, marked by slightly different temperaments until she settled into being a happy, glowing, outgoing young woman, not afraid to face every challenge life would throw her way—and there would be many of those to come, including one in particular that would threaten to undo it all in a single crushing blow.

It's important to know, though, that anyone who met her as an adult would hardly have believed that she was once so different. But because Tillie shared her life's story and took time to come alongside Beth on a sunny afternoon in May of 2005 in a village called Compact, New York, Beth was not doomed to the decades of misery that Tillie had known all too well.

Rhonda

Rhonda Greenfield was only a few months older than Beth and her family belonged to the church in Compact. Several times over the years Rhonda had reached out to Beth in friendship. However Beth's shyness had prevented them from ever founding any kind of a real relationship but for some reason Rhonda never gave up. A month or so after that missions conference in 2005 that all changed. Beth was beginning to come out of her invisible shell and show more interest in the people and goings on around her.

"Hey, Beth!" a young woman's voice was heard calling as Beth left church on a hot, sunny June day, heading home to the nearby parsonage. Stopping and turning around, Beth noticed Rhonda almost running in her direction. She did not know it but Rhonda was going to try *one more time* to reach out to Beth. Rhonda was relatively tall with long sandy-blonde hair, always made up in an attractive arrangement of one kind or another. Her clothing was always likewise careful and attractive; she could easily have been a model. She had blue eyes, fair skin, and a beautiful soprano voice.

"Hey, Beth," she repeated, "a few of us are going to a concert on Friday night. My mom's gonna drive us. Do you want to come too?"

Rhonda almost could not explain why she even bothered to ask. The answer was always "no thanks." She had begun to even feel hurt by Beth's consistent refusals of her and the other girls at church.

Beth thought for a moment. Her impulse was to decline the offer but she actually thought better of it this time. As she stood there holding her Bible against her chest with both arms folded before her, others walking past, she smiled and said, "Yeah. Yeah I would." The thought of it still made her nervous but she did not bow to it.

Rhonda's eyes popped and her smile widened as she asked, "Really?"

"Yeah, really," Beth chuckled. It now felt surprisingly good to say "yes" to something—to see Rhonda so happy with her response.

Rhonda gave her the name of the band (a well-known contemporary Christian group) and the time and place of the concert.

"I'll ask my folks and give you a call," Beth promised.

"Great," Rhonda replied with a very satisfied look on her face, "I'll talk to ya later!" Then off she happily went as Beth continued toward the parsonage.

Dan and Ginny were so glad Beth actually *wanted* to go that they simply could not say no. It helped that an adult was driving and they approved of the band.

"You're gonna be so glad you went," Rhonda promised Beth on the phone Monday evening. Her statement would prove to be prophetic.

Beth was the first one Mrs. Greenfield picked up on Friday afternoon in her family's minivan. It was a long drive all the way to Syracuse but it went by in a flash for the group of laughing teenaged girls. Beth was friendly and warm but a little reserved at first. That eventually was overtaken by the silliness of those around her simply enjoying themselves and each others' company. Beth did not even notice how caught up she was in all the fun.

There was a quick fast food supper on the way and ice cream afterwards. In between, the concert was lively and exciting but also reverent and encouraging. It was after midnight when Beth arrived home—a new experience for her.

Dan was asleep sitting at the end of the sofa. Ginny was also asleep stretched out on the sofa with the side of her head on Dan's lap as if it were a pillow. The television was still running. It woke Ginny when Dan startled awake. They promptly, through yawns, asked Beth about the evening and they spoke together for a few minutes before all going upstairs to bed. Dan and Ginny were overjoyed to see Beth so happy and excited. They had literally prayed that it would be another turning point for her. They thanked God for it.

On Sunday Rhonda sat next to Beth in Sunday School. All the teens usually sat together on a back pew during worship. Beth joined them this time, for the first time, and so her circle of friends began to grow.

Thus a true friendship was born. Much to everyone's surprise and delight, Beth and Rhonda became best friends. They looked for each other at church and at school. They studied together and drove to malls, movies and concerts in Syracuse, Watertown, Utica, and even once all the way to Albany. Usually there were three, four, or five girls altogether on those long outings.

One weekend the following summer, their seventeenth year, Rhonda, Beth, and their moms went on a day trip to Alexandria Bay and the Thousand Islands. Two years before Beth would never have boarded that huge boat for fear of it sinking. But she not only boarded it, she loved the cruise through the countless islands, large and small. But later that summer Rhonda's and Beth's friendship was threatened by a devastating loss and the changes that immediately began to follow, some expected, some startling.

* * * * * * *

It was Thursday afternoon on a pleasant August day. Beth was home from her summer job that day. The church and the parsonage were located on the main road through town and most traffic passed by their front porch.

Ginny and the kids heard the fire whistle blowing downtown shortly after lunch. It had been so long after it had stopped that they just assumed the trucks had gone the other direction out of town. Then it blew again. A couple of minutes later a single fire engine screamed by the house. They stood on the porch following its trajectory when Ginny said, pointing, "There!"

A column of black smoke rose from the horizon. The fire whistle blew yet again but then all was strangely quiet. Many minutes later a fire truck from another town went by, then another one from Compact, followed by two more from neighboring towns. The smoke on the horizon got worse, not better.

Ginny went inside to answer the phone. Beth had a bad feeling about the fire but she was not sure why nor prepared to hear what was coming next.

"Calm down, Rhonda," Ginny said forcefully.

Beth became even more concerned.

"Oh no, Oh no," Ginny exclaimed. "Where are you? Is everyone okay? All right."

Beth heard only half of the conversation but she already knew what had happened. Ginny came out to the porch, the phone to her ear, a panicked looked on her face, looking off in the direction of the smoke.

Tipping the mouthpiece back she said, "I'm sorry, Beth, it's Rhonda's place."

Beth turned back to the ever blackening horizon and, putting her hand to her face, began to cry for the thought of what her friend was going through right then.

"Dan," Ginny was heard saying into the phone, "the fire department went to Greenfields' and it sounds bad."

There was a pause.

"Okay," she ended the call and said, "Dad's coming. I'm calling the prayer chain."

When Dan finally got back to the house, he and Beth climbed in his car and headed in the direction of the Greenfields' to see what they could do. The road into the small development was closed down. Fire trucks and hoses covered the blacktop up the short hill and water was running down the street and out onto the road. Finding an empty driveway, Dan parked and he and Beth walked over to the blockaded intersection.

"I'm the family's pastor," he said to the fire police captain stationed at the corner, "they called me."

The captain told Dan who to speak with once he got up the street. When Dan and Beth reached the neighbor's yard Rhonda was spotted watching the progress of the firefighters. For some reason she turned just in time to see Beth approaching her. Rhonda ran to Beth and the two just held each other.

"It's all gone," she cried, "everything's gone." Then as they pulled apart from each others' arms Rhonda, wiping away her tears, unknowingly corrected herself. "The neighbors got the dogs out and the firemen pulled out the living room furniture, but the rest is ruined."

Looking around the gathered neighbors, crisscrossed hoses, and busy firefighters, Dan spotted Mr. Greenfield speaking with one of the firemen who was wearing a solid white helmet. His back was turned toward Dan and his yellow coat said, in three lines of reflective characters, "Chief," "C.F.D.," and "Station 13."

"It shouldn't have turned out this way," the chief told Mr. Greenfield apologetically, "But we have so few volunteers any more. I have half the men I did fifteen years ago when I became chief. They can't work, sometimes two jobs, have a family, and meet these ever-increasing training mandates. We're volunteers, not career firefighters. I can't even recruit new guys because they know they can't meet the necessary hours for certification. Daytimes have always been bad with so many of the guys at work."

"I know, I know," Mr. Greenfield interrupted, "I had heard some about those problems and I can see your recruitment signs up all over the place."

The chief resumed his apology, "I'll tell you plain," his gloved index finger thumping into the opposite gloved palm, "if just one more man would have brought that one truck I needed, just five minutes into this, it would have ended differently. Instead I had to wait for the mutual aid to arrive—just minutes too late."

"I understand," Mr. Greenfield assured him, his left hand on the Chief's shoulder. "Thanks for everything you did; we *do* appreciate your efforts."

Mr. Greenfield extended his right hand and the chief accepted the gesture. The two men shook hands briefly then the chief walked away obviously frustrated and angry that he had lost this battle, when he knew it could have been won.

Dan and Mr. Greenfield also shook hands and one of those brief side-to-side hugs. Then the two men plus Beth walked up to the edge of the yard where Mrs. Greenfield and Rhonda's sister, Rita, were still looking on in virtual disbelief. The sight was enough to take Beth's breath away. She knew that house so well, inside and out, and now it was just a blackened shell, the charred garage collapsed to the ground, the windows all missing and the vinyl siding hanging in melted sheets. The two Golden Retrievers nervously stood at the family's side. The hum of diesel engines filled the air. Water laid everywhere and several firemen milled around inside and outside the smoldering house.

"*Everything* for Rita's wedding was in there," Mrs. Greenfield said, looking over to Rhonda's older sister, "it's gone now. I don't even want to see whatever is left."

Rita's wedding was only weeks away.

The newspaper's account told how the attached garage was engulfed in flames when Compact's first truck arrived with only three men and seven hundred fifty gallons of water. There were no water lines or hydrants in the rural area and the truck's tank was empty after barely making a dent in the fire. Then the firemen waited helplessly as the fire grew even bigger than before, spreading into and throughout the house. The next truck also had only a small tank of water. When the first of several two thousand gallon tankers arrived, the house was almost fully involved. The fire was quickly suppressed after enough personnel and equipment was assembled but the irreversible damage had already been done. The three initial firefighters had begun retrieving furniture while they waited but soon had to pull back due to the flames and smoke. One was seen stomping, punching the air, and cursing while the fire advanced, he was so frustrated and angry.

* * * * * * *

The insurance company put the family up in a motel for a few nights but Rhonda had been invited to stay at the Mortons' home. Then Mr. Greenfield rented a small apartment for a couple of weeks. The church members collected money and clothing for the family. The Deacons gave them a generous check to help the very day of the fire. The church members also loaned or gave Rita everything she needed for the wedding. It was not the way Rita had pictured it but anyone who did not know what had happened would have thought it had been planned just the way it actually turned out. Rita was the first to say that no matter the dress, the shoes, or any other item, she was to be married to the love of her life and that was all that mattered, no matter what they wore to the ceremony. She said she knew it was a wedding, not a fashion show or a photo op, anyway.

Mr. Greenfield made a very difficult decision in light of the fire. He had been resisting a promotion to a new position for some time because it would mean moving to the Rochester office in western New York. But now, instead of rebuilding, he accepted the promotion and moved the family. It was to have been Beth and Rhonda's senior year together in the Compact Central School District.

But a surprising decision was made between the two fathers and at Dan's suggestion. Rhonda would be allowed to attend her senior year in Compact, as she wished, by staying with the Mortons Monday through Friday.

It was an adjustment but a mostly pleasant one for Beth. Rhonda was relieved but also missed her parents through the week. Patty, being five years older than Beth, was not as close to Beth in many of the ways Rhonda was. In the months that followed Rhonda was like the sister Beth never had. As sisters they disagreed sometimes and competed for the bathroom a lot but they treasured the last-chance opportunity to be so close in so many ways before graduation.

The weekends were still different, though—most of them. Each Friday after school Rhonda was permitted to drive to Rochester and spend the weekend with her parents, not to mention holidays and breaks. But when December brought Lake Ontario's brutal lake effect snow squalls, sometimes dropping several inches per hour, Rhonda would stay in Compact, at least whenever they hit on a Friday or were even predicted for Sunday. Folks in upstate New York are accustomed to such conditions but Rhonda's parents viewed her as too young and inexperienced as a driver to take on the combination of the Thruway traffic, the darkness, and the blinding snow. Beth often prayed for snow, though she knew it was somewhat selfish to do so.

After the mountains of lake snow had melted and graduation came, Rhonda moved to Rochester fulltime and attended a Christian College there. Dan announced the end of his ministry in Compact; he and Ginny would start their "empty nest" years in northwestern Pennsylvania—a place called Blueberry Haven. Patty would marry Daryl in July and move to Cleveland. Billy had already decided to strike out on his own, though in anger and rebellion and with no intention of "looking back." To him happiness was his parents and the church and God in his rear view mirror. Now Beth would make the bravest decision of her life to date—to leave home to attend nursing school.

Beth and Rhonda called, emailed, and even visited many times. But Rhonda's attention was soon diverted to a man, an upperclassman at the college and hers and Beth's contacts thinned to just occasional. Both were busy--busy finding their own place in the grown-up world.

Up on the Farm
(for Barry)

Whenever the Archers spoke of Jack's farm they always called it "*up* on the farm..." Peter's family lived on that turn in Elm Street right in Laingeville Center. Elm Street connected State Road with Slocum Road and by doing so formed LC's only "block." From the house one traveled the short distance (about a half dozen houses' worth) to the "T" intersection with Slocum Road and turned right. The Farm was about three-quarters of a mile north of the village on the left. The brief trip was up a gentle hill all the way there and, of course, downhill all the way back.

Grandpa and Grandma's house, where Peter's dad had grown up, was located on the upper end of the farm near where Brick Silo Road went to the left and over "the slope," as it was called, until it intersected with Wright Road. The property was over two-hundred acres in size and rectangular in shape, with the short side along Slocum Road.

Another house was at the lower corner. It had belonged to a neighboring farm until 1990 when that house's barn burned to the ground in an overnight fire, taking the entire herd with it. When the family could not afford to rebuild due to inadequate insurance, Grandpa bought the house and a small strip of the property—about forty acres (Percy Romig bought the rest of the land). He rented out that house. It was simply called "the rental."

The Archer's farmhouse was actually fairly small. It stood two stories high with the roof's gables facing north and south. The long front faced east, parallel to Slocum Road, with a full length porch the roof of which visually separated the first and second floors. Three windows equally spaced across that front wall sat between the porch roof and the main roof. It was the same below in the first floor except that it was a door in the middle position, rather than a window.

There were only four rooms in the main part of the house, a dining room in the left half and a living room in the right half. A bedroom was directly above each in the second floor. A hall with a stairway divided the structure right inside the front door.

An intersecting two-story wing off the back contained the kitchen with the master bedroom and the only bathroom above on the second floor. A single story unfinished, unheated room ("the back room") continued from the back of the kitchen. The whole house was clad in white clapboard siding and a dark standing-seam metal roof. Though the home was comfortable enough for two, it was desperately crowded on holidays. It had not been much better when Peter's Dad, uncle and aunt were growing up in it.

The barn sat directly behind—a "bank barn," built against the side of the hill. The tractors would enter the second story hay mow from a ramp behind and the cattle were housed below in the fieldstone basement which was at ground level only on the front. A white silo and a small square milk house stood at the left end of the severely weathered board-and-batten sided barn and a single story addition was on the right end, it increased the original barn's size by more than half. Several sheds and outbuildings of varying sizes and states of repair were scattered around. Rugged pastureland stretched up the right half of the slope behind the barn and fields of corn and alfalfa grew on the left half. Between the farmhouse and the rental was the "willow bottom." It was a formerly swampy area that Grandpa had dried up by planting weeping willow trees along a line about fifty feet away from the road. It was also a pasture area.

Grandpa maintained a herd of between seventy-five and one-hundred dairy cows. He virtually lived half his life in the barn and when he was not in the barn feeding or milking the cows, he was in the fields. From time to time he might hire a local teenager to help with milking or haying but largely he worked alone. The earnings were meager. Some have been overheard calling farming an expensive hobby due to the financial return seen from it. But it was demanding—often sixteen-hour days, depending on the time of year.

Peter loved the farm. As a young boy he would have gone up everyday if his parents would have allowed it. At family meals Peter would ask Grandpa questions and try to discuss the farm's operation as if he were an adult or even an equal partner with Grandpa. Jack feasted on Peter's interest and spoke back to him as if Peter were, in fact, another adult. Every decision and plan was carefully explained to the young boy.

Ten was a special year for Peter. When school ended in June, he was allowed to help his grandfather almost everyday, except Sundays, but only if he was caught up on his chores at home. Sometimes he rode his bicycle up and back and other times his mother or grandmother drove him. He had to be home for supper each evening.

In those earliest years he helped with simple tasks like feeding the cows or fetching things for Grandpa. He also mowed the lawn, took care of the chicken coop, and helped Grandma in the garden. When school resumed in September he was limited to Saturdays, holidays, and snow days off from school; Peter lived for Saturdays.

Thirteen was another special year. Not only had the teenage years arrived just as Pete was approaching his mother's height, but on his thirteenth birthday Grandpa gave him a special gift: his very own calf to raise and do with as he wished. He could raise it and milk it, keeping a proportional amount of profit, or he could auction or sell it when it reached maturity, or he could either sell it to a butcher or have it butchered and keep the meat for the family. (Peter had started calling himself Pete about this time because the boys at school teased him about his name to no end.) Pete raised that calf until it was old enough to sell and with the profits he bought two more calves. Each year on or near his birthday, Grandpa gave Pete another calf to add to the others.

Over the course of years, Pete formed a tiny herd of his own in the midst of Grandpa's larger herd, always selling them and buying two more calves for each cow sold. Grandpa called him "the wheeler-dealer" and eventually announced that at the age of eighteen he would have to "cap" Pete's herd at twenty-five because the farm could not support an infinite number of cows. That was when he first started raising cows for meat and experimenting with breeding his own animals right on the farm. Early on, he tried different breeds from Holstein to Jersey and Guernsey, then on to meat breeds like Angus, settling eventually on Polled Herefords as his favorite.

By sixteen Pete was not only shaving a couple times or so a week and as tall as his dad and grandpa but driving the tractors, baling hay, milking cows, and truly acting like an equal alongside his grandfather. Some days his dad needed his help on a job and he gladly went with him but otherwise he was at the farm or, later, also at the firehouse. Grandpa never hired another boy to help him as he was busy quietly cultivating Pete as his successor. Pete had managed to save enough money between his wheeling-dealing, his allowance, and a couple lawn-mowing jobs to celebrate the arrival of his driver's license by paying for his first vehicle: a very used small red pick-up truck. He even paid for his own insurance and repairs for that truck.

There was no doubt that Pete loved farming: working outside, the physical exhilaration of hard work, selling and buying livestock, making and managing his own money, and being his own boss. But he hated milking. Pete found the daily milking routine not only boring but also as a kind of dictatorship. The milking times had to be followed precisely, seven days a week, for the cows to be as productive as possible; there were no sick days, holidays, or vacation days. Grandpa would get frustrated if Pete was even a little late to help with milking. Even at a young age Pete also discovered the dairy farmer's dilemma: a very small financial reward in comparison the monumental amount of time, effort, and investment put forth.

This love-hate relationship to dairy farming left Grandpa with pestering doubts and fears about asking Pete to take the farm someday.

It also left Pete with many unanswered questions. Would he somehow take over Grandpa's farm someday? Would he be a dairy farmer or try some other type of farming? Grandpa could not afford to pay him a living so how would he make a living one day, as long as he was on Grandpa's farm? Where would he live as an adult? Every sixteen-something teenager has similar unanswered questions, of course. The man-to-be was taking form and trying to find his place. Many other changes would come—some pleasant and some definitely not. The most exciting one of all was just around the corner during that sixteenth summer.

In the meantime, Pete was by everyone's estimation a "good kid" and every superficial measurement confirmed that. But there was also a dark side—a side kept hidden from all but one other. It threatened to eventually steal all his dreams and goals and he would come to find it incredibly offensive, even to himself. This darkness certainly took hold because, while Pete was very successful and wise, he had failed to give God much of a place in his life. He went to church, Sunday School, and Youth Group without protest and he was far from being labeled a rebel. He could quote at least some Scripture from memory but a personal relationship with God was not a priority for him. The farm and, later, the firehouse were, and one other thing, too—the dark thing—were his priorities. He made room for this thing wherever and whenever possible and always secretively for it had come to control him.

Also at sixteen Pete had his first girlfriend, Melissa, a sixteen-year-old girl from the East Side. The two spent a lot of time together—almost every spare moment of which there were not many. Melissa's family went to one of the many other churches in Colsonburg. She professed to be a Christian. If she had not, Pete's parents would not have let him date her. But in reality her only basis for saying she was a Christian was, like Pete, that she went to church—in her case only once a week. (Funny thing: Pete was in the barn every *day* but that still did not make him a cow!) Her parents were nice people but her older sister had a reputation for being on the wild side, especially where boys were concerned. John and Joanie did not know this at first. Pete made sure they did not as that might derail his plans.

Company Five

At some point in his life every boy is enamored by fire trucks and the excitement that comes with flashing lights, screaming sirens, blasting horns and what he thinks it is like to be a firefighter. Peter was no exception but he had the advantage of growing up with a "front row seat" since Lainge's Creek was all that separated his home from *Station Five: Lainge Township Volunteer Fire Company.*

From the time he was a baby "Company Five" was a constantly recurring presence in Peter's life. Laingeville Center was only a tiny rural village so fire calls were not frequent; they came in only two to four times a month. But the fire company tried to be ready for any emergency: fires, accidents, and rescues. Though they were not needed often their necessity was proven time and again when the call would come in.

When there was "a call" the fire whistle (some would say "fire siren" or "house siren") began its deafening, cyclical wail—helping, along with pagers, to alert local volunteers to the need and warning everyone else to get out of the way. The volunteers rushed in by vehicle or on foot and the fire trucks, one by one, rushed out to answer the call.

If Peter was home when a call came in anything he was doing stopped as he watched the response. He was required, though, to remain on his own side of the creek and away from the road. His bedroom window faced the firehouse so at night he went to that window and watched the excitement.

Peter had many questions about the things he saw but John knew only a little bit about the fire service. One Thursday evening, when the firemen had their regular work night, John took his seven-year-old son over to the firehouse. John knew Rick Harrington, one of two local automobile mechanics, was the new fire chief so he introduced Peter to Chief Five-one.

"Hey, Rick," John called out as he and Peter entered the firehouse. It was a long single story building sided with blue corrugated steel. Four tall overhead doors filled the front wall. Where there could have been a fifth one at the right end, a regular door and window showed where the radio room and offices were located instead. The garage-style doors were all opened, a red truck perched just inside each one. A social hall with a kitchen stretched across the entire back half of the building.

"Hi-ya John," the Chief responded coming over to meet John and Peter in one of those open doorways. He shook hands with both of them. Peter looked, wide-eyed, around the neat, orderly garage. A row of shiny fire trucks sat at the ready and turn out gear—coats, helmets, bunk pants, and boots—was on the wall behind the trucks.

"This lad," John started, "has been asking me a lot of questions about what's going on over here. A lot of them are way over my head."

The short, bald Chief looked at Peter with a very pleased expression on his face.

John continued, "Any chance of his getting a five-cent tour before you guys start your work?"

"Five-cent?" the Chief exclaimed, "why tonight we're giving ten-cent tours at the five-cent price! Come on in buddy," the Chief invited.

Putting his hand on Peter's shoulder, Mr. Harrington directed him to the far left end of the building. The truck next to the Chief was huge; the hood was higher than the top of his head! The driver's door said in two rows of yellow-gold reflective characters, "Lainge Township Tanker 5."

"This is our tanker," he pointed to the first truck in the tour, "Out here in 'the sticks' we don't have hydrants so we get all our water from creeks, ponds, or tankers. If we have a big fire, each company all around us sends their tankers also. That way we have plenty of water. This one has two-thousand five-hundred gallons. It sounds like a lot but it's not much at a big fire. It can also pump five-hundred gallons of water a minute."

Just behind the driver's door was a small set of valves, gauges, and places to connect hoses. Two sets of fire hoses, with nozzles, were folded up in layers above the pump panel. The rest of the truck looked a lot like the one that came to get the milk from Grandpa's farm—a huge silver cylinder-like tank taking up most of the back part.

Turning around, he pointed to "Engine 5-2" saying, "this is an 'engine/ rescue.' It's brand new this year. It can fight fires just fine but it also has everything we need for vehicle accidents and other rescues. It has just seven-hundred fifty gallons and it can deploy six hoses at a fire. See that on top? Those are big, bright lights we use to give light at an accident at night."

A ladder was attached to the passenger ("Officer's") side actually lying on top of the truck. There were big doors all along the side and there were three places to connect hoses. Two hoses were, like the tanker, folded up above the pump connections. This truck had a hood and two doors on each side. It was not as high as the tanker.

Walking between Engine 5-2 and the turn-out gear, Peter looked up and saw all the hoses folded up on top of the truck with their ends carefully set where they could be grabbed easily and quickly. Most of the hose was very wide and yellow but the rest was just regular fire hose, one stack each of folded-up blue, red, white, and yellow-colored hose. Giant red characters "E-5-2" filled the otherwise silver-colored area below the hose bed.

Coming around the back of the third truck, the chief introduced Peter to LTVFC's pride and joy, "Engine 5-1" or, as they called it, "Old Faithful."

"This one used to be a big city fire engine," Rick explained, "we bought a few years ago. All it does is fight fires and pump water. It can easily deploy eight hoses and carries one-thousand gallons but can pump out every drop in one minute. See those?" He pointed up to the long, black tube-like pieces attached to the driver's side above the rear wheels. "Do you know what those are?"

Peter shook his head, indicating he did not know.

"They are called 'hard bars.' They are like giant straws we use to suck water from ponds or creeks so we can send it out to the hoses."

The pump panel was very complicated with countless gauges and valves and lights. Peter wondered how one would remember what each one was for. Hoses were likewise folded above the pump panel—three of them on this truck, each one a different color. The front was flat without a hood and the the front wheels were actually slightly *behind* the driver's seat.

"Finally," Dick gestured toward two comparatively small trucks that looked like oversized pick-up trucks, "we have the brush truck—like a miniature engine with four-wheel drive that we use for brush fires, field fires, and such. In front of it is the squad. It has first aid stuff, stretchers, backboards, and extra air tanks for the men's air packs."

The chief opened the door to Engine 5-1 and invited Peter to sit in the driver's seat. He needed a boost to get all the way up there. He sat holding the wheel, twisting it right and left.

"Pull that chain up there to your right, Peter." Then Rick looked at John and winked. With no idea at all what would happen, Peter pulled it—hard. The air horn let out a deafening blast that had everyone ducking and/or giving surprised glances. Peter looked out the open door with gigantic eyes *and* a big satisfied smile. Rick laughed so hard he was doubled over wheezing and had to wipe his eyes.

Recovering, he offered to Peter, "sometime you can hold a working nozzle and spray some water but tonight we have to do our small equipment checks," the chief explained, helping Peter back down to the floor. "But come any time and ask anything you want to. Maybe mom and dad will let you join when you turn sixteen." Rick looked at John who did not protest at all.

"Mom! Mom!" Peter exclaimed as he came into the kitchen, "They showed me everything!" He went on to brief Joan on every piece of apparatus.

He accepted Chief Harrington's offer and was frequently at the firehouse.

* * * * * * *

One night, not too long after his tour, Peter was surprised awake by the fire whistle's roar. He went to the window for the usual show. In a couple of minutes men were seen running into the firehouse from both directions but, oddly, each one kept looking over his left shoulder. Cars and pick-ups with flashing blue lights on top raced into the gravel parking lot skidding to abrupt stops. One by one the overhead doors opened, head lights and flashing red lights filled the doorways. Peter could see the men running to the trucks and climbing in.

From the front hallway Peter heard his mother, alarmed, say, "Oh John, look…is that at Percy's place?"

"Ohhhh boy," was his dad's worried reply.

Peter raced to the hallway window which was above the front door. Looking down the length of Elm Street toward the stop sign at Slocum Road, all he saw was a glowing, dancing, wall of orange and a bright glow above it.

"I bet it's the barn," John surmised.

Peter then raced down to the front porch in his pajamas. Engine 5-1 had stopped at the bridge. Peter was at first confused by this but then a fireman pulled down some of that huge yellow hose and wrapped it around a sign post. The engine then crawled down Elm Street rhythmically dropping a trail of hose behind it. When Engine 5-2 came out it also stopped at the bridge but it stayed there. In the darkness the men connected the yellow hose to the truck and put the hard bars into the creek—accompanied by the clanking of metal meeting metal and the men speaking with one another. Peter guessed this engine would suck out the water then send it, through the hose, to the other one. He overheard the communications radio which was full of odd messages about someone or another "responding on the five box" and something about "defending the exposures," and a call for a "second and third alarm assignment," whatever all that meant. Tones for additional fire companies could be heard on the radio as well.

John came down, sloppily dressed with Peter's slippers and jacket in his hand. The tanker raced down the street staying to one side of the still flat yellow hose. The squad soon followed.

"Let's go see," John suggested.

As the two walked up Elm Street toward the dancing flames and flashing red lights, the yellow hose next to them hissed and jumped from side to side like a giant snake as the water filled it and rushed up to Engine 5-1. It quickly became apparent that the giant wooden barn at the Romig's was fully involved as the wooden siding seemed to be melting away due to the flames behind it. The fire roared, snapped, and popped. The flames rose high into the sky where they became thick smoke. Two hoses with two men at each nozzle, one right behind the other one, were already spraying water on the nearby house and the other barn, steam rising from both structures. Two men were pulling down another hose from the engine. Rick Harrington in his solid white helmet and turnout gear was walking back and forth, observing, and talking into his radio and pointing this way and that occasionally stopping to talk to another fireman who would then go off to do what he had been instructed to do usually with a slight pat on the back of his shoulder.

A huge blue fire engine came up Slocum Road from State Road and stopped perpendicular to Engine 5-1. The side of the cab said in reflective white characters: "Lainge's Gap Fire Co. Engine 19." Below this was added in italicized black letters *"Big Blue!"* It, too, was leaving a line of yellow hose behind it; Peter guessed that they would get water from the bridge on Slocum Road. Two men climbed on top of the engine which had a deck gun on top behind the cab. Two others pulled a hose from above the pump panel and took it inside the house but it did not fill with water. The men on top of the truck aimed the giant nozzle then the engine roared to life and water sprayed from the deck gun right over to the main fire. In one minute the water sputtered and quit before making any difference in the flames. Engine 19 was out of water. When the stream started again Peter peered down the road and saw red lights flashing in the vicinity of the bridge on Slocum Road. It turned out Engine 16-2 from Colsonburg was sending water to Big Blue. To the right there was another group of fire trucks that had come down from the north from companies eight, fourteen and ten. Tanker 5 was with them. They were getting water from Grandpa's pond. The tankers shuttled back and forth from the fire to Grandpa's pond where Engine 14 was pulling water for them. The road was now submerged in a sea of water, tangled hoses and the reflections of flashing red lights.

One by one the burning beams collapsed into a heap. The main floor inside collapsed all at once under the weight of many giant round bales of hay and then one whole wall fell in flames against the house, but the streams from the hoses and deck gun quickly subdued that serious complication.

When the flames finally began to diminish somewhat John said, "Well, we best get home and get you back in bed. It's three o'clock in the morning now and you have school tomorrow."

On the way home they passed a parked fire truck that said "Colsonburg Ladder & Hose Company Rescue 16" then an ambulance, also from Colsonburg—both parked right on Elm Street, diesel engines humming loudly. Neighbors lined the street watching it all and Engine 17 from Trasston was standing by at the Laingeville Center firehouse. That truck was yellow. As they walked, Peter explained everything he saw to his dad. He was only partially correct in his observations but not too far off for a child.

Percy Romig lost three tractors plus any hay left from the last season in the overnight fire, but no animals. The big barn was a total loss but the single blackened spot on just the side of the house gave testimony to the fact that the firemen had succeeded in keeping the fire from engulfing *three* other nearby buildings. Ironically Percy and his son, Garrett, were both firefighters.

* * * * * * *

Just about nine years after the fire at Percy's, a sixteen-year-old young man known as Pete went into the firehouse on a Thursday evening. He was the better part of six feet tall; he really needed to shave his chin and sideburns. No adult accompanied him that day. Finding Rick Harrington, he said with a man's voice, "Here's my application."

"Excellent," Rick said, receiving the form from him and quickly looking it over. "I'll have the chairman of the membership committee call you."

A month later, after Pete had completed the remaining forms and had been interviewed by the membership committee, Chief Harrington knocked on the front door at nine o'clock on Thursday evening after the monthly meeting. Amy answered the door.

"Is Pete home?"

Pete recognized the voice and rushed to the open door, nudging blonde-haired Amy aside.

"Pete," the chief began, "here's your membership card. Randy McDonald will call you to make a time to get your gear and so on."

"Thanks," Pete answered, excited, taking the card, "I'll see you soon."

"Probably...," Rick agreed, "...probably."

The next time Pete would ride in the truck and not just watch it from a distance.

* * * * * * *

The fire whistle did not blow for three weeks.

One Monday afternoon after school Pete and Pat helped their dad load some scaffold into the back of John's truck for a job he was starting the next day. They were almost done when the fire whistle began blowing next door. Pete just froze and looked at his dad as if to ask, "What now?"

"You better get over there," John swung his head to the right.

Pete removed his gloves and took off running for the firehouse.

"Be careful," John called but Pete was long gone.

44

The other men had pagers and therefore a head start on Pete. Percy and his adult son, Garrett, were already there, along with Randy. Only the far right door was open. Percy was in the driver's seat of the squad; Randy and Garrett were in the front seat of the brush truck. After pulling the squad out, Percy parked it and, getting out, said to Pete, "Come with me."

Percy walked swiftly into the firehouse, right past the engines, to the tanker. Pete put his gear on and jogged over to the tanker as its diesel engine rumbled. Pete was sitting high above the ground; he put on his seat belt. The brush truck drove away turning left toward State Road as Percy hit two or three of the black toggle switches above the windshield. Pete heard the details: a tractor on fire and spreading into the field and nearby woods.

"You know what to do?" Percy asked, pointing at the communications radio.

"I think so."

"Good; you talk, I'll drive."

Pete keyed the mic and waited for the subtle beep indicating it was ready.

"County, this is Tanker 5."

"Tanker 5..."

"Tanker 5 is responding with two." He replaced the mic in its clip on the dash board.

The dispatcher acknowledged his message and repeated the location and details.

"You want to operate the siren and horn?" Percy asked.

"Sure," Pete replied plainly, calmly. Inside, though, he was as thrilled as that seven-year-old blowing the air horn.

Pete was back in time for supper. It did not always work out that way, though.

For the next several years many of Pete's evenings were spent in training and classes. There were long nights, missed meals, and missed sleep from answering calls. But Pete had a passion for firefighting. He proved himself a team player and a willing worker on the fire ground.

But it was not all just fun and games; it was serious. For him it was also a way to help his friends and neighbors in a practical and necessary way. Some calls were routine, even mundane like pumping out a flooded basement. Other calls were bizarre like a tractor-trailer truck full of boxes of plastic-wrapped heads of lettuce catching fire in the middle of the night—burned lettuce was sure a messy thing to wade through! But still others were pretty tough—like losing a long, desperate fight to save a home out on Wright Road one Sunday morning or helping to extricate a deceased victim of a car accident. Leaving for a barn fire at bedtime and returning home after breakfast was not pleasant either. At a garage fire on a sub-zero December night, Pete slipped on the frozen water and bruised his tailbone; he hobbled around for days afterward.

Eventually a day would come when Pete's part in the fire company would make the biggest difference of all for one person. The funny thing about it was that that man was himself a fellow firefighter and his rescue did not involve any sirens or hoses or stretchers; the pager did not even ring first.

Lessons at Camp

Youth Group at 3C was held every Wednesday evening at the same time as Prayer Groups and the Kids' Clubs. About eight or ten high schoolers came on an average night. It was still May when a flyer was distributed for a youth retreat at the denominational church camp in west-central Pennsylvania. This was held each year but Pete had never been able to attend. The year before was the first time he was old enough (fifteen) but the family had planned vacation that week. He would go this year, though. After all, it sounded like fun and his parents were encouraged to send him, in part, by the keynote speaker: The Rev. Daniel Morton, though Pete barely remembered Pastor Dan.

The planners of the retreat selected Dan because of his youth ministry credentials and his availability.

* * * * * * *

Four teens, Pete, Brad, Erin, and Deanne, went to the retreat riding with the youth leaders, Mr. and Mrs. Wilcox, who doubled as chaperones. They slept in crowded dormitories on narrow bunks. Meals were in the dining hall and the gatherings in "The Tab," short for the Tabernacle. The event lasted from Monday through Saturday. There was free time every afternoon following lunch, worship early each morning and each evening, and the teaching sessions were held the second half of each morning and afternoon.

But on the first day there were two sessions in the afternoon. The first session was based on First Timothy 4:12, "Let no one despise your youth, but be an example to the believers in word, in conduct, in love, in spirit, in faith, in purity." It was both an overview of the verse that was the basis of the whole week and a general challenge to live in a godly way as a teenager.

Pastor Dan combined humor, slide presentations on the computer and projector, stories, and illustrations to catch and keep the teens' attention. He had no difficulty getting them to hear the message he sought to present. Ginny was with him to both be supportive of Dan and to help teach the girls. Patty and Billy had both graduated and now had jobs at home in Compact, New York, so they stayed behind. Only sixteen-year-old Beth came with her parents to the retreat.

It was the second session that first caught Pete's attention in a very serious and personal way. It focused on one of the words in 1st Timothy 4:12 and applied it in a typical teenage context; it was called "Purity—in Relationships." It was a bold, direct, and blunt plea in favor of saving sex for marriage.

Dan started with some statistics about teen sexual activity. He quickly transitioned to an overview of the Biblical teaching about premarital sex beginning with establishing the purpose of sex for procreation and the uniting of a husband and wife as "one flesh." (Genesis 1:28 & 2:24). He especially focused on the word "fornication" in the New Testament showing that it primarily referred to premarital sexual relations. He also presented a couple references from the Old Testament that demonstrated God's clear disapproval of premarital sex and the harsh judgment Israel was to exercise over those who did not wait for marriage. He was careful to remind the young people, though, that the Bible spoke a lot about sex and that most of it was in a positive sense, but that sex could be very destructive if not maintained within God's revealed purpose. He also was firm that *not* handling it according to God's will caused it to mean far *less* to the people involved than God intended.

His central illustration, though, captivated the imagination. Dan taught them that sexual intercourse was the closest form of physical affection available to a man and a woman. He called it "love, all grown up." With that concept in mind, he told how affection should only follow the other steps taken in a growing relationship. Those steps included knowing one another's pasts, dreams, values, sharing time together, making mutual decisions about the direction of the relationship, and making increasing levels of commitment. Affection, in appropriate forms, could and should follow each step of growth in the relationship but that sex should only follow the greatest decision and commitment of all: the wedding.

Dan told how easily teens fell into the trap of premarital sex but it was really about one part of the relationship "growing up" before the rest of it. To illustrate his point he put some cut and pasted pictures on the screen. One picture showed a baby with an adult arm; another showed a preschooler with a full beard; others included animals and even plants with similar problems.

"Now we would all agree something is terribly wrong in these pictures, right?" he asked his audience.

Still laughing, they all agreed with that conclusion.

"So what's wrong is that one part is trying to be all grown up while the rest is still far behind. That's what happens with all premarital sex; part of the relationship is trying to be all grown up while the rest is in infancy or childhood or adolescence, in terms of intimacy and commitment. If we would agree that something is desperately wrong in these photos—I think we would call them 'mutations'—then why wouldn't we agree that something's very wrong with premarital sex?"

He concluded with a few of the problems that result from premarital sex, the myths about 'the first time' perpetuated by society (especially the movie and music industries), and a few tips on how to avoid falling into the trap of unexpected, unplanned sexual intercourse as a teen and young adult.

The young people, guys and girls, alike listened and many took notes in the packets Dan had provided. This gave Pete much to think about and reflect upon, though he was actually quite skeptical. At Dan's invitation several teens went forward to pray for strength to stand against this powerful temptation and a few for confession and forgiveness from God and self because they had already allowed themselves to fall into that trap; they wanted a new start.

* * * * * * *

For the session the next morning the audience was separated. The girls went with Ginny to another meeting area where she taught about modesty in their appearance, especially in how they dressed. She stressed the strong visual aspect of a guy's personality and the effect a girl's appearance had both in attraction and in a guy's attitudes and responses to her. Ginny also taught how visual attraction had a role in some of the cases of rape and even murder of women, especially girls, even offering quotations from criminals themselves as to how it affected their decisions and actions toward women, especially teens and pre-teens. She gave them specific suggestions and guidelines about dressing and presenting themselves in an appropriate, safe and godly way.

Back in "The Tab" with the guys, Dan's text was from Job 31:1-3 (NIV), "I made a covenant with my eyes not to look lustfully at a girl. For what is man's lot from God above, his heritage from the Almighty on high? Is it not ruin for the wicked, disaster for those who do wrong?"

For only a few minutes he spoke from the guys' perspective about the modesty issue, about guys dressing appropriately but also about avoiding giving improper attention to a girl's body. He was again plain and blunt, only more so since it was just the guys now.

Seizing on the phrase "look lustfully at a girl," he talked to them about the problem of viewing girls as sexual objects to feed the mind's fantasies. He was sympathetic to the guys' curiosity and vulnerability to lust because they were so visually-oriented. But he warned them about the problems associated with lust—what it leads to, how it consumes the mind and the imagination if it is not kept under control. He explained how a man can actually become a slave to sexual thoughts very easily. There probably was not a senior high boy in the place that had not struggled with this problem, some more than others, of course.

Pete was riveted by Dan's frank discussion. He had heard plenty about this from time to time at home, in Sunday School, sermons, and youth group. But he had never heard a whole talk reserved only for this subject that was also so plain and straight-forward. But even more, he began to feel almost like everyone else had left the room and Pastor Dan was talking only to him—straight at him. It was not a comfortable feeling. It was a mixed feeling of anger, guilt, feeling like he was caught red-handed, like someone had been watching him and sending reports to Pastor Dan about their observations.

He did not like the feeling and wondered what he could do about it. He could not flee. He would have to listen and decide from there what his response would be.

Dan did not miss seeing the look on Pete's face. He saw it on the faces of others also. Dan could tell he was hitting his mark: the consciences of guys with a very real problem. Many of these problems would begin to be solved that day. Sadly many would remain, depending on how those young men responded.

But the presentation would only get more difficult for Pete. Only a short way into the time, Dan switched his focus to the problem of pornography. Again he quoted statistics about how common the problem of pornography was among fifteen- to eighteen-year-olds.

He went on to point out the sources of pornography in guys' lives: from friends, fathers who have it, finding it accidentally, the internet, email, webcams, and camera phones. He gave suggestions on how to control those sources.

In the final phase of his talk Dan talked about the problems pornography leads to. He compared the energy aroused in a man by pornography with the energy that builds up in a cloud during a thunderstorm. That charge of energy needs to go somewhere so a lightning bolt results. The longer the charge builds the more powerful, destructive, and loud was the strike. So the longer the pornography goes on and the more severe and/or frequent the images, then the more serious and damaging the bolt or bolts that result.

The problems that result start small, he explained, almost naively, but go on to become more frequent and destructive. Some of his examples were a little embarrassing to hear or think about and often did not appear very serious at first. But snickers and blushes disappeared as Dan told of instances where men, charged up on months or years of pornography, committed heinous crimes including even serial murders. He cited actual news stories that almost everyone had at least heard about.

When Dan invited the guys to come forward for prayer at the end, several went down. Pete stayed in his seat and watched; there was no way he was going to let Brad from church see *him* go forward over *this* issue! What would Brad think—or *say*. Eventually Dan dismissed all but the ones at the makeshift altar and they left quietly but quickly—most glad that was over but secretly relieved someone had finally said a serious word to them about a very common problem. It was a problem most had questions about, but many were too embarrassed or afraid to pursue their questions with an adult.

* * * * * * *

Finishing his lunch, Pete crossed the dining hall and quietly, politely stood near where Dan and Ginny were seated with some of the other adults. Catching a glimpse of Pete, Dan cheerfully called out, "Hey, Peter!"

Approaching Dan he sheepishly asked, "Can I talk to you about... something...sometime?"

"Sure," Dan answered wiping his mouth with a napkin, "can you come to my cottage during free time? The sooner the better; I may get other callers too!"

"I guess so," he replied, not expecting such a prompt response.

Dan described the location of the borrowed cottage and wrote down the name of it and the lane where it was located.

"Thanks," Pete said.

"Sure. I'll see you later."

Pete's Big Day

Stepping up to the porch of the cottage, Pete nervously approached the wooden screen door. He reached up and rapped on the wood sash with the knuckles of his right hand. Though no voice was heard, there was movement inside in response to his knock.

Carrying a book in her hand, Beth appeared from a far corner of the dim living room. Lest she ask any questions, he spoke up immediately saying, "Pastor Dan is expecting me."

Beth immediately diverted to her left where the narrow, steep wooden stairs went up to the tiny upstairs rooms. "Dad, Peter Archer's here!"

"Okay," was the invisible response descending from the top of the steps.

Turning toward the screen door, Beth said, "He'll be right down."

She immediately returned to the corner to continue reading in the natural light from the window, leaving Pete standing on the porch waiting. Then feet were heard pounding down those bare wooden treads.

"Hey, Peter," Pastor Dan happily said as he reached a hand up to the wooden sash and pushed the door open with that legendary long squeak. After he stepped out onto the porch, the door instantly swung back to its closed position with the loud slap of wood hitting wood. In Dan's left hand was his Bible.

"Do you want to sit on the porch or go for a walk?" he inquired of Pete.

Pete knew he did *not* want their conversation overheard, especially by a sixteen-year-old female just on the other side of the screen door, so he simply said, "a walk, I guess."

Dan gestured forward with his right hand and he and Pete headed down the steps, along the gravel lane for about twenty yards, then between two cottages and onto a rough trail that ran between the summer homes and the small, shallow river still near its source, forested mountains all around them. At first Dan just asked questions about Pete's family, school, and his interests.

But, knowing Pete wanted to talk about more than just his grades, 4-H, and the fire company, he asked him, "So, what's on your mind, Peter?"

After a brief hesitation Pete started, "Well…I've *really* been thinking about those talks yesterday and this morning," Pete answered.

"Oh?"

"Yeah."

This whole exchange was starting out on an awkward note as Pete did not know how to say what he *knew* had to be said. He had never done anything like this before.

"Why don't we sit down?" Dan pointed out some large rocks at the river's edge. The only noise was the flow of the water over the rocky riverbed and an occasional car passing on the nearby blacktop road on the other side of the water. The sky was solid blue and the sunlight sparkled on the playful water; it was hot that day. Dan sat hunched forward with his elbows on his knees, his Bible hanging down from his left hand. Pete sat on the rock looking out over the water as Dan watched him. Moments seemed like hours.

"What's wrong, Peter?"

Pete began to quietly cry as he watched the glittering water. Dan silently prayed for him. In shaking words Pete started "fessing up."

"All that stuff you were talking about and what it does to a guy," he struggled to say, "...that's...well...that's...me." Pete closed his eyes as if wincing in pain. The direction of this conversation was now set and could not be altered; for the first time the secret was out.

Dan clarified what Pete struggled to say, "You mean the lust—"

"All of it!" Pete blurted out emotionally so Dan would not be able to say the rest. He did not want to even hear the rest of the words. "*All* of it, almost all of it, anyway," Pete summarized, "nothing, you know, criminal, but *everything* else."

"How long has it been going on?" Dan asked him.

"About four years now...it wasn't that much at first but...well, like you said, it just gets more powerful. The truth is by now I think I've seen everything there is to be seen. And even some of the things I've *done*...you wouldn't believe it," he said in subdued tones.

"You could try me, but I doubt you're right about that," Dan offered.

"I don't even want to *think* about it, much less say it."

"Okay. You don't have to. But I have a hunch I know already anyway."

"I knew it was wrong and at first I guess it was just curiosity—you know. I was just, like, twelve or thirteen."

Dan nodded, asking, "How did it start?"

"My friend, Bryan, has his own computer in his room. His parents don't really monitor it or filter it or anything. I'd go to his house and he'd show stuff. I never could have gotten it at home; my folks had no idea. He printed me stuff and made a DVD and a CD—even gave me an old DVD player that didn't have sound anymore. I stashed those at Grandpa's place. I couldn't keep it at home. I really thought it was no big deal but things are getting out of control now—in a lot of ways. I've experimented with some stuff I never would've until the porn came along. I got pretty scared a couple times this summer—just before coming out here."

"What happened?" Dan asked calmly.

"The stuff I hid at Grandpa's—in one of the sheds—disappeared so I think I might be busted. I know Grandpa knew I was going in there a lot."

"Hmm. What else?"

"I had a girlfriend, Melissa," Pete said. Dan's countenance fell as he feared he knew what was coming next. "And one evening I was taking her home but we didn't actually go straight back to her place. We both knew what it was we wanted to have happen. I know, especially, now, that all that stuff just had me so stoked, I felt like I *had* to act on it—like one of those programs on your computer, you know, that just runs automatically, without even having to tell it to—act, besides just…well…you know."

Dan nodded indicating he understood what was too embarrassing and difficult for Pete to put into words.

"So we started, you know, kissing and stuff—really carrying on. It was getting pretty heated. If we had had just a few more minutes alone things would have somehow gone, you know, 'all the way'. I was trying to make sure of it. I really thought I could just 'get it out of my system.' I don't know why. None of the rest of it worked that way."

Slightly relieved, Dan asked, "So what happened instead?"

"We were just about ready to, I guess, when lights flashed into the truck. The guy whose field we were near was coming down the hill in his tractor. When we looked out he was getting down and studying my truck from across the way. I hope he didn't figure out it was me; it's a small town, you know. We took off pretty quick. Of course we were both pretty frustrated afterward…you know…"

Again Dan nodded.

"I was so upset I could have just exploded somehow. She was kind of ticked off. I know *she* wanted to, maybe even more than I did. We didn't try it again—partly out of *my* fear of being caught and partly because we just didn't have enough opportunity I guess. But about a week ago she broke up with me. My parents still think she was a nice girl; they didn't realize."

"I'm sorry she hurt you but it probably spared you from a big mistake and for that you can be thankful," Dan observed, gently pointing in Pete's general direction with his index finger, as if emphasizing the point.

"Yeah."

"So you still have never—"

"No. That was the closest I ever got."

"I'm relieved to hear that; do you have a lot of lustful *thoughts*?" Dan inquired.

"*All... the...time*," Pete admitted. He had never looked Dan in the eye the whole time. He just kept staring out over the water. He was too embarrassed to even look in Dan's direction.

"And now you're scared that you've been caught on both counts, huh?"

"Yeah. And I can see how what's been happening is like that stuff you said about those criminals, sex offenders especially, who got started just like I did. I can see how it might actually go that far someday."

"So you're scared of that, too?"

"Yeah. I want a decent life—you know, a family and stuff," Pete really started crying.

"But this isn't the way to that dream is it?"

"No," Pete sobbed, almost angrily.

"Look at me, Peter," Dan requested.

Pete turned to him at last, his face red from trying, very unsuccessfully, to hold in his tears.

Dan continued, "Do you want to get things right, get on the right track, and get your mind straightened out again?"

"Yeah," Pete said through his tears, "this isn't worth it—the sneaking around, the lying, not knowing what I'll turn to next. And what if me and Melissa *did*? What if she got pregnant or something—oh that would've really been bad. What would my parents have thought? What would I, *we*, have done? But we weren't thinking about that—just about *one thing*. People talk about 'safe sex' but that's the last thing on your mind right then. I mean you take the opportunity when you see it, ready or not. At least it was that way for us. And I *have* tried to quit thinking about all that stuff but I can't. I just can't." Pete cried out of frustration and desperation, not to mention self-disgust, flinging his hands down in front of him. "It's like a constant slide show or video in my head. It drives me to do, well, stuff. Even weird stuff—at least think about it or even just plan it."

"Okay. Take a minute to calm down." Dan handed Pete his handkerchief and then stayed quiet so he could get composed.

"I bet you can't believe what a bad apple cute little Peter Archer turned out to be," Pete sobbed, wiping his face with the handkerchief and looking back out over the water.

"That's not true, Peter," Dan said compassionately. "You got caught up in something that a lot of young men have, but most don't deal with it the way you are right now. We've all had our dark times of one kind or another."

"Even—?"

"Even me," Dan assured him, "I wasn't always saved you know and I was a teenaged boy once, too. I've talked to a lot of young men caught in the stuff you're caught in and some are in worse shape than you. One was already in jail—for rape of a younger girl who's having a really tough time now. Some are fathers at *your* age. You are right to take this seriously because it doesn't sound like jail fits into your dreams and this isn't going to just go away either. Peter, I'm sure God wants you to have a wife and a family and a wonderful, beautiful relationship with that wife—not like the junk you've been seeing—but *real* intimacy, a healthy affection, and mutual tenderness."

"I hope so but I got to get this stuff out of my head, first." Pete could barely say.

"You're right and I'm sure you will," Dan encouraged him.

"But *how?*" Pete pleaded.

Dan changed the course of the discussion. "Peter, has there ever been a time that you turned your life over to Christ as your Savior and Lord?" He needed to know.

"No," Pete admitted. "I should have. I've had a hundred chances to. I've had the chances and I know the whole story, the whole plan of salvation. I just never did it. I wanted to do other stuff more, I guess and I knew I couldn't do both."

"Do you think if you had, things might have been different for you?"

"I'm *sure* they would have been somehow but I've just been coasting along—spiritually—you know. And now it's done and I'm all messed up."

"You and a whole lot of other kids, too; you're not the only one. You know the story inside-out but let's review it anyway, okay?" Dan asked, opening his Bible.

"Okay," Pete said sniffing.

"There are a lot of problems in our world—things like we've talked about already and other things too like corruption, stealing, murdering, and cheating. God calls all those things sin—so sin is the problem."

"That's for sure," Pete agreed, more calmly now.

"And God judges sin. Romans 1:18 says, '...the wrath of God is revealed from Heaven against all ungodliness and unrighteousness of men.' Sin makes God angry and He's doing something about it. Hell is real and it is God's eternal wrath, or anger, for those who sin and never repent. Also it says in verse twenty four that '...God...gave them up to uncleanness,' and in verse twenty-seven that they received '…in themselves the penalty of their error which was due.' So God lets us be miserable in our sins while we wait for Hell. Romans 3:23 says, '…all have sinned and fall short of the glory of God,' not just Peter."

"I suppose so," Pete acknowledged, though it did not feel that way just then.

"And God says in Romans 6:23 that '…the wages of sin is death…' There's no future, no eternal life in sin; it separates us from a right relationship with God and ultimately separates us from Him forever in Hell."

"But," Dan continued, "Romans 5:8 says 'God demonstrates His own love for us in that while we were still sinners, Christ died for us.' God loves us and doesn't want sin to ruin our lives like it's doing to yours. Christ died for us *because* we were sinners and the time to receive Him is now—as a sinner. And he died *for* us—in our place. You see, Jesus took our personal penalty for sin on Himself and suffered what we each should have suffered. When we rely on that fact, that's faith, believing. Then God puts that payment against our account so that the debt is settled."

"Further," he pressed ahead, "First John 1:9 says, 'If we confess our sins He is faithful and just to forgive us our sins and cleanse us from all unrighteousness.' Do you want that, Peter, to be forgiven *and* cleansed?"

"Yeah."

"Finally the Bible also says, '…if anyone is in Christ he is a new creation; old things have passed away: behold, all things have become new.' That's in Second Corinthians 5:17. You need to realize that if you do this, God sees you as brand new, clean, and untarnished by all that stuff. You'll be able to remember it but eventually you'll get your mind clear of it and God will *never* bring it up to you again. The Devil might but God won't and *I* won't. This is all called being born again. Do you want that, Peter?"

"Do you mean *now*?"

"If not now, when? Has waiting *this* long helped?"

"I guess now makes sense," Pete consented, though Dan would have let him wait if that was what he wanted to do.

"That's right—nothing to lose, huh? Let's pray," Dan suggested. It was he who started, "Thank you, Heavenly Father, for my friend Peter and for showing him he needs to get forgiven and start over, repent of these things and probably some other things, too. I know he's sincere and that today's his big day with You. So help him now and honor the prayer he brings." He paused then said, "Peter, why don't you pray to God now and admit again what's been going on in your life."

It was Dan's intention to prompt Pete through each step he had laid out in his talk, reminding him what to pray about with each prompt but letting him do it in his own words. Pete did not give him that chance though because he did not stop praying until he was good and done. This is the sign of someone who is very sincere and definitely ready to take that step.

"Dear God," he started, "I know You know what I've been doing and thinking about and that all of it's wrong and it's really messing with my life and making a lot of problems. I am so *ashamed* of myself for ever starting with that stuff and letting it take control of me. And I've done a lot of other sinful things too besides that." He cried as he prayed. "Please forgive me for all of it. I want to start over and get my life where it needs to be. I want Your will for me. Help me stop and help me forget all the stuff I've seen and done. I want to be clean and be that new creature Pastor talked about. I believe Jesus died on the Cross to pay for all those sins so forgive me, please."

Pete's prayer was not eloquent or well-crafted but it was from his heart and he meant every word of it—even more than he was able to say in words. It got kind of quiet and finally both looked up at each other. They stayed quiet for a few more moments.

"Happy birthday, Peter," Dan finally greeted him.

"Huh?" Pete wondered out loud.

"Today, right now, you've been born—again. Happy Birthday."

"Wow, I guess so." Pete let a slight grin escape along with a nod.

"Look, this is what you need to do next; I'll write it down for you: You need to tell your pastor, Zed Jackson, right?"

"Yeah."

"Tell Zed about your decision today and see if he can help you get some discipleship or follow up. You also need to be baptized as soon as possible. You need to start disciplining your mind about sexual thoughts and get rid of anything that is pornographic to you in any way. Pray, too, for new friends and for this Bryan and Melissa to get saved also. You need to find a way to be honest with your family about what was going on. Remember this day; whatever it takes, don't forget these moments, they will help carry you in the tough times. Later I'm going to give you something else to help you out a little okay?"

"Okay."

"I'm going to mention to the Wilcox's that you've made a decision but that's all I will say."

"Thanks."

Standing up and patting Pete once on the side of his arm, Pastor Dan said, "I'm going to leave you alone for a while. Okay?'

"Yeah." Pete smiled politely.

Dan walked back to the cottage where he happily announced that Pete had just "got saved." But he offered absolutely no details of their conversation—

that was a sacred confidence and only Pete could ever tell those things and only when he was ready to and only to whom he wanted to.

Pete sat on that rock and watched the water go by. He thought how he somehow actually finally felt clean and fresh like that pure water. Everything looked the same and he was otherwise just Pete Archer but he also knew he *was* different now and that his life *would* be changed. Already it felt as if a gigantic weight had been lifted from him and indeed it had been. He prayed a little more, just letting his thoughts and feelings about it all go up to God. But eventually he had to leave. Walking back up the path everything was the same but at the same time everything was different.

Later Dan gave him a Bible arranged into three-hundred sixty-five daily readings in an easy to read translation. Inside the front cover Dan had written: "To Peter from Pastor Dan Morton on the biggest day of your life, August 16, 2005; never forget." There was also a paper with the steps Dan said he needed to take all written out for Pete to remember.

Back home Pete did tell Pastor Jackson about getting saved and asked about being baptized. He told his parents he was going to get baptized because he "decided to get saved while at camp." It was a long time before he was able to tell them everything but eventually he did—as much as they needed or had a right to know. Pastor Jackson gave him some workbooks to complete and asked Jim Corbin, one of the elders, to meet with him and go over the answers from time to time. He was baptized on a Sunday evening in September along with three others: a very young girl named Megan, a fifteen year-old girl named Christine, and an eighty-year-old man who had never been baptized.

He never experienced Sunday School, worship, or Youth Group the same way ever again. Instead it was better and more rewarding than ever. He continued to struggle with lust but less and less all the time, eventually finding victory over that habit. He never found those missing items and Grandpa never mentioned them. The neighbor must not have reported to his parents seeing Pete's truck in that field. Pete and Bryan had already started to drift apart as Pete spent more and more of his spare time up on the farm. Pete intentionally let that relationship slip away. Eventually the memories of all those images he had seen became foggier and foggier and one by one they disappeared from his mind altogether. There *would* be other struggles and a period, not so far in the future, that would test him in a profound way about his decision to turn from pornography. He frequently had to ask for forgiveness for some sin or another, like anyone else. He made a lot of mistakes, too, but his life *was* changed—forever.

Going to Court [4]

Before it was time to go home, however, there were several other lessons to listen to, each one based on a section of 1st Timothy 4:12. Dan also took one timeslot to teach about one of his favorite topics but it was something Pete had never heard before. He initially saw the wisdom in what Pastor Dan was saying but also felt it was impractical for most people. Because the outline was in the packet he would be able to refer back to it one day but for the next several years he largely ignored the advice.

* * * * * * *

"How many sitting here tonight think that they would want to get married and have a family someday?" Dan asked boisterously, thrusting his hand in the air to demonstrate the response he was looking for.

Almost every hand went up.

"How many dream of getting divorced?" he asked next.

Almost every hand went down; a couple jokers kept theirs up, thinking they were being funny.

"I thought so," he responded. "So if I'm a teen or young adult how am I going to find someone to marry?"

Choosing one of the raised hands he called on the young man who stood and said, respectfully, thoughtfully, "You, like, go out with a girl and find out if you like her or not. Then you fall in love and then you decide to get married."

"Thank you," Dan said pointing the direction of the answer-giver. "Now, does the system work? Are we getting married and living happily ever after?"

The reaction was mixed but a lot of the young people seemed to understand the point he was making and said "no" to the latest question but most still said "yes."

Dan then talked about the frequency of divorce in society and reminded them that almost no one *wanted* to get divorced someday.

"So what's the problem? Why are we getting divorced so much?" he asked.

Several answers came from the audience, most of which he agreed were part of the problem.

"Another part of the problem is *how* we choose our spouses—the dating phase."

He described the dating pattern. One kid thinks another one is nice or cute so they go out. Or a person wants to fall in love or get married so they go out with someone they think might be a good one to consider.

"But you want them to *like* you right?"

"Right," the audience agreed in unison.

"So you act like a jerk, right?" he asked hypothetically.

"If you do, you won't get a second date," one female voice called out.

"Exactly. You act perfectly—or try to—and put your best foot forward so the other one will like you and the relationship will move ahead. But that may not be who you really are and you might not find out what they are really like until it's too late and heartbreak cannot be avoided anymore. By the way you also start holding hands, and kissing, and the next thing you know you're 'in love.' But really a lot of it is just hormones and excitement. So what happens next? I *am* assuming this to be a *Christian* relationship, by the way."

Taking the bait, one male voice called out, "You get married!"

"Okay," Dan agreed, "that's right. And *why* did you get married?"

"Because you're in love!" another voice reminded him.

"And how did you 'fall in love'?" Dan asked as if uninformed on the subject.

"You feel it in your heart," a young lady responded.

"You *feel* it in your heart…" Dan repeated it pensively. "Not to mention in your hands when you're holding hands or in your lips when you're kissing." Then he added the question "Is this system working? And before you answer, remember how many marriages today end in divorce and that many of the rest are very unhappy."

Perhaps sensing a trap no one dared answer this time.

"It doesn't help, by the way, that my observation is that teens usually go through serial relationships—that is, one after another—falling in love, breaking up, falling in love, breaking up, and so on. It's like rehearsal for divorce!"

"Okay…let's look at the alternative. It's called *courtship*. Now, there are a lot of resources that teach about courtship. This is just my own version, based on my own experiences, observations, and Biblical teachings. So let's look at this one form of 'courtship'," Dan proposed. "Open your packets to the section called 'Going to Court'."

The outline was in three sections called "Never", "Always", and "Suggestions for Courting." As Dan spoke, the outline appeared on the screen with each point blank eventually appearing as a completed statement as he finished talking about it. When it was finished it looked like this:

1. <u>Never</u> go out with someone just because they are cute, nice, smart, or because you were set up.
2. <u>Never</u> go out with a stranger or someone you barely know. This includes most people you meet on the internet.

3. <u>Never</u> kiss or hold hands on a first date with someone new to you.
4. <u>Never</u> make decisions about a person based on feelings or emotions.
5. <u>Never</u> go out with someone you will not realistically marry someday.
6. <u>Never</u> go out with someone who does not believe and live the way you do.
7. <u>Never</u> allow yourself to become *"desperate"* for someone—be content in and by yourself as a single person.

Then the "always" list was presented:

1. <u>Always</u> maintain *friendships* with both guys *and* girls.
2. <u>Always</u> go out with someone you've already come to know very well, so there's no pressure to be Mr. or Miss Perfect.
3. <u>Always</u> reserve affection until you've both agreed, out loud, that you belong together, are in an official courtship and start very slowly.
4. <u>Always</u> pray for God to guide your decisions about a relationship.
5. <u>Always</u> date a person you already know could be a potential spouse; if they could not be a spouse to you, do not get romantically involved with them.
6. <u>Always</u> go with a person who shares all your most important beliefs and priorities in life.

"Courtship," he explained, "unfolds like this:"

1. You don't look for a boyfriend or a girlfriend.
2. You wait for God to show you someone from your circle of friendships whom He is drawing you toward, and they toward you.
3. You both pray individually about it and ask God to lead both of you in your friendship.
4. If God continues to bring you closer and your friendship is getting deeper and more personal then…
5. You discuss it, pray about it, and decide what to do next: stay friends or start a courtship, based on God's leading.

6. Once in a courtship you both expect and agree that you will *probably* eventually decide to get married so everyone has the same perception.
7. *ALL* affection is reserved until the courtship has actually been launched and the relationship remains sexually pure—no sex before the wedding night.
8. Engagement is the last phase of the courtship—the decision to make it final and set a wedding date.
9. Love and attraction will become apparent at the right points along the way but maybe not at first.

Each point was explained thoroughly and he answered questions after he was done speaking. He also made it clear that he believed no one should be involved in dating or courting until they were *at least* sixteen years old and preferably older because anyone younger than sixteen was still way too far away from making any permanent decisions about their life.

"Courtship is a very serious decision," Dan admitted, "but if everyone courted then there would be a lot less pressure, short-term, and heartache, both short- and long-term. It's not fool-proof, though. Courtships do fail also but I believe the failure rate is a lot lower than with typical dating." He concluded by giving a brief account of the courtship between him and his wife during the late 1970's.

The final session at camp was a lesson on becoming a Christian—on the new birth. Afterward several teens demonstrated a decision to trust Christ as their personal Savior, but not Pete—he had already made that choice. But it was a good ending to the retreat.

Geoff

School started, as usual, the day after Labor Day. Though Pete had friends at school, it would appear that that year's schedule had conspired to keep him away from most of them. Many were attending the vocational-technical school while he followed a college-preparation track, staying in the high school all day. There were two lunch periods and he was assigned to a different one than almost everyone he knew well. His junior year would take some getting used to but a blessing was hidden in it as well.

Since Pete brought his lunch from home most days, he was able to be seated ahead of most of the students who were buying theirs. Pete bought lunch only occasionally since his parents required that he pay for his own when he bought.

Most of the tables were still empty and students were only slowly filing into the long room filled with tables and chairs. One very long table ran the length of the room in the center with chairs on each side. Tables were placed along the side walls perpendicular to the walls and seated eight or ten to a table.

Pete selected a place at one of the side tables that was near an open window and looked out over the teacher and staff parking lot. He was the only one at the table but that would soon change. The sounds of voices in conversation and chairs sliding back steadily increased until reaching a slight but constant roar. Four other students, seniors, approached Pete's table, trays in hand. Pete knew them by name at least; they were all from Colsonburg. There were three girls, all popular, pretty, and smart, one a cheerleader and the other two played basketball. The guy was someone Pete had seen at some of the combined church services in Colsonburg as well as at school. He was Geoff Gilberton.

Geoff also was popular, smart and a renowned athlete. He could play anything except for football, but he had slowed down his athletic schedule during his senior year, much to the dismay of many. Geoff was tall, trim, with short jet-black hair and always clean and well-dressed. His dad was a doctor, a general surgeon at a nearby hospital and his mother was an attorney with an area law firm. Geoff was the youngest child in his family and the only one still living at home fulltime. He was outgoing and active in the school; everyone was familiar with the name Geoff Gilberton.

"Mind if we sit with you?" Geoff asked.

"Help yourselves," Pete replied.

The group of four sat with their trays in front of them. Geoff was to Pete's left and all three girls sat opposite Pete and Geoff. The girls chattered away but suddenly became quiet and seemed to be waiting for something. Pete looked at them inquisitively and one of them tipped her head in Geoff's direction, rolling her eyes slightly. Looking to his left Pete saw Geoff raising his head and opening his eyes; he must have been quietly praying before eating! The girls' chatter resumed and Geoff chimed in with them.

Looking over at Pete, Geoff said, "I've seen you at some of the church services, haven't I?" Pete agreed that he had. Geoff continued, "I'm Geoff Gilberton. What's your name? I should know but I can't think of it." Pete did not have the name recognition Geoff and these girls had.

"Pete Archer," he reminded Geoff.

"Pete," Geoff said, nodding his head. "Your family goes to either Grace Center or Colsonburg Community, right?"

"Yeah," Pete acknowledged, "Colsonburg Community Church."

"My family goes to Light and Life Church," he explained.

"Okay," Pete said, "I've seen you at some of the services, too, besides here at school, of course."

One thing about Geoff, it was always easy to pick him out of a crowd around Colsonburg.

Geoff and the girls resumed their talk, apparently about a class they were in together that morning. Geoff must have noticed that Pete was being left out.

"What are your classes, Pete?" he asked.

Pete recited his class schedule. The four seniors all added their comments and advice on the classes and the teachers. After a while, however, the girls all left, one to see her guidance counselor, another to take a note to the nurse, and the third to meet yet another friend.

"The youth group leader at my church is starting a Bible Study on Tuesdays after school. Do you think you'd be interested? I mean since you obviously go to church and all," Geoff asked Pete.

"I might be. Is it here at school?"

"No, it's at my church since it's just a few blocks from here anyway, then no one can start that separation of church and state junk," Geoff explained.

"Let me talk to my folks about it. They don't like me to drive to school too much."

"Cool. Let me know," Geoff replied.

On Tuesday of the following week Pete drove to school. After the last bell he drove the short trip down School Street to Light and Life Church. Signs on the doors pointed the way to the gathering.

As Pete came into the designated classroom Geoff told everyone, "This is other the guy I was telling you about, Pete Archer." Taking a seat at the table and putting his Bible down in front of him, Pete looked around and recognized most of the dozen or so faces from school plus Ted from church—all sophomores and older, guys and girls alike. There were introductions around the table, then they were all asked by the man leading the meeting to share prayer requests first. Everyone had something that they wanted the others to pray for. Pete mentioned getting used to the changes in his schedule and that he would be baptized Sunday night. They went around the table and each young person prayed for the person on his or her right. A super tall senior girl prayed for Pete and Pete prayed for a sophomore guy whose grandmother was very sick out in Coudersport. The leader shared only a short devotion at the end then they dismissed.

"Thanks for coming, man," Geoff told Pete after.

"Thanks for telling me about it," Pete answered.

"So I'll see you next week, too, then?"

"Yeah, I think so."

* * * * * * *

On Sunday night Pete was baptized with the others and each gave a brief testimony of how they came to faith in Christ. Pete told about talking with Pastor Dan beside the river at camp but, of course, didn't tell all the details he had told Dan. Pete was surprised but pleased and impressed when he looked out over the congregation and saw Geoff sitting there with his dad! No one else from the group was there, except Ted.

Pastor Jackson gave a brief exhortation to the baptism candidates and told them that this represented the biggest and most significant decision that they would ever make: the decision to follow Christ. Then, one at a time, the candidates came into the waist-deep baptistery. Pastor Jackson said each one's name then he or she dropped to their knees and he said, "I baptize you in the Name of the Father, and of the Son, and of the Holy Spirit." He gently pressed down on the top of each one's head and he or she went beneath the surface of the water for only a moment or two. One of the elders assisted. Poor Megan was terrified of water but nervously went along with it and did just fine. The congregation sang a hymn afterward while the newly baptized went to separate rooms to change into dry clothes.

"Good job up there, man," Geoff said to Pete in the vestibule afterwards where all the people were greeting and congratulating the ones who had been baptized that evening.

"Hey, thanks for coming; that was cool of ya," Pete said back to him.

"See ya tomorrow," Geoff said as he turned and started to leave. Mr. Gilberton shook Pete's hand and congratulated him on his decision to follow Christ then followed Geoff out to the parking lot.

"Wow," Pete whispered to himself

"What?" Christine, one of those who was baptized, asked him.

"Oh, nothing—just talking to myself," Pete answered her.

* * * * * * *

Over the weeks and months the Tuesday afternoon gathering seemed to become more of a prayer meeting than a Bible Study but that was apparently all right with everyone. About ten to twelve teens came each week.

Pete and Geoff frequently ate at the same table during lunch. When it was cold or raining, Pete would drive Geoff home from the prayer group's gathering, though it wasn't far to Geoff's house. They found several interests in common including a similar taste in music and a fondness for science fiction movies. One Tuesday Pete drove Geoff home and stayed for supper. The two went up to Geoff's room where Geoff showed him his set of DVDs—including many of Pete's favorite movie titles. They played music—all contemporary Christian music, some soft, some loud and crazy, and some stirring and worshipful.

Geoff also had a gift for making music. He had an electronic keyboard and could immediately play any number of songs, traditional or contemporary, without any sheet music in front of him. Pete found out later that Geoff also could sing and was a part of the choir at Light and Life Church and even sang a solo now and then. His voice was versatile and he could switch around from tenor to baritone to bass but he could not hit the lowest bass notes as Pete could.

Geoff's room sure was different than Bryan's. Geoff was really trying to lead a pure life; Pete never had to worry about what would happen in *that* room. Geoff likewise came over to LC on another Tuesday. Pete's family was not well-to-do like Geoff's so Pete did not have as much to show off but Geoff did not seem to mind. Pete took him up to his room and they explored Pete's modest collection of music CDs and they went out to Grandpa's farm for a little while. From time to time they would go, along with other friends, to a movie or for ice cream. This helped Pete to expand his circle of friends, as well. They even double dated once but it wasn't anything serious—just for fun.

By winter the two had become fast friends. Geoff was popular but did not have deep *friendships*. Pete was not popular and needed a deep friendship with someone who would be an encouragement to him. So the two were good for each other; they talked about *everything*, including things that guys talk about only between themselves. Geoff told how he came to Christ and what it was like to be from such a unique family on the Colsonburg scene. Geoff was the first person, besides Pastor Dan, that Pete ever told about the pornography and other issues, at least in any detail; he had told Pastor Jackson but only in sweeping generalities. Geoff was very understanding and said he could see how a guy could get caught in that pretty easily.

"I knew you were hanging out with that Bryan," Geoff observed once, "that worried me because a lot of people know what he's into and it's only getting worse."

"I guess I found out too late," Pete admitted.

"And that Melissa girl…" Geoff said, "She's definitely trouble waiting to happen. It's a good thing you're done with her—and before it was too late."

"Yeah, for sure," Pete agreed.

"But we should remember they both need the Lord big time," Geoff pointed out. "We should be praying for them."

By spring Geoff and Pete had become best friends. It was a friendship many would never have guessed but their common bond was their faith in Christ and that surpassed all the other superficial differences between them and confirmed their equality no matter what.

Pete went to Geoff's graduation but it was hard to think that Geoff would not be around next year. It was very hard to say good-bye come late August.

Geoff had decided on a private Christian college in the southern part of the state; he wanted to be either a pastor or a teacher. He and Pete emailed frequently and occasionally called one another. They got together at least once every time Geoff was home for a break. Geoff often asked Pete if he was doing okay—keeping himself pure. Knowing Geoff would ask motivated Pete to be extra vigilant about his life but if he failed in some way he could always confide in Geoff. Geoff even shared his own struggles with purity, though he did not have the mental baggage and memories that Pete had. They always helped each other in that area and others as well.

Pete felt somewhat empty that first week of senior year but the other members of the prayer group and his Sunday School class provided increasing levels of friendship. One day in September Pete and two friends, a girl from the prayer group and a guy from his Sunday School class, sat with a new student, Kaleb, in the lunch room. After introducing themselves, they invited him to the prayer group, and he came—every week, faithfully. Kaleb and that girl who was with Pete that September day even started dating and they did so for a long time. Though it did not work out past high school (they originally had big dreams about one another), they really enjoyed and appreciated their relationship and they learned a lot from it. They remained friends.

Off to School

Now it was Pete's turn. The end of senior year kept getting closer and closer. He knew that his whole life would change come that Saturday afternoon in mid-June. He had been to Geoff's graduation and so he knew what it would be like. Geoff had told him quite a bit about college life; it did sound interesting, fun, and very challenging but still largely a mystery.

But first there were decisions to be made. John and Joanie wanted their children to receive as much education as possible and a degree of some kind to show for it. John did not attend college at all and often wished he had. Joanie had a certificate from a business school. Pete's grandfather, Jack, always said there was so much Pete could learn to make himself a better farmer if he would go to college.

Pete was uncertain about it. He just wanted to farm fulltime. Down inside, though, he knew his family was right but he was nervous about starting something so new and different. But if he was indeed a man now he needed to rise to meet the challenge and not just play it safe and comfortable.

If Pete was to attend agricultural school it was almost a given it would be at the university and not at a branch campus either. So he applied and was accepted. The problem was paying for it. He wanted to graduate debt-free and also not burden his parents with debt either, especially since Pat and Amy would have to have the same opportunity as well.

The Archers ran the numbers and could see him realistically attending the two-year associate's degree program, making it the one he applied for. This was a good start anyway and maybe he could transfer the credits into a bachelor's program later if he wanted to. The problem was that the savings and financial aid they could count on would cover most of the tuition costs but not room and board; they were out of dollars by that point. He was expected by the financial aid experts to work and borrow for the rest of it. The only debt the Archers had ever held was the mortgage for the house. Everything else was paid for on a cash basis. It was too far to commute from home so they decided together to pray about it and wait on the Lord for His direction.

Gathered around the dining room table at Jack and Dorothy's on Easter Sunday afternoon Pete was quizzed about his college plans.

"Your folks tell us you're going to the university," Aunt Judy informed Pete.

"I hope so," he replied, quickly popping a forkful of ham into his mouth.

"What do you mean by 'hope so'?" Uncle Jerald cross examined him.

Pete explained the limited finances and his commitment to not going into any unavoidable debt. Joanie added her own doubts about dormitory living anyway—the party atmosphere. She trusted her son but still nurtured a fear he would lose his way if he was immersed in that environment.

John, Jim, and Jerald were visiting together in the living room after dinner. Pete and his grandfather were, predictably, out in the barn to begin the afternoon milking.

"You know, John," Jim started, "if you want to send Pete to the university he could stay with me, if wants to."

Jim was tall, like his brother John and their father, Jack, but he was clean shaven and virtually bald. He had never married and continued to live in Centre County in a borough called Centre Hall, not far from where Pete wanted to go to school.

"In fact," he continued, "it might benefit me in some ways. I travel a lot for work so having someone around to watch the place might be a nice change of pace for me. Last winter the furnace quit while I was away and I came home just before the point the pipes would have started freezing. Having someone around to watch things would definitely be reassuring."

"To be honest," John replied, "we never talked about it."

"Well, why not? We're family, aren't we? And Pete and I always got along well. I have a spare bedroom that he can stay in and it wouldn't cost him a dime for utilities or even groceries as far as I'm concerned. Besides, in a couple of years he'll move on. It's up to you guys but it sounds like it would be just enough to fill the gap if he can get some work too."

"I'll mention it to him," John promised.

"You do that."

It did not take long for Pete and his folks to decide to accept Uncle Jim's offer. It sure "smelled" like an answer to prayer. There could be little doubt it would be of benefit to all involved. So Jim was called and a date for Pete to move in was set.

* * * * * * *

Dan, Ginny, and Beth came into Aunt Cynthia's living room and quickly set Beth's bags down so hugs could be shared all around. Cynthia had been praying for Dan since he was a child, then for his family, too. She had been a widow for many years and was, herself, a nurse. She had actually been a role model for Beth and a source of over-the-phone advice on fevers, coughs, and rashes for the Mortons for the last twenty-five years. She was short, kind of plump, with short grey hair that was fairly curly. Her face always had a blushing appearance and she *loved* to joke and laugh.

Aunt Cynthia lived in one of the neighborhoods surrounding Lewistown, Pennsylvania in the central part of the state, between State College and Harrisburg. Though retired now, she had been a nurse at the Lewistown Hospital and a graduate of its School of Nursing. After her husband died she moved into town to be closer to the work she loved so much. After retirement she volunteered her skills for church camps and substituted as a school nurse in several nearby districts.

Most of the walls were paneled and the bulky woodwork in the old home was all painted white. Plain white sheers hung over every window.

The Mortons had left Blueberry Haven early so they could drop Beth off and be back by bedtime. Dan had extensive commitments to keep at the new church.

When it came time to choose a nursing school, Beth had carefully weighed and prayed about her options. She could have lived at home and commuted to a program that was closer but she truly believed she needed to leave the nest and try her wings a bit. But the cost to move somewhere and pay rent or room and board was just not going to work out.

Finally, with her parents' blessing, she swallowed her pride and asked her great aunt Cynthia about staying with her if she could get accepted into the local program there were several features to it that she found attractive. The high pitched sounds of happiness and approval were audible all the way from the phone to the far reaches of the parsonage, still in Compact at that point in time. Given Cynthia's excitement, Beth was almost irrevocably locked into the arrangement. She offered to pay toward utilities to which Cynthia simply replied, laughing, "Oh, come on now!" Beth was accepted into the program.

Beth and Dan carried her bags up the narrow open stairway to the second floor. The room was plain, like the rest of the house, with a long, low dresser with a mirror and a twin bed with a painted metal headboard; the bed was all made up in a set of floral print sheets and a matching comforter.

"So this is your digs for the next couple years, huh?" Dan observed, straightening his back and looking around.

"I guess so," Beth said with trembling words. She was full of excitement and terror, both.

"It'll be fine kiddo," Dan said putting his arm around her shoulder and giving her a little shake.

Beth felt like she was going to cry so she suggested they get downstairs again. After some conversation over lemonade it was finally necessary to admit that the time for Dan and Ginny to leave had arrived.

Ginny looked at Beth; all she had to say was "oh…." Instantly everyone was crying. Dan and Ginny assured Beth of their love and prayers. Cynthia hugged both the parents at once, one arm around each of them and said, "don't worry—I'll take *good* care of her."

Beth stood in the door as her folks walked across the porch and down the steps. She thought to call out, "see you at Thanksgiving!" She could not stand to close the door so she did not until her parents' car had gone around the corner and out of sight. She missed them already.

"There, there, dear," Cynthia put arms around Beth, "you'll be fine and so will they."

As Beth pulled away she silently nodded her head and wiped her eyes. She told her great aunt that she wanted to go get unpacked. She lied. She actually went upstairs to sob. Later Cynthia took her to a little nearby diner for a nice supper out—her treat.

Dan could hardly drive he cried so. He did not know if the was crying for Beth, for him and Ginny, or all three of them. Ginny wouldn't have done any better as she was in the same condition herself. But after they got onto the expressway they each began to calm down again.

On Sunday Cynthia took Beth to church with her to a rural place called Paintersville. She showed off her great niece to everyone she could. All the parishioners greeted her warmly—some with a gentle handshake and others with a quick hug. This might be her church for the next two years. It was the first time Beth sat in a pew and heard someone else preach, knowing her Dad would not be taking over again the next Sunday. It would definitely take some getting used to.

* * * * * * *

Beth came into the classroom and picked a seat as all the other new students were doing. It occurred to her that she actually knew *no one* in that room. In the past when she started at a new school while growing up she had met at least one classmate at church first. But today she was totally and completely on her own. But God was with her and she knew that. She was counting on it, but still it was so very, very new.

She was terrified but not in the old way. The devil was not going to win—she was. No matter what he threw her way she was determined to prevail—and he wasn't done with her yet.

"Okay…" the instructor began….

* * * * * * * *

Out in the pickup truck Pete had carefully set his new laptop computer bought with money he had received as graduation gifts. It was carefully nestled between his two duffle bags. A pair of slacks and a white shirt were draped over the top of it all so he would have an outfit for church—somewhere.

Pete's departure was being spread out over a matter of a couple weeks; this made it a little easier to tolerate. The previous week he left early Friday morning to care for any business he could ahead of time. He stayed with his Uncle Jim then spent Saturday acquainting himself with the area and even looking for opportunities for work.

Now it was Wednesday afternoon. As he said good-bye he knew his parents would be down soon for Parents' Weekend. But he himself would not be home for weeks, or more, to come. He hugged his parents, then Pat and Amy hugged him—*that* was a surprise. It still wasn't sinking in yet.

He went from the house to the farm. This was where his life had been spent more and more over the last years. He would not see this place or, especially, his grandparents again soon. Grandma came out, wiping her hands on a towel.

"On your way?" she asked.

Sighing, he said, "I guess so. Where's Grandpa?"

"He's up at the top, cutting hay," she explained.

Grandpa knew Pete was leaving that day and at that very time. He had done this on purpose to avoid saying good bye or the emotions that go with it. Pete shook his head.

"I know..." Grandma sympathized.

"Well, maybe I'll see you in a month or two," he suggested.

"We'll be counting the days," Grandma promised. As he hugged her good-bye she whispered over his shoulder, "We're *real proud* of you."

She made him wait while she went inside to retrieve a zip bag of homemade ginger snap cookies.

"Share them with Jimmy," she warned, pointing at him.

"I will," he assured her.

He put the cookies in the cab and then walked up to the barn. He leaned on the barnyard fence. Grandpa's tractor was droning along at the edge of the woods, near the top of the slope. One of Pete's Herefords came over to him and he patted her on the head.

"Take care guys," he whispered, "Grandpa will be looking out for you."

His throat was tightening and his eyes were wet. He looked around at the barn, the cows, the fields—all of it.

As he got in the truck Grandma waved to him from the back porch. Pete turned the pickup around and turned right onto Slocum Road, then left onto Elm Street. He made the turn past the firehouse and his home;

everyone was inside now. It was all hitting him at once. He cried all the way to the stop sign at State Road but it started getting easier after that.

Uncle Jim was not home. It was to be a common sight. Pete let himself in and plated the only three cookies still left after the drive. He organized his room but it still felt like a strange place. It would be suppertime soon and he was not sure what he should do. He did not have Uncle Jim's cell phone number. He looked in the refrigerator and cupboards then, without thinking, ate another ginger snap!

Pete remembered there were several fast food restaurants on the way to school and just as he was about to grab his keys and go, Uncle Jim finally arrived home. The two men grilled bratwursts for supper. Then Uncle Jim buried his face in his laptop; his work was never quite done.

Pete was bored crazy so he took a walk around the borough. It seemed odd not to be in church on Wednesday evening. Come Sunday he would start visiting some local churches and maybe they would have Wednesday night activities like at home.

* * * * * * *

The first day of classes was now upon him. Pete was part of a line of vehicles flying up the on-ramp onto the expressway; using the freeway everyday would take some getting used to. There was a light fog and the traffic was thick and fast. He had left earlier than technically necessary in the event he became stuck in traffic or could not get parked quickly. He actually walked into his first class just at the announced starting time. Countless others came in late and many seemed not to care very much. The professor marched in and set his stack of papers, notes, files, and a laptop on the stand next to his lectern and started the class.

Not long after the first day another first arrived: Uncle Jim's first business trip since Pete had moved in. He would be away in Europe for two weeks. Pete left in the morning and Uncle Jim was gone when he returned. The house was completely silent and still. Pete had reading and other schoolwork to do. But it was not enough. He was used to the other people at least being around—the laughter and the conversation. Here there was none of that and it would continue that way for two entire weeks. Pete wondered how he would manage, especially since this was only the first of many such stretches of solitude.

3C

Pete had many new things to begin and he was starting each one by himself. While he could call or email his parents, he was largely on his own as he launched out into these new areas. It was both exciting and very intimidating at the same time. Of course he only outwardly expressed the excitement side of those emotions.

Besides his classes, he needed to find some work and a church to attend. He got busy with both as soon as possible but one was decided quickly while the other was much more difficult to find an answer to.

Pete wanted to work in an agriculture-related job. He spent his first Thursday and Friday looking for openings that would fit his schedule and occasional need to go home. He did not want to work Sundays, especially in the mornings.

He stumbled on something Friday afternoon. Pete never would have sought that particular job but he needed work and it *was* agriculture-related. There were two openings at an area greenhouse and vegetable farm. The fulltime student help had left with the conclusion of summer and the owner was looking for a set of part-timers for the rest of the year.

Pete would work in the fields picking corn and squash and other vegetables. He would also be helping as needed in the stand, ringing up orders, watering plants, selling Christmas trees in November and December, helping start the new sets and pots of plants in February, and beginning to plow and plant in the spring. He would have January off and other students would work fulltime in the summer, allowing him to return home for those three months. There would be no Sunday work, except as absolutely necessary, like watering the plant sets. He was surprised at how much he enjoyed it.

* * * * * * *

The first church Pete went to was Uncle Jim's church. It was a lot like Grandpa and Grandma Archer's church. The service was very stiff and formal almost everyone was his uncle's age or older and not very friendly. The sermon was short and not very informative or helpful. It felt like just going through some religious motions. Pete had a different expectation from church.

The following Sunday he visited another area church. It turned out to be very small—only about twenty people. It was their only service all week long. The people complained right in front of him about how small their church was; Pete did not know how to respond. The pastor rushed in from another church and with hardly a word darted into the pulpit to lead the service for the people. The sermon had very little to do with the several

Scriptures that had been read earlier. Then the pastor left in a hurry for yet *another* service in yet *another* church—his third one that morning.

Church number three had a large congregation in a relatively new building. There were Sunday School classes (they called them "cells") and everyone was very friendly. The atmosphere was casual and relaxed. They used a band for the music which was fine with Pete but it got a little wild at times, especially when they started flashing rotating colored lights around the room in time with the music. The Scripture was put on the projection screen and Pete realized he was the only one looking down at an actual Bible. It was exciting and the sermon was helpful in many ways but something about it just did not feel like church. It was like something was still missing.

In another church the people were unrestrained, very emotional and excited but it was very uncomfortable. The next one was stiff, legalistic and judgmental—almost downright angry. Pete felt like he was being scrutinized, like he was suspect of some heinous sin simply by virtue of being young, an "outsider," and in college.

This was the way it went week after week. Pete was discouraged. *Why should it be so hard to find a good church to attend?* He wondered many times. It was no wonder Bea Tanner warned him on his last Sunday at 3C that "even the good kids fall away during college."

It felt so good to go home in October. In some ways it was like he had never left—like someone had just pushed a "pause button" while he was away. But things *had* changed. Pat had his driver's license now, all the haying was finished. The township had painted the iron railings on the bridge in front of the house and Holmes' Country Market had new blacktop. The fire company, he was told, had not been busy except for a couple of brush fires. The leaves had turned colors a little more up home than back in Centre County.

Church was something everyone in the family looked forward to. When the kids were younger it had a lot to do with seeing friends but eventually it became more than just that. That is the way it is when God has touched a person's life and a true loving relationship has resulted—worship becomes a way to show love, gratitude, and appreciation to God in the way He wants to receive it. People get excited about watching a team play a game at a stadium. Christians also get excited about celebrating Who God is and what He has done for them and countless others.

Preparations began Saturday night. Everyone made certain that he or she had an outfit for Sunday—not fancy but nice. Sunday dinner was planned. That week it would be at Pete's home so a large roast was set to thaw. Joanie finished her Sunday School lesson as she taught the third through fifth grade class each week. Everyone was in bed by ten or ten-thirty.

In the morning Pete was at the farm by four-thirty for milking. He and Grandpa got caught up as they worked. At home the roast was already in the crock pot along with potatoes, carrots, and an onion. Pete got his shower and a quick, light breakfast. Everyone was ready by eight-thirty and the last preparation before leaving was for each one to get his or her Bible. Pete, Amy, and Joanie also took tablets where they recorded important points from Pastor Jackson's sermons.

At the last second, John had to go back inside to get his offering envelope. On the front it was carefully marked with the amount for *general expenses* (which was his tithe), and the amounts for *Missions* and *Benevolence Fund* (his faith promise and offering respectively). Pete had already set apart ten percent of his last check to put in the offering at 3C; but he always did this at any of the churches he attended. Pete was certain that this service would not be a disappointment.

At the church the parking lot was slowly filling up with people from Colsonburg and the surrounding area including other towns, as they were the only church of their denomination in the county. Inside the door Bob Crowley was the greeter—shaking hands and giving each one a weekly bulletin. He happily greeted each person, speaking even to the children and babies.

"Hey Pete," he exploded with excitement, "it's soooooooo good to see you again! How's the college man?" Then one person after another was welcoming him home.

"Excuse me," John said, departing from the family, "looks like visitors." John had to take a turn with the others to greet them and introduce the rest of the family to them.

Pete knew right where he wanted to go next: the kitchen. There the coffee was strong and hot. There was also hot water for tea or cocoa plus orange juice and even chocolate milk for the children.

Everyone retrieved his drink and sat casually in the Fellowship Hall, talking and laughing together. In the middle was a table with some of the few fresh vegetables still coming out of the church members' gardens. Each one brought extra if they had any and picked up something else they did not have. In June, July, and August, that table would be covered from end to end.

The buzzer sounded and everyone headed off to their classes. Pete had technically been promoted to the Young Adults Class while at school. He left most of his old class behind and rejoined some who had moved up the last couple of years. Only grumpy Deanne had moved up at the same time as he did. The teacher was someone he knew well: Jim Corbin. Both were glad to see one another.

The comfortable chairs were arranged in a circle around the bright room all facing toward the middle so they could see one another as they discussed the topic of the lesson. Coffees and cocoas were carefully set on the floor and Bibles on laps. There was Brad, Erin, Deanne, Ted, Punjab, several "older" but still single young adults and of course Pete. A large coffee mug was the "offering plate;" the mostly dollar bills went to the cost of buying Sunday School curriculum.

Jim welcomed Pete then asked for prayer requests. Each class member prayed for one or two needs. Then the Bible study in Exodus resumed where the class had left off the week before. They were up to the place where God called to Moses in the burning bush. The discussion was lively and not everyone agreed with everyone else's conclusions. One thing was for sure though, they all new a lot more about Moses' calling than they knew the day before.

The church hallway and restrooms were busy as the parishioners moved from class to worship. Everyone, it seemed was welcoming Pete home. He made a point to say something to the visiting family. There was a constant exchange of good mornings, handshakes, quick hugs, and laughter. But in with it all was also a sense of anticipation, a feeling of something good and wonderful coming.

Pete went through the double doors to the bright, airy sanctuary. The tall frosted-glass windows were glowing white with sunlight. The ceiling was a high one; the walls and ceiling were both white. The pews were a light-colored oak and the floor was carpeted in a rich plum color.

At the front (which was at the end closest to South Main Street) was the long altar rail that extended most of the way across the width of the sanctuary. About two feet higher than the floor was the chancel with its matching oak pulpit exactly in the center. The organ and piano were behind the pulpit, one on each side of the chancel. Behind all this was the opening in the wall that revealed the baptistery area with a tall cross in the center and the words "Be holy" permanently placed under the arms of the cross. Other people were milling around in there as well as in the hallway.

Eventually the Archers all found each other and took their usual place almost halfway up the center aisle and on the right side. Jim Corbin was the leader that day. He took to the pulpit and proclaimed, "Good morning!" before diving into a quick review of the announcements and upcoming events. The talk among the congregants was now finally beginning to calm down. Then the organ played as everyone silently prayed and prepared for worship. A child suddenly shrieked out, "Mommy, no! Let me!" followed by a strongly issued "Shhhhhhh!!!" from the mother. Then it was quiet again.

Jim returned to the pulpit and asked everyone to stand as he prayed, asking God's blessing on the service and on Pastor Jackson's sermon. Immediately after that the worship team took their places, two persons on each side of the pulpit, a soprano, an alto, a tenor, and a bass. A few people who could play instruments joined the organ and piano with a string bass, a guitar, a drum set and a trombone. One of the song leaders brought a tambourine up with her. But they were careful not to dominate the more traditional piano and organ, seeking only to softly complement their sounds.

Then it was as if a kind of invisible Presence had filled the room (and indeed *He* had). There was a continued hush as the words to the first song appeared on the screens on either side of the chancel area, near the corners of the sanctuary. It was a contemporary song, often heard on the Christian radio station.

The room was filled with the reverent but vibrant singing of the one hundred-plus voices. The sound was one but how each one participated was a little different. About ten or twelve worshiped with one or both hands raised high. One woman bellowed and wailed like a dying cow but no one ever said anything about it to her (no one *ever* sat in front of her either)—she was making a "joyful noise,"– joyful to her anyway, and to God. One man stood with his hands in his pockets looking very mellow and relaxed. Another stood holding the back of pew in front of him with what looked like some kind of a death grip. Some of the older people sat for some or all of the singing, as did a young woman holding a little baby. As the song progressed both the volume and the harmony rose, reflecting the people's enthusiasm for worshiping God.

The song was over but the music played softly as the words on the screen changed to those of one of the old hymns. Back and forth the songs were older hymns then newer ones, about six or eight altogether. Then everyone sat down again as seventeen-year-old Christine Spieglemeyer came to the chancel and sang a solo—a rousing, touching song that was also commonly heard on the radio. She sang to an accompaniment track played on the sound system. When Christine was done it was quiet again except for a flurry of "amens." The people never clapped for a song since that implied entertainment rather than worship.

Then came the offering, Jim asked for the ushers right after announcing the beginning of Children's Church in the Fellowship Hall (the youngest children and a pair of adults quietly left the sanctuary). John was one of the ushers that day. Jim asked John to give thanks before the offering. John turned, faced the congregation and prayed a simple but appropriate prayer. A musical solo was played on the organ while the tithes and offerings were received in the plates which were then given to a pair of "counters" who quickly totaled all the amounts given for General Fund, Faith Promises, Benevolence Fund, and any other designated purposes. The totals were posted on the bulletin board and the money locked in the church safe until the Financial Secretary retrieved it and took it to the bank's night deposit box on his way home. The people of 3C were faithful tithers, giving ten percent of their income to the support of the local church. Since they tithed, all the church's income came by way of the offering plate. No money was ever raised by merchandising of any kind. In fact it was prohibited to do so.

Finally Pastor Jackson went to the front and happily skipped up the steps to the chancel, taking his place behind the pulpit. He was of average height and weight with dark brown hair that had a natural bald spot on top that spread down his forehead. He was always clean-shaven and well-dressed. In worship he would wear a dark suit and tie with a white shirt. Pastor Jackson was very personable and spoke easily with children, adults, and every other age group in the church.

Putting on his reading glasses he first announced two requests for prayer that had been made of him that morning. Joanie made a note of them on the list of prayer requests distributed on Wednesday night (the list also served as her Bible bookmark). He prayed, first for the requests then for God's blessing on the sermon—both on him as the speaker and on everyone as the listeners.

With the "amen" everyone was ready. Pastor Jackson asked enthusiastically, "Got your Bibles, Church?" He held his up and almost everyone in the pews held up a Bible brought from home. "Good," he said, pleased.

There was no single set reading this time; he was doing a character study on Mark. So he would read a verse or passage pertaining to Mark in order through the course of the sermon. He read it, then described the points it made about Mark's life. He highlighted Mark's failures as well as his successes as recorded in the New Testament but especially emphasized that, despite his weaknesses, God ultimately used him in a mighty way, resulting finally in the Gospel that bears his name. The point was that everyone makes mistakes and fails from time to time but they should not be discouraged by these problems. Instead they should overcome them with forgiveness and the Holy Spirit's guidance and empowerment. Pete made several notes about Mark's experiences and underlined in his Bible each verse Pastor Jackson had read. The service ended with the singing of the hymn "Make Me a Blessing."

It was good to be home again for church as well as for family and a rest, obviously. It was refreshing to experience church the way Pete was used to it: the warm welcome, enthusiastic worship and the sermon that was Biblical, encouraging, challenging and practical.

Dinner with Grandpa, Grandma, Aunt Judy and her family was followed by a short nap, afternoon milking, and then the evening service. During the evening service the music director led in a hymn sing with several shouting out numbers of hymns they wanted to sing, then the evening offering and another message by Pastor Jackson from the book of First Samuel. Only about half the people came back out for the evening service but they did so because they knew they benefited from the additional teaching.

* * * * * * *

But what about church while he was at school? Pete finally settled on a small white church along the road on the way in to his uncle's near a place called Mingoville. He had noticed it along the way and decided to give it a try too. It was smaller than 3C but many of the aspects of its services were similar to what he appreciated about worship. It felt at least a little bit like home.

Course Correction

The diner was very busy. The roar of voices, clanking china, sizzling burgers, and sliding chairs was almost deafening. Pete waited next to the cash register for Pastor Jackson to arrive.

"Hi-ya, Pete!" Pastor called out, removing his coat as he approached.

"Hey," Pete answered back.

When he reached Pete, the two shook hands.

"Let's see if we can get a table in the banquet room where it's quieter," Pastor suggested, looking around for the hostess.

The hostess was happy to oblige the request. So the two men shared that back room with only two other parties.

It was late January of Pete's first year at school and he was home for a weekend. The two had hoped to get together for some time but their two schedules had never coincided until then. It was just as well as Pete was ready for that talk more then than he would have been any earlier in the year.

Looking over his menu, Pastor said, "I'm sorry it's taken so long to get together, Pete. I've been anxious to check in with the college man, though….So how's it been going?"

Right at that moment the waitress came and took their orders. Pastor Jackson had been a great help to Pete since the day Christ had saved him from his doomed pathway in life. Not only had Pastor Jackson shown a personal interest in the young man, but he had also used his position to help Pete get to know other older men in the church that were an additional help to Pete, such as Jim Corbin. Pastor had gently nudged Pete along in his spiritual growth over the last few years.

Waiting until the waitress was finished, Pete said only, "Pretty good, I guess."

"Are you happy with your grades?"

"Yeah, I'm doing pretty good there."

"Keeping the faith and going to church?"

"Yup."

Pastor prodded a little more. "A little bird told me you have a girlfriend," he teased, as he added some cream to his coffee.

"Musta been Mom," Pete surmised, rolling his eyes slightly.

"Well, you know about pastors having to keep confidences."

But Pete knew it was his mother.

"So…?" Pastor pressed his latest question.

"Sorta," Pete hesitantly replied.

"Sorta?? How does one 'sorta' have a girlfriend?" Pastor asked half laughing at the notion.

Pete explained, "it...didn't actually work out."

"Oh, I didn't know that part. I'm sorry to hear that." Pastor paused a moment and then continued, "Was your mom sorry to hear that?"

"Probably not," Pete uncomfortably admitted.

"So what was Joanie's problem with this ah...ah..."

"Mandi."

"...with this Mandi?"

"Mom just didn't think she was a good match for me—not really as church-oriented as I am and from out of state, wants to have a career and stuff," Pete explained what Pastor already heard.

"I see and how did *you* feel about those things?"

The waitress brought their plates and Pastor offered a short prayer of thanks.

"I suppose mom was right but we just liked each other so we started going out and all," Pete answered before taking a bite of his BLT sandwich.

Pastor paraphrased, "so you didn't think it was serious, then?"

"What do you mean by 'serious'?" Pete inquired.

Pastor tried to eat some mashed potatoes and talk at the same time.

"You know, like maybe you'd want to get married some day or something to that effect," he answered waving his fork in a small circular motion.

"Oh, no, not serious *that* way, not yet, anyway," Pete said a little surprised, "We never even mentioned the subject once, at least not in terms of *us.*"

"Oh," Pastor acknowledged as he cut up his meatloaf. Then he stopped and looked at Pete curiously asking, "so how do *you* define 'serious'?"

Pete very matter-of-factly explained, "you know...like...holding hands, kissing, just that sort of thing." Pete shrugged as he said it, then crammed a pinch of potato chips into his mouth.

"So you two were 'physical' with one another..." Pastor echoed Pete's words back to him.

"Don't get me wrong," Pete immediately began to explain, "It wasn't sinful; we both knew how far was too far."

Pastor seemed convinced of that--and he was.

"If you don't mind Pete," Pastor requested, "tell me a little about this Mandi."

Pete explained, as Pastor listened to him while sticking forkfuls of meatloaf and mashed potatoes into his mouth, that she was from southern

New Jersey, pursuing a four-year degree and hoping to work for the state some day in the area of agriculture. She was from a major mainline denomination and a professing Christian. She always wanted to go to *her* church but only went two or three Sunday mornings a month and never to Sunday School. They spent a lot of time hanging out at her apartment or at Pete's uncle's house, studying and "stuff."

"So what went wrong then," Pastor wondered when Pete was done.

"I guess she was nervous about the whole relationship thing," Pete began, "She had had a lot of relationships that either weren't good for her or that went too far. It all kinda spooked her I suppose."

"How did you two get together?"

"I noticed her—she was pretty stunning—and we had a couple classes together. Then we started seeing each other around campus."

After some further conversation about Mandi, the food was finished but Pastor was not.

"Look, Pete," he started cautiously, "I've known you well for a couple years now and I really value our friendship. But I'm going to take a big chance here and ask you some tough questions."

"Okay…" Pete consented nervously, suspiciously.

"Did you actually think that Mandi was a good, you know…equal, match for you?"

"I guess," Pete answered, "We were both Christians. Doesn't the Bible say 'as long as you're both Christians'?"

"Sort of," Pastor partially conceded, "Second Corinthians 6:14 says, 'do not be unequally yoked together with unbelievers.'"

"So if she's a Christian and I'm a Christian, what's the harm in it?" Pete challenged Pastor.

"Well, two people, a man and a woman, can both be believers, but not equally so. I've watched you, Pete, you were always here every time the doors were unlocked—Sunday School, morning worship, evening worship, youth group, everything. But Mandi sounds like one who was doing just the minimum to get by. I mean, what would happen if you two really fell in love and got married? How would you work that out? Either she would have to take the extra steps to become like you or you would have to slow down to her pace. Neither one of you should plan on the other changing for you, that's not fair. It should be 'what you see is what you get' – take it or leave it. The other option, of course, is that you would be at continual odds with one another in that area."

"But nobody said anything about marriage yet," Pete answered back.

"Yet—but feelings of love have a way of sneaking in and convincing people to do things like that. Would she move here? Would you follow *her* back to New Jersey? Would she join your church or would you join hers?" Pastor pressed him even farther.

"We hadn't really talked about anything that serious."

"But by your own admission you two were 'serious' in terms of the physical part of your relationship. You've got to be careful there. Things can happen—all kinds of things, positive or negative. Becoming 'serious' in that way can make you feel like marriage is a good idea, even if it isn't."

"But we were only having fun, enjoying one another."

"But was it fun breaking up?"

"No," Pete confessed, remembering how torn up he was that night and the next week or so after Mandi had called it off.

"It was a kind of a set-up for heartbreak, then, wasn't it?"

"I guess you could say that," Pete had to admit.

"Then, I say it. Look, Pete I'm not scolding you. I'm just concerned for you. I don't want to see your faith just implode over something like a girl or see you being heartbroken unnecessarily. Life is already full of enough pain without going and looking for more."

Pete knew that his spiritual life had definitely taken a beating the last couple months and he *had* lost ground—just so Bea Tanner did not find out!

Pastor continued, "you know that God calls us to be filled with the Spirit, but it's hard for Him to do that in us until we *let* the Spirit fill everything about us—you know, be fully surrendered to Him, which is all about our choices as believers including choices about relationships. Romans 12: 1 says to "…present your bodies a living sacrifice, holy, acceptable to God, which is your reasonable service." You and me," he said pointing his finger back and forth between them, "we need the Spirit's power to live the Christian life, overcome the Devil and those temptations back to the old ways, and make it to the finish line with our souls intact. That's where a lot of people make a crucial mistake and then begin falling away from the faithful life they once had."

Pete knew that Pastor Jackson was right, though it was hard to admit it. It was hard to admit, as well, that he took up with Mandi mainly because he was lonely and enjoyed her company and the comfort of her affection not to mention that there was some expectation that one goes to college, gets a degree, and falls in love along the way. But Mandi was only a couple steps removed from where Melissa had been only two and a half years ago while Pete was now *dozens* of steps removed from that point. As far as he knew Melissa did not even so much as go to church anymore.

"Jesus," Pastor admonished, "needs to be Lord of *everything* in your life. You can't go wrong that way and you'll never regret it. I would encourage you to think about making that deliberate, full consecration of your whole life to God, including your love life, making Jesus Lord, boss, of it all. You've been delivered from the immediate threats to your soul. Now it is time to live proactively against, not just outright sin, but against any *possible* threats to your life in Christ. It would be so rewarding if you would do so. What do you think?"

Pastor Jackson was unusually forceful with Pete but God was in it and he was being led by the Spirit of God to say those things. It was not offensive, though it was very unexpected.

"I'll definitely think about that," Pete tentatively agreed.

"Good, you do that and if you need me to talk to or pray with you, just let me know," Pastor offered.

"I will," Pete promised.

Somehow Pastor Jackson knew just how far to push Pete and when to step back and take off the pressure. It seems some do not push at all and some push too hard; Pastor had found the balance.

"Let me also counsel you to be careful about spending too much time alone at a young lady's place or alone with her at your place. When feelings are involved and when there is a physical dimension to the relationship it is very, very easy to suddenly find yourself having gone too far. You know what I mean?"

Pete agreed that he understood what Pastor was saying.

"It sounds like she might have had a past in that area and you were once involved in some things that could drive that situation over the edge pretty quickly. Sexual things don't just shut off and there is a natural tendency in man to immediately return to where he left off in the last relationship and then go from there. That is a reality about which you need to be very intentional, deliberate, in your choices. I'm sure your parents would never have let you take a girlfriend up to your bedroom. That's wise and that's because they understand human nature and the risks that you would be walking into."

"Yeah," Pete agreed. Pastor was right; no girlfriend would have been allowed to go with him into the privacy of his room at home.

"Anything else you want to talk about?" Pastor asked.

Pete was surprised he had asked—as if all that had not been enough already.

Pete shook his head, looked his pastor straight in the eye and said, "No, not really."

But Pete had just lied. There *was* something he needed *desperately* to talk about but he was too proud, too embarrassed and so he chose that morning to continue suffering at the hands of the even larger, more threatening problem that he was facing. He was almost to the breaking point and soon he would reach it. But someone else would also arrive to help, just in time.

Later Pastor Jackson wondered to himself whether he had been too hard on Pete. He feared it would become an obstacle to their relationship. He prayed that Pete would, in fact, receive his words in the spirit of love in which they were offered and that Pete would have his eyes opened to the imminent danger he was facing in his relationships and the potential danger to his spiritual wellbeing.

Pete thought about Pastor's words several times over the weekend. At first he was shocked and then even a little bit angry. But the problems he was having were obvious and frightening to him. Slowly he began to see that his relationship with Mandi was a reckless decision and doomed to failure, sooner or later. He wondered whether Pastor's advice about making a "full consecration" of himself to God might help, too, with the rest of his struggles.

He remembered the point he was at when Pastor Dan led him in receiving Christ into his life. He never wanted to go back, but finding his way on his own was more complicated than he ever imagined. It was no wonder that so many men and women his age fall into all kinds of traps when they got out on their own. Would he become one of them?

Finally back in Centre Hall, overwhelmed by a feeling of defeat and isolation, he made another choice. He bowed at his bedside alone in his room at Uncle Jim's house. He was crying and asking for God to comfort and guide him and somehow it just worked its way into the prayer.

"...and, God, Pastor was right. I haven't let you have full reign over all of my life and some of the choices I've made are the kind that could take me back a couple years. I don't want that, Lord. So, God, I'm going to start making all my decisions more carefully and with Your will for me in mind and with Your Word guiding me. Show me when I am wrong and I will do all I can to right it. I'm going to let You lead me in everything, relationships..., everything. You *will* be Lord, I promise. Just, please, help me with all this stuff and help me see Your will for everything in my life. I yield all of me to You so You can fill all of me. Amen."

Even Pete did not fully comprehend the significance of that prayer and the effect it would have on his life. There were a lot of unanswered questions about how and where and with whom God would lead him but Pete would patiently trust his Lord.

The only mistake he made in his thinking was that this prayer would work like some instant cure and that the problem he was having would simply disappear as a result. It did not, in fact the struggle become more intense, not less—the devil was fighting back. Sometimes he wondered where God really was in his life, whether God even heard his prayer that night. A "voice" actually suggested to him that maybe God did not hear or even care.

He may have been discouraged, but Pete did not give in. He went to church every time he was able. He joined a Sunday School class. He prayed. He read in his Bible regularly and he tried to make decisions with God's will in mind as he waited for a breakthrough.

* * * * * * *

Class was over and it was time to move to another building for the next one. As Pete left the building and entered the bitter winter air, Mandi approached him from the left. She was barely visible inside her parka, scarf and knit hat.

"Hi, Pete," she greeted him, though quietly.

"Hi," he replied rather flatly.

"Can we talk a minute?"

Pete could not simply refuse her. He wanted to be on civil, even friendly, terms with her.

"I guess."

The two sat on a bench that had been dug out from under a deep bank of snow.

"Look, Pete, I'm sorry for what I said right after Christmas. I was only thinking about myself; I didn't mean to hurt you."

"It's okay," Pete dismissed.

"I've been thinking about it a lot and I wondered, if you're not too mad at me or anything, if you would want to try to let bygones be bygones and maybe we could start seeing each other again."

Pete was speechless. This was not the "breakthrough" he was looking for. He missed Mandi—a lot. But he *had* been hurt and he had made some new decisions in the weeks since she had broke up with him. He wanted to say "no" but could not find the strength to do so.

"Let me sleep on it," he decided, though he was only stalling for time.

"That's fair," she replied, her small rosy face grinning out through the scarf and cap, a few locks of that long, shiny, jet-black hair stuck out on each side of her face.

* * * * * * *

For two days Pete struggled with his feelings. He was lonely. He missed Mandi's company. But the thought of his choice he made in prayer and the remembrance of Pastor's words would not leave him alone either. If he said "no" it might be a long wait for someone else to come along but what would be the price of saying "yes?"

* * * * * * *

The two of them stood off to the side of the glass doors safely shielded from the snow that was falling heavily now; the next class had been cancelled due to the storm.

"I've thought about it," he confirmed to her.

"And...?"

"And...well...I don't think it's really a good idea."

Mandi's countenance fell. She had hoped and believed he would say yes to her.

"You're a nice person and I *do* like you and spending time with you but I just don't think we're right for each other. I've had a chance over the last few weeks to just re-evaluate what I'm looking for and I really think it's in another direction. I don't think I'm right for you and the other way around—at least in that way, you know, 'seeing' each other."

She was not crying but she looked like she could any second.

After a few awkward moments she asked, "Is there someone else now?"

"No," Pete gasped, "no one else."

"Well, okay then. I guess that's your final answer," she summed up his answer as she saw it.

"Yeah, my final answer. Still friends?"

"Friends," she answered with a nod.

Walking through the thick snowfall Pete reflected on what he had just done. He sure hoped he was right in thinking that there was someone better suited to him than Mandi. He had bet all he had in hopes that there would be.

Though friendly toward one another, Pete and Mandi never went on to enjoy much of a true friendship with one another. After graduation, Pete lost all contact with Mandi.

Capturing the High Ground

Pete happened to be looking out the window the very moment Geoff drove up to Uncle Jim's garage. By the time Geoff reached the top step Pete already had the front door open.

Pete's talk with Pastor Jackson had been just two weeks ago. Now it was Geoff who was returning home for a few days and had made a point to stop and see Pete at the house in Centre Hall. Uncle Jim was away so the distraction was very welcome.

"You got it *made*, dude," was Geoff's verdict when Pete had finished the tour of the house. He made a big deal about Pete having an entire house to himself while Geoff shared a dormitory room with three other men. Pete had seven rooms and three bathrooms all for himself.

"It's all right, I suppose," Pete shrugged as he replied.

The two sat in Pete's room talking about college life but Geoff had something else on his mind and he was not sure why. When the conversation reached a lull he broached the subject.

"So…how's it going with you—you know, with your thought life and all," he asked somewhat haltingly.

The look on Pete's face told it all in a second. His smile went away, his head dropped, and he looked away.

"I wish it were better, man; I wish it were better," Pete admitted.

Pete was seated in an office style chair and Geoff was leaning back on his elbows as he sat on the bed. Geoff then sat up and leaned toward Pete, a look of concern in his eyes.

"What's up?" he asked almost afraid to find out. Any time he had asked in the past the answer had been generally positive. Geoff had actually stopped showing as much interest in the topic as Pete's progress had been so good.

"Right there," Pete said angrily, accusingly, pointing one finger in the direction of his laptop computer.

"Uh-oh," Geoff responded, "the computer again, huh?"

Pete explained the problem: "At home there was just one computer. Mom and Dad watched it like a couple of hawks. It had a filter and only *they* knew how to get around it—you know the password. Now I have my own and only *I* know the password."

"How bad is it?" Geoff interrupted.

"Not as bad as it was before I got saved but I'm literally getting afraid that I'm gonna completely give in to it all one of these times.

"What happened, man?"

"I was doing some searching one night for a paper, real late, and some links came up that were really bad. I didn't choose any of them but it was just enough to tip things out of my favor. I was really lonely and discouraged. You know how that stuff, the porn, sets something off in you—a euphoria, like a drug does, makes you feel better for a little while."

Geoff nodded that he understood what Pete was describing.

"Then it happened another time. I knew exactly what I was doing and did it anyway; I clicked one of those links. Sure enough, the filter blocked it. Like a crazy man I put in the password and, yup, that's what it was. I don't even know what I was thinking or what was wrong with me. I closed it right away but I also knew it was there, too—not good. I felt so guilty and dirty. I prayed and asked for forgiveness right away. Then one night there I was actually watching a video! I was suddenly so overcome by guilt and anger. I just felt out of control. It kinda scared me, you know."

Geoff nodded.

"I tried everything I could. I prayed. I even wanted to just smash the thing to bits but I literally *need* it for school. One night I actually cut the Ethernet cable. I got a new one, of course but it got me through the night. At least there's not a wireless connection right here."

Pete was ashamed and embarrassed. Then he explained the effect Mandi had on all of it, how it diminished and virtually disappeared when he was seeing her but within forty-eight hours after they broke up it was creeping back in again. He even told Geoff about his talk with Pastor Jackson and how he hoped his prayer afterward would have changed things, only to have the problem get worse.

"What can *I* do?" Geoff longed to know.

"What would *you* do? I feel so trapped. I feel like that machine sits there and mocks me to my face, calls out to me."

The two brainstormed all kinds of ideas: prayer, accountability, giving up the computer, they even reviewed the spiritual armor of Ephesians 6:13-18 and did a checklist for Pete: Truth? Check. Righteousness? While Pete knew his actions were not, and did not feel, righteous, he also knew he had the righteousness of Christ "accounted" to him (c.f. Romans 4:3), so...check. Gospel of peace? Check. Faith? Check. Salvation? Check. The Word of God? Check. And prayer? Check. The two did not know what else to do. Pete was too embarrassed to talk to anyone else.

Eventually Geoff had to get on the road home to Colsonburg. He prayed for Pete and promised to keep praying, instructing him to "hang in there." He hated to leave Pete behind. There was a part of him that simply wanted to stay and watch over him. But he needed to go, like it or not.

Geoff redoubled his efforts. He prayed for Pete more and more. He also called or texted him every couple days to ask if he was living above it. Most days Pete was but many he was not and the struggle was unrelenting.

Pete was so humiliated he wanted to just give up and give in to it rather than fight it all the time. But in his heart he knew that was not the answer and instead a recipe for a long-term disaster.

* * * * * * *

Pete's phone showed a missed call when he finished working at the greenhouse. It had been three weeks since Geoff's visit; his calls were frequent. Pete knew he needed to return it but he already knew what it was about so he was in no particular hurry to do so.

"I thought you'd *never* call back!" There was excitement and energy in Geoff's voice.

"What's up, bro?" Pete asked curiously.

"You gotta here this. I think it's the answer!" Geoff loudly proclaimed.

"What's the question?"

"It's about your problem with the porn and the computer and stuff."

"Oh." Pete was not excited about being reminded of his "problem."

"We've been having this special chapel series on spiritual warfare and some of the stuff the speaker has been talking about sounds a lot like what's happening with you."

"Okay, I'm listening."

"He started with Jesus being tempted out in the desert by the devil (Luke 4:1-13). He pointed out that Jesus was alone and said that it's in times when we are in isolation, like you, that we are most vulnerable. He said, too, that even Jesus was tempted so we shouldn't be surprised if we are. Then the devil left him until another 'opportune time' (Luke 4:13) because he always takes advantage of the weak points and times in our lives. That's kinda where you are right now—in an opportune situation—for the Devil. That's one of the reasons why the Bible always talks about stuff like "one another" and "each other" and says we should not stop coming together with other Christians like that verse in Hebrews about "not forsaking the assembling of ourselves together" (Hebrews 10:24).

"That sounds like more about the question," Pete observed, "when do we get to the answer?"

"Now," Geoff promised. "It was there all the time and it's like I never heard it until the sermon he gave in chapel today. You know about demons, right?"

"Sure. Doesn't everybody?"

"Well, they're like angels in reverse. Instead of helping, they tempt and torment," Geoff started.

"You're not going to tell me I'm possessed are you?"

"*No, of course not* because you're a believer. But, listen, demons still creep in around the edges if they can and the devil uses them to try to wear us down with temptation, hoping we'll give up and turn our backs on Christ. You know how in the New Testament some of them talked and had names? That's because they are personal. Remember what you said that day? You know, how the computer 'mocked' you to your face? I think Satan knew you were alone and kinda down and that you had a computer so he came after you by using a demon to attack you at your weak point. It was his 'opportune time'—a 'perfect storm.'"

"I don't know. That's kinda scary but if it's true what does your speaker say about *that*?"

"Go nuclear, man!" Geoff proclaimed.

"Nuclear?"

"Yeah, you know how you did everything you should but the problem stayed? There's one more option—the nuclear option."

"Go ahead," Pete invited.

"You got your Bible there?"

"Yeah."

"Look at Luke ten in verse seventeen. It says the seventy disciples told Jesus that 'even the demons are subject to *us* in Your Name.' (emphasis added) You know how the demons had to obey Jesus and Paul? Well they had to obey these guys, too. You see when a serious Christian uses Jesus' Name against a demon it *has* to obey him. He can actually *command* it!"

"I never did anything like that. Sounds kinda, I don't know, fanatical," Pete responded.

"Well you don't do it like every day or anything. It's for serious situations and when it's definitely demonic. You don't like go around all day long 'in the Name of Jesus this' and 'in the Name of Jesus that.'"

"Okay."

"He said it's all about the 'believer's authority' from verse nineteen."

Pete read the words aloud, "...I give you the authority to trample on serpents and scorpions..."

"Those are symbols of evil," Geoff interjected.

"...and over all the power of the enemy..."

"He said it's about us taking a position of authority over evil, demons, even Satan himself and it all checks out Biblically. He's not some weirdo. His sermons are on the school's website. Check them out, especially days one and four."

"Okay. I will," Pete agreed.

* * * * * * *

Pete watched the sermons on the computer. In fact he watched *all* of them. He knew there had been a lot of teaching about spiritual warfare and the Name of Jesus at 3C but apparently he just had not paid enough attention.

He knew he had to do something though. The battle was wearing on him. He felt an urgency in it, like he was fighting for his very soul. If he gave in and turned his back on all God had done in Him what would become of him? He was not sure he wanted to know.

But Pete wanted to be sure. His concordance was home but he found one at a bookstore. He had learned how to use one in church and he had been given his Grandma Wilmor's copy.

Sitting down at a table in the bookstore he looked up the word "name." The phrases showed him which references might be of interest and he wrote down the book, chapter, and verses for each on a sheet of notebook paper. Having collected several references, he looked them up in his Bible, circling the ones that seemed to be the most informative.

Pete especially noted Luke 8:31-33 where Jesus was commanding the demons to come out of a demon-possessed man. They begged not to be sent to the "abyss." A footnote in his Bible sent him to Revelation 20:1-3 to read more about the abyss. Instead the demons went into a herd of swine and interestingly the swine were destroyed by the demons that took control of them.

The other interesting one to him was when Paul commanded a demon to leave a girl in Acts 16:18. Paul simply said, "I command you in the Name of Jesus to come out of her" and it did.

Pete was not possessed but the Devil definitely wanted him back. He could not take Pete by force because Jesus said, "...neither shall anyone snatch them (Christians) out of my hand" in John 10:28. But Pete did not want to find out would happen if he sold *himself* out to the Devil.

The final conclusion? Go nuclear.

* * * * * * *

Pete felt awkward and self-conscious even though no one could see him. He knew nothing except what he had read and heard. He was doing this strictly by faith. He had spent the day mentally preparing himself. He did not know what to expect or what he would experience.

He prayed a while in his room at Uncle Jim's. Then he finally stood and, facing the direction of his computer, he took the authority that the Bible said was rightfully his.

"I know you're here," he said forcefully, though also nervously, "and you don't want to leave. But I know who you are and I know who I am—I'm a child of God so I don't have to do what you say. In fact *you* have to do what *I* say. So I'm taking up my authority over you. So *in the Name of Jesus* I command you to leave this place and *never* come back. In fact, get yourself to that abyss where you can't harm anyone else anymore. And I mean it! In Jesus' Name, Amen."

He paused to see what, if anything, would happen—like in some Hollywood horror film, but all was strangely quiet. Pete was actually a little disappointed at the lack of "special effects."

He somewhat doubted his efforts. Maybe he needed to be more dramatic. Pete had seen video of preachers shouting and yelling in prayer. But maybe it was not the drama, but just the Name, and the simple faith in God's Word that counted the most. He sure hoped so because that was all he had—faith.

Pete went to bed and slept soundly. The next week was very busy with no spare time whatsoever. He even forgot to think about the confrontation with his personal enemy most of the time.

About a month later he suddenly realized that somewhere along the way the "mocking" had ended. He suspected he was still able to go to any website he wanted to but he had captured the high ground in his battle for purity so he felt suddenly empowered and free *not* to go and the taunting had ceased.

In prayer he thanked God for the victory and he committed himself to a set of standards for purity as he was sure that temptation would return at some point or points and he was *very* right. Pete also prayed for, claimed, and received the forgiveness and cleansing promised in 1st John 1:9.

It was a turning point and he actually felt launched forward in his spiritual life like no other time since the day Pastor Dan prayed with him at camp.

Yet again, nothing would ever be the same for Pete.

Grandpa's Proposition

At the conclusion of a Sunday afternoon dinner at the farm, Jack asked John to come with him to the barn as he started the afternoon milking. He said there was something he wanted to discuss.

Jack began the milking by cleaning the udders of several cows. Then he connected the milkers to the overhead pipes and then to each of the cows' four teats. He continued down the line preparing several more udders as the milk began splashing through the clear piping toward the tank in the milk house.

Though helping in small ways, John mostly followed his father up and down the central aisle with a row of Holsteins along each side—their tail ends toward John. The barn was cold as February's winter air overtook the drafty old structure. But the cows did not mind at all.

As one milker finished, it was moved to another animal, "hop scotching" past the others that were still not finished. The whole place smelled of a combination of manure, hay, and grain, tempered by the sterile, frigid air of midwinter. From time to time one of the cows lowed or a fresh deposit of manure was heard slapping down into the gutters that ran parallel to the aisle and were strategically positioned right beneath the cows' tails. Outside the late afternoon sun was bright on the snow cover.

"Has Pete let on any more about what his plans are after college?" Jack finally initiated the discussion as he gently patted one of the cows on her side.

"Not really," John replied, "he's looking forward to being out here again, come summer. I know that much."

"Likewise," Jack echoed the sentiment. He continued, "I've had my Medicare for a couple years now, first health insurance in quite a while, and I'm thinking about getting this hip fixed."

He slapped his left hip. His limp was more pronounced all the time.

"Maybe after Pete graduates....He could care for the place so I could recuperate."

"He would probably enjoy that," John answered, "it would be a good opportunity for him to spread his wings a little."

"Well...that's not all," Jack admitted, "the other side bothers now, too, and I'll probably need to eventually get that one worked on. It could go on for a year or more. I actually think I'll finally start my Social Security around the same time. There's no longer any benefit in delaying anymore. Pete would be able to collect the earnings from the farm—such as they are."

"I bet he would *really* appreciate that chance. It'll get him some experience on his own and let him earn his first fulltime wage. Maybe God's plan for him will emerge during that time."

"Look, this isn't easy for me," Jack said, shaking his head and limping over to the gutter to look his son straight in the face, "I'm talking about retiring here. I can't sell this place—I've lived here and worked it all my life, Dad, too, not to mention my own grandfather. And I can't just ignorantly work and work until I die. Then who does the milking the next day? I also can't take the chance that all this will be sold to take care of me or Dot someday."

"All good points but what can I do about it now?" John wondered. He actually feared a guilt trip about not taking over the farm, for launching out in another direction.

"Nothing. And don't worry," Jack replied, "this is not some guilt thing—I was over that a *long* time ago."

"Okay, so..."

"Look, Pete would take care of this place. You *know* he would. Where else is he going to turn after college? No one can just go buy a farm anymore and this one has no future apart from him. Jimmy doesn't want or need it, nor do you. Judy's kids are interested in other things."

"So you want Pete to run the farm," John echoed his father's words, or so he thought.

"Not run—*own*," Jack clarified.

"Oh." John was otherwise dumbstruck.

"I know he's young but he's wise and he would have me around to guide and even help him for a while. He's had a lot of experience—just needs neatened up a little."

"It's a lot of responsibility for a twenty-year-old," John retorted, referring to Pete's age upon graduation from college.

"But look at what you accomplished; you're virtually famous in this county!"

"That might be a bit of an exaggeration," John again retorted, "plus I worked for someone else for almost seven years before I struck out on my own. I was twenty-five when I started the business."

"Twenty, twenty-five, big whoop, and Pete's been working out here for what, six years now?" If I died right here, right now, he could start running this place in the next minute and know *exactly* what to do and the herd would never know any the better."

"You're probably right."

"Darn tootin' I am!"

There was a brief time with little talk between the men.

Jack again broke the silence. "I know this farm is mine and I can do with it as I wish but you kids all have a stake in it as my heirs. So do the grandkids. I don't want bad feelings from anyone and Pete won't do it if he thinks there would be. So I'm going to talk to the others first and come up with a plan all can live with."

"Does Pete know about any of this?" John curiously inquired.

"Absolutely not," Jack said firmly, almost disgusted, "I would never have done so without talking to you first. Give me a *little* credit. Dot's the only other one who knows. Pete wouldn't do it without your blessing and the others' too—because of the inheritance."

"So...you want me and Joanie to pray about it then?"

"I guess that'll do for now," Jack agreed. He always accused his son's family of wasting a lot of time praying instead of just deciding.

Joanie was as surprised as her husband. It did not take long, though, to see how the Lord might actually be at work in the situation and they cautiously agreed to cooperate with Jack's idea, keeping an open mind about it, either way. They both knew that Jack and Pete were both adult men and could make any arrangement they wanted to about the farm. They could not stop it and trying to do so could only potentially create hard feelings at best or rifts in the family at worst. At least the way Jack was looking at it, everyone's interest was protected to some degree. So what would be the point in challenging the idea?

* * * * * * *

Three weeks later the scene out in the barn was virtually replayed. But the weather was warmer and the snow not so deep now. The day was cloudy. Jack worked as John again largely watched.

"So Jimmy and Judy are on board," Jack abruptly reported. "I'll show you the same plan I sent them if you can stay after milking for a bit."

Inside Jack had sketched out the property and had drawn some new lines in red ink. He set the large page on the dining room table and began describing it to John as the two men sipped coffee.

He began the overview, pointing at the various lines. "The house would be made a separate parcel. You three kids would jointly have that; I'll put it in your names. There would be a series of building lots up Brick Silo Road to the rear of this house—one for each of you and each grandkid, except Pete. Jack pointed toward the kitchen, which was also the general direction of the proposed lots. "The township requires a minimum of two acres. Pete could work the ground on them until one of you guys decides to build on that plot." Each square had a name on it: John, Jim, Judy, Pat, Amy, Mike, Susan.

"The balance of the farm would be transferred to Pete's name. But he only gets the ground, the equipment, use of the barn, and whatever's left of the rental—he'll probably want to tear it down. The direction he's pointed now, he may end up raising beef instead of dairy. Whatever he does he'll need to make up his mind because if he does go with beef, I'll sell my herd and the milking equipment. He can have the calves plus his cows. But all the cash proceeds from selling anything go to the expenses in all this and I'm getting anything that's left over so me and Dot can finally go on a trip together."

* * * * * * *

The email from his father worried Pete somewhat. "When you get home for Easter your grandfather wants to discuss something with you about the farm."

* * * * * * *

Pete could not get home in time for the Good Friday service but he was waiting for the rest when they got home at nine o'clock. Not long after the family's return Pete inquired of his dad about the mysterious email.

"It's nothing bad," Pete's dad assured him as they sat at the kitchen table.

"At least that's a relief." Pete finally relaxed.

John was ready. He produced the document Jack had asked Joanie to type up. It was called *A Proposition Concerning the Archer Farm*.

"Uncle Jim, Aunt Judy, and I have all signed it," John said. Pete was *really* bewildered.

John watched his son read Jack's proposition. At first Pete read as if looking at nothing more than a newspaper. Then he began to look more studious. Next his eyes popped and his face moved closer to the page. He turned the page over to the other side with the speed one uses to swat a fly. His face moved slightly from side to side. He turned the document to view the diagram stapled to it. Then he was frozen looking down at the whole thing.

"He wants to do *what*?" Pete asked almost breathless, raising his face from the page.

"What he wants is for the farm to stay a farm and stay in the family. You're the only one qualified to run it as such," John explained.

"Wow."

"You realize that you would agree to give up any stake in my business or in this house—they would go to your brother and your sister exclusively. You also get just the ground, the equipment and whatever stock he wants you to have. You also would be obligated to give the others certain things like the building lots and give each household up to a quarter of a beef each year."

"Yeah but it still looks like I come out ahead," Pete observed.

"Until you calculate your costs, that is. It's not cheap to run a business," John cautioned him, "and a farm *is* a business."

"True," Pete admitted.

"It's a lot to think about," John said sympathetically, "you best pray about it awhile first."

"Oh absolutely," Pete quickly affirmed.

"Your sister and your cousins are too young to weigh in on it. Your brother, who's more interested in the business here, is okay with it. If you have questions you best take them to your grandfather."

All alone in his room that night Pete sat thinking. He knew he needed to pray but he could not come up with any words. But he had recently read in his Bible about King Hezekiah spreading Sennacherib's letter out before himself and praying over it (2nd Kings 19:14).

So Pete took the proposition and, kneeling beside his bed, he laid it before himself and smoothed it out with both hands. He finally found some words.

"O Father. I am just *blown away*. I can't believe this is happening! I almost don't know what to do. On the one hand, I want to just seize the opportunity but, on the other hand, it scares me so much I wouldn't dare touch it. But it also seems like an obvious answer to what I should do next. I just don't know if I'm ready for this. But if not *me*, then *who*? But *now*? It's maybe a once-in-a-lifetime opportunity but I would also have a *lifetime* to either regret doing it, regret *not* doing it, or be *glad* I did it. *PLEASE* show me the way, *please*. In Jesus' Name I pray. Please. Amen."

Pete could not sleep; he was overwhelmed. A phrase, a plea, echoed through his mind: *please send someone else*. When had he heard that? It at last occurred to him that it might have been Moses.

He opened his Bible to Exodus and flipped slowly through the pages of the opening chapters. He went past it at first but when he looked again his eyes did, at last, land on the statement in chapter four, verse thirteen.

His eyes also happened to slip down to the beginning of verse fourteen: "So the anger of the Lord was kindled against Moses..." God wanted Moses to trust Him but Moses would not and it displeased God.

It did not take long to inventory all God had done through reluctant Moses. Pete remembered the passage Pastor Dan was teaching from the day he got saved, First Timothy 4:12, "Let no one despise your youth..."

Surely most of Pete's fear of being inadequate was based upon his age and comparative lack of experience.

Timothy was a young man. So was Jeremiah, David, John-Mark, Daniel, even Mary and Joseph—and look what God entrusted to them! So being young was not to be the deciding factor. Besides, Grandpa and his own parents could still advise him and he *would* ask for their help—that is, if he decided to do it.

* * * * * * *

Pete and his grandfather were doing the morning milking when Jack asked him why he was so tired. Pete had been yawning since they had started.

"I had a lot on my mind last night," he explained.

"Oh...?"

"Yeah..., Dad showed me the proposition about the farm last night," he further explained.

"Well, don't let it keep you up nights," Jack chided him, "I wouldn't have proposed it if I didn't believe in you—you've proven yourself already, so you have."

Pete did not know how to respond and Jack did not pressure him to. Instead, Pete went home and fell asleep for a couple hours. When he awoke he called Geoff then emailed Pastor Jackson, explaining it to both and asking for their prayers. On Sunday he spoke with his Sunday School class about it, again requesting their prayers.

Geoff told him right on the phone that he should "go for it."

On Sunday Pastor Jackson said simply, "it sounds like the Lord is 'giv[ing] you the desires of your heart' (Psalm 37:4)."

Immediately several in the Sunday School class encouraged him to accept his grandfather's offer. But some were cautious.

Peter kept praying about it and nothing arose that seemed to say to him "no" or "stop." Pete was nervous but otherwise at peace about it.

But since there was no impending deadline, and therefore no hurry, Pete waited until school was over for the year to make a final decision that way God would still have a chance to tell him "no.".

His first day home for the summer he brought the proposition to Grandpa. Pete set it down on the kitchen table. Jack looked down at it and saw that Pete's signature was *not* on it. He looked up at his grandson as if Pete had just shot his favorite dog for no reason.

Pete reached into his back pocket. He had bought a fancy brand new pen. Twisting the top so as to reveal the ball point at the tip, he signed it right there in front of Grandpa, who smiled from ear to ear and reached out to shake Pete's hand. Then, even emotionally reserved Grandpa, reached the other hand up and put it behind Pete's shoulder. He *almost* hugged him but then just patted him on the back and said, "Thanks."

* * * * * * *

The only other thing Pete prayed for was someone to share it with and very soon it would appear that the answer to that prayer would show up right in front of his face.

Disappointments

After another winter of shoveling snow, Cynthia decided to hire someone to handle the upcoming summer mowing and the snow removal the following winter. After receiving a few estimates, she settled on a little-known firm that would handle all the groundskeeping needs.

When the end of April brought the first warm days, two young men came to the house to rake and begin mulching. Beth was surprised by their presence as she rushed out of the house for an early afternoon class but she quickly smiled and said "hi" before hurrying down the steps to the sidewalk and eventually to the hospital a few blocks away.

As April turned into May the two men showed up each week to mow, trim, and sweep the walks. Beth saw them almost every time they came. She was careful to thank them and compliment them for their work.

One of the young men, Rob, took an increasing interest in Beth and actually hoped to see her when he came to work. He was of medium height and a slender build, very tan with brown hair, cut very close, a slight mustache and brown eyes.

One bright day in late May, Beth was enjoying the front porch like her family always did back in Compact. She was reading and taking notes in the pleasant early summer air. The landscapers' truck pulled up to the curb and Rob got the mower out and ready. The two exchanged a quick "hi." Rob's partner was not with him that day.

When he was done, Rob introduced himself and the two talked for a short time. It was enough time for Beth to tell of going to the School of Nursing and hoping to be a missionary. Rob asked where she went to church and she told him. He quickly told of going to another area church of the same denomination, but then he had to go to his next job.

Rob was finishing when Beth returned to the house the next week and they spoke again for a while. Then the next evening when the phone rang it was Rob calling Beth!

"Don't tell the boss, but I got your number from work," he confessed. Continuing, he asked, "would you like to go out sometime—maybe to supper or a movie?"

Beth was very taken aback. She did not know him very well but she thought they had a lot in common. She had embraced her father's ideals of courtship but so few men her age actually knew much about it. However she liked him well enough so far that she was willing to accept his offer but determined in her mind it was just a way of getting to know him a little better.

Rob picked Beth up on Friday afternoon after class. It was obvious he had no huge intentions as he simply got in his side of the car as she got in her side. He took her to a place along the Susquehanna River called Selinsgrove where they had a nice supper, watched a movie at the mall, and then they had a quick dessert.

They talked the whole time. He told her an amazing thing: He also wanted to be a missionary some day! His work was just a temporary phase. Beth could not believe how such a thing was actually happening. *Maybe* he could eventually be "the one," but not yet.

Rob walked with her to the porch and told her he had a nice time. Then he completely startled Beth. Rob began to try to kiss her! This was totally unexpected and premature as far as Beth was concerned.

Stopping him, she said, "Don't get me wrong. I think I like you and I had a nice time. I appreciated it all but I don't kiss on a first date."

Rob looked surprised and puzzled as he blurted out, "Oh…I'm sorry. I just thought...well, you know. I thought we hit it off pretty well. Could I still go out with you again?" He was worried he had ruined his chances with Beth.

Smiling, Beth said, "Yes."

So the next weekend they went out again, this time to Harrisburg. Again Rob dazzled Beth with dinner, a movie, and dessert. Over the meal Beth explained her reaction to him at the conclusion of the last date by trying to describe courtship to Rob. She especially stressed the friendship stage and her father's adage about "relationship before affection." It was obvious he had never heard of this concept before.

In an odd way Beth was taking the lead but felt she had to help set the pace, though she technically believed that responsibility was the man's. What choice did she have except to simply end a potentially promising relationship? Rob intentionally refrained from trying to kiss her when he took her back to Aunt Cynthia's that evening. He, chuckling somewhat uncomfortably, extended his hand to her; laughing, she accepted it and shook it.

The following week Rob called and they exchanged emails and text messages from time to time. On Saturday he took her for another exciting evening, this time in State College. The next day he picked her up and they went to her church in Paintersville. His presence with her garnered a lot of attention and a couple of questions that were answered simply, "We're just friends right now."

But when Beth asked about going to his church the next time he replied dismissively, "Oh you don't want to go to my church. Your church is a lot better than mine."

At the same time, however, on the inside, Rob was losing patience. He expected to be able to kiss a girl he dated. He did not understand courtship and did not think he liked it. But he liked Beth, even if his expectations were not being met. Unfortunately other things were going on in Rob's mind, too. For some reason he was willing to do or say anything to win Beth and he had done it before with other girls. He always got what he wanted but unfortunately he would become quickly bored and eventually move on to another. He was consumed with a desire for physical affection and he wanted that from Beth, too.

On Friday they stayed in Lewistown for their date and went for a walk in a local park after dinner. Beth finally convinced Rob to take her to his church; she wanted to see it for herself. Come Sunday morning Rob called to say his alarm had not rung and that they would have to miss Sunday School. At worship Beth was struck that there was no warm welcome for her and Rob or questions about their status, as at Paintersville. In fact several said to Rob, in an awkward sort of way, that it was "good to see you." There was something odd about this reception. Further, Beth thought the church and the worship service was not much different than the one at Paintersville, though Rob apparently disagreed. For the evening service they went back to Paintersville, then he took her for ice cream.

Beth was falling for this man, though. Everything he was telling her seemed to match what she was looking for but she was so overwhelmed by his romancing of her that she began to lose track of her priorities and her doubts. Beth enjoyed being liked by Rob. She had never had a boy show so much interest in her before. Beth reckoned it was a small compromise but she made the decision: she would let him kiss her. He had compromised with her to this point and she thought she would meet him "half way." It would be her official "first kiss."

So on Sunday evening on the porch she gave a couple of hints and Rob eventually figured it out and moved his face toward hers to kiss her. What happened next horrified Beth. Instead of the simple, sweet, innocent "peck" she dreamed of, his kiss instantly became more serious and involved than she had prepared herself for. She had to pull away from him. She even had to slightly *push him* away from her.

"That's plenty," she said shocked.

"I'm sorry...I just thought that..."

"It's okay," she said, "I understand but I didn't intend to kiss you like that so soon. I'm not ready for that much yet."

"Okay. Okay," Rob said, his hands in the air like he was the object of a hold up. He was obviously flustered, disappointed, and maybe downright put out.

"It's all right," she assured him, "Just so you know, I want more of a commitment before we share anything even approaching *that.*"

"Fair enough," he agreed. Then saying good night, he left for home.

Rob was restrained but also more quiet on Saturday. She let him kiss her but only a brief, light peck. She told him it was nice.

Beth was excited when Rob called on Monday evening. She was anticipating what they might do together come the weekend. The relationship was progressing well again.

"You know," he started, "I don't think we're right for each other. I guess I'm just not ready for a relationship right now." He said several other similar things as well.

Beth mostly just listened, though tearfully. When he was done she simply said, "Okay; I understand."

But she did not, at least not at first. She was devastated. She had dared to take a chance on this man and to even hope for the *possibility* of a serious relationship someday, despite Rob's heightened interest in physical affection. But things would only get worse for her.

When Friday night came Cynthia took Beth to dinner over in Juniata County to help fill up her now empty time. On the way home she stopped for gas. Beth sat in the car as Cynthia went inside to pay.

Not far away a couple was locked in an embrace and kissed several times. Beth thought it was a disgusting display for a public setting. But it took her breath away when the couple came apart and got in the woman's car to leave. The man was Rob!

Beth was crying when Cynthia came back to the car. She dismissed it as just an expected emotional reaction to being "dumped." Inside Beth felt betrayed and used. She was overwhelmed on the way home with a powerful feeling of self-doubt. That half-hour drive home set her back years, emotionally. She took a chance; she trusted. She had even prayed about it; and it ended in disaster. She wanted nothing more than to just go home—home to her parents. But it would not be home to Compact. It would be home to an unfamiliar, therefore uncomforting, place. She soon began to doubt nursing school and even missions. It would take weeks and weeks for her to heal and get her bearings back.

Ironically it helped when she came to eventually learn that Rob was not at all the man he presented himself as being. It turned out he was known for his "tall tales" about himself and his numerous and passionate romances. He seldom ever attended church and had no intention of being a missionary some day. Beth wondered how she could have ever fallen for such a "straw man." Maybe she should be like Aunt Tillie: fifty-something and single; maybe it would be best that way as a missionary anyway.

* * * * * * *

Soon after these things, the disappointments continued and grew even more profound. They shook Beth to the very foundation of who she saw herself as a person and how she looked at her future.

Beth began to receive replies to her inquiries into various missionary organizations. She knew she could not go with her own denomination, not yet anyway. She would need more education and a time of service in a local church. But Beth was anxious to get her feet wet and press forward with her life so even before Rob showed up she had applied with several groups and ministries that could take her soon after she had finished nursing school.

The theme of these replies was a consistent "no." Two said simply that they could not take her at that time. Another two cited the poor economic conditions as a reason not to accept her as financial support was uncertain at best. One noted a major difference in doctrine between herself and the organization—a difference that she had initially underestimated.

But the one that stood out the most was the one that stated very bluntly, "We understand your sincere desire to be involved in missions but also believe that you lack a clear and concise call to fulltime career missionary work. The mission field is demanding and doubts will inevitably arise; the certainty of your calling is what will carry you through those tough days. Even with it, many ultimately leave the field feeling defeated, never to return to ministry again. You may want to consider short-term missions work, work trips, other missions-related work, or finding a way to participate in and promote missions through the local church at least for now."

The letter cut like a knife. After the initial shock, and even anger at the agency, Beth was forced to evaluate herself against the statements in the letter. They were right. The hardest thing she ever had to do was to admit that *she* had set her heart on being a missionary but God had not set *His* heart on it; He must have had another purpose—but what? Beth also reviewed in her mind the many testimonies she had heard over the years of those called to become missionaries; they had all experienced a moment and a place where they knew that it was God's plan for them to serve in that way. Beth had no such moment or place, just a desire. But that was obviously not enough.

But there was no other dream, so she decided to make further inquiries and see what, if anything, resulted—if God would open the door for her to go. The real problem now was she suddenly felt like a boat adrift on the water with no map, no radio, and no engine or sail. A year ago everything seemed so clear. Now almost nothing seemed clear and the halfway point of nursing school was already past.

So where would she go and what would she do? God only knew and He had not shown her yet.

Lauren

Since Pete and his grandfather began working more closely in the business part of the farm, Pete decided to move his bank account to the same bank that Grandpa used. It just seemed it would simplify things somewhat when transferring money.

It was the first Monday after school ended when Pete walked into the Savings Bank. He asked a teller about opening a new account and was told to take a seat in the waiting area and "Lauren" would be with him soon.

After a few minutes the sound of women's shoes rhythmically clapping on the floor was heard and getting closer.

A young woman asked, "Did you want to open an account?"

"Yes I do," Pete replied.

"Come with me them," she said as she gestured with her hand.

Pete stood and she stuck out her hand to him, saying, "I'm Lauren Thomasen and I'll be helping you with that today." They shook hands politely.

Pete could not help but notice how attractive this woman was. She was thin, shorter than him, fair skinned, with straight naturally blonde hair, and well dressed in a pant suit well tailored to her job as a customer service representative. It was *her* shoes that were making that sound. Her voice was sweet and chipper. She gestured toward a desk in the corner of the lobby.

The conversation was a normal business transaction. He told her what he needed and she described the various accounts then began the paperwork on the one Pete selected. Pete observed her closely; he was definitely taken with her appearance and demeanor. He noticed that no rings were present on her left hand (he had learned to look there first) and that several Christian symbols were around her work area, but no pictures with men in them. But he kept it all business and never let on that he thought she was attractive. He even dismissed the idea of anything other than a business connection.

But Pete was forced to return to the bank when the checks failed to arrive in the mail as expected. It was Lauren who helped him again that day; the problem was resolved with the check printing company. Pete was on his way again. A week later he stopped by Lauren's desk on the way to the teller to let her know the checks had arrived and he thanked her for the help.

Then a week after that he came into the bank and asked to speak with Lauren. He was seated across from her desk when she came and sat down.

"Is everything okay?" she asked him.

"Well, maybe," he replied.

"Okay...how can I help you?"

"I have a question I think you might know the answer to," he said, mystifying her.

"And what would that be?" she asked.

"Is there any chance that you might be interested in maybe...ah...going for a movie or something sometime?" he nervously and haltingly asked her. "With me?" he thought to add.

"Oh!" she exclaimed with a smile. "Why would you want to do that?"

"I kind of assumed you might not be married or engaged and I noticed that you seem to be a Christian."

"Yes, I am a Christian. Are you too?" she asked, her face lighting up.

"I sure am. But if you have a boyfriend or something, I understand," Pete answered.

"Well, I don't," she assured him.

"Would you maybe be interested?" he inquired again.

"I think so but I can't answer you here—on work time," she explained.

Pete was horrified at himself for not thinking that it might not be appropriate for him, a customer, to ask her, an employee that question on work time.

"Oh, I'm sorry," he apologized.

"I get off at four," she hinted.

Pete was back at the bank at four.

"The sidewalk is borough property," he observed to her as she left the bank at a little after four.

"And I'm off now," she said smiling.

"Do you like miniature golf?" he asked as she stood across from him.

"Sure."

"If you wanted to, we could get a burger and mini golf for a while."

"Okay."

"Could I meet you on Friday after work? I could pick you up at your house," he suggested.

She wrote her address and some basic directions on a page from her planner. The address revealed why Pete had never met her before. She lived all the way on the *east* side of the Susquehanna River!

"You have a quite a drive to work, don't you?" he asked.

"It's not too far for you is it?" she asked alarmed, "Because I could meet you there or something."

"No, that's fine," Pete assured her, though he had not anticipated such a long drive just to pick her up.

Pete found the house that July evening nestled in a modest but comfortable subdivision. She must have seen him coming because the door opened even before he reached it.

"Hi," she greeted him with a smile.

"Are you ready?" he asked.

"Sure. And, oh, this is my Dad. Dad, this is Pete Archer." She introduced the two, each man on a different side of the threshold.

"Good to meet you, Pete," he said cheerfully, reaching out to shake Pete's hand.

"Likewise," Pete responded respectfully, shaking Mr. Thomasen's hand.

"See you later," she told her father as they headed to Pete's truck.

The evening went without a hitch. They just talked and got to know each other a little more as they ate and putt-putt golfed.

Lauren still lived with her dad. Her parents had been divorced since she was twelve and her father had always had custody of the children. Her mother lived in Binghamton, New York. Mr. Thomasen was a good man, friendly and agreeable, a good father, but not a Christian. Lauren was about a year and a half older than Pete and became a Christian when she was fourteen. She was attending a Free Methodist Church where she also helped with the Children's Church program. As far as Pete knew, the Free Methodists had very similar beliefs to what 3C held. Both were very open about their relationship with the Lord and their beliefs. It was fun, refreshing, and got Pete's hopes up a little about a potential relationship. He was over Mandi after all and had learned his lessons there; he was not making the same mistakes all over again. But Lauren was still more a stranger than a friend, though it seemed they were instantly moving in the right direction, relationally.

Both agreed when he brought her home a little after dark, that it had been a good evening. Pete asked if she might want to do something together again soon and she agreed she would like to.

Pete called her Sunday afternoon and they set up another date. They went out five Friday evenings in a row. Each time they seemed to just get closer and enjoy each other more. Each kept becoming so familiar to the other as they shared even about their families, the joys and hurts from the past, and even their own dreams for the future.. They called and emailed each other during the week but Pete did not see her at the bank anymore as she was transferred to another office on Route 6 and much closer to her home.

On their fourth date, Pete took her to LC to meet his family and see the farm. This looked like a critically important step to him.

At the conclusion of the fifth date, Pete sat with her on her front porch. They talked and enjoyed the warm evening.

"I won't be able to see you next weekend," he lamented to her. "We're all going on a family trip out to Erie."

"It's going to be strange to not see you," she said.

"I think I'm going to miss seeing you too but I'll be here the next weekend—with bells on," he promised her.

Finally they got up from the porch swing and walked over to the door.

"Good night," he said.

"Good night," she reciprocated.

All of a sudden, without any fanfare or awkwardness at all, they exchanged a short kiss. Neither one seemed to mind it at all; it was completely mutual.

"See ya," he said.

"See ya," she returned the promise with a smile.

* * * * * * *

Pete did not see Lauren for almost two weeks. He called her several times. The whole time the family was in the Erie area he thought about her constantly. He was so anxious to get back so he could see her again and pick up where they had left off. He was confident that this relationship might actually be "the one." But he knew it would take a lot of time to unfold and grow. Considering he had another year of school to go, that was okay; he would wait.

Their sixth date came with the frightening realization that Pete was returning to school. But he had already thought about that. While he stayed in Centre County most of the time last year, he told Lauren he would come home every single weekend he possibly could, even if for just a day so he and Lauren could maintain their relationship. It would be hard but worth it, he figured. If she was *the one* he needed to make her a priority, whatever the cost, he thought to himself. Their kiss was still soft and gentle but a little longer and a little more serious that evening.

Pete began to imagine finishing college in the spring. He would be back north to stay. He began to dare to imagine a life with Lauren. He was sure she was experiencing the same things. He was thrilled by the thought. He also decided it was time. When he returned home that next weekend he would tell Lauren the truth, that he loved her. He was sure she loved him, too. It seemed he could see the future stretching out in front of him and with Lauren in the middle of it.

Presque Isle

It was a Saturday morning in mid-July and the Archers had just sat down for the biggest breakfast of the week. The windows were wide open and the birds sang as the cool morning air poured into the house. On that morning it was sausage, pancakes, grapefruit, coffee, and juice that they enjoyed.

Joanie spoke up with the news, "We got an email from the Mortons last night," she started, "remember they moved to northwestern Pennsylvania a while back. Anyway, they've invited us to join them for a weekend and spend some time with them on Presque Isle."

John inserted, "Presque Isle is a beautiful place. You'll all enjoy it."

After a sip of coffee, Joanie continued, "We discussed some dates and wondered what everyone thought. We won't always be able to continue to travel together so we hoped that everyone could make this one a priority." She looked at Pete, the eldest, as she said it.

The dates were reviewed and the calendar passed around the table. Pete knew he would not see Lauren the weekend they went so he wanted to avoid the last weekend before college resumed. Everyone agreed to set aside the first weekend in August. So Joanie called Ginny and the date was set.

* * * * * * *

The family and their bags filled the van shortly before lunch and they started for Blueberry Haven, the new home of the Mortons. Lunch was fast food in Mansfield and then the almost nonstop drive west.

Joanie had printed directions from the internet but they were wrong and she ended up calling Dan and getting old-fashioned directions instead; they worked. They arrived in the late afternoon.

The parsonage was nestled in a suburban area a few blocks from the church. The garage, living room, kitchen, and dining room were at ground level. Inside a half flight of stairs went up to three bedrooms and two bathrooms. Another half flight of stairs went down below grade to a family room, study, and another small bedroom. It was built as a nice, comfortable home, about thirty years old with a modest yard, including a patio.

John and Joanie took the small spare room downstairs. Amy slept on a trundle bed in Beth's room. Pete and Pat used the twin beds in the other upstairs bedroom.

Beth was the only one of the Morton children still at home, though she was away at school much of the time. Patty had been married for about a year now; her husband, Daryl, had been transferred by his company to Seattle, Washington as part of a downsizing.

Ginny explained that Billy had opted to move to Albany before the family's relocation back to Pennsylvania. In the years at Compact he had become very antagonistic and rebellious toward his parents. They seldom heard from him now and had no address for him. His cell phone number changed from time to time so the only contact was whatever he initiated and that was not very often. Dan and Ginny thought he had moved again already—they thought maybe to Baltimore but they were not certain. It was a very sad topic for the Mortons and not discussed much beyond an explanation of "What's Billy up to these days?"

After a walk around the neighborhood and a quick tour of the church, everyone went out to a local restaurant for supper. They went to bed early. Dan wanted to get to Presque Isle early the next day so he could return to "Blueberry" and to his office for the evening. The Mortons rarely ever did social events on Saturdays because of the pressure on Dan to be ready for Sunday. Besides preaching Sunday morning and Sunday evening, Dan was expected to teach a Sunday School class as well. He tried to get a substitute for that week but could not find anyone who was both willing and available. It was unfortunate that he was under so much pressure right when the families were trying to spend some time catching up with one another.

After a quick and early breakfast the two vehicles headed in tandem to Erie, about forty five minutes away. They drove out onto the peninsula and staked out a picnic area on the east shore where the breeze was gentle and the waters calm. They enjoyed a sightseeing boat ride on the lake then returned to the tables for Frisbee games. Beth, Amy, and Pat went swimming at the adjacent beach. Lunch was done on the grill and they all sat at the table together enjoying the outdoor feast of picnic food that Pete had helped to prepare. The city of Erie rested on the opposite side of the bay complete with marinas, their boats coming and going all the time.

After lunch was the exciting west shore. The winds off Lake Erie were strong and the waves pounded into the beaches. It was just like the ocean except that the water was not salty and the tide was steady. Looking out over the lake was like looking out over the Atlantic; it was impossible to see the other side and it was dotted with boats of various sizes and types.

Pete, Pat, and Beth sat at a table together talking about school and such. Pat was excited about starting his senior year of high school. Being in two-year programs, both Beth and Pete would be graduating, Pete in the spring and Beth in the late summer. Pete told about going to the university and living with his uncle in Centre Hall.

"Isn't that near Lewistown?" Beth asked.

"Yeah, about twenty miles, I think, why?" he wondered aloud.

"Well I'm going to the Lewistown Hospital School of Nursing—in Lewistown," she explained, "I've seen the signs for Centre Hall on the way."

"Really?" Pete asked surprised, "Isn't that weird?"

Beth explained how her great aunt Cynthia lived only blocks from the School of Nursing and Lewistown Hospital. That gave Beth free room and board and eliminated most of her commuting. She was, like Pete, trying to get her education on a very tight budget.

"It's a small world," she observed.

Dan chased blonde-haired Amy around in the surf as Ginny, John, and Joanie looked on but finally stopped to catch his breath.

"Your Dad's as crazy and fun as ever," Pete said to Beth.

"Yeah, he likes to goof around," Beth replied. "Mom worries about him, though. He gets winded so easily anymore."

"Is he okay?" Pete asked.

"He had some tests done but they didn't show anything except some high cholesterol and high blood pressure which are both typical for a man his age. So they put him on blood pressure medication and he's watching his diet. Other than that they just figure it's his age; he's in his fifties now. I just wish he would have gotten more preventive care over the years. He only goes to the doctor when he's really, really sick"

Dan came over and sat down with the young adults gasping for his breath after his romp around the beach. He asked Pete how he was doing.

"Real good," he said confidently.

"Glad to hear it. I'd enjoy talking to just you a little more later on, if you have time," he proposed, his breath back again.

"Sure," Pete affirmed. "I've started seeing someone," he couldn't resist adding.

"Well good for you!" Dan trumpeted, "Is it serious?"

"It looks like it." Pete went on to describe Lauren in grand detail including how they met and what they had been doing and planning together.

Pat, looking over at Beth, rolled his eyes, shook his head, and said, "She's all he talks about anymore."

Beth grinned at Pat. But she was only hiding her own hurt over what Rob had done to earlier that summer. It was hard to hear about someone else's success in the very thing she had experienced such disappointment and hurt.

Ginny called to Dan so he got up to see what she needed.

"So you're gonna be a nurse?" Pete asked Beth, more to confirm what he had already heard.

"I want to work in a missions hospital or clinic but I'm having a hard time finding an organization to go with. The economic downturn has really hurt missions support and a lot of workers actually have come home for lack of support."

"Wow. I guess I heard *we* had called some of own missionaries back," Pete said, referring to the denomination's overseas workers.

"Yeah," Beth confirmed, "It would be almost four more years before I could qualify to go through them with no promise that there would even be space or money for me to go. I hate to wait that long and I can't afford the extra schooling right now. But if I go with an outside organization I have to raise my own support. I guess I'll just see what happens, how God leads. I'll get the RN to start. Maybe I can work my way through more schooling or find an agency that would send me with just the RN."

"Well, I'll support you if you go with another group," Pete promised.

"Thanks," Beth said, "I'll remember that."

Beth was the last to leave the Morton nest. She had grown to be about five and a half feet tall with wavy red hair hanging down just below her shoulders. She was average build, fair-skinned, with just a "sprinkling" of freckles and had a big bright smile. Her voice was soft and comforting. She laughed frequently and had a happy demeanor.

Pete, the first to leave the Archer nest, was about six feet tall now with short brown hair, combed with a part on one side. He had brown eyes and was clean shaven. He was tan and strong from working on the farm. His voice was deep but gentle. Pat was similar to Pete but blonde and not so tan. Pat was experimenting with a small beard on his chin but John and Joanie had said it had to come off before school started again in the fall.

"Look at them," Ginny said to Joanie, indicating the table where Beth, Pat, and Pete were seated, "They're so grown up."

"Where is the time going?" Joanie wondered in response.

Amy, though, was at that awkward age of fourteen. She was still a child but slowly becoming more and more woman-like in appearance and conduct.

Before leaving, Dan and Pete walked together along the beach for a while. "How have you been doing with the Lord and with your private life, Pete?" he asked directly.

"Good overall," Pete summarized. "It has been a battle against the old stuff a couple times," he admitted.

"The battle means you're not just giving in," Dan observed.

116

"No, I'm not," Pete confirmed. "Last year was rough. The loneliness made me really vulnerable and the temptations were almost overwhelming. I got involved in a relationship that wasn't really the best but the Lord helped me get out of it and now Lauren has come along instead. I can truly say I am saving myself for my wife in every way."

"That's good," Dan affirmed, "but more battles may be awaiting you so don't let your guard down. Remember the Word says, 'No temptation has overtaken you except what is common to man; but God is faithful, who will not allow you to be tempted beyond what you are able, but with the temptation will also make the way of escape, that you may be able to bear it'." (1st Corinthians 10:13) Dan said the whole verse from memory. "If you have not memorized that verse by now then start working on it."

"I will," Pete promised.

"I look forward to meeting this Lauren of yours someday."

"Me too."

"Just be careful, Pete," Dan warned. "You don't really know this young woman very well. It takes a long time to get over the whole dating mystique. In the meantime there are more than enough opportunities for disappointment, disillusionment, and even heartbreak."

"I will but I'm really confident of this relationship," Pete answered.

* * * * * * *

It was like old times for John and Joanie to see Pastor Dan preaching away so passionately on Sunday morning—for Pete, too, as he remembered the Youth Retreat at the camp just three years before. But the congregation of a hundred or so seemed very subdued and reserved.

Over dinner at the parsonage, Dan and Ginny shared how hard the Blueberry Haven church was turning out to be. It was not at all what they had expected. The leaders were critical and slow to assist Dan with the ministry as they should. Shortly after he came, the board abruptly made several changes to his compensation. The problems seemed centered on one outspoken, intimidating, and wealthy man, Walter. Dan theorized that he and the board were merely exerting their sense of authority over him or, worse, the original package and the other issues were just false promises from the start. He had confronted them about it all but they were determined to stand their ground. He didn't see how he would be able to stay there more than a couple of years under those conditions, especially the lack of trust. All Dan's pastorates had been generally positive so this was very unsettling to them. The stress (emotional, spiritual, and physical) on Dan at this church was unprecedented.

Lunch was followed by homemade ice cream and then hugs good-bye with the promise of future get-togethers. The Archers headed east again, refreshed by their reunion with the Mortons. Joanie and Ginny began to maintain a regular friendship again by email and phone and even went Christmas shopping together one time later that year.

An Unexpected Email

Returning to school was a completely different experience compared to the previous year. Not only was Pete familiar with the routine and the setting but he was in love! After he arrived at Uncle Jim's, the two men got caught up with one another. Then Pete took his bags to his room and got everything put away. He sent Lauren an email to let her know he had arrived safely and he told her he looked forward to seeing her on Saturday. He also emailed his folks. That was on Wednesday.

On Thursday morning Uncle Jim left for a trip to Australia for his company. But Pete did not feel empty this time. He was anxious to hear back from Lauren and even more to see her.

Thursday evening he finally saw what he was waiting for—an email from Lauren. Pete hurried to open the message but was disappointed by the first statement: "I won't be able to see you this weekend." But always the optimist, he tried to think that he could wait until the following weekend, though it would not be easy.

But then he read on. "I don't think we can continue to see each other." His eyes popped open. He gasped and began to plead again and again "no!" There were more rambling lines about it not working out for them, and Lauren not being ready for this and similar things. Everything had been going so well. "How? Why?" he begged to know from himself, God, someone, anyone.

She was breaking up with him! All the hope and anticipation was starting to vaporize right before his eyes. The proverbial rug was pulled out from under him.

But surely this could be changed. He could convince her not to break up with him. Pete whipped out his cell phone and speed dialed Lauren. It went to voice mail. He left a message begging her to call him back right away. He waited and paced and cried and prayed. Lauren did not call. She and her dad used only cell phones and did not have a land line. He did not know her dad's number so he was stuck. He called her again and left another message. He now feared she was refusing to answer his calls which could only mean she did *not* want a resolution. The situation looked worse by the second. This *was* actually happening and it might be irreversible. He called everyone he knew: his folks, his grandparents, Geoff; he could not reach *anyone*. He had *never* felt this alone his whole life; he felt utterly abandoned.

As the darkness set in, he crawled onto his bed without so much as turning down the covers. Still in his clothes and shoes he cried himself to sleep. Then he woke up and it was morning. He heard the birds singing and saw the sunlight streaming into the bedroom. But then the realization hit him, it was true and not just a nightmare. He cried again.

Finally Pete got up and found the strength to go to the laptop. He read the email again. He looked for a new one—nothing. He checked his cell phone—nothing. He typed an email begging Lauren to call him—begging to talk about this. He even proposed that they slow down the relationship a little maybe just be friends for awhile. Maybe that would ease whatever was on her mind. He heard nothing.

The only reason Pete did not just go home early instead of staying alone in Centre Hall was that he could not face telling everyone that Lauren had broken up with him. But he was expected by Saturday and Sunday so he had to go then or else face the question about why he did not come home "to see Lauren." What Pete really wanted was to just disappear.

So he started for home on Saturday morning. What else could he do? Telling his folks was like telling them someone had died and in a way it was true. He was dying inside and he felt like Lauren had died in an instant, without a warning. His parents were understanding and saddened; they both had liked Lauren and were as confused as Pete about it all.

Instead of seeing Lauren on Saturday afternoon, Pete went over to Jim Corbin's house. Through tears he told Jim and Holly what had happened and what he had hoped for in this relationship. They were sympathetic as they had watched their own kids go through similar experiences. They tried to reassure him that God had another, even better plan. They meant well but their words were wasted on brokenhearted Pete.

In Sunday School Jim mentioned Pete's disappointment, sparing him having to go through telling it again. Punjab was the one who prayed for him.

Pete returned to Centre Hall later Sunday night. His classes and work kept him occupied most of the time. But those lonely stretches were starting all over again—especially the nights and even worse the weekends when he was in Centre Hall and Uncle Jim was off in another state or another country. At first he wondered "why?" almost everyday but slowly he recalibrated himself to life as it was the previous year. He knew how to survive. Thankfully the spiritual battle against lust and pornography did not rear its ugly head like it had last year; that was the last thing he needed now. He remembered 1st Corinthians 10:13.

 Sometimes someone would suggest "setting him up" or encourage him to consider dating some certain girl. But Pete avoided all this; he had had it. As far as he was concerned the only way to avoid heartbreak was to avoid love. So that's what he started doing.

* * * * * * *

It was late October and fall was in full swing. Pete was home for the weekend. While in town he stopped in the pharmacy. They sold a certain tart candy he liked so well and he had an appetite for it. He was not prepared for what he saw inside. With a shopping basket on her elbow was Lauren! He saw her in one of the aisles and he quickly passed by, sure she had not seen him.

But then she came out of the aisle and lingered in the area near the register. Now he would either have to wait until she left or risk her seeing him. As he thought about his options he became overwhelmed by an urge to speak to her but he was not sure it was a good idea. She was not leaving anytime soon so he finally stepped forward and said, "Hi Lauren."

Her response was quick and full of surprise. She had no more planned to see him than he had planned to see her.

"Hi," she said but no smile accompanied either one's greeting.

Pete could not decide if he was hurt or angry or afraid. Lauren was embarrassed because she knew she had not treated him fairly and now she had to face him. She had tried to avoid any personal encounter.

"What brings you to Colsonburg?" he asked in a very subdued tone.

"Some of us are taking turns filling in for a gal on maternity leave. How about you? I figured you'd be at school."

"I just took a weekend off to see my family and all," he replied.

"Oh," was her only response.

Pete knew it was a long shot but he finally asked, "Is there any chance you'd want to grab a bite at the Diner or someplace—just casual, no big deal."

"Oh, I don't know Pete," she seemed to protest the idea.

"Please. I need to talk to you. I've *been* needing to talk to you. You ought to give me that much—just one talk. That's all. I promise."

Seeing no graceful way out of it she finally consented to meet him at the Diner at eleven-thirty.

Pete was waiting in a booth in the north end of the Diner. Lauren came over to Pete who remained seated as she sat down across from him.

"I already ordered," he said flatly, "I did ask her to bring you a diet cola, though."

"Thanks," was all she could say.

Not much was said until after Lauren looked over the menu and had placed an order. Pete just watched her. He used to look at her differently and he felt the change in his thinking. It was like she was a stranger.

Looking down at the table she finally said, "Pete, I'm really sorry."

Pete knew he should be forgiving but he was also hurting and not feeling very diplomatic.

He simply asked, "Why?" When she did not immediately answer him he pressed the point. "Why did you dump me after leading me to believe we really had something? Why did you do it by email? Not cool at all. Then why didn't you respond to my calls and email? I don't understand. What did I do to you to deserve that?"

Finally looking up at him she admitted, "You're right. You didn't deserve it."

"Then why?" he pressed the question again.

"It's complicated Pete," she replied. Continuing she said, "I've just got some things I need to deal with in my own life."

"Like what?"

"I can't talk about it now."

"Can't? Or Won't?"

"Both."

The orders arrived. Each gave their own quiet thanks before eating but it sure did not feel "right."

"I shouldn't have let you get so close to me—not now anyway," she said.

"Why?"

"Pete, don't, I—"

"I would have listened—been there for you."

"I'm sure you would have but I'm just no good for you. You need someone else."

"Well, I don't *want* someone else. I *want* you." Pete was struck by his own use of the present tense. "Now I don't have *anyone.*"

"Don't say that."

"I just did. It's the truth. Was I too fast, too slow?"

"No. I thought that you were appropriate."

"Is there someone else?" he dared to prod.

"No," she answered very sincerely and convincingly, "there's no one else."

"Lauren, I loved you," he boldly but almost hesitatingly proclaimed.

"Don't. That's what I wanted to avoid."

"Love?"

"No....oh...*You*, falling in love with *me.*"

"I wish you would have said that maybe in July or the beginning of August, not now. Didn't you love me—at all?'

It was quiet a moment then she admitted, "I did. That's how I knew I had to break it off."

"I don't...I don't understand, especially *now.*"

"I wish I could explain."

"Me too."

Realizing there was little hope of getting an answer or explanation, Pete turned his attention to his meal but he could only eat part of it. Lauren ate even less of hers.

He looked up at her at last, "So we're really done—forever—no chance of trying this again?"

"It's best that way."

The waitress left two bills at the table.

"I wish I agreed. Oh, how I wish I agreed," he said shaking his head.

"I'm really, really sorry, Pete. I hope you find someone who will love you as much as you love her."

"Well, we'll never know about that someone else you're speaking of because I'm 'off the market'."

"Please forgive me," she begged, "and don't give up just because of me."

"Oh, I do forgive you. It's just that I don't understand and I don't think I ever will. You know, maybe I better just go. Maybe we shouldn't have had lunch after all." The emotions were starting to swell within him. He feared breaking down in the middle of the Diner or making an angry display; he *was* both sad *and* mad.

He stood up and put on his coat and said to her through the beginnings of tears and a broken voice, "I really, really loved you...You know how to find me."

She looked up at him but said nothing. He wished she had. Just a simple "okay" would have been enough.

He picked up his bill, put down a tip and headed to the register. As he paid and answered the usual questions about "How are you today?" and "How was your meal?" he fought further tears. But as he crossed the parking lot the emotions began bursting forth. He was sobbing when he got to his truck. Once inside a gust of wind brought a shower of falling leaves. Like summer, the dream was over. Pete put his head down on the steering wheel and cried. Then afraid he would become a scene, he took control of himself and started the truck. As he passed the Diner on the way to Main Street, Lauren's silhouette was visible still sitting at the table. That was the last he ever saw of her. Pete drove up to the farm to find something to do with himself.

He never spoke with Lauren again. He forgave her and hoped the best for her. For a while he hoped she would call and ask to start again but she never did and he was done begging. He never knew the outcome of her life or the mysterious struggle that had gripped her so. He wondered if he was too harsh on her. But now he could only pray for her. He wondered from time to time what kind of a life she had found—if she was happy or not, if she ever married, if she did was he good to her? All of that remained one of life's mysteries to him but less and less important with the passage of time and the events of his life.

Things could now revert to how they had been but only for a time for Pete would graduate in May and start his farming career. Then everything would change again. But Lauren would not be part of the next season in his life. He could not find it in himself to trust his heart to someone else again—not after that. The life he saw stretching out before him looked pretty lonely but what could he do about it? Nothing.

The Finish Line

The Phone Calls

When Beth's cell phone rang the display said, "Mom." It had been a little over two weeks since Christmas.

"Hi!" Beth happily greeted her caller.

"I thought I better let you know what's going on," Ginny began, very seriously, a little winded, and with a shaking voice.

"Why? What's wrong?" Beth's tone instantly changed.

"Your dad hasn't felt well since Thursday. I wanted him to rest today but you know him, always on the go," Ginny began to explain. "But he just *had* to go see someone at the hospital today and of course he had to clear the driveway first. Then that blasted Walter called and gave him a hard time about something your Dad said at the last board meeting. He was really flustered when he left."

"At about eleven they called me to come get him. He got real sick up on the third floor so they had taken him down to the E.R."

"So what's wrong?' Beth interrupted.

"Well, that's the thing. When I got here," indicating that she was still at the emergency room, "they said he was having a heart attack."

"How bad is it?" Beth begged to know.

Cynthia had begun to watch Beth closely, inquisitively.

"Oh, how do I start to…" Ginny struggled.

"Is he okay?" Beth demanded to know.

"Yes and no." Ginny was searching for a way to explain the situation. "His heart had stopped before they got him to the E.R."

Beth gasped, "Oh, no!!!"

Cynthia jumped up and came to where Beth was standing.

"They got it going again but he's unconscious and they have a bunch of equipment on him." She hesitated, her voice breaking, "You better come, honey. I'm lost in all this stuff and don't know what to say or even ask. They wanted to know if he has a living will. Neither of us does. I'm really scared."

"Right away!" Beth ended the call soon after.

It was just as hard for Beth to explain it all to Aunt Cynthia, who insisted on going with Beth, not only because of her years as a nurse, but as a comfort and help to Beth.

They both wanted to go straight out the door but they could not do that. A bag had to be packed but how many nights? One? Three? More?

Attempts to reach Ginny failed, probably because her cell phone was off while in the emergency room. But about an hour and a half into the drive, Beth's phone rang. Cynthia, as the passenger, answered it.

"Where to?" she asked.

"How do we get there?...Oh dear....all right; we'll do our best. Keep in touch."

Ending the call she updated Beth: "They've flown him to Pittsburgh; that's not a good sign. I don't know a thing about Pittsburgh, do you?"

Beth, through tears, simply said, "No."

So continuing a ways further they then headed south toward Pittsburgh, searching the hospital signs for the one Ginny had told them of. They got lost twice in the city but finally found it shortly after dark.

Pittsburgh

After winding up through the parking garage and hiking to and through the hospital, Beth and Cynthia finally reached the intensive cardiac care unit. The nurse directed them to the room where the scene took their breath away: Dan unconscious, IVs, a respirator, pipes, tubes, wires, monitors, and a plethora of slight beeps, hums, and hisses. These were not good signs. The most disturbing sign of all, though, was the one posted over Dan's head: "DNR." Do not resuscitate.

After an emotional greeting, Ginny updated Beth: "I called Patty; she's trying to get a flight into Pitt. Your Uncle Curt said he would bring Grandma Morton tomorrow morning. Billy's latest cell phone number is already out of service again. I don't even know for sure if he's still in Charlotte or not. All we can do is wait—and pray."

So they prayed and begged for Dan's life to be spared. But it was a serious looking situation. None of the numbers on the monitor were right and suggested a chaotic and unstable situation inside Dan.

The cardiologist's update confirmed Beth's and Cynthia's worst fears. The heart attack had been "massive" and the damage to the heart muscle was "extensive." The doctor said that "if he survives" his life would be "severely altered." That one phrase shook all three to their very cores: "if he survives." Surgery was not an option, not now anyway; his condition was too unstable. All the hospital and doctors could do was to provide him with "every advantage" in hopes that his heart's condition and function would eventually begin to stabilize. Their whole lives were instantly changing forever, right before their very eyes.

There was not space for all three in the tiny ICCU room so Beth and Ginny took turns waiting with Dan. Beth stayed first so Ginny could get a break. Ginny slept in the waiting room, then Beth and so on it went all night.

Beth had her mother's phone with her whenever Ginny was with Dan. At about six a.m. it received a text from Patty: "In Chicago awaiting flight to Pitt. Will text again when there."

Ginny entered the waiting room soon after the text had arrived. She came in slowly. The look on her face enough to cause Beth to jump up from her seat—her mouth opened and her eyes terrified.

Ginny looked at Beth and said, softly, flatly, "It's over. He's home now."

Cynthia covered her mouth as she gasped. Beth shook her head violently, her face already drenched in tears as she shrieked again and again, "No!" The two were instantly locked in a desperate embrace crying on one another's shoulders.

Finally pulling apart, Beth tried to clear some of the tears from her face saying, "Patty's on her way to Pittsburgh. Someone will have to get her... and...tell..." Her tears started again.

Ginny went to Cynthia who was alone in the chair and crying. Then the two of them leaned on one another sobbing.

The nurses removed all the equipment so the three of them could see Dan in a slightly more natural state. There in the now quiet room it was decided that Beth and Cynthia would go to the airport as there were papers to be signed and decisions to be made that only Ginny could make.

It was Cynthia who broke the news to Patty, who had already read it on the faces of her sister and her great aunt. The emotional scene was repeated back at the hospital but then with four women instead of three.

By noon everyone was headed back to Blueberry Haven, Patty riding with Beth and Cynthia driving Ginny back in her car. The news was already spreading across the church, the borough, and the district. Before dark returned that night Ginny had received a call from both the District Superintendent and the denomination's president, not to mention almost all the church members (except Walter) and her neighbors.

The next two days were mostly a blur with the four women moving from meeting to meeting and task to task almost like robots just executing a program. The only difference is that robots don't just stop in their tracks to cry.

At the Church

The funeral was on Wednesday. Visitors came to the funeral home on Tuesday evening. The funeral director reserved two hours but the line did not stop until three and a half hours had passed. The callers included parishioners, neighbors, and fellow pastors.

The scene started again on Wednesday at nine a.m. but this time at the church. Patty and Daryl were at the head of the line, the first to greet the guests. Beth was next then Ginny, right before the open casket. On the other side of Dan's body were his mother and siblings, along with Aunt Cynthia.

It was during this period that people from Dan's other churches began showing up. Several came from Maryland and even more from Compact. One dear, thoughtful couple came all the way from Kentucky. Numerous people from Colsonburg were there as it was actually the closest church of all of them to Blueberry Haven. Beth and Patty remembered the people from Maryland and Compact the best but still recognized some from Colsonburg.

The family was constantly asked where Billy was and the sad story had to have been repeated several hundred times. Patty had spent the entire day on Monday trying to locate him but to no avail whatsoever.

After speaking with a couple from Maryland Beth turned to look down the long line again and saw a true, but thoughtful, surprise—a couple she knew from Aunt Cynthia's church!

"Oh my, you didn't have to come all this way," she exclaimed, though happily because of their thoughtfulness and sacrifice.

"We've *all* been praying for you, dear," the woman said. "We've known a lot of loss ourselves. We truly understand what you're going through. There *is* comfort in knowing he's in Heaven." Beth just nodded in acknowledgement. They spoke a few more moments.

Then the lady reached into her large purse and presented Beth with a stack of sympathy cards bound together with a large rubber band.

"These are from the people at church," she explained, "they're all praying for you and we'll all be there for you if you're able to return to Lewistown after all this."

The man simply said plainly, but sincerely, empathetically, "We're very sorry for your loss."

Beth introduced them to her mother. Then another family caught her eye, still down the line a ways—John and Joanie Archer and Pete. Pat and Amy, who had school anyway, did not know Dan as well as the other three so they stayed home rather than taking the day as an unexcused absence. No one came in cheerful or laughing but there was a look of downright dread on Pete's face as he drew nearer to the Mortons and to the casket.

Joanie hugged each of the girls. John took each of their hands, in turn, between his two hands as he greeted them. Joanie and Ginny hugged and cried together a few moments. No one in the Morton family fully grasped how important Dan had been to Pete. Pete barely spoke as he acknowledged Patty, Beth, and even Ginny. He silently went to the casket and looked in for a few moments. He then walked off silently by himself until the start of the service.

"He's really torn up," Joanie told Ginny.

Then a face was visible to Beth down the line and she could not hold back. She left her post and rushed down the line calling "Rhonda!" They just held each other for several moments.

Beth was heard saying "Thanks so much for coming!"

Rhonda was likewise heard saying, "Oh Beth—I can't imagine, I just can't imagine!"

The Service

The church was filled to capacity and beyond. Folding chairs were added around the perimeter of the sanctuary and people stood in the vestibule, the doors to the sanctuary propped open.

A fellow pastor from the area led the service and the District Superintendent preached. The congregation sang *Amazing Grace* and, though it was an unspeakably difficult time, they had never sung it with more conviction than they did that day. The superintendent gave a greeting and offered prayer. The congregation said the twenty-third Psalm together in unison and another pastor read from 2nd Timothy 4:7-8, saying, "I have fought the good fight, I have finished the race, I have kept the faith. Finally there is laid up for me the crown of righteousness, which the Lord, the righteous judge, will give to me on that Day, and not to me only but also to all who have loved His appearing."

During his sermon the superintendent applied the first verse as a testimony to Dan's life and ministry. He applied the second verse to the certainty everyone had that Dan's soul was in heaven, paradise, the presence of Jesus even right then. He also added in Romans 8:28, "...we know all things work together for good to those who love God..." He explained that, though Dan was now absent, his ministry would live on in the lives of those he had touched. He asserted, with confidence, that great things would result from all of what had happened, even if indirectly or in the distant future. His words would one day prove to have been prophetic.

Several tributes followed the sermon. Ginny displayed incredible strength and composure as she told Dan's life story from her perspective—

from growing up next door to each other in Garrett County, to their courtship and marriage, and the various churches they served in together. She spoke of his faith in Christ and pleaded for people who had not come to rely on Christ as Redeemer, to do so and to do so *soon*.

Patty and Beth stood together at the pulpit giving their tribute as Dan's children, Patty first and then Beth. They were obviously shaken and emotional but through the Holy Spirit they found the strength to do what they felt compelled from within them to do.

The opportunity was given for anyone who wished to stand and share a few words. Many did from all over the congregation. Some were humorous anecdotes, while others recounted ways Dan and/or Ginny had been there to help in times of need.

His voice and his mouth, not to mention his hands and his knees, were shaking as Pete finally stood. He did not feel up to the task and was not one to speak to a crowd. But Pete also knew that if he failed to say what was on his heart he could not change his mind tomorrow. This was the only opportunity to do it and to do it properly.

"I am who I am today," he began, "because the Lord became everything to me starting one August afternoon in 2005. But I made that decision because..." He had to pause to a couple moments to regain his composure. "...Pastor Dan was there and he gave me the opportunity to make that choice." His voice was halting but he continued. "But the only reason I even thought about it was because he told the truth about some things that a lot of people probably wouldn't even discuss or take seriously. If he would have played it safe and polite and not taught those things or just thought the way the rest of the world thought about that stuff, instead of being true to the Word, I *know* my life would have become a total train wreck. I'll *never* forget that day or his being a part of it. I thank God for him." The things he alluded to in his words were a mystery to all but his parents, who knew even less than Dan ever did.

Pete had to stop both as a courtesy to the others who wished to share and because he was losing his ability to contain his emotions. He sat down, his head bowed and his shoulders shaking. Soon the congregation was standing again and singing the hymn "It Is Well with My Soul." They sang so heartily that it seemed the roof would come right off the church.

There was dinner in the fellowship hall after the service. Due to the cold weather there was no public graveside ceremony. The mood was lighter over the tables and many happy memories, stories, and quotations were shared. But slowly the crowd thinned, though no one left without speaking to Ginny and the girls for a few moments.

Ginny came to where the Archers were seated. "Thanks so much for coming all this way—it meant so much," she told Joanie.

"So what are you going to do now?" Joanie inquired out of genuine concern.

"I'm not entirely sure," Ginny admitted. "The district superintendent said I should just stay at the parsonage until I have some place else lined up."

"Will you have an income?"

"Nothing reliable until I can find some kind of work. Dan opted out of Social Security, though he later wished he hadn't. Between college tuitions and the funeral expenses I have nothing left in the bank, but God will provide somehow."

Joanie looked at her friend with deep and obvious worry. John was writing; it was a check for one hundred dollars. He handed it to Ginny.

"Oh no, I couldn't," Ginny protested.

"God wants us to and I've had a good year. Please—even just to help with the funeral and such."

Ginny knew better than to outright reject the gift.

"Thanks, John. I can't deny that it will be put to quick use."

The truth was that, while John had had a good year, he really technically could not afford to give that money. But it was also true that God was moving him to give it, even if by faith. The Archers left soon afterward.

It was almost dark when Ginny, Patty and Daryl, Beth, and Cynthia finally returned to the parsonage. Ginny fell asleep in the living room chair while reading through the mountain of cards she had received. Several had cash or checks inside them.

Afterward

Cynthia took a bus back to Lewistown. She offered for Ginny to come live with her there, even temporarily but Ginny felt it would be a burden, despite Cynthia's protests. Besides, Ginny needed to stay put awhile to settle Dan's matters in Blueberry Haven. The generosity of friends would provide food and the church would provide the home and utilities until she discerned her next step, though only because the district superintendent forced the matter..

The hardest thing Beth ever did in her life was to leave her mother behind in Blueberry Haven. Beth wanted to quit the nursing program but Ginny insisted she had to finish because "...your Dad would have wanted you to get your R.N." If she was to return to Lewistown it had to be soon; she was already in danger of not being able to catch up and finish the already accelerated program. The only reason she could leave at all was because Patty had received approval to use her whole year's vacation to stay with Ginny for a little while. It would prevent her being able to return for the rest of the year but Beth promised to return home at every opportunity she could manage. Patty's departure all the way back to Seattle was infinitely harder than Beth's—for both Patty *and* Ginny, though Ginny did not let it show.

When Beth left on Sunday she cried all the way to Clearfield. Then she drove into an ice storm that had arrived sooner than predicted and it demanded her undivided attention as she drove.

In the dark, and exhausted, she followed two snowplows down "the mountain" toward Lewistown, one plow in each lane, clearing a safe passage through the sleet and slush. She was part of a long, two-lane row of cars and trucks that crawled down the long, steep, winding slope. Shortly after this, the mountain was closed for several hours due a set of tractor trailers that had become stranded on the uphill side.

Beth walked into the living room, to Cynthia's relief, and virtually collapsed into her aunt's warm hug. There she cried and cried. Cynthia stroked her long red hair saying in teary words, "I know, I know, dear. I never had children of my own but he was like a son to me...But don't tell your grandmother I said that." Beth actually grinned a tiny grin.

The next morning Beth prayed for the strength to go on and then she left for class. The landscape was grey with the sloppy combination of sleet and freezing rain from the night before but the snow plows and salt trucks were out in force.

Everyone was kind to Beth and her instructors were patient with her as she got caught up on her work. Eventually she settled back into the comfort of her normal routines. But the struggle to recover from this stunning loss was far from over.

The end of Part 1

Part 2

The Months Following Lunch in Lewistown

Prologue to the Section
The Sunday night before Thanksgiving, 2009

"...I just wish I knew what was next—what God really wants me to do with my life"

"You'll get it figured out," he assured her.

"I sure hope so," she said softly, looking down into her lap.

* * * * * * *

"...but sometimes I still just wonder 'why?' You know..."

* * * * * * *

"...But at least some things have gone right. Thanks for everything you and Fred did for us."

"Oh...I almost felt like just a spectator, not one of the players," Pete replied, "God just took over control and made things fall in place."

Beth responded saying, "It's no surprise His Word says, '...all things work together for good for those who love God...'" (Romans 8:28)

"So true," Pete had to agree.

--from *Milkshakes*

Lunch in Lewistown

It was the first full week of March so Spring Break had arrived at last for Pete. Since returning to school after Christmas, he had been home only one time. The only other break from school, if it could be called that, was to attend Pastor Dan's funeral in Blueberry Haven. Pete was anxious to see everyone again. It had been a difficult year to say the least: the break-up with Lauren, sickness, Pastor Jackson moving to Vermont, then Pastor Dan dying so suddenly, the last two so close to Christmas, and the loneliness that so often enveloped him. A week or so to relax and recalibrate would be of infinite value to Pete. Little did he know, though, that this Spring Break was to be very different than the last one, very different from what he had expected. It was indeed to be a break with another purpose than just rest and relaxation.

Anxious, though he was, to return home for the vacation, Pete wanted to use the first day to do something he had never done before—visit the State Fire Academy over the mountain in Lewistown. A group of firefighters from Colsonburg and surrounding fire companies, including Laingeville Center, was training at the academy and the ones from LC, Sonny and Lerch, suggested Pete come down for awhile. He would not be so close after graduation and the daily routines of a farmer would not easily lend themselves to such expeditions and training.

After leaving Centre Hall, Pete drove over "the mountain." After climbing the slowly twisting and turning two-lane highway through rock cuts and forestland, he came to an area that passed through the tops of where many different mountains came together. The road became a spacious four-lane expressway. Passing more forestland and camping areas he crossed into Mifflin County. The highway remained four lanes but narrowed severely and the lanes were separated only by a jersey barrier. Trucks were required to come to a complete stop before descending at only twenty miles per hour. Surely this was the sign of a mountain that should be taken very seriously. The highway swung in long but narrow curves around the face of the mountain and down to where even more steep peaks came in from the left and the right, the highway snaking its way through the winding groove formed where they met. The reservoir below and to the left was still white with winter's ice and framed by the bare, brown trees, all waiting for central Pennsylvania's spring to truly arrive. As far as the eye could see, long mountain ridges stretched across the horizon, one after the other. Surely this could be a beautiful sight in another stage of the seasons.

The road widened again and leveled out as it crossed the floor of a great valley framed on each side by a long, continuous, tree-carpeted mountain. Farmland stretched out to Pete's right and to his left. Two white-topped Amish buggies followed a side road off to the right. The mountain ahead of him was broken in two by a natural gap that gave level passageway to a parallel valley. As he finally came into the edges of Lewistown, hills came in from the right and left while another great mountain ridge rose up perhaps a couple miles straight ahead.

With lunchtime upon him, Pete exited the highway to a busy three-lane avenue with several fast food establishments on both sides. He seemed to know that Beth Morton must be over here somewhere but that did not seem important now—no time, no need, no pressing interest in seeking her out. Lewistown Hospital was ahead on the left but before he got that far he instead turned left into a fast food burger place. It seemed the easiest way to get back to the on-ramp when he was finished—a right turn back into the first lane of traffic instead of a left turn against all three. He actually would have preferred to have gone to the chicken place on the right but the traffic was so heavy. He also would have gone to the chicken place had he known that there was a traffic signal enabling him to reenter the avenue with ease. So he accidentally chose the burger place; if only he had known.

Being lunch hour, the place was busy. Not far ahead of him a small group of what appeared to be nurses was ordering, one at a time. The railings directed the customers in a kind of sideways S-pattern. As that railing forced him to the left, Pete noticed that one of those nurses had the same distinct hair as Beth Morton's—long, wavy, and red. He watched this one for a moment, as a person watches anyone that seems familiar, only to discover that the reason she looked like Beth was because that was who she, in fact, was! Leaning to the left he half whispered inquisitively, smiling, "Beth?" He figured that if he was wrong she would not respond to the name. The young woman turned only slowly at first but her jaw dropped open and she suddenly spun around, tray in hand, as she incredulously exclaimed, "Pete!"

"Can you hold up a moment?" he inquired.

"Sure," was her cheerful and surprised response.

Ordering his simple meal, Pete hastily worked his way past the other customers to where Beth was waiting. The others in her group observed this and whispered, smiling, to one another about what they wrongly assumed to be happening.

"What in the world are you doing in Lewistown?" Beth asked in amazement.

"Well, it's Spring Break and I'm on my way to check out the State Fire Academy before heading home," Pete explained as they began to walk toward the tables.

"Since I saw you here, can you talk a minute?" he asked her.

"Okay," was her simple reply. "Do you mind?" she asked her classmates.

"Oh, be our guest," the unofficial spokeswoman replied, all of them smiling among themselves.

One jeered, "Ask him if he has a brother!"

"He does, actually," Beth quipped, "but he's still in high school!"

"How have you been?" she asked as they spread their meals out before them on the small table. She sat directly across from him. She looked so different in her nursing uniform, still more grown-up than ever. He likewise was, as she remembered, tall with short brown hair, visibly strong and speaking with that deep voice. But the tan that the summer's work on the farm had brought was long gone now. It was strange to think that they were both to graduate soon and pursue adult lives complete with careers. They each paused to offer their own silent thanksgiving before eating their meals.

"I guess I'm hanging in there," Pete answered her. "I'm anxious for some time back in LC."

She looked little confused.

He realized he needed to interpret his lingo, "Laingeville Center," he clarified.

"Oh."

"It's been a tough year." He had no more than said it when he realized how stupid and thoughtless it was to tell a nineteen-year-old woman whose father had died so suddenly and tragically only two months before that *he* had had a "tough year."

"I know the feeling," she was already thinking out loud, her voice trailing off slightly.

"I'm sorry; I didn't..." Pete started.

Snapping back from her momentary trance, as it were, she tried to assure him that she was not upset saying, "We all have our struggles and I know how Dad's passing also touched you and your family."

"Yeah. He was the best," Pete remembered. He started eating.

"My mom hasn't heard from your mom almost since the funeral," Pete continued, a half-chewed french fry rolling around in his mouth. "So, how are you guys doing?"

He expected a simple and standard set of answers including the predictable "We're getting there," or "It's been hard, but..." and also,

"God has been faithful," and so on. It would be a simple, harmless, and fleeting conversation. They would conclude that it had been good to see each other again, one more time, and they would each finally go their own way. However, it was not to be so this time. Beth's mood instantly changed. The question brought her back to a cold hard reality that the busyness of school allowed her to push to the back of her mind most of the time.

"Things aren't good...aren't good at all," Beth started, her cheerful demeanor quickly melting away.

As she tried to continue, she stopped abruptly before the first syllable could be formed. A sound like a small gasp came out instead of words. Leaving her salad fork on the tray, Beth transferred her hand to a position just barely in front of her mouth, her fingers slightly below her nose. It was as if having her hand there would hide the sadness surfacing from within, or somehow contain the flood of emotions suddenly stacking up and getting ready to pour out. She looked off to the side, staring out the greenhouse-like windows. Outside the bare mountains stretched, one after another, endlessly, with Lewistown in the foreground. The sky was grey and low. It was like she was traveling off to another world with her thoughts.

"I don't know what I'm going to do," she whispered, through her fingers, in shaking words.

Pete, initially filled with pure selfishness, thought, *Oh no, what have I done?*

He wondered what he would do if she started to weep. His initial instinct was to flee this flash flood of emotion—he was already on his own emotional overload now—but he knew he could not. In almost the same instant he was convicted in his spirit of this self-centered response. He was being so selfish, even if silently. No, he would listen, for whatever it would be worth to Beth, he would listen.

"Why? What's wrong?" he pleaded to know, tipping his head so as to look more squarely at her face, his own face filled with concern.

It was all Beth could do to rise above the physical effect her emotions were having on her. She spoke alternating between shaky words and miniature sobs. Her hand remained just before her mouth.

"Dad's...gone," she fought just to say it. "Patty and Daryl are back in Seattle and she used her whole year's vacation at once so she's out of the picture for awhile. We still haven't heard a word from Billy and we don't know for sure where he is—if *he's* even dead or alive. There is a mountain of bills, mostly medical, and no salary to pay them anymore. Mom has no idea which way to turn. She can't stay in the parsonage indefinitely. Now she seems to have fallen into some sort of depression. She's suddenly all alone for the first time in her life. I wanted to quit school and go home to her but she won't hear of it—says Dad would never have permitted me to quit now with only until August to go. She isn't working. She only ever helped Dad and raised us kids. And she can't pay her bills. The church *did* let her stay in the parsonage rent-free but they have already been reminding her that they will need it back for the next pastor. But it could take up to a year or more to find one. I understand their situation but they also have not been as supportive as they should have been. Mom always said it was the coldest church they ever went to."

"Oh wow," Pete said, horrified, "we had no idea…"

"I know," Beth said apologetically, "We have both been pretty quiet about it all. Sometimes that pressure that you have to be perfect, problem-free, *always* victorious because you're 'the pastor's family' is just too overwhelming. Besides I have been just swamped here; it's an intense program. You're the first one I have talked to about it, besides my great aunt, of course, and my friend Rhonda. I don't have time to talk. Right now I'm the one keeping things together up there. Sometimes I've had to go up and back in the same day and it's a five-hour drive, one-way. Not to mention that it can be really rough country in the winter."

She continued to explain the depth and severity of the problem. Pastor Dan had paid her tuition in full through graduation but at a terrible price; there was no savings left when he died and she did not realize that he had taken a loan to help pay her tuition. The church had tried to save money by switching him to a cheap health insurance plan that paid very little of her Dad's medical bills for those last two days. His churches had always provided life insurance, but not this one and he had not planned to purchase his own until Beth graduated and the loan was paid off. Ginny had done okay through the funeral but then the combination of the initial shock, combined with the string of sudden, and major, decisions only to be followed by the enormous bills and the stark loneliness had taken their toll. Now she faced a virtual eviction from the parsonage, unprepared emotionally to decide where to go next. A pastor's family has no real home, she explained.

Putting her hand down at last she turned back to look Pete straight in the face. Looking at him, she asked with pleading eyes, "What am I going to do?"

There was no answer for that question—not yet. *No one* knew. It was obvious that only God knew. The issue was finding out what *His* answer was.

"Hey Juliet!" one of the other students yelled to Beth, "Break's over!"

One of the others slapped her on the arm, her eyes flashing disapproval. "What's wrong with you?" she demanded to know of the heckler.

"I'm going to have to go," Beth resigned, wiping her eyes. "I'm sorry…" she began.

But Pete stopped her, reassuring her, "It's all right."

"Thanks." She answered quietly.

"How else can we reach you guys?" Pete asked on a whim.

Beth quickly wrote out two phone numbers, designating one "Aunt Cynthia's," and the other one, "Beth's cell." She also wrote an email address that began "bvmorton," indicating it must be hers.

She observed, "I know your mom has the landline at home and Mom's email address. I have to go. Thanks Pete."

She rushed off to throw away her uneaten salad.

"Anytime," was all he could muster as she departed with the others, one of them placing a comforting arm around Beth on the walk back up the hill to the hospital, about a couple blocks away.

Pete felt empty inside as he ate his now cold meal in silence. He took another expressway over top of one of those ridges with Lewistown directly below him as if he were passing over in an airplane, the valley stretching ahead and behind him. The Juniata River dove into a narrow gap in the next mountain ridge and disappeared on its way to the Susquehanna River and Harrisburg. Finding Fourth Street, he caught up with Sonny and Lerch at the Fire Academy.

A few hours later it was time to go home. He "flew" back over Lewistown then crossed those cold frozen valleys again to the foot of the bare-treed mountains and made the winding ascent back over to Centre Hall, stopping only to pick up his bag, laptop, and cell phone charger. He made the trek back north—past Lock Haven and Williamsport then in the direction of Mansfield and Corning. Eventually he exited the four-lane highway to a state highway then through several miles and turns to ever-smaller roads, through Singleton Flats, over Spring Hill Mountain to Lainge's Gap, following Lainge's Creek, arriving at last in Laingeville Center.

But all the way there his thoughts were about his lunch back in Lewistown. He was haunted by the images of Beth struggling just to speak and his imaginations of her mom frozen in a state of confusion, loss, and pain. He remembered Beth begging just to know, "What am I going to do?" He didn't even recognize these people anymore.

Earlier the radio had played one of his favorite Christian radio stations from the State College area. The song was familiar but suddenly it was personal, too. It told of someone who had been through a great trial but in the refrain it seemed that God Himself was saying that with His help it was going to be all right, that He was soon coming to the rescue.

He wanted to believe that the song was right or even prophetic. But he felt like *he* needed to do something to help with that, but what? Later somewhere near McElhattan he got a notion of what he could and should do. Even as he drove he prayed for a confirmation of this hunch. If it would be confirmed to him he was certainly going to the right place to do it.

Later Pete's mind wandered to a sermon on this subject that he had heard recently. He was sure it was in the opening chapters of the Book of Acts that it was told how the believers sold even land and homes to provide money for the needy. The Bible talked a lot about Christians helping other needy Christians. That was all the confirmation *he* needed. He would, however use his concordance to track down the exact chapter and verse for that account in Acts when he got home. Yes, he knew what he should do. But he could never have imagined how that passage of Scripture would be fulfilled right before his very eyes in the coming days and weeks.

It was dark long before he drove into the driveway. The night was crisp and silent—more like winter than spring—and the steam from his breath hung in the air. He almost forgot it all, though, when he cracked the front door open and was greeted by the toasty warm interior, the golden lighting, and the cheerful voices of Mom, Dad, Pat, and Amy welcoming him home. Even Grandpa and Grandma were there.

Back on Call

When Pete went to bed that night he first looked up the passage he remembered on the way home. It was in Acts 4:34-35. He also made a mental note that he needed to retrieve his pager from the firehouse tomorrow. He kept it there while at school so it could be loaned to someone else if, for instance, their own pager was out for repairs. It was not likely that he would need it but it was better to have it, just in case.

He did not notice the time as he began to drift off to sleep but it was 1:59 AM when he was shocked awake from a deep sleep. The fire whistle had gone off, filling the night with its shrill call—climbing quickly to a loud, high-pitched peak, holding it for a few seconds, only to fall off to a low, quieter moan. Bottoming out, it immediately took off on the upward climb again. And so the pattern repeated itself maybe a dozen times.

Pete switched his lamp on and pulled on his sweat pants and shirt, a pair of wool socks, and an old pair of laceless work boots. All these items were kept carefully arranged next to his bed for just such a time as this.

He came down the stairs as quickly as he dared and threw the front door open. The cyclical wailing filled the air. Running next door to the firehouse, the sound completely filled his head. Tapping the combination into the lock, he pulled the door open and found at least some refuge from the noise in the dark garage. He wondered what the call would be for: an accident? a house? a barn? a first or second alarm assignment to a neighboring district?

Someone else flung the door open as Pete began pushing the buttons opening the overhead doors in front of each truck; it was Percy.

"What do we have Percy?" Pete called out.

"Chimney fire out at O'Connor's on Spring Hill Road," he called back to Pete.

"Okay."

In the moments that followed more men were scrambling into the station. Pete was at the back wall where the turn-out gear was kept. Having put his feet into the boots of his assigned set of gear, he simultaneously pulled the suspenders for his bunk pants over each of his shoulders. One truck roared to life behind him, the diesel engine purring roughly as the men began to scamper to the trucks. Another engine started, running in harmony with the first one. The red and white emergency lights flashed all over the walls. Pete could hear one or two of the truck doors slam closed. He jogged down the driver's side of Engine 5-1, his yellow helmet on his head now and his unzipped coat flapping to the sides. Guy Madison was right behind him carrying his helmet and coat each on one arm.

Reaching up to almost eye level, Pete pulled the silver-colored door handle down and pulled the door open. He climbed up into the front of the crew compartment and sat facing the opposite direction the driver faced. Guy climbed up and sat directly across from Pete, the two of them facing one another. It was cramped quarters in the older six-man pumper, the one called "Old Faithful." Just before Guy slammed the door shut someone was heard yelling, "I'll get the tanker!"

The shoulder-high steel box next to Pete and Guy contained the rumbling engine. Looking over the top of it, Pete observed Curly and Hank seated and getting their turnout gear situated. Pete pounded his hand on the steel engine box to get the attention of the men in the two front seats. Zeke, the assistant chief, in his white helmet, was in the officer's seat next to Percy, the driver. When he and Pete made eye contact, Pete gave the "thumbs-up" and held up four fingers, indicating four crewmen were in the rear compartment, ready to go. Zeke said something to Percy and motioned forward. The parking brake hissed as it was released. The engine next to Pete suddenly roared and the truck rolled forward. The doorway quickly went past the windows and they entered the dark night.

Zeke's voice was heard on the speaker, "County, this is Engine 5-1."

A pleasant, relaxed, almost sing-song female voice called back, "Engine 5-1, go ahead."

Zeke replied back, "Engine 5-1 is responding with six."

The invisible voice responded, "Engine 5-1 you're responding with six at zero-two, zero-two hours to two-two-two-three Spring Hill Road, in Lainge Township, for a chimney fire. Your cross streets are East State Road and Swamp Lane. Chief 5-1 is on the scene and has command post five on fire ground one."

"Copy," Zeke acknowledged, "Fire ground one." He reached up to change the channel setting on the communications radio to the designated frequency, then flipped on the electronic siren whose controls were mounted right next to the radio. Zeke sat back for the nighttime ride out to the O'Connors', obviously talking, and even laughing, with Percy up front. The truck's warning lights flashed against every tree and building they passed. The engine next to Pete became quieter, then louder, as it approached and pulled out of curves and turns and as the automatic transmission changed gears.

Pete finished putting on his gear and then laced his arms through the straps of the air pack implanted into the back of his seat. He fastened the buckles and pulled the cords that snugged it tightly against his body. He would not need to turn it on but he, like the others, would have it with him if it became necessary. Chimney fires occasionally turned into house fires.

He grabbed his flashlight and portable radio from the chargers next to, and slightly behind, him; there was one set for each crew member.

So many homes were heated by woodstoves or wood furnaces because it was a fuel that was local, abundant, and cheap or even free. But the chimneys needed regular care and cleaning or they would surely clog or catch fire inside, heating them up to dangerous levels. While most chimney fires were benign they did from time to time spread into an adjacent wall or the roof and once in awhile became full-blown house fires. The Lainge Township Volunteer Fire Company responded to one or two chimney fires a month during the winter and each one was taken very seriously.

"When did you get home?" Guy asked Pete as they wound around the rural roads.

"I just got back tonight," Pete spoke loudly over the sound of the engine next to him, also volunteering to say, "and I go back a week from Monday."

"Welcome home!" Guy joked, referring to the early-hours expedition.

Guy, like Pete, was a young man of about nineteen or twenty. He was slightly shorter than Pete with sloppy medium-length blonde hair that had a slight tint of red to it. Guy had been raised by a single mother who had had live-in relationships with several different men. He did not even know who his father was and he had lived with his mother in many different men's houses, trailers, and apartments over the years. He was normally a quiet, shy person but he had a taste for beer and when he had been drinking he became silly and a laughingstock. His "friends" liked to get him drunk and then sit back and watch the show. He seemed to not notice, or else not care, that they were simply using him. He also smoked—a lot. He and his girlfriend lived together in the apartment that John and Joanie once rented above Holmes' Market.

Curly and Hank were swapping the usual stories about drinking and womanizing. Pete suspected that their accounts were mostly fiction or exaggeration as they each tried to impress the other with a more sensational tale. While none of the men in Engine 5-1 that night were Christians, except Pete, most were respectful of his faith. Curly and Hank, however, respected no one when they had a choice and were often sarcastic toward Pete. They sometimes made fun of him and called him names. These epithets did not have their intended effects as Pete refused to be discouraged by them. Instead Pete actually felt sorry for them, though he never said so in so many words. But most of the guys paid no attention to Pete's Christianity. A few even went to church themselves, at least sometimes, like Sonny and

Lerch who had also just returned from the Academy that same night. But they were in Engine 5-2.

Guy and Pete chatted back and forth, pausing at times to listen to the things being said on the radio. Chief 5-1 was on the scene with heavy smoke evident and wanted both engines to stage in front of the house. Tanker 5 and Squad 5 would stay near the road, at the ready if needed along with Ambulance 16-3. According to what they heard, Engine 5-1 would have a hose pulled and charged—that was in case the hot chimney should ignite the house's timbers or roof. Engine 5-2 would use its lights to illuminate the roof as a crew worked from the top of the chimney. Another crew would work at the bottom of the chimney—in the basement. The Chief and any spare men would be watching the walls on the inside, using a thermal imaging camera, to be sure the fire was not also in the walls.

"Engine 5-1 on the scene," Zeke called to the county dispatcher as the truck rolled down the long, bumpy driveway.

"Engine 5-1 on the scene at zero-two, zero-nine hours," the familiar but invisible voice answered.

Everyone jumped from the truck and met the Chief next to the driver's door. He gave everyone his instructions. Guy pulled the hose from the bay above the pump panel and Pete helped him stretch it out, eliminating any potential kinks. Pete took the nozzle as Guy put on his gloves. Then he grasped the hose behind Pete ready to help him move and direct it, if necessary. That was all Pete and Guy did the whole time, except drizzle some of the water onto the hot materials extracted from the chimney and contained now in a metal wash pail.

Curly, Hank, and Zeke began setting up the ladders enabling Sonny and Lerch to climb up and begin their work in the center of the farmhouse's roof. Others retrieved tools and equipment from the engines as needed by the crews working on the chimney. The pungent odor of burning creosote hung in the air and snow was seen in Engine 5-2's lights—only light, but steady.

Everyone knew what had to be done. If anyone had a doubt or a question, he would ask an officer. They all knew how to take orders or find a task to be completed and begin working at it. No one was without an assignment of some kind. Some assignments were exciting, like being up on the roof dealing directly with the fire, and others were plain or even dull, like holding a hose and never having to use it. But every task was important and needed someone attending to it.

It took about an hour and half to finish extinguishing the fire, clean out the chimney, and put the equipment back on the trucks. Back at the firehouse, the drivers and the Chief completed their checklists and reports while the others finished putting things back in order on the engines. One by one the men returned home. Pete was back in bed shortly after four in the morning. He brought his pager home with him but it did not ring even once for the rest of Spring Break!

* * * * * * *

Pete called Grandpa to let him know he would not be out to the farm until after lunch. Under the circumstances, Grandpa understood. He had been milking without Pete most of the time anyway. For now Pete could do this but someday soon he would not be able to skip milking time because he missed two hours' sleep. He also would not be able to *stop* milking to answer a fire call. This was a struggle for him. During the days, especially, the Fire Company desperately needed men available to respond with no notice since not many were around at that time because of their jobs. Pete had seen farmers not respond to a call that was close to milking time or leave a call to tend to the milking. But the farm was his primary vocation, not the fire company.

Pete had been having his doubts about being a dairy farmer long before this—the long hours versus the meager earnings. But he loved the farm—working the land, the family heritage it represented, being his own boss. He was beginning to pray and think about a new approach to running the farm when Grandpa retired. Pete hoped this new approach might, if God would lead him down that pathway, enable him to survive doing what he loved and continue to serve in the Fire Company, the church and perhaps in other ways, too. He also hoped it would net him at least a decent living.

A family was not included in this vision. He had trained his mind to see his life without a wife or children. Living with his bachelor uncle in Centre Hall for almost two years had given him an example to follow. If God would surprise him with those blessings that would be fine but he was not planning on them. Pete knew that the odds were slowly, but steadily, stacking up against him. He would graduate in a couple of months, leaving the college setting that afforded many opportunities to meet women his age. Back home in LC his schoolmates and other friends were already pairing off—some married or engaged, some dating or living together. Others were not suited to him because they were not Christians or their personalities clashed with his own. He was done trying to start a relationship "from scratch" with a stranger. That approach had failed twice in the last year or so. His new approach was to seek no one and then no one could hurt him again. Loneliness was not easy but it was predictable and stable. Pete felt he could adapt to it, even long term.

An Unlikely Partnership

After one of those typical Saturday morning feasts of homemade waffles and bacon, Pete headed into Colsonburg. He needed to cash a check from work to supply his needs while on break and to get him back down the road to Centre Hall at its conclusion. The March sun was warming the air now but last night's snow lay sprinkled around in the shady areas.

Done at the bank, he drove over to Fred and Meredith Holt's home on the north end of Colsonburg. The colonial style house was very old and large but in perfect condition. It stood impressively behind a waist-high hedge with the sprawling lawn perfectly landscaped and groomed, even despite the torturous winter months. Parking in the semi-circle driveway, he approached the dark green front door, banging the brass knocker three or four times.

It was Mr. Holt who answered the door.

"Pete," he declared, "what a pleasant surprise!"

He was a tall man and always well dressed, even on this Saturday morning in a pair of blue slacks and a white dress shirt. His skin was fair and his hair white. A newspaper was folded over and held in one hand and he was wearing his famous reading glasses—the ones with a black cord attached at each end of the glasses and draped around behind his neck. He always wore those thin, half-circle lenses, it seemed, halfway down his nose, looking over the tops of them whenever he was not actually reading.

"Do you have a few minutes?" Pete asked.

"Certainly," he graciously replied, "Come on in"

The interior was as perfectly appointed and maintained as the exterior. Mr. Holt motioned to a doorway located to the right of the banister-graced central stairway. Through that doorway was his home office. A large brown desk, perfectly organized, was positioned straight ahead in such a way that as Mr. Holt sat there he could look directly at anyone who entered. Various antlers, stuffed animal heads, and other hunting trophies dotted the walls. There were well-stocked bookshelves behind the desk. In the corner to Pete's left were four wing-back chairs with a brown coffee table in the center of them.

"Have a seat," Mr. Holt gestured toward the wingback chairs, "What's on your mind?"

"There is someone I hoped the Deacons could consider helping," Pete started as they both took a seat diagonally across from one another. Mr. Holt was the chairman of the Deacons at 3C and requests for their assistance usually started with him. Pete had never presented a need before. He hardly knew how to proceed.

Mr. Holt sunk down into the chair, his elbows on the arms and his fingers laced together just before his chin. Having removed the glasses from his nose and allowing them to hang from around his neck, he asked, "And who would that be?"

"Actually," Pete started carefully, "it's Mrs. Morton, Pastor Dan's wife."

"Oh?" he responded with a half-curious, half confused look on his face. Pete related the account of his unplanned meeting with Beth down in Lewistown just the day before. He repeated all she had told him. He explained the emotion in Beth, his own emotions seeping through a couple times. Mr. Holt's countenance fell to a very sad and grave appearance.

"I think the Deacons will be very interested in hearing this," he concluded very seriously, "If only we had known before now."

"We had no idea either," Pete offered, as if he had to explain.

Mr. Holt walked over to his desk to pick up a legal pad and pen and returned to the chair. He placed the glasses back in their typical position on his nose, and reviewed the main points of Ginny's situation and needs as he wrote them down, frequently looking up at Pete for confirmation of their accuracy.

"Our fund is unusually well-stocked for this time of year. I am sure we can help in some way," he concluded. "I'll call the other Deacons and ask them to meet with me either before or after services tomorrow," he explained to Pete, "We'll discuss it, agree on a plan to respond, and then I'll let you know what we have decided."

"Thanks a lot Mr. Holt," Pete said.

"Oh, no, thank *you* Pete," Mr. Holt responded, adding, "And two other things: One, I am Fred; we are both grown men here so you may speak to me as I would to you. And, two, I'll need a phone number or other contact information for Ginny."

"Oh yeah," Pete remembered. He took a three-by-five card from his shirt pocket on which he had re-written the phone numbers and email address Beth had given him.

Fred held the card at the top of the pad as he copied the information onto the page.

"Here," he said, handing the card back to Pete, leaning forward as he held it over the coffee table for Pete to retrieve.

"Anything else, Pete?" he asked.

"I guess that's it," Pete replied.

"Okay. Let's have a word of prayer for Ginny," Fred invited. He immediately led out: "Father, we are so saddened to hear of the plight of our dear sister, Ginny and her family. We pray now in Jesus' Name that even today You would please pour out Your grace upon them all. Make them overcomers in this trial, Lord. Give them strength beyond their own; give them hope. Lord, guide us as a church to know how to respond to this need for Your Word teaches us to care for widows and orphans in their distress. Bless our meeting tomorrow that we might have Your mind on this and be a blessing to these dear people. Amen."

"Amen," Pete agreed. "Thanks again," he added.

They stood and shook hands and Pete was on his way again. He did not realize it was already past eleven o'clock. At home he explained why he was gone so long. Pete and his folks sat at the kitchen table as he related the story of his surprise rendezvous in Lewistown. John looked blankly off into the distance but Joan dropped her head to her hands and began to cry quietly about her friend Ginny. John rubbed her back softly to try to comfort her a little. Pete showed them the phone numbers and the email address, leaving them on the table so he could get ready to leave for the farm.

* * * * * * *

Jim Corbin was the worship leader the next day, announcing the different parts of the service as they went. He mentioned that Ginny Morton had a need but did not elaborate at that time. After worship Fred asked Pete to see him in the church library.

Fred explained, "Pete, I met with the other Deacons before Sunday School and this what we are going to do. Bob will write a check for five hundred dollars and send it to Ginny as soon as we can confirm her mailing address. We are also going to announce a special Deacons' Offering for Ginny. My wife will work with the Women's Fellowship to try to find a way to encourage Ginny—maybe a card shower, for starters."

"That's great Mr.—er—Fred," Pete answered.

"But that's not all, Pete," Fred continued, "Could you maybe meet me here before the evening service, say at six or so? I have an additional possibility I want to discuss with you as well."

"Sure. Six," Pete agreed.

* * * * * * *

Pete was waiting in his truck in the church parking lot by six o'clock when Fred pulled up next to him in his light grey sedan, motioning Pete to join him in his car.

"Good evening," he greeted Pete, stretching his right hand to Pete who grasped it and shook it firmly.

"Good evening," Pete returned.

"Let's take a quick ride," Fred proposed, putting the car in gear as Pete buckled his seat belt. They started toward downtown but soon turned right onto East Luzerne Avenue and then left into Holt's Trailer Court, one of Fred's property holdings. Pete was puzzled but stayed quiet.

The trailer court was simple and plain but decent and well-kept. Soon they stopped along the gravel street. Pete got out of his side, following Fred's lead. Fred led the way toward a simple yellow trailer with a small wooden porch on the left side. No cars were in the parking area next to the steps. Fred walked up to the door, unlocked it, and walked right inside; Pete followed. The trailer was completely empty of furniture, pictures, heat, or anything that indicated someone lived there. They seemed to be standing in a living room surrounded by dark paneling and carpeting. The kitchen was to the right, a counter separating the two rooms. The kitchen was brighter with a light-colored vinyl floor and light-colored walls; the cabinets were brown. A light hung from the ceiling where a table and chairs might sit. Opposite the kitchen, a narrow hallway left the living room, following the sidewall. Presumably the bedrooms and bathroom were down that hall. A window looked out onto the porch with another one on the opposite wall, a neighboring trailer visible maybe fifteen feet away.

"God has blessed my business," Fred started, "I have a good life but it's all because of His blessings. When I became a Christian I promised God I would honor and serve Him and His people with the blessings I receive. I follow the principle of Leviticus 19:9-10 in regard to the needy. I have never regretted that decision."

Pete was beginning to get a sense of where this might be heading but he continued to listen; he wanted to be sure he was right.

"My wife and I have prayed about Ginny's need," he explained, "what she needs now is a safe place to go with no pressure and no fear of eviction, where she can recover and get her matters sorted out. This place just became available this week and God has simply laid it on our hearts to offer it to Ginny rent-free for a year."

"Oh wow," Pete exclaimed, otherwise speechless.

"I'm offering it," Fred continued, "should she want it or need it. If she is not interested or it does not suit her needs, or if she has other plans, that is fine. But it is here if she needs it. It has two bedrooms—one for her and one for Elizabeth to stay in when she comes home on breaks—and one full bath. There are hook-ups for a washer and electric dryer. The range and refrigerator are included. The carpet cleaners are coming this week. Since utilities are included in all my rents, she would have no expense for those either. Now I don't want this publicized; it is just between us and the Lord. I don't want any glory—let God have it. He gave the idea after all."

"I never would have dreamed…" Pete contemplated out loud, "I would never thought to ask you to…"

Fred stopped him, saying, "I know. You did not. But God has granted me the ability to help and we want to do this," indicating he and Meredith. "What do *you* think?" he asked looking to Pete.

"It's ideal," was all he could say.

"I will call Ginny and Elizabeth tomorrow to make the offer. If Ginny accepts, we may need to help her move here, so be ready to help out if necessary."

"I am so there," Pete agreed, still flabbergasted.

That evening at church the need was explained, the offering and card shower were also announced. No one mentioned Ginny moving to Colsonburg yet since it was not known if the offer would be accepted. A lengthy and emotional prayer was offered by one of the other Elders and the evening congregation of about sixty gave almost three-hundred dollars that would be added to the gift already approved by the Deacons. Pete was in awe. He never dreamed the hunch he struggled with on the way home Friday night would have grown to this kind of response in just forty-eight hours!

* * * * * * *

Beth was sitting at one of the lunch tables at the hospital when her cell phone rang. She did not recognize the "570" area coded phone number on the display. Home was in the "814" area code.

She had just finished a first draft of a letter telling the administration of the School of Nursing that she felt she was needed at home right now, that she was resigning from the program until further notice. It broke her heart but family needed to be first. Still, she was not ready to send it just yet.

"Hello?" she answered suspiciously.

"Elizabeth?" the mature male voice asked.

It had to be either a stranger, like a telemarketer, or someone from her childhood who did not know that she now went by "Beth."

"Yes…" she continued to sound suspicious.

"You probably do not remember me," the voice explained itself, "my name is Fred Holt and I am the Chairman of the Deacons at the Colsonsburg Community Church up north where your father used to pastor. My wife Meredith and I were at the funeral but you and I didn't get a chance to talk."

"Okay…" she consented. She still vividly remembered Meredith Holt from her Colsonburg days and seeing her at the funeral along with her husband.

150

"I want to talk to you about something before I discuss it with your mother," Fred started. He went on to explain what the church was doing for her mom. Beth's mouth dropped open as she listened. The only reply she could manage was, "Pete."

"I am not at liberty to say," Fred replied, "but that is not all." He concluded by explaining the offer of the trailer in Colsonburg.

"I need your opinion. Do you think I should go ahead and make the offer to her?" he asked.

Beth was crying now—filled with emotion, relief, and thanksgiving. A raspy "Yes" was all she could say.

"I'll let you go then," Fred decided not to cause any more emotion than she could handle; "You may call me if you need anything at all or have any questions of any kind."

"Okay and...thank you," was all she could say, and that just barely.

She wept into her hands as soon as she ended the call but managed to get out a short but very sincere "Thank you, God!"

She saved the draft but decided not to return to it—not for now anyway.

* * * * * * *

Ginny was crying when she called Beth that evening to report Fred's call to her.

"Are you going to do it?" Beth finally asked.

"I don't know," Ginny replied with that all-to-familiar overwhelmed sound in her voice.

"I think you should," Beth explained. "It will get the pressure off you and it's pretty obvious that those people care a lot. You would definitely be among friends."

"How would I get all this stuff ready?" Ginny asked curiously but horrified.

"We can figure that out later," Beth assured her, "God provided this much. He will certainly provide for that too. You know I'll help."

"Maybe you're right," Ginny conceded, "I'll think about it. You know, I had about given up hope but maybe..." She never finished the sentence.

Two days later Ginny announced, first to Beth, then to Fred, that she would move to Colsonburg as soon as it could be arranged—maybe during Beth's Spring Break in April. For the first time in her life she was moving somewhere that felt like home already—more now than ever. But this time she would do so alone, without her husband. It was humbling that it had come to this point but also that God and these people cared enough to reach out to her in this way.

The decision, minus the specific details of Fred's offer, was announced to the Church Sunday morning. Immediately the plans began to take form and people came to Fred, who was obviously taking the lead, after the service to offer help of every kind: some to move furniture into the trailer, others to travel out west to help Ginny pack, still others with more financial assistance, and even an offer to prepare a meal for all the people who came to help Ginny move into the trailer.

Pete watched his church come together and team up to address the crisis. He remembered the fire call last Friday night, and all the other times, and how his church reminded him of the instant teamwork of the fire company—everyone taking their place without hesitating or arguing, rushing from what they were already doing to "save the day." He was thankful, yet again, to be a part of a close, loving, and active church.

So it was to be. Ginny would come home to Colsonburg. The folks there would minister to her until she was ready to stand on her own again. She would find a new life, a happy life and so much more than she would have dared to ask or imagine. It was her turn now to be the one ministered *to*.

Homecoming

It was April and the land was beginning to come back to life. The grass was becoming greener with each day. The spring flowers had all appeared and a green "mist" began to shroud the mountains of Centre and Mifflin Counties as the trees' leaf buds opened up into the tiniest of leaves. The days were brighter and longer, too, lifting the mood of everyone.

Pete had just turned twenty. For him the privilege of that birthday was that he could begin driving the fire trucks, albeit under limited conditions. He received his training ahead of time on weekends home so he could be approved by the chief the moment his birthday arrived. He could now drive the four-wheel-drive brush truck, the squad, and the tanker (if an officer was with him). The engines required additional amounts of training so they would wait until summer, following graduation.

It was a Monday evening when Pete's cell phone rang.

"Pete?" Fred Holt's familiar voice cheerfully inquired, "This is Fred. How are you tonight?"

"Fine, and how are you?" Pete answered.

"Very well, thank you," Fred replied and then continued, "How busy are you next weekend?"

"Not too bad, I guess," Pete said, "I was even thinking about coming home. I have some time off that I can take. Why?"

Fred continued, "Well I heard they're letting you drive the tanker now."

"Just started," Pete confirmed.

"Would you like to drive another large truck?" Fred asked.

"Maybe, what did you have in mind?"

"Ginny Morton is moving back to Colsonburg this weekend," he began, "and the Deacons wondered if you might drive the moving truck. It's a little more of a vehicle than most want to tackle if they don't have to. Besides you kind of started this thing so maybe you would like to help finish it."

"I might be able to do it," Pete thought out loud. "What's the timeline for this?"

So Fred told him, "We would leave first thing Saturday morning. Some folks are going out to help her pack on Thursday and Friday so we should be able to just load things up and be back here by suppertime. It will be a full day, though, no doubt about it."

"I don't mind driving the truck, I guess," Pete replied, "I know it's not for everyone. I suppose I can....so I'll come up Friday evening after class."

"Wonderful!" Fred cheered, "I'll have everything reserved and ready to go. We are all going to meet at my place at five A.M. We'll have breakfast in Mansfield right before we pick up the truck and head west on Route 6."

"Okay. I'll see you Saturday," Pete confirmed.

"I will see you then, Pete. And thank you."

* * * * * * *

It was late morning when the truck and Fred's car, filled with men from the church arrived in Blueberry Haven on the mountainless but gentle and rolling land well south of Lake Erie. Pete stopped the truck along the curb in front of the parsonage and carefully backed it into the driveway with only minimal guidance from a man he had never met before—he must have been from the Blueberry Haven church.

The house was a beehive of activity. A few of the "bees" were women from Colsonburg. The rest were from the Mortons' church, though none appeared to be leaders or officers. Pete climbed down from the truck's cab and stood on the driveway stretching. When he turned to enter the garage, Beth was standing there.

Looking straight at him she said sternly, "This was all your doing, wasn't it?"

Pete was fearful that she was *unhappy* with this change in events so he answered her saying, "I had absolutely no idea it would come to this, though."

"Thank you so much," she said through choked words and threw her arms around him.

"You're welcome but this part was Fred's idea, not mine," Pete emphasized speaking over her shoulder.

"I have a hug for him, too," she said, her voice very near to his ear. Pulling away from Pete she went off to find Fred, who was generally not much of a hugger, except with his wife, of course. This should be interesting.

Ginny was in the open garage inspecting some still open boxes when she saw Pete. She looked tired and sad, maybe a little thin, too—worse than she did even at the funeral in January.

"Thanks, Pete," she said hugging him but only weakly.

"How are you doing?" he asked, mostly out of convention.

"What can you say?" she shrugged, returning to oversee the packing process.

Pete was struck by this one who now appeared to him as almost a stranger. The happy, strong woman his family had known for years was absent and someone else was here in her place it seemed. He was struck again by his own grief as well as the grief he felt for these two women. It was as if it were all just a story. But it was time to rise above all this and get to the tasks at hand.

They all worked together until noon when someone brought two buckets of fried chicken and some cold sodas. They ate the simple lunch on the front lawn and then went back to work, finishing by one-thirty.

Jim Corbin led everyone in prayer for their journey east. Pete feared the packed truck would climb the hills only slowly so he suggested the cars go on ahead of the truck. One of the Colsonburg men drove Ginny's car and Beth followed the truck, her mother riding with her; Ginny felt better being able to watch the truck on the hours-long journey. It was similar to so many other times over the years but now Beth was driving and Dan was *not* in that truck ahead of them.

So Ginny left the last place she moved to with her husband and actually started to strike out on her own now but she could hardly, if ever, have done it without the support, prayer, and help of her brothers and sisters in Christ. Blueberry Haven had been a hard assignment—the hardest of Pastor Dan's career—but it was still emotional to see it disappear from sight as they pressed eastward back into the mountains. So many dreams and hopes faded along with that home. For Ginny, the hardest part to leave behind was her husband's grave. It held only a shell now, his soul with Jesus, but it was a place to go to remember and honor his life with her on earth. She would have to find a way back there from time to time. Still she partly felt like she was abandoning him in some way.

They reached Mansfield again around suppertime. When they reached Colsonburg the Deaconesses were already at 36 East Holt Lane. They had brought crock pots of chili and soup, plus bread, fresh vegetables, and plenty of cold water, punch, and coffee. Everyone was so hungry that they did not even care there was no place to sit comfortably. It was remarkably similar to that cold June night back in 1992 when Colsonburg first became a part of the two women's lives but there were five of them that night and only two this night.

Ginny reacquainted herself with several old friends from 3C but especially her dear friend, Joanie Archer. It was very emotional for everyone who saw it as the two of them cried on one another's shoulders for a minute or two. Ginny's heart was broken and Joanie's was broken *for* her. After this, Meredith Holt took Ginny through the trailer. Meredith knew it was not much, compared to what Ginny was accustomed to, but it was a place to start again. Maybe she could get something nicer in time, Meredith suggested, almost apologetically.

Ginny was very emotional. Part of it was the completely foreign feeling of moving somewhere without Dan. She had never done this before and it was terrifying to her. But somehow Ginny knew this was God's will for her life now, hard as it was, and it was His provision. So she tried to be as brave as possible, under the circumstances. The doting help and encouragement of her daughter gave her the edge she needed to move forward but Beth was tired and burning out fast. She hoped this would stabilize her mother's situation so she could sort out her own and get some rest again.

Beth and Ginny agreed which bedroom belonged to which one and the men, including Pete, began moving that furniture in first. The other women helped them unpack the most necessary items that they would need for that night and the next day. Some of them would return on Monday to continue helping. Ginny reached the point that she could not stand to make any more decisions so Beth gave direction to the arrangement of the living room and kitchen. Extra items such as Pastor Dan's books, seasonal things, and furniture that simply could not fit in the relatively small trailer, went to the garage of one of the men for storage in an upstairs loft area.

After Pete had left with the truck, Beth began putting some items in the refrigerator and freezer. But the freezer had one corner taken up with several packages wrapped in brown freezer paper. There were handwritten labels on them such as hamburg, rib steak, chuck roast, and so on. A note on top said: "Hope this helps a little. Pete."

Exhausted physically and emotionally, Ginny went to bed early. It was dark as Beth thanked and hugged everyone who helped. Pete had to return the truck to Mansfield before coming back to spend the night at home with his family in LC. It was after midnight when he came in the house, utterly worn out. He went straight to bed and slept very well.

* * * * * * *

Ginny did not want to go to church the next day. She was tired and self-conscious of all the attention she was already receiving. Most of all she did not want to see another pulpit her husband had once preached from so enthusiastically for five years and not see him in it, and knowing why, remembering she would never see that sight ever again. But in the end courtesy to everyone who had helped won the day and she forced herself to go. It was a decision she was ultimately glad she had made. Beth stayed by her side the whole time. The only exception was when Holly Corbin pulled Beth aside to assure her that everyone would be taking care of her mother and that everything would be fine; she had sensed Beth's anxiety.

Many faces were familiar even after all the intervening years. The children were the most difficult to recognize, all grown up now. There were new, unfamiliar faces as well—some young, some old. Some were no longer there—they had moved or died. But it was also the first time Ginny had ever moved and went to a church already knowing at least half the people there. That was actually a refreshing phenomenon in a sea of chaos.

It seemed that everyone welcomed her, even the strangers, many stopping to talk a few moments. Almost everyone affirmed that they were praying for her. Bea Tanner, a seasoned widow herself, though much older than Ginny, took the two women to the Pancake Palace for lunch. Ginny and Beth did not normally eat out on Sundays but chose to accept the invitation rather than offend the thoughtful woman.

Unbeknownst to Ginny, the Deaconesses had a plan in place for her. For her first week in Colsonburg someone was ready each evening either to take Ginny out to supper or have her over to eat with their family. Each Sunday for four weeks one person or family would have her for dinner. After that it would be left to each one to offer as they felt able. This way Ginny could gradually adapt to her life in Colsonburg.

*   *   *   *   *   *   *

It had occurred to Pete that Beth may not know the way back to Lewistown from Colsonburg. He sought Beth out after the morning service before she and Ginny left with Bea for lunch.

"Hey, when do you have to be back to Lewistown?" he asked her.

"I better go back yet this afternoon," she contemplated out loud, "I have an early class tomorrow morning."

"Well, if you want to, you could follow me back as far as Centre Hall. Lewistown is only twenty miles or so from there," Pete suggested.

"I just might take you up on that," Beth answered, "I don't have any knowledge of the roads from here."

"When do you need to leave?"

"Maybe about three," she replied, "Is that too early for you?"

"That's fine," Pete said agreeably, "I'll look for you here at the church around three then?" he confirmed. Actually Pete had hoped to wait until Monday to go back.

"Okay, thanks a lot," she said with a smile.

Beth's grey compact car was sitting alone in the church parking lot as Pete pulled in driving his small red pickup truck. He pulled up alongside her car so both drivers' windows were facing each other. They each lowered their window.

"All set?" he asked her.

"I guess so," she answered him. It was obvious that her farewell to her mom had been very difficult. She had definitely been crying.

"I'm going to stop on the north side of Williamsport for gas," he let her know. "If you need any, either there or Lamar or Zion are good places to get it. Do you have my cell phone number? I know I have yours."

"No," was the simple reply.

Pete entered her number into his phone and pressed "send." Beth's cell phone rang.

"Now you have mine," Pete observed.

So off they went—Pete in front and Beth never far behind. They wound through the rural roads, eventually joining U.S. 15 toward Williamsport. Beth parked her car and went inside while Pete filled his gas tank on the north edge of the city. As he went inside to pay, she returned, carrying a bottle of iced tea.

"I'll be right out," he assured her. Having used the restroom, he poured a coffee and paid the clerk for his gas and drink. He came out and they snaked their way back onto the highway. Pete watched attentively to see that all was well in the rearview mirror as they journeyed through Williamsport, Jersey Shore, Lock Haven, and Pleasant Gap.

Arriving at last in Centre Hall, he led her all the way through the borough until they reached a convenience store at the far end of town. Parking his truck, he walked over to her car and gave her directions back to U.S. 322 which was the route she knew so well.

"Thanks a lot, she said just before she closed the window. "I really appreciate it—everything."

"Anytime," Pete called as he turned back to his idling truck.

Her little car drove out onto the road and right at the light, now bound for Potters Mills and the turn that would take her over that familiar mountain to Lewistown again.

* * * * * * *

Uncle Jim's house looked dark and quiet as Pete pulled into the driveway. It was a sight which was all too familiar to him. A note on the kitchen table explained it: "Emergency business trip to Phoenix, Arizona," it said. "Be back by Wednesday night—hopefully."

It looked like another stretch of lonely evenings again. "'He should be accustomed to it by now but somehow it was still difficult. The contrast between the fellowship of the men working to help Ginny all weekend or the time with family in LC was striking when held against this empty house and Pete sitting in that vacuum, the stillness swallowing him every moment it seemed.

Looking at his watch he judged he could make it to the little white church in Mingoville for the evening service without being late. So he turned around and left again retracing many of the miles he had traveled that day.

A few people from the church went for desserts at a diner in State College after the service. Pete knew this diner well by now. It reminded him, in some ways, of the Colsonburg Diner back home. They laughed and talked and sipped milkshakes until almost ten. It was a nice distraction and they were good to include him, delaying the inevitable return to that dark house.

Back at the house in Centre Hall, Pete finally called home to confirm that he had arrived safe and sound. He quickly slipped into bed, almost numb with exhaustion by that point.

* * * * * * *

Beth's great aunt Cynthia was at church out in Paintersville when Beth arrived at the old house just outside Lewistown. She was exhausted and changed for bed right away. She called her mom to tell her she was okay. She caught up on a little studying until Aunt Cynthia arrived home. They spoke for a while in the living room until Beth just had to succumb to her exhaustion. Going upstairs, she slid under the covers and just before drifting off to sleep, she prayed simply but oh so sincerely, "Thank You, Father, *so much*, for everything You have done for me and Mom. I was almost ready to give up, Lord, but now I feel like I can see hope on the horizon again. Thank You for the people at Colsonburg and for Your provision to Mom through them. Thanks for Fred and Pete and the Deacons and Deaconesses. You're so good, Father. Thank You. Thank You."

She was too tired to go on any more. Turning off the lamp, she pulled the covers close and quickly dozed off into a deep, peace-filled sleep.

The Healing Begins

Five weeks had passed by since Ginny moved to Colsonburg. The people tried to be there for her but there were still so many lonely stretches. Grief is an odd thing. Nothing can be done to stop it. Like a virus it must simply run its course though there is much "medication" that makes it easier. But sometimes even a simple virus gets out of control and takes over. Grief can do that, too. That is what happened to Ginny. 3C, however, was like a medication used of God to help and comfort Ginny until the debilitating condition was healed, allowing her life to go on.

In the meantime, Ginny slept a lot and watched far more television than normal. She did not feel like cleaning and the trailer was in disarray. Many boxes lay on the floor still unopened after the move. She was embarrassed by the condition of the home and did everything she could to keep it from the view of others. Most knew, but most of them understood.

On Mother's Day weekend Beth came home Saturday afternoon. After church on Sunday she made a simple feast for Ginny, featuring one of the steaks Pete had left in the freezer when she moved to Colsonsburg. Soon after that Patty called from Seattle and spoke with her mom and sister quite a while. Beth left again before the Sunday evening service to get back to Lewistown on time.

* * * * * * *

Pete arrived home that same weekend on Friday night. He worked with Grandpa on the farm all day Saturday, stopping only for an hour or so to respond with the Fire Company to a car fire along East State Road, on the way to Colsonburg.

After church the whole family gathered at the farm to honor all the moms, but especially their matriarch, Grandma Archer. Uncle Jim was there from Centre Hall along with Aunt Judy and Uncle Jerald from Wellsboro, their son and daughter, Mike and Susan, with them. Pete and his whole family were there.

Being a wonderful day, the tables were set up in the yard and the men cooked hamburgers, hotdogs, chicken, and sausages on the grills. The meat joined a spread of macaroni salad, fresh vegetables, and potato chips on the serving table. Everyone ate way too much and then had ice cream anyway. Pete stayed for the evening service and then left straight from the church to return to Centre Hall well after dark.

* * * * * * *

The church had still not called a new pastor and many different men were lined up to fill the pulpit at 3C from Sunday to Sunday. But the Saturday evening after Mother's Day, Jim Corbin received a call that the next day's preacher was too sick to make it. Turning to his list of emergency substitutes, he tried in vain to find another. Only one name remained but he was all the way in the Tunkhannock area—a long drive exacerbated by the very short notice. If he could not come then the elders would handle the service and the sermon.

"No problem!" the retired Rev. Lilly declared. "We'll just see what God gives me for a message between now and then."

Rev. Lilly was not even from the same denomination and knew no one from the church or even where it was, apart from Jim's directions.

"Brother Corbin didn't give me much notice," Rev. Lilly joked as he stood at the pulpit, "but this morning the Lord confirmed in my spirit the message He wants me to bring for Corsonburg today," he said, mistakenly "renaming" the borough.

He cracked his tattered Bible open and set it down on the pulpit desk. Thoughtfully, deliberately, he turned the pages one by one. Stopping, he looked down on the page he had sought, announced the reference and read with dignity from Jesus' words in Luke 4:18, "The Spirit of the Lord is upon Me, because He has anointed me to preach the Gospel to the poor. He has sent Me to heal the brokenhearted." He abruptly stopped and burst out in prayer asking for the Lord's blessing on the sermon he was about to proclaim.

He preached long and hard without any notes at all on that line, "He has sent Me to heal the brokenhearted." He strutted back and forth across the chancel, gesturing frequently and his voice sometimes rose and sometimes softened according to the emphasis he was making at that point. He occasionally bent down and occasionally stood tall and straight. What little hair he had on his balding head flew back and forth across his forehead in thin grey locks. Giving illustrations and stories that made even his own voice crack with emotion, he delivered with conviction a rousing message of how God can miraculously heal and restore the brokenhearted soul.

Ginny sat transfixed by him, missing not a single word. She suspected several sets of eyes took turns looking her way—most with concern and prayerfulness, others just nosey.

Suddenly Rev. Lilly began to pray again. He was finished but the sermon had actually lasted for forty minutes. He asked God to speak to anyone suffering a broken heart. He invited people to come forward for prayer at the altar rail. Sitting down, bowing his own head in prayer, he had asked the music director to come and lead the hymn "The Comforter Has Come."

The congregation stood and sang with gusto and conviction but Ginny stayed seated, her head dropped, tears falling all the way to the floor. Then a warm presence was sensed on the pew beside her and a gentle hand was felt running across the backs of her shoulders and resting on her left arm. Joanie's voice was heard whispering straight into Ginny's right ear, "I'll go with you if you want me to."

Ginny simply nodded and the two stood up in exact formation and made their way down the aisle to kneel at the rail. Immediately they were joined by Meredith Holt and Holly Corbin. Joanie's hand never departed from Ginny's arm for even a fraction of a second. Rev. Lilly came down and knelt opposite the rail from the two ladies and inquired how he could pray for Ginny.

Speaking in only half sentences, split by sobs and gasps, Ginny poured out the horror story of the last months, one tissue after another being plucked from the box always there at the ready.

"Oh sister," even Rev. Lilly was touched, "you have come to the right place today!" He proceeded to pray, crying out to God with great emotion for his broken sister in the Lord. No one at the rail noticed that the hymn was over and almost everyone in the congregation had sat down or come and knelt beside or behind Ginny, some extending a hand to touch her or one next to her or even one next to one next to her. In fact, a great throng of people had gathered around her, though she was not aware of it. Of those seated in the pews, some watched, some prayed, or did a little of each.

Finally Rev. Lilly asked Ginny to pray as best she could. Her prayer was short, fragmented, and unpolished but sincere. Rev. Lilly looked at her and said, "Sister, this is a day God has chosen to give you a new start. I know it. You're gonna make it, sister, you're gonna make it," he almost shouted but gleefully so, and convincingly.

Ginny cried all over again when she stood and witnessed the gathering of friends also standing up behind where she had been. She also let a smile escape as she embraced Joanie, a sister in so many ways except biologically. Many other hugs were shared and the whole box of tissues was consumed. Only now did the congregation begin to depart.

"Come have dinner with us," Joanie pleaded. But Ginny politely declined explaining that she wanted to make some calls. Joanie understood and proposed ice cream after the evening service. Ginny nodded in agreement and the two hugged one more time.

* * * * * * *

Pete's mom was on the other end of the call he answered on his cell phone Sunday afternoon. He was outside. A large shed had burned in the neighborhood and he, along with several others, were watching the firefighters from Centre Hall, Boalsburg, Spring Mills, and Pleasant Gap extinguish it. Pete wanted to help but, not having gear that fit and since many local men showed up, he stayed back.

"We've had quite a Sunday up here already," she started, an air of intrigue in her voice.

"Oh," he asked, "how's that?"

"Well…" she started, delivering the entire account with pinpoint accuracy.

"O, wow!" he exclaimed, "That is *awesome!*"

They agreed in their interpretation of the way God had engineered the events leading up to that day. Their conclusion was that, as far back as that disheartening lunch in Lewistown, more than two months ago, God had been bringing Ginny to that very moment in time to touch her, heal her, and give her a new chapter in life. Pete immediately thanked God for it all after he ended the call.

* * * * * * *

Beth was napping when her cell phone woke her that afternoon. The display said, "Mom."

"Hey," she started cheerfully, through a yawn.

"You got a few minutes, babe?" her mom asked.

"You bet," Beth promised.

Ginny related the whole account from the time the regularly scheduled preacher had called off sick all the way to the moment she placed the call to Beth. Beth listened in stunned silence, tears coming down her cheeks.

Satisfied her mother was done, she half-sobbed, half-laughed, "that's wonderful, Mom. Praise the Lord!" They spoke a while longer when Ginny suddenly changed the direction and tone of the conversation.

"Beth," she began, "I'm so sorry for everything I've put you through."

"Oh no, Mom," Beth protested.

But Ginny protested back, "No, I let it all take control of me and I caused you to have to take care of me instead of the other way around."

"Mom…"

"Let me finish," Ginny said firmly, "I'm sorry for the burden I put on you. I just hope you found time to grieve for yourself."

"I did," Beth assured her, "maybe I'll come up next weekend. I understand about everything. I really do."

"It's up to you if you want to come up," Ginny answered, "you're always welcome and thanks for everything you've done."

Ginny decided to end the call so she could tell Patty the same story. Just before leaving for the evening worship service, Beth's phone range again. This time the display said, "Sis." Patty and Beth talked and laughed and cried and thanked God together long enough that Beth missed the service.

* * * * * * *

When Ginny had finished speaking with her daughters she looked over at the end table next to the chair where she was seated. This had been her husband's favorite chair. She looked at the mess on the table, reached over and starting picking the items up from the tabletop. Some things she put back but in a more orderly fashion. The other items she moved to the coffee table. On the newly ordered end table she stood up the last photograph taken of her and Dan together. Then she set her Bible in the middle in front of the lamp and the picture. She liked the appearance so well and it was so encouraging to her that she got up and sat on the far end of the couch and organized the other end table. But then she stopped and lay down for a nap. The day had been very good indeed but also draining.

After the evening service she and the Archers went to the East Side Ice Cream Stand and enjoyed their cones, seated at a picnic table. It was like a whole new feeling to enjoy herself again.

It is interesting, perhaps, to note that Rev. Lilly never preached again after that day. It was his final assignment. Within a month after that Sunday morning, his wife found he had passed away in his sleep. But surely great was *his* reward in that Promised Land.

* * * * * * *

Ginny's car was not in its parking spot when Beth arrived home late Saturday morning. The note on the door said, "Gone to the market—be home soon. Mom." Letting herself in, Beth was pleasantly surprised. She had dreaded coming to the cluttered trailer. But today the living room was tidy and orderly; the end tables and coffee table were clean and polished. The shades were pulled open and the room was bright. Many things still sat out but in carefully organized stacks well on their way to further organization.

In the left tub of the sink only a frying pan, plate, cup, fork, and knife lay dirty. The right tub was filled with clean dishes that had been carefully set to drip and dry. The countertops were clean and ordered.

On the kitchen table lay stacks of what appeared to be bills, each stack from the same creditor in descending months from May down to February or January. The top, and most recent, copy on each stack had, in Ginny's handwriting, a phone number and a small dollar figure followed each time by the words "per month." A newspaper lay open to the want ads with stars scribbled next to several entries. One was circled. It told of the Colsonburg Diner hiring two cooks. Written next to this ad were the words in her mom's handwriting, "Monday at 2:00, see Ray."

The right side of the hallway was stacked with boxes and piles of papers and clothes. But opening the door to her room, Beth realized why. It was perfect. The dressers were cleared on top and the bed was made with freshly-washed sheets and a comforter. Curious, Beth peered into her mom's room and found it still quite cluttered but the bed made neatly and the end table carefully organized, as if this room was still being worked on. Something was definitely happening around there.

"Hey," a happy voice called, "who broke into my house?" After a quick hug, Ginny asked, "Are you hungry yet?"

"Sure," was Beth's simple answer.

"Well, I went to the store to get some buns," Ginny began to explain, "I have two hamburgers left plus I sliced some potatoes for French fries.

So Beth fried the burgers in a skillet while Ginny tended the French fries and retrieved two plates and poured two glasses of iced tea. They sat on the steps to the porch in the early summer's warmth to eat their lunch. As they talked, Ginny told Beth about the two cook positions open at the Diner and how she had a time set to talk to the owner on Monday about maybe working in the kitchen there.

After lunch, they walked all about town—around the square and all the way out past Holts' and back through town all the way out to 3C. They stopped several times to talk briefly with those out tending their lawns, preparing their flower beds, or just sitting on their porches. Ginny told Beth about how different she felt and how each day that she made progress in getting her life organized again, she felt better still.

They talked about Patty and Billy and, of course, Dan and the people at 3C. Back at the trailer, Beth took a nap while Ginny tidied up from lunch and caught up on some reading. For supper they had salads with chopped ham and cheese and then watched some television, finishing off the evening with a batch of popcorn.

That very day Pete was graduating and there was to be a cookout at the Archers' after church the next day. Ginny had bought a card for him and wrote a lengthy note of appreciation and encouragement in it. She and Beth signed it and set it out to go with them to church tomorrow, along with a small cash gift—all that Ginny dare try to give at that point.

* * * * * * *

The next morning Pete's Sunday School class presented him with a card signed by all the class members, complete with a cash gift inside that they all contributed to. It was standard procedure for a class member who graduated. Jim Corbin recognized Pete's milestone during the worship service and everyone clapped to show their congratulations. Many handed him cards before and after church.

By one o'clock the gathering had begun at the Archers' home in LC. The whole family was there all over again. In addition, several neighbors, friends, and people from church filled the side lawn. John had borrowed tables and chairs from the fire company to supply the need. Everyone brought a card and most of those contained cash or gift cards.

Among the friends present were Ginny and Beth. It had been more than a decade since either one had been to that house. The weather-worn swing set still sat in the same spot it occupied all those years ago. For Beth it was like visiting somewhere almost for the first time. Ginny was actually happy and outgoing in the crowd of only partly-familiar people. There were hotdogs and hamburgers, chips, cake and a "speech" from Pete's dad. Several others joined in with encouraging words, congratulations, and advice. By four o'clock Ginny and Beth said good-bye so Beth could get back to Lewistown.

"Thanks so much for your card," Pete emphasized before they left, "you didn't have to do that."

"I wanted to, Pete," Ginny answered with a gentle pat on his arm.

"Thanks for the words especially but I don't think I deserve them."

"Oh yes you do—and more. You and all these folks mean a lot to us, Pete," she said gesturing toward the group of remaining guests.

Pete just smiled—an expression of satisfaction that his willingness to follow God's leading had made such a difference. Ginny gave him a gentle hug.

"Bye, and congratulations again," Beth said smiling as she and Ginny turned to head for the car.

Tomorrow things would change yet again. Ginny would interview for the cook's position at the Diner. Pete would start his post-college life and soon start the transition of the farm's ownership from his grandfather to himself. Life was definitely going to be different in the days ahead.

After everyone left and before the chairs and tables were returned, Pete just stood in the now abandoned yard. He thought of the days gone by: his high school graduation party, games with his brother, sister, and friends, campouts, and snow forts in the winter. Those chapters were long over. Tomorrow would start the new chapter in his life. The first steps in taking over the farm would begin. This would be an ongoing chapter as he planned to be a farmer his whole life. Would anything else change or would the rest of his life look more or less like tomorrow? He did not know the answer to these questions. He was excited and pleased but did not have a strong sense of hope for his life; he felt as if he would just spend the rest of his days farming and that was it. However that was what he had decided to expect and he chose to make the most of it.

Back at the trailer, Beth had much more confidence and peace about leaving her mother behind. The difference over the last two weeks was like night and day. Her old mom was coming back but somehow different. She was different because she was on her own now. But her strength, peace, and cheerfulness had been resurrected; she was finding her way again.

But what about herself? Was Beth finding *her* way? The door to the mission field appeared to be quickly and finally closing and she had no "plan B" right now. The only plan was to finish nursing school and get her RN. At one time she felt such purpose and drive when she had a specific goal. Now the future was shrouded in an impenetrable fog. She would need to take a day at a time and listen for God's leading from this point. At least the burden of responsibility and concern for her mother was lifting and she was becoming free to do whatever God would set before her.

Ginny was excited about the possibility of becoming a cook and putting one of her skills to work for pay and for the enjoyment of countless others. She prayed she could get this job. It would pay her bills, fill her time, and give her some fulfillment. She had spent her life getting up and helping others get ready for school or work but now she would be the one heading out the door every day. That is, if she got the job.

The Summer of Transitions

Beth's Short Summer

Ginny was able to get one of the cook positions at the Diner, working the breakfast shift. It was part time at first and while it did not provide health insurance, it did provide a wage, work to fill her time, flexibility to have time off when she wanted it, and the promise of a fulltime position in the future. There was a lot of pressure but she enjoyed preparing meals as she had done for her family for many years. The job provided enough money to buy groceries, gas, and start paying her now past due bills, but no extra at all.

Beth still did not know where her life was going next. There were no indications that the mission field would open up to her. God had closed that door and His decision increasingly appeared to be final. She would, however, be a nurse but she did not know where. She decided that she would return home to help her mother get reestablished while she waited to find her own calling. If she could get work of some sort she could help with the bills but she hesitated to take a fulltime nursing position since she did not plan to stay in the Colsonburg area long-term.

Beth was home once in June and once again in July, right after Independence Day. She graduated in mid-August. Turning down the offer of a fulltime position at the Lewistown Hospital, she returned home to help and wait on the Lord. She had not been there in her mother's darkest days, at least not in the way she would have wanted, and she needed to take the time now that she was in transition and could afford the time to do so.

Ginny had heard of a family, the Ericsons, in which both parents worked in two opposite directions from Colsonburg and desperately needed a babysitter for their three children, the youngest for all day and the two older ones when they came home from school. The cost of daycare was wiping them out financially and they needed to do something different. Beth met with the family first thing and was hired on the spot. She would be paid a flat amount per week, less when she was not needed each day. She would have weekends, holidays, and snow days free for her. The Ericsons understood that she would be moving on in a couple of months or so, but it gave them some time to explore their options.

Independence Day

Pete had become familiar with the Central Pennsylvania Fourth Fest in State College from living with his uncle. The year before he had convinced his family to go for the fireworks and they loved it so much that they planned for it again that year. In fact they decided to leave in the morning, park for the fireworks later on and spend the afternoon exploring the displays and stands. Grandpa watched over the farm while Pete was gone but the milking herd had been sold by that time so the workload Grandpa assumed was greatly reduced.

Joanie convinced Ginny to go with them. It did not take long to realize that Beth was right over "the mountain" in Lewistown so Ginny invited her to join them. Beth could not come over right away but was able to join them by late afternoon. Then they all took a stroll through the heart of the university campus near downtown, Pete guiding the tour. Then they walked up into the area where the cars were continuing to park, reaching the top of a small hill Pete gave them a tour of the views. He pointed out the barns and pastures associated with the campus, the hospital, beautiful Mount Nittany to the east and the Nittany Valley extending north and east before abruptly "dead ending" between Salona and Mill Hall. He reminded them about earlier passing through the narrow gap that was the only access from Nittany Valley to the valley that was home to the West Branch of the Susquehanna River, Lock Haven and Williamsport. Later that night they would pass back through there again on the long drive home.

After seeing these many sights and needing some rest, they returned to the parking spot in one of the university's fields. There they grilled burgers and hotdogs on a portable gas grill. They ate on blankets spread out on the grass, next to the vehicles, as the sun began to set. The weather that night was chilly as was that whole summer—the coldest summer anyone could remember.

At the designated time Pete tuned the portable radio to the required station. As darkness took hold, the music started with every single firework firing off in time with the music. But the first song played was the National Anthem. Pete was surprised at the number of people who did not stand or place their hand on their heart as the precious tune played but he did what he knew was right and proper as did the rest of the Archers and the Mortons. The bursts and booms were virtually nonstop for well over half an hour. It was so constant it was almost like an ongoing grand finale. But *this* display's grand finale was far and away grander than any other these families had ever seen before. Ginny and Beth were speechless at the sight.

It took hours for the traffic to clear so they all talked, snacked, played games and listened to a local Christian radio station. It was three in the morning when they arrived back in LC. Beth followed them back and then followed Ginny home to Colsonburg. In church on Sunday Beth made sure to tell Pete how much she and her mom appreciated being included and how much she herself enjoyed the day. It was the nicest distraction she and Ginny had had all year.

Pete only said, "I'm glad you got to come and spend the day with your mom."

The Farm

Almost as soon as graduation was over Pete and Grandpa began the complicated process of transitioning the farm to Pete according to Grandpa's proposition. First Grandpa applied for his Social Security. Then entered the surveyors and the attorneys to measure the ground and draw the lines separating the farmhouse from the rest of the farm. Jack and John rewrote their wills to accommodate the plan. Documents were drafted, signed, notarized, and filed. The herd was sold—all but the weaned calves and cows approaching butchering age. The milking equipment was sold next along with any equipment Pete deemed unnecessary. Even the excess hay was sold. The proceeds paid for the fees incurred by Pete's grandfather and father, any taxes and other expenses associated with the transition. Pete was not allowed to enrich himself by this endeavor; he would have the farm itself that was all. The extra money was turned over to Grandpa. The farm became Pete's free and clear but it was also almost incapable of making any money—yet.

Pete knew that several cattle would soon be sold as beef, but would it be enough to cover the land taxes that would be due in the fall, not to mention insurance, investment in new calves, the multitude of other taxes and expenses, plus a meager living for him? There was the old rental house he was going to renovate and rent but it would not be ready for months or a year and it would take money for the materials to do the work. It kept Pete up night after night, worrying about it. He often doubted what he had done. He wondered if he had taken on too much. He feared it would all end in disaster and humiliation for him, not including the heartache and perhaps even anger of his grandfather, should he fail.

One day in mid-July he could take it no more and did what he should have done from the moment he graduated. Pete was working near the top of the slope, building a new fence line across the width of the farm. Grandpa had a doctor's appointment that day so Pete was all alone. His mind was filled with concern. He looked down the slope at the barn and the farmhouse and the land between. LC lay nestled in the small valley below the farm. He sat down on a stump and said, "Oh God, please help me. I want to be successful—for me and for Grandpa. Please don't let me fail now."

It occurred to him how self-centered much of this short prayer really was. Then he begged, "Please forgive me, Lord, for my selfishness." He sat for a spell just thinking and reflecting. God needed to be central to it all he concluded, as Pastor Jackson had shown him after his breakup with Mandi, but how? He looked and thought about this. Then it just began to come to him almost automatically.

He got down on his knees, the stump between himself and the farm. He folded his hands as he had been taught as a child. He was overwhelmed and humbled by a sense of gratitude. Pete had received all of this, not as a gift but as a trust. However it was *his.* Not everyone could say that. In fact, it was almost inconceivable that he, at age twenty, was allowed to be the sole owner of this farm. He knew of no acquaintance who could say that. Even well-to-do Geoff was still in college and would graduate with nothing but a degree and a car. But for some reason this was allowed to happen and God had led him to accept the challenge of owning and running it. There had to be a purpose in it all and it had to be about more than just him or even him and Grandpa.

"I don't ask to be rich, God," he prayed, "I ask only not to fail."

He thought a little more and said, "And God, no matter how You choose to answer my simple prayer, I promise, as long as I have this farm that," and it just began to happen, unrehearsed, unscripted, completely spontaneous, "it belongs to You and I will be no more than a trustee of it....I will seek to glorify and exalt You with my life and with this farm....I will declare Your Gospel in any way I can to anyone I can as You give opportunity....I will, to the best of my understanding, farm according to Your ways based upon Your Word and Your design in creation, and not only according to the ways of man.... Of every dollar I earn, ten cents will go to You through Your church, 3C. It will be, and already is, Your tithe. For every dollar I return to You in this way, ten cents more will be given to missions in my faith promise....I will help the poor and needy with Your blessings to me....I will incur no debt I cannot repay in three months' time....My life will be simple, plain, and humble so I can serve You better. And I will maintain my purity, never letting the old garbage back in. And if You never give me a wife and I live single all my days, I will stay pure. This pledge I make without condition, God, because You are worthy of it all. I am Yours for as long as I live and this farm, too, as long as I have it. In Jesus' Name, Amen." It actually took at least five minutes for him to say all of it.

Much of what he said he was already doing but he had never actually *promised* to do it in just so many words so some he was now deciding to do for the first time or in a new or deeper way. He was being intentional about how he would live as a Christian. It helped that much of it was already being modeled or had been demonstrated to him in his life experience and training up to that point. But now he was doing it all in his own right.

Pete realized this was actually a great moment in his life but that he could never remember all he had promised God. Pastor Dan was always so big on "remembering" things so he made note to himself in his cell phone and wrote down one to three key words for each point before returning to work. That night at home he made a new document on the computer: "Peter's Pledge," he called it, using his more formal name. He numbered each point in his pledge, chose a handsome font for it, and a pitch large enough to make it fill a page. He printed it then signed and dated it. Later it would be framed and hung in his office but it would need an amendment before that time; for now it was tucked safely away in the desk in his bedroom, but where he would encounter it frequently and be reminded. Pete never disturbed that stump. Though it slowly rotted away and eventually disappeared, he visited the spot frequently enough that all his life he never forgot where he made those promises to God.

Pete worked hard. He started early and worked until dark but always ate supper with his family, took Sundays off—that day doing only the most essential daily chores. And he never missed any worship service, fire call, or fire company meeting if he could help it. He helped with 4-H, as a leader now. He lived with his parents and drove back and forth to the farm. When it rained he did paperwork or worked in the old rental house, stripping the interior down to the bare studs. If he had free time he tried to find ways to relax and enjoy himself with it.

Waiting

After Beth's graduation from nursing school in August, Ginny hosted a reception in the Church's picnic pavilion. The Archers were careful to attend, as the Mortons had attended Pete's reception, including a card from the family complete with a cash gift and the signature of each one of them.

Beth was anxious to put her new training to work. She became the unofficial church nurse and occasional advisor to an ill or injured church member or neighbor.

One time Pete developed an infection in one of his fingers from a splinter. He thought he had removed it all but the infection grew worse anyway. Beth noticed it in Sunday School and she asked him about it after worship. He dismissed it saying the splinter was out and it only needed time. Beth disagreed and would not leave him alone until he peeled back the bandage he had on it.

"Oh, Pete," she exclaimed, "that's not right!"

She retrieved her first aid kit from her car and, sitting at a table in the fellowship hall, dug until she found the source: a small part of the splinter deep in his finger. Poor Pete winced and writhed as she mined for the remnants of the splinter. She cleansed it, applied antibiotic ointment, and a fresh bandage. She instructed him on how to change the bandage, cleanse, and disinfect the wound regularly until it healed completely. And heal it did.

Another time she helped a lady who had fainted during Sunday School. When the ambulance and paramedic arrived, Beth had already completed a full evaluation, speeding the woman's trip to the Emergency Room which was over half an hour away, adding urgency to every minute and second.

Beth decided she would continue babysitting until her mother was either financially stable again or had fulltime work with health insurance. Then she would seek a nursing job, be it near or far. She tried to imagine the positions that might await her where she could be a nurse and minister to others spiritually too. It was an odd time, a kind of self-imposed exile. She found comfort in knowing it would only be temporary.

Beth became even closer to her mother in those days. Patty was thousands of miles away. No one knew where Billy was, and her Dad was gone. It was just the two of them for now and for the foreseeable future.

Ginny was strong again but Beth could not stand to leave her alone— not yet anyway. She might never have a time like this again in her life; she would make the most of it.

With September summer began to melt away and fall slowly filled its shoes. But not much else changed, at least not immediately or suddenly.

The Busy Months of Fall

September through December were the busiest months of the year in 3C's calendar. Events included the Sunday School Picnic, preparation of the Christmas cantata, the Fall Fest, Missions Conference and Thanksgiving.

Sunday School Picnic

The first Sunday after Beth's graduation, Jim Corbin reminded the class that this was their year to host the Sunday School Picnic. Each adult class took a turn at hosting this event; each one added its own special touches so no two picnics were identical. They discussed what they wanted to do and who would coordinate each activity. They were careful in their plans to include something that the older generation would also appreciate, in this case a hymn-sing.

Brad, Deanne, and Punjab would handle the set up, including washing all the picnic tables. With Deanne cracking the whip on them all, they certainly would not fail to be ready. Erin was to manage the serving table. Pete would do the grilling. Andrew was to get all the buns, hot dogs, and drinks (water and sodas). The church paid for them. Pete donated the hamburgers from the stash of frozen homegrown meat he kept in the freezer at the rental. Christine and Adam took charge of the games. Beth was attending regularly, at least for now, so she offered to lead the hymn-sing at the end.

The Picnic was the first Saturday after Labor Day and held in the church's pavilion. The setup crew had everything ready by Friday night. People started showing up by eleven AM. Some of the older people brought lawn or parade chairs to sit in while they talked about the weather, politics, and so on. A few of the games started by eleven-thirty but stopped for the meal, shortly after noon.

Pete manned the large gas grill, in a cloud of aromatic smoke, getting the hamburgers and hot dogs "just right." Deanne changed everyone else's plans when she insisted that the meat had to be placed in the buns before being put on the serving table. It had something to do with "the presentation."

"Some help!" Pete cried out as he could not manage the extra step alone. Beth stepped up to assist, holding each bun open as Pete placed the meat in it. Beth passed the sandwiches to Deanne who arranged them on the trays "just so." Erin was not at all happy with Deanne. The extra step made the meal later than expected and the meat quickly grew cold sitting in the open buns rather than being stacked in serving dishes, but it looked nice.

"Thanks for the mutual aid," Pete told Beth just before the meal began, "I owe you."

"I'll remember that," she teased, and she soon would call in that debt.

Harold Van Horn gave thanks before the meal and everyone lined up at the buffet-style serving table covered in homemade side dishes and desserts. Later when someone commented on the meat being cold Pete mumbled to Beth as she passed by, "If Deanne had stuck to *her* job and just let us put the meat in serving dishes it would have stayed warmer."

Beth leaned over to him and discreetly replied, "I could see that coming but there's at least one in every group."

Pete made a very big deal about how good the carrot cake was; carrot cake was one of his favorites. Ginny spoke up and said that Beth had made it.

"My compliments to the chef," Pete said looking down the table, holding up a fork full of his favorite dessert.

"Thanks. But it's Mom's recipe," she humbly responded.

After the meal and the games, Beth led the songs. Adam played a guitar and Erin played an electronic keyboard. The singing was handled "hymn-sing" style; people called out numbers from the books when Beth asked for another selection. There was a mix of newer songs and choruses and the older, traditional hymns.

Everyone in the class worked together on cleaning up afterward.

Cantata Rehearsal

On the next day it was announced that the time had arrived to sign up for the annual Christmas cantata. In the cantata the choir sang a series of songs with short narrations or readings between; it typically lasted close to an hour. It took weeks and weeks of rehearsals to be properly prepared since the songs were written for soprano, alto, tenor, and bass parts so each group had to learn the song, their part, and how to sing in harmony with the other ones.

There was a sign up sheet in the vestibule, divided into the four parts. Pete had sung in the cantata during high school but not during college since being away kept him from too many rehearsals so he was ready to sign up again. He put his name under the bass heading. Looking over the list he saw several familiar names and a few new ones but two newcomers stood out to him: Beth on the alto list and Ginny on the soprano list. He thought they would enjoy the rehearsals, the fun and the camaraderie among the singers.

The Sunday afternoon rehearsals were always a good time, though they cut everyone's Sunday afternoon short. There was laughing, joking, teasing and some singing too! The director, Jack Pringle, joined right in the fun but still made sure they actually sang enough to be ready for that last Sunday evening before Christmas. The accompaniment music was moving, stirring the soul, though much of it was also light and happy. It was recorded on CDs by an orchestra and the sound assistant would play it on the sanctuary sound system, pumping it throughout the room as the choir sang to it.

The altos stood in front of the basses and it was common for them to tease and joke back and forth with one another, as the tenors and sopranos also did. The basses got somewhat rambunctious one afternoon, though all in good fun.

Smiling, Beth spoke up for the altos saying to the basses, "Hey, don't make me come back there!"

The basses led by Pete, all acted shocked and afraid as he teased back, "Ooh, we're *soooo* scared!"

To this Beth replied, "You should be. I aint red for nothin', you know!" referring to her red hair. "Don't make me take you down again, Peter Archer," she warned actually recollecting the day she took him on during duck-duck-goose, all those many years ago.

This routine continued for most Sunday evenings starting at five-thirty right up until the night of the cantata. Everyone hated to see it end.

The Fall Fest

After returning to Colsonburg, Beth was asked to help with the Wednesday night Kids Clubs as the games coordinator. In this role she was one of the main planners of the annual Fall Fest. The Fest was a special time of fun and games for the kids but also used as an outreach to the community as all the local children and teens were invited to join in.

Though it took place on the Wednesday evening closest to October thirty-first, they were careful *not* to call it a Halloween Party and did not encourage the children to wear costumes. This was because the church did not believe in observing Halloween (it was known to them as 'the Devil's holiday'). They did not want anyone to think that was what they were doing, celebrating a holiday that actually belonged to the Devil.

There were hotdogs, games, a short Bible message, a hayride, a bonfire complete with toasted marshmallows, and, of course, candy. The others on the planning committee suggested asking Pete to do the hayride. Beth said she would ask him about it in Sunday School the next weekend. As Pete was getting a coffee in the kitchen before class that Sunday, Beth asked him about it while she made a hot chocolate.

"Remember how you 'owe me'?" she asked.

"Yes..."

"Would you consider doing the hayride for Fall Fest?"

"Sure," was his immediate and enthusiastic response. "I've been on a lot of hayrides but this would be the first one I actually conducted. It sounds like fun. Call it a done deal!"

The morning of the Fest, Pete drove the tractor and hay wagon all the way to Colsonburg. Grandpa followed him in the pickup with the flashers on to warn drivers that came upon them. He also took Pete home for lunch. Following soup and sandwiches with Grandpa and Grandma, Pete drove back to the church to make sure the wagon was prepared for the children in advance. He arranged the bales of hay around the perimeter of the wagon, two bales deep against the sides then he put a second row one bale deep inside the first one. This made two big steps to sit on, like bleachers all the way around the wagon.

Pete had just finished doing this when Beth came to the church's playground with Haley, the youngest of the Ericson children. This trip was a daily routine for the two of them, interrupted only by rainy days. Pete waved to the pair. Bringing Haley over with her, Beth asked if they could help in any way.

"Sure. I have one more thing to do here," he answered.

He jumped down and gave Haley a boost up to the wagon. Climbing back up, he offered Beth a hand to help pull her up. Pete cut the twine on the remaining bales and showed Beth and Haley how to separate the flat sections within them and lay them out as a kind of carpet on the floor of the wagon.

Haley whispered something to Beth who motioned her to be quiet. Beth snuck up behind Pete with an armful of hay and dumped it on his head and then quickly ran as far as she could, which was only a matter of a few feet. Haley squealed with delight.

"Why, you..." Pete grabbed two handfuls of hay and tossed them straight at Beth.

An all-out hay fight ensued with even Haley joining in. Finally Beth called a truce so she could get Haley cleaned up before the older children came home from school.

"You better watch your back tonight, lady!" Pete warned, lightheartedly.

But nothing happened to Beth that evening. The kids piled in the wagon and they were off. Crossing Main Street, Pete took them down Columbia Street to Creekside Drive and crossed the bridge on Susquehanna Street over to the East Side. Now out of the borough, he took them about a mile or so on one of the township roads and came back around on a different road still returning to the Susquehanna Street bridge. Beth led the kids in songs and games as they traveled along in the dark. The bonfire was waiting for them when they returned to the church.

"What does everyone need to say to Mr. Archer?" Beth prompted the kids.

Pete thought to himself, *Mr. Archer? I didn't know Dad was here.*

"Thank you, Mr. Archer," the children cheered in unison.

As everyone gathered around the fire, Beth approached Pete, seated on the tractor. "Thanks, Pete," she said to him.

"Anytime."

The Barn Fire

The next Wednesday right after lunch Pete's pager rang. Numerous other tones were heard following his station's alert. The number of tones suggested a large fire. The fire whistle began wailing down in the village. Pete started running for his pickup truck. The call was for a barn fire on the East Side near where the hayride had been. Several fire companies were being paged together to go and help the Colsonburg Ladder and Hose Company. Lainge Township was to send a tanker and an engine.

As Pete arrived at the fire station, Percy was already leaving with the tanker. Randy was in the driver's seat of Engine 5-1. It looked like another low manpower day; Chief Harrington was on vacation. The second page went out so Pete finally took the officer's seat next to Randy. He was about to request permission from the commander at the fire scene to respond below minimum manpower. But Curly showed up and took a seat in the back; that made a minimum crew.

Randy, the senior member of the officerless crew, said, "Let's go."

"County, Engine 5-1 responding with three," Pete called on the radio and they joined the race to Colsonburg, siren wailing and horn blasting.

The radio was alive with reports from officers at the scene and orders to the many pieces of apparatus pouring into the borough. It was a working barn fire with other structures endangered. Engines 16-2 and Aerial 16 were to lead the attack on the fire. There was not enough manpower for Engine 16-1 to even respond but the aerial was actually a quint and therefore capable of acting as both an aerial and an engine. Both units were to lay five-inch diameter hoses behind them as they went down the driveway. Engines 11 and 4-1 would relay water down the five-inch lines from tankers meeting them on the roadway. Tankers were coming from companies sixteen, five, two, eight, seventeen, nineteen, fourteen, four, and eleven; one each was coming from three other counties as well. Most came with only a driver. If one or two others were on board they were left at the fire scene to assist the meager daytime crews. Several engines were transferred in to standby in some of the emptied stations in event of a second fire. Engine 5-1 was assigned to fill tankers at the square in Colsonburg. The hydrant there had an exceptionally good flow and the square provided a way to turn the tankers back around without having to take time to back them up first. The creek was low anyway so it would be easier to use the hydrant. From the top of the Narrows the column of smoke and even a few flames were very evident on the other side of the valley.

Beth and Haley were at the church playground. They had watched the fire trucks leave the station and were now watching the others racing in from the south. One truck said on the side across three lines: "Lainge Twp. Vol. Fire. Co. Engine 5-1." The siren was wailing and the diesel engine was growling loudly. That truck was soon followed by tankers 17 (from Trasston, it was yellow) and then 19 (from Lainge's Gap, it was blue) and then 2 (from Singleton Flats it was white).

When they arrived at the square, two tankers were already waiting to be filled. Randy staged in front of the Presbyterian Church. As he started the pump Pete, Curly, and the tanker drivers set up the hoses: a five-inch diameter hose from the hydrant to the pump then another five inch line to the manifold that would split the five inch line into two three-inch lines. Curly took charge of the valves on the manifold and Pete connected the three inch hoses to the tankers to put fresh water into each one in turn. It was hectic and nonstop hard work for many hours. A constant supply of water was crucial to saving the other structures and the house, even though the main barn itself was a lost cause and began crumbling under its own weight as the fire continued to engulf it. Comparatively little effort was put into it at that point.

After leaving their payloads at the fire scene the tankers raced back to the square, coming in alongside Engine 5-1. When they were filled full again they went all the way around the square and took off back out Susquehanna Street to return to the fire. Sometimes the tankers waited in line several deep waiting to be filled. Pete and Curly added extra hoses to try to accommodate the need. Sirens filled the air all afternoon. Susquehanna Street was closed by Fire Police, who also stopped traffic on Main Street every time a refilled tanker came around the square. Each tanker was filled multiple times that afternoon.

A crowd gathered and watched. Among them were Beth and Haley, who were walking back to the Ericson's home, north of downtown. The two of them sat on the steps of the Episcopal Church. Beth recognized Pete as he used hand signals to direct the tankers and tell Curly when to turn the hoses on and off. Pete connected the hoses to the inlets on the backs of the tankers and opened and closed the valves on the trucks accordingly. Beth and Haley watched for about half an hour. The Colsonburg Fire Auxiliary members brought coffee and sandwiches to all the firefighters with bread, meat, and cheese donated by several store owners in the borough.

Eventually the parade of tankers slowed and one by one they were sent home. The column of smoke had slowly diminished and Pete and Curly put the extra hoses back on the truck. It was almost eight o'clock when they reloaded the remaining hoses and headed home again. So Pete missed church that Wednesday night. Thursday was a very hard day as all the work missed on Wednesday had to be caught up again. The rest of the week was busier and harder as a result—just so they didn't have another large fire.

On Sunday Beth asked several questions about what she had observed on Wednesday. Pete then gave her quite an education in the basics of initial fire attack and rural water supply. But it helped her understand and was somewhat interesting if not very "foreign" to her.

Milkshakes
(my kids' favorite chapter)

During Sunday School the first week of November, Ted suggested everyone from the Young Adults Class get together at the Diner for ice cream when the evening service was over. At about eight-thirty the group of young adults, plus a few others each from the Senior High Class and the Couples Class, gathered in the north end of the Diner. There were enough there that they put several tables together to accommodate the group; the rest sat in the nearby booths. Some ordered fries or just a drink, but most ordered milkshakes.

It was one of those times when after a few jokes and talk of current events far and near, one person said something like, "Remember that time when…" Then, back and forth, across the table stories of growing up were compared. For those who grew up in the Colsonburg area, like Pete, the talk surrounded 3C or attending the Colsonburg Area School District (there were plenty of stories about teachers they had). There were also discussion questions like, "Whatever happened to Susie?" or, "Didn't Thad move to Towanda?" or, "Didn't Craig join the Navy?" People like Beth who had not lived their whole life in Colsonsburg pitched in stories of their own. The talk was constant, hearty, and boisterous. Beth talked and laughed a lot with Erin who was next to her.

But gradually, one by one or two by two, the group dwindled. Eventually it was just Pete, Beth, and Punjab left. Then even Punjab succumbed to the need for sleep because of his class schedule. He had to get up early for a morning class at Mansfield University. Pete and Beth should have likewise left by then, too, but it did not happen that way. They each meant to finish the story he or she was telling but each story led to another and on it went.

The subjects got deeper and more personal. Beth talked about her Dad, about Rhonda and the fire that destroyed her friend's home. She even talked about what Rob had done to her and the uncertainty she felt about her future. Pete also remembered Pastor Dan and that day at camp when he trusted Christ as his Savior. He told about Geoff, and even Mandi and Lauren and the talk he and Lauren had "right over there," pointing to the booth where they sat that day. And he talked a lot about the farm. The milkshakes were long gone by then. Neither one intended to go on like that—it just worked out that way.

Pete noticed that the Diner was getting darker as the lights on the outside were off now as well as the ones on the south end. So he finally glanced at his cell phone: almost midnight! The Diner had closed at eleven!

"Wow! Look at the time," he exclaimed with shock.

When he tried to pay his bill he was told that the register had already been closed out for the night. Ray, the owner, told him they could pay their bills tomorrow; he said he trusted them.

Pete's truck was the last vehicle in the parking lot. As he and Beth left, Ray locked the door behind them. It was getting frosty out so Pete offered to drive Beth home. He would pass near her place anyway.

As he pulled up in front of the trailer, Beth said to him, "That was fun; I'm glad I went along."

"Yeah, me too," Pete reciprocated, "but I never shut the place down before," he said with a laugh. He continued, "I guess I'll see you Wednesday night."

"Yep," she agreed, "I guess I will see you again then. Good night."

"You mean 'Good morning'," he corrected her; "it's twelve-fifteen."

"Good morning, then," she happily made the correction, "Thanks for the ride."

"Anytime," was Pete's simple and predictable reply.

He watched to make sure Beth had no problem getting inside. After she disappeared inside the trailer, he drove away. When Beth stopped at the Diner the next day to pay her bill she was told that the young man had been in earlier and had already paid both their bills.

* * * * * * *

Missions Conference at 3C generally took place the week before Thanksgiving, starting on a Wednesday evening and ending on Sunday evening. A missionary or missionary couple that was home for a year between terms would come tell about what was happening in their field. They would tell especially about the conversions taking place but also about challenges faced in that country and other progress in the work. There were always lots of pictures and stories in addition to sermons and challenges to become involved in the missionary work of the denomination. There was always an invitation for people who thought God was calling them to become a missionary, to respond to that call. But most people, admittedly, are not called to go. They are called to stay and support those who do go by prayer, financial support, and mere awareness.

There was a meal before each service and a dessert social at the close of the conference, all prepared by the Socials Committee. Wednesday night was "Kids' Night" and on Sunday morning everyone pledged financial support for the fund that paid the missionaries and met their ministry expenses. It was an exciting time. The stories were always riveting and educational. Everyone was encouraged in the command to "...make disciples of all nations...." (Matthew 28:19)

This year's speaker was a single woman serving in one of the African nations. She was the kind of woman that, as a child and a teen, Beth always admired and wanted to imitate, like "Aunt" Tillie. Many wondered if Beth would finally enter the mission field as a result, perhaps, of this conference, given her interest in missionary work.

But Beth did not respond that way. She had already heard God's oft-repeated "no" to her. It was a bittersweet conference because she watched and listened to this woman realizing that she would *not* become like her. She was forced to reconcile herself to the fact that this might be as close as she would ever get to the actual mission field.

On Sunday evening Beth returned to the sanctuary after the dessert social. Everyone had either gone home or was helping to clean up the Fellowship Hall. She was praying and trying to let God speak to her spirit. Her Bible was open to Acts 13, specifically verse two: "...now separate to Me Barnabas and Saul for the work to which I have called them..." She had always wanted God to make her the Saul or Barnabas figure in that account but tonight she was led to consider, *What about all the others, the majority, mentioned in verse one, specifically Simeon, Lucius, and Manaen? They must have stayed while Barnabas and Saul left. God must have had a calling for them right there in Antioch of Syria. Maybe they are my role models, not Barnabas and Saul.* She had come to feel clear in her conscience about *not* going because she had at least offered herself sincerely and eagerly to that work, something many Christians never consider doing.

Her hymnal was also open and she was crying--tears of loss over a dream to never come true. The tears were also for the mixture of fear and excitement for what God would certainly do with and in her life instead. But her tears were silent; she did not want any attention.

From behind her a familiar sounding male voice asked, "Are you all right?"

She jumped just a little from the sense of surprise she felt. She quickly and discreetly wiped her eyes so he could not tell she had been crying. Beth turned ninety degrees to her left. Taking a seat on the pew behind her, and watching her as he did so, was Pete.

"Yeah," she said through blurry eyes, "just thinking about some things."

"Okay," Pete replied, acting as if he might get back up again and leave.

Beth made that unlikely when she told him, "I was looking at this hymn. I must have sung it a thousand times but never really heard these words here in the third stanza."

The hymnal was open to "If Jesus Goes with Me". Pete reached over the back of the pew and retrieved the open book; he read that third stanza silently.

> *But if it be my portion to bear my cross at home,*
> *While others bear their burdens beyond the billows foam,*
> *I'll prove my faith in Him—confess His judgments fair,*
> *And if He stays with me, I'll stay anywhere.*[5]

That stanza was a far cry different from the first two which seemed to celebrate *going away* to some distant land.

"Wow," Pete started, "that hymn spoke to me once, too. You know, I once considered becoming a pastor, soon after I was saved? It was just a fleeting idea."

"Really," Beth sounded shocked.

"Yeah, I wanted to be just like your Dad. But this song helped me see it wasn't to be so and that it was okay to sorta stay behind."

Beth smiled a strange smile that looked like approval, sadness, and surprise all rolled up in one.

Pete finished, "But God never gave the call so here I am in Laingeville Center finding my way as a farmer because I love it and for some reason *that* is what God wants me to be."

"I never knew that about you," Beth admitted.

"Remember," Pete instructed her, taking the focus back off him, "one of the greatest men in the modern missionary movement was never a missionary, though he once dreamed of it."

"Yeah?" she said curiously.

"Yeah. A.B. Simpson," Pete answered.

"Really?" she said surprised, "Who told you that?"

"It was part of the membership class Pastor Jackson taught a year or two before he moved to Vermont."

"And here I am the pastor's daughter. I should know that," she said almost ashamed. "But it certainly might change the picture a little to look at it that way."

"You know, it also says at the end of the fourth stanza of this hymn,

> *But if to go or stay, or whether here or there,*
> *I'll be with my Savior, content anywhere!*[6]

Beth responded, "I guess that's what really counts, huh?"

"Yup," was Pete's simple acknowledgement.

Then Pete changed the course of things a little, "You know they're going to be closing down *this place* pretty soon. Do you want to finish this over a couple more milkshakes?"

"Sure," she smiled back at the idea, "but we better get them 'to go' and *I'm* paying this time."

"Ooh," Pete feigned a severe tone, "I don't know about letting a woman pay my way."

"Oh, come on," Beth scolded him, "it's not like it's a date or something."

"True," Pete had to agree. It was just two friends enjoying one more snack together.

* * * * * * *

The owner of the Diner and the waitress at the counter looked worried when Pete and Beth came in at about nine o'clock. But their fears quickly melted away when they heard that the shakes were "to go."

Beth paid and they went back out to Pete's truck. He drove her over to the trailer but left the engine running as he did not plan to stay for long and it was cold so the heater felt nice.

"Thanks for being such a great friend," she said to him

"Right back at ya," he replied, taking another sip of his mocha shake.

"You know it's funny," she contemplated, looking out the windshield, "we've known each other since we were three, at least off and on, and only now that we're twenty can we say we're friends. How did we grow up so fast?" She wondered, shaking her head slightly and getting another sip of her teaberry shake. Changing subjects she added, "You know, I don't know what we would have done if it weren't for coming here. This church actually reached out to us and just loved us so much. It was the perfect place for a couple of heartbroken women to find a new start."

"It's been great to have you guys here for a while," Pete replied. "And we have problems here, too. We're far from perfect at 3C."

"I suppose every place has issues," Beth conceded. She continued in yet another direction, "I just wish I knew what was next—what God really wants me to do with my life."

"You'll get it figured out," he assured her.

"I sure hope so," she said softly, looking down into her lap.

Pete thought to mention to her, "Did you hear that Dr. Ramsey is planning a big expansion of the Colsonburg Medical Center? Maybe he could use you there for a while. At least you could do some nurse stuff while you figure everything out and help your mom."

"I hadn't heard that," she answered. "Maybe I'll look into it sometime." After a pause she continued, "But sometimes I still just wonder 'why?'"

You know…why Billy left, why Daryl and Patty had to move so far away, why Blueberry Haven was so hostile, why I couldn't go to the mission field yet, why Rob did what he did, why…" her voice cracked and her shoulders shook a little, "why Dad had to die and everything had to get so messed up. I really thought I knew where life was going." She had to stop as the emotions were too much now.

Pete did not quite know what to do at that point. Sometimes there is nothing to say and it is even better to stay quiet. In that moment he remembered that day at camp over four years ago—he and Pastor Dan sitting on those rocks down by the river, the day that changed everything for Pete. He was not even the same person anymore.

Regaining her composure she looked at Pete and, sniffling once, said, "But at least some things have gone right. Thanks for everything you and Fred did for us."

"Oh…I almost felt like just a spectator, not one of the players," Pete replied. "God just took over and made things fall in place."

Beth responded saying, "It's no surprise His Word says, '…all things work together for good for those who love God…'" (Romans 8:28)

"So true," Pete had to agree. Then he changed the course of the conversation yet again asking, "So, what are you guys going to do for Thanksgiving?" He was really thinking of inviting them out to LC if they did not have plans. He was sure his mom would approve, even appreciate, the idea.

"We're leaving Wednesday to see my Grandma Morton in Cumberland, Maryland. We'll be back late Sunday night."

"Oh," Pete was slightly disappointed, "Are you guys close?"

"Not real close," Beth had to admit, "Dad's family isn't a close one but it's all we have now. Mom is an only child and her parents are both gone, too and with Billy, Patty, and Daryl scattered to the winds…"

"Sheesh," Pete interrupted, "you guys really are kind of out there alone, aren't you?"

"Yeah," she agreed. "Be thankful you have a close family—close in both senses of the word and that you have a real 'home.'"

"I am….I am."

"Well, I better go," she decided, "it's getting late again and the neighbors might start talking."

"Oh let them talk," Pete sneered. "They're gonna talk about something anyway. So I guess I won't see you again until a week from Wednesday."

"The Lord willing," she chirped, a new tone taking over.

"Well, have a safe trip and try to enjoy yourself as much as you can."

"I will," she assured him. "And...you were right about A.B. Simpson!"

Beth got out of the truck and headed for the door. Again Pete waited until she was safely inside before he drove away.

* * * * * * * *

John, Pat, and Amy were already in bed when Pete arrived home. Joanie was in her bathrobe shutting off any extra lights before retiring herself. "Another late night," she observed as Pete came in to the kitchen.

"Sorry. I just lost track of time again," he explained.

"I saw you were talking with Beth," she remembered. "Is everything okay with them?"

"Yeah, it's just a tough time. You know, it's the first Thanksgiving since the funeral and all. She just needed someone to talk to" he explained.

"I'm sure it's harder than any of us can imagine," Joanie replied, "at least my parents had lived a long life before we had to start spending holidays without them. And it's your time," she abruptly changed subjects. "You know when you have to get up tomorrow so as long as you don't wake us all up, I guess it doesn't matter to me when you get back, within reason, of course." She was resisting the urge to "mother" her now adult son. "Good night."

"Good night," he wished back as she headed for the hall and the stairs.

* * * * * * *

On Monday, Beth had the afternoon off so she took the long way home, walking as usual. It was cool but not too bad for late November. Coming to the Square, she sat down on the steps of the Presbyterian Church looking out across the square (the gazebo was decorated with pumpkins, hay bales, and corn stalks) trying to consider what God wanted her to do next. The Ericson children would someday grow up—they wouldn't always need her —and she had a brand new RN that she needed to put to work soon, but where? There were so many possibilities: one of the rural hospitals in the region or a large hospital center. She could move to a city like Scranton or Harrisburg, work in a doctor's office, or be a visiting nurse. The possibilities seemed endless. If only God would give a sign of some sort. She was excited but also terrified by the prospect of truly striking out on her own, all alone.

She also thought about Pete—how hard it was going to be to say good bye to him when it finally came time to move on from Colsonburg. He had been such a good friend; she would certainly miss him.

Getting up from the steps she started out Susquehanna Street, planning to follow Creekside Drive to the trailer. The medical center was on

Susquehanna Street directly behind the Church. In fact the two shared a parking lot. Walking past it she noticed a change; it had to be relatively new. The sign had been replaced and the new one said at the top, "Colsonburg Medical Group." Dr. Ramsey's name was near the bottom of the sign with two spaces under it where additional names could be added. The tanning salon that occupied the other half of the building had moved out and their sign was completely removed. Pete must have been right. She memorized the website on the sign figuring that any openings would likely be posted there. She would look up the website sometime to see what was really going on with the expansion, if anything. She was only curious and anything she found there would only be temporary.

The Change in Seasons

Thanksgiving was usually seen as the change in seasons, the unofficial transition from fall to winter. Preparations were made ahead of time and everything was in place for the new season of cold, snow, and ice, though sometimes all of those arrived even before the holiday did.

In the Archer home and at 3C there was indeed a great sense of gratitude for God's blessing and provision, for the nation and its Christian heritage, and for every "good and perfect gift…from above." (James 1:17)

All the supplies for the Thanksgiving Day dinner were gathered and in place by Wednesday. As always, everyone would gather at Grandpa and Grandma's for the feast.

But first things first: On Wednesday night 3C, Light and Life Church, and Grace Celebration Center would join together for a Thanksgiving Eve worship service. A key part of this service was the offering. Every family was encouraged to bring canned and boxed food items plus financial gifts for a "Harvest Celebration." One-hundred percent of this offering was divided between the local food pantries and the Salvation Army; the churches received nothing from it. This year 3C hosted the event, the pastor from Grace preached, and Light and Life provided the choir and musicians; their pastor also led the service.

As before, this gave Pete and Geoff a chance to at least say hello and chat a few minutes, as Geoff had returned home from college earlier that day for the extra-long weekend. Geoff and his family sat behind the Archers. John called Grace's pastor "hyper" because of his more Pentecostal style but Pete thought it was a nice, but temporary, experience. The altar rail was covered with the food items. It was interesting to see all the new faces but also notice who was not there. Seeing Beth and Ginny every time there was a service had become so normal. It seemed odd not to see them or talk with them.

Instead of talking with Beth after the service, Pete left the sanctuary with Geoff. They agreed together that Pete would go to Geoff's house on Friday after his chores were done on the farm. More science fiction movies would be the centerpiece of their short time together, plus a lot of catching up about their lives.

* * * * * * *

Beth and Ginny arrived at Janet Morton's townhouse in the early afternoon. After some grocery shopping and a light supper the three of them went to Janet's church. The service was stiff and formal. Every movement and syllable, it seemed, was scripted ahead of time. All the prayers were read, the sermon was read by the pastor, and the whole thing was over in less than an hour. The service was poorly attended in Beth's opinion.

Uncle Curt's family would host the dinner. Janet would take the dessert: store-bought pumpkin pies heated up in the oven! There were only two bedrooms at Janet's so Ginny and Beth shared the guest bed.

All the aunts and uncles and cousins were at Uncle Curt's. Some drank beer—something Beth and Ginny were not at all used to being around. Not all the stories and jokes were wholesome or clean either. There was a lot of cigarette smoking by Beth's aunts, uncles, and cousins. In some ways it was good to be done with it all. On Friday Janet took Ginny and Beth "Black Friday" shopping for the whole day. Janet seemed to plunk down the money quite freely despite the fact that she never helped a bit when Ginny was struggling just to survive in Blueberry Haven, but at least she bought lunch and a couple of gifts for each of them. Janet had some of the relatives for lunch on Saturday. There was more dry, dull worship on Sunday, but no Sunday School. It was good to leave for home but important that they had spent the time with Dan's relatives. There were times of tears for both Ginny and Janet. Beth got through fairly dry-eyed though which actually surprised her somewhat.

Beth wondered what it might be like to have Thanksgiving back in Colsonburg—what the church service was like, especially. She also tried to imagine what it was like to have dinner at Pete's home. Surely *those* pies were homemade!

* * * * * * *

On Thanksgiving Day Uncle Jim and Uncle Jerald asked Pete about the farm and so the three men plus Pete's dad went outside and Pete shared his continued plans for the land, the new barn he would build when he had enough money saved and the old rental house down the road. They drove down to the rental and toured it briefly, noting the work Pete, with John's help, had well underway. The two uncles were very interested in the changes though mostly out of curiosity.

Just the table and chairs alone nearly filled the small dining room, which also doubled as Grandpa's office. Those seated farthest from the two doorways had to slide back to their seats first then others filled in until everyone was seated. Everyone who needed to used the single bathroom upstairs before dinner because getting up might require the movement of a half dozen other people. Grandpa recited one of his memorized prayers. A brief rest after dinner was followed by homemade pies, cakes, and ice cream then everyone began to head home. Uncle Jim stayed overnight at the farmhouse.

Pete frequently wondered how it was going for Beth. She got so upset on Sunday night. He did not know if her day would be miserable, merely tolerable, or actually enjoyable. He was concerned about her—and Ginny. When he went to bed that night he prayed for them.

* * * * * * *

Friday was the second day of doing only essential chores at the farm. Saturday promised to be a very long day of catching up, made even more so because the next day was Sunday—the day off. Pete awoke early and worked all morning. After a lunch of leftovers with his family and grandparents at the farmhouse, he got ready to head to Geoff's. Just before he left the house in LC his cell phone rang.

"Hi Pete," Beth's voice was heard saying to him.

Pete was very surprised and it probably showed in his simple but startled "Well hi!"

"I hope you don't mind me calling you," she started, "I just needed to talk to someone normal—besides Mom, of course."

"So...should I go find a normal person for you to talk to?" he chuckled. She was heard laughing, too. "How's it going?" he asked.

"Okay, I guess," she began. "Most of my Dad's family aren't Christians so it's a little different here than what we were always used to."

"So where are you now?" Pete asked curiously, because he could not believe she was sitting in the middle of the living room saying those things.

"Grandma has been dragging us through the mall and every other store in the area all day long; there's no end in sight," she explained. "I'm just sitting on a bench in the mall waiting for Mom and Grandma right now."

They continued by sharing brief accounts of their respective Thanksgiving Eve services and the family dinners.

Eventually Beth said, "Here they come now. I better go. It was nice to talk to you, though."

"Same here," he agreed.

"Bye."

"Bye."

It felt so good to talk to her—to know she was doing okay.

Pete and Geoff watched their movies in the Gilberton's rec room until late evening. The two friends said good bye with a quick "man hug" and a promise to see each other again at Christmas.

Beth was very comfortable sharing her opinions and insights during Sunday School. It seemed so odd without her there. Punjab and Deanne were away, too, but Pete did not sense their absences as much as Beth's. He rode to the services with his folks because he did not plan to stay around at all afterward. During the evening service he briefly imagined Ginny and Beth traveling over the dark roads. He knew many of those roads quite well. *Where might they be now,* he wondered. He silently prayed for them.

* * * * * * *

"Welcome home?" Pete asked when Beth answered her cell phone late Monday morning.

"Yes," she said, "we got in late last night. I'm glad the Ericsons have school off for the deer season opening. That way I can get caught up on my sleep."

"I'm glad you're home safe," Pete told her, "I'll see you Wednesday night."

"I'll be there," she confirmed.

"Well, bye, then."

"Bye."

He found himself wanting to see her but he was so far behind from having three days out of four having been days he only did the minimum necessary. There were not only chores but also paperwork and banking to catch up on, too.

Things returned to normal by Wednesday but even "normal" was changing somehow. Pete had to admit that Beth was somehow changing his "normal." But did it mean anything, really? He was not sure. He was reserving judgment on that for now. But he had to admit that something besides just the seasons was changing, but what and to what extent?

A Colsonburg Christmas

The Class Party

"Okay," Jim Corbin started at the beginning of class, "most of you know the procedure: write your name and something you would like. Fold the paper over and place it in this offering mug. We'll each draw a name and purchase a gift for that person along the theme they provided. It should not cost more than about ten dollars and all *givers* are anonymous."

Writing his name, Pete also wrote the words "coffee" and "mint" on his paper. He folded it and tossed it in the mug with the rest. Jim stirred the names and passed the mug back around the room, reminding them, "If you draw your own name put it back and draw again."

Beth retrieved a paper and opening it read the words: "Pete," "coffee," and "mint." Pete, however, drew Brad's name; he had secretly hoped to draw Beth's.

That Saturday evening the class gathered in Jim and Holly's home for pizza, wings, games, and the gift exchange. Beth was placed in charge of handing out the gifts. She looked at each tag, said the name, and passed it to that person. Pete felt that she looked at him a little differently when she passed him his gift and he immediately suspected it might have been from her. When it was his turn, he unwrapped the package and found a box from one of his favorite Colsonburg businesses: *CTC!* (which stood for Coffee, Tea, Cocoa—no one knew why there was an exclamation point on the end). Upon opening the box he saw a sample-sized pack of mint-flavored coffee, another of mint-flavored hot cocoa mix, and some chocolate-covered espresso beans.

"Thanks a lot. It's perfect," he said.

He was sure Beth grinned a little more than when the others opened their gifts. Their eyes met for only a quick moment right after he opened his gift.

Everyone else seemed in such a hurry to leave that night. After everyone else left Beth offered to finish with the cleanup. Pete stayed too. Finally, when everything was clean and put away, the two headed out to their frost-covered vehicles.

Pete looked across the hood of his truck and took a risk. He said, "Thanks for the coffee and stuff."

She smiled with a look of surprise and pleasure, saying, "How did you know?'

"Call it a hunch," he replied, "and, by the way, I didn't draw *your* name."

"I'm glad to hear that," she said. "That was weird—soap and perfume. My theme was 'cats.'"

"Are you and your mom going to the Christmas Social after the cantata?" he asked her about the following weekend's main church activities.

"I'm sure we're planning on it."

"When do you guys leave for Cumberland?"

"The twenty-third."

"You'll be back for the New Year Party at the Holts', won't you?" He sure did hope to be able to spend at least some of that evening with her.

"I hope so," she was cautious but optimistic.

"You'll like it. It's a lot of good, clean fun," he explained to her. "I hope you can be there."

Beth hoped she could, too. Her thinking was like Pete's, hoping to just hang out with him.

A Tough Spot

After Wednesday prayer groups, Pete went to the Fellowship Hall to help clean up after the Kids' Clubs Christmas Party. Beth had been there for the whole event and was picking up cups and plates from the tables. Pete snuck up behind her and draped a small piece of garland over her shoulders.

Her reaction was not at all what he had expected. She turned around, ripped the garland off and handed it back to him forcefully saying, "Not funny—now let me get done!"

Pete was dumbstruck. He stepped back and simply said, "Sorry."

He put the garland back where he found it and went across the room to help fold some of the chairs. He was definitely hurt and bewildered. This did not seem at all like Beth.

After a short time he turned around to get a couple more chairs and observed Beth coming toward him. He did not know what to do or say. He wanted to just flee, stomp away to demonstrate his hurt, or pour out some vindictive words back at her. He did none of those. He just continued with the chairs, pretending not to notice her, remembering to practice that fruit of self-control (Galatians 5:23).

"Pete," she began, still approaching him, "I'm sorry for snapping at you. It's just been a tough couple days. I didn't mean to take it out on you."

"All's forgiven," he replied sincerely, "...but what's wrong? You look really beat." From that vantage point he could see her eyes were marked by dark circles. She looked tired and a little red in the face.

She looked around and then walked into the kitchen. Pete assumed he was to follow and did so.

She whispered to him, "Mom and I are just beginning to feel what it will be like to have Christmas without Dad," she explained. Beth stopped abruptly and looked Pete in the eye and exclaimed through an instant torrent of tears, "I miss him so much!"

Pete was choked up too but wanted to be a help or comfort. He reached out with his arm and tried to give her a small reassuring hug or a pat on the back. Instead she buried her face in the corner of his neck and shoulder and sobbed and shook uncontrollably. Pete just kept his arm around her back and let her cry it out.

Meredith Holt came in the kitchen and stopped in her tracks, a surprised look on her face. She then gave Pete an inquisitive look and he responded by silently mouthing over Beth's shoulder the words, "Her dad."

Meredith mouthed back the single word, "Oh." She came up behind Beth and, putting her hand on Beth's shoulder, asked, "Do you want to talk about it, dear?"

Pete stood by as Meredith took over the lead in the situation. Beth poured out her memories of how they would all spend their Christmastimes together right up through last year. Meredith stood listening, rubbing Beth's back as she shared.

Eventually Beth regained control over her tears and finally, wiping her eyes and blowing her nose with a paper towel said, "I'm sorry…but thanks. I better just go."

"I can walk you home," Pete offered.

"You don't have to do that, Pete."

"Why don't you let him?" Meredith suggested.

"Well, okay. Let me get my coat and purse," Beth consented.

Beth talked most of the way back and Pete just let her. Part of what she told him was, "The really dumb part about all this is that we wanted to put up a fresh-cut Christmas tree like always but Dad always cut it for us and we don't even know how to cut down a Christmas tree!"

Pete stopped. Beth followed suit. Turning ninety degrees to face her he said, "Elizabeth Morton. You mean to tell me you didn't get a tree because you never cut one before? All you had to do was ask. I would have helped you guys get one."

"Oh, we wouldn't have bothered someone else over a thing like that," she explained.

"Look," he replied, "a Christmas tree would be a nice, fun distraction for you two. Why don't I take you guys tomorrow to get one? It won't take long and I'll help you stand it up, too."

"That would be nice—if you have time," she consented.

It started to snow. When they reached the trailer she stopped and said, "Thanks Pete, you're a good friend."

"Anytime," he answered.

She turned and went inside. As he walked back to the church, and his truck, Pete prayed for Beth and Ginny to be comforted. The snow was falling steadily but only lightly.

The Christmas Tree

Pete awoke early and got as many chores out of the way as possible before lunch. Then after lunch he retrieved his bow saw and headed down to Colsonburg. He was not afraid to drive in the snow but was still thankful to be able to follow the snowplow down the steep winding "Narrows." He could see the wing plow sticking out and funneling the snow up in a curl and down into a long neat line off the side of the road. The spreader on the back tossed salt and sand down on the plowed but still slick road. The salt crystals ticked and clicked on the bottom of his truck as they were kicked up by the tires. At the intersection with Main Street the plow turned around and went back up the narrows, clearing the other lane now.

At the trailer, Ginny and Beth were all bundled up and ready to go.

"Boy, it's perfect weather to cut a tree," he said cheerfully, trying to lift the mood a little.

The women had retrieved the ornaments and tree stand from storage and had them waiting; they were obviously anxious to get that tree.

They piled into Pete's truck—Beth in the middle and Ginny next to the window. Pete drove them over the bridge on Susquehanna Street and about four miles out into the East Side.

Arriving at the tree farm Ginny was alarmed at the fact that they were at the base of a steep hill and all the trees were on, or even over, the hilltop.

"Oh," she said, "why don't you kids go up and pick one for us and I'll wait here and in the gift shoppe." Company Four's fire auxiliary was selling hot cocoa and other treats from a small food truck

So Pete and Beth climbed the hill. The snow was not falling as hard now.

"We won't be able to see the trees for all the snow," she mourned.

"Actually a light snow like this" (it had only accumulated about four inches) "helps you see how the branches lay and spot openings and flat spots better," Pete explained.

"I didn't know that," Beth said, a little surprised.

"Yeah, it's in deep snow that this gets really tough," he further explained.

Finally Beth picked a tree near the top of the hill. It was perfectly shaped and layered, a blue spruce only about five feet high.

Pete lay on his side with his head under the edge of the branches and reached up with his bow saw. It only took a few seconds of sawing until the tree gently fell over.

"Wow that was quick," Beth exclaimed.

Pete stood it up again and tamped it on the ground. All the snow fell off its branches at one time.

"It's beautiful," Ginny declared back at the bottom of the hill.

As Ginny and Beth noticed some of the wreaths and other decorations, Pete threw the tree in the back of the truck and paid the twenty dollars for it. Coming back out, Ginny handed him a twenty dollar bill and asked him, "Would you be willing to run in and pay for it, Pete?"

"Already done," he said, "my gift to you guys."

"I can't let you do that, Pete," Ginny protested.

"If you're worried about it," he suggested, "put the twenty in the can over there for the Salvation Army."

"Okay, and thanks a lot Pete," Ginny consented with a smile.

The main roads were beginning to clear out, with just slush and salty water covering most of them. Back at the trailer, Pete put the tree in its stand and adjusted it until it stood straight.

"You should let it stand for a spell so it dries out and comes back into its shape again before you decorate it," Pete advised.

"Before you go, have some homemade Christmas cookies," Ginny offered, heading toward the kitchen, "but you have to frost the ones you eat. I'll make some coffee, too."

"Sounds like a fair trade to me," Pete said, following her to the kitchen.

The three of them sat at the kitchen table frosting the various shapes of thin Christmas cookies. Ginny got up to retrieve the mail when it arrived and then got distracted looking through the tree ornaments. Pete and Beth sat at the table frosting cookies and comparing their families' Christmas traditions and memories.

But Pete's afternoon with the Mortons ended abruptly when his pager rang. It was the kind of thing no one wanted to hear, especially at Christmas time.

The dispatcher announced, "Lainge Township, box 5-F, in the area of two-five-zero North Back Hollow Road. Possible house fire. Heavy smoke evident. Company Five; engine, tanker, and rescue from Company Sixteen;

engine and tanker from Company Eight, tanker from Company Fourteen. Ambulance Sixteen, one unit. Engine from Company Nineteen to Station Five." Then the next round of the tones sounded.

Pete jumped up, even as the dispatcher was speaking and, putting on his coat, said, "I better go—you never know who will be around on a weekday and this could be bad and that's *way* out in the boonies *and* on bad roads."

As he rushed out the door, Colsonburg's fire whistle began blowing. Beth did not know what to think of all this. She knew Pete was a firefighter but she did not understand or relate to the fire service. It was something she and Pete did *not* have in common.

A few minutes later she took some trash out to the garbage can and heard the siren and horn of one of the units from Colsonburg heading over to LC to lend a hand. She thought about the fire at Rhonda's; it was on a Thursday afternoon too. She remembered how the fire chief said if he had just one more man respond with one more truck that day he could have stopped that fire. She decided it was good that Pete did this. Most did not. Maybe it would make the difference for that family in Lainge Township. Who knew? She stopped and prayed for Pete, for the family who lived in the home, and for the firefighters to be successful in putting out the blaze in time.

Later, when Beth answered the phone, it was Pete.

"It was a false alarm. I'm sorry for having to leave like that," he said, explaining, "the man was burning rubbish and the neighbor thought the smoke was coming from the house. That kind of thing happens a lot."

"I'm glad it wasn't serious," Beth replied. "Oh, and you left your cookies here."

"I'll get them from you on Sunday, then," Pete suggested, "I'm going to the livestock sale tomorrow. Pray that I get a good price."

"Consider it done," she assured him.

The Gifts

Several times on Saturday Pete thought about going down to Colsonburg to get those cookies. But he struggled against the idea. He knew that he was interested in seeing Beth more than having those cookies. He felt shock and even fear over how much he wanted to see her. *Just wait until tomorrow* he thought to himself. That's all he had to do.

At home later Pete wrapped the small gift he had bought for Beth on his way home Friday. He hoped it would please her. He felt odd buying her something so personal and special. Would she feel like he was saying "too much" when he gave it to her? Would it be so much that it would cause her to pull away to a "safe distance" from him? Or would it simply show her what he meant. That he cared about her and wanted to share a token of that for Christmas?

Also on Saturday, Beth stopped in *CTC!* to pick up her special order. Mr. Johnson retrieved the two items from the back room for her inspection and approval.

"They're perfect," was her simple but convincing reply.

Mr. Johnson rang up the amount and Beth handed him the cash to pay for them.

"Would you like a box to put them in?" he asked.

"Sure. Thanks," she replied.

"This one holds two nicely," he said as he put them in the box and added some shredded paper to help protect and conceal them. Then he placed the lid on it and put the box in a brown paper bag.

The whole time Beth wanted to ask someone if she was really doing this. She had never bought such a flattering gift for anyone but a family member. She wondered if it was too much, too sappy, too much perhaps for Pete at this point in time. What message was she sending him? She didn't even know for sure. But she knew she wanted to do this and felt that she should.

"Thanks and come again," Mr. Johnson said, startling Beth from her contemplations.

"Oh…yes, thank *you*," she said as she turned for the door.

It was a typical Sunday morning at 3C. Pete and Beth sat next to each other in Sunday School but that was not unusual; everyone knew they had become good friends but Beth was not planning to stay in Colsonburg long term so one made any kind of a big deal about it. During worship Beth sat with her mom as usual—across the center aisle from the Archers and two rows forward, Ginny next to the aisle and Beth on her left. Pete sat on the aisle with his dad to his right, then his mom, Amy and finally Pat. When the service ended and after both families had taken time to greet the morning speaker, Pete sought Beth out in the crowded vestibule.

"I think you have something for me," Pete reminded her.

"They're at home in the fridge," she explained. "Can you stop over?"

"We all rode down together today…"

"I can run you home if you need me to," she offered.

"Well, okay, if you don't mind," he consented.

She assured him, "It's no problem."

Pete explained his new plans to his folks and walked with Beth back to the trailer. Ginny was still at the church but sure to arrive home any moment.

"Here they are," she said reaching into the refrigerator to retrieve the zip bag of about a dozen or so cut-out cookies of various shapes and colors of frosting.

"Thanks," Pete said, "and I believe this should cover it," he continued as if making payment for the cookies. He reached into his coat pocket and produced the thin, square package wrapped in white paper covered with the images of small candy canes.

"Oh Pete," she responded, "you didn't have to do that!"

"I know, but I did—so you won't forget about me after you move on."

She unwrapped the small paperboard box and removed the lid revealing a fine gold necklace with a gold pendant clearly in the image of a cat in a sitting position with its tail wrapped around in front of its paws, its head turned as if looking up at her.

"Oh, it's beautiful," she said through an approving smile.

"Turn it over," he instructed her.

Turning the pendant over, she saw the small but clear engraving: "From Pete. Christmas '09"

"Oh..." she seemed to almost sing it.

Beth took it out of the box and let it hang in front of her.

"Here," she said, handing it to Pete so fast he simply had to take it or let it fall to the floor.

Suddenly she was standing with her back to him and her hair pulled up from the back of her neck.

"Put it on me?" she asked.

Pete did not expect this but carefully reached around and brought the ends of the chain together and closed the clasp. He was very careful, though, because he did not think he would be comfortable touching her face or neck and she might not either.

She turned around to present it to him on her and then went to the mirror in the hallway and looked at it on for herself. She said thanks again with that big bright smile of hers.

"But you're still in debt," she teased, "because I have something for you too."

She disappeared down the hallway. Pete heard what sounded like a drawer open and close. Beth reappeared carrying a much larger and heavier box wrapped in green foil-like paper.

"Oh boy," Pete exclaimed.

He needed to sit down to open it. Removing the wrapping, he opened the box and pushed the packing aside to reveal two coffee mugs. One said on the side: "World's Greatest Farmer."

"Look at the other one, too," she directed him.

"World's Greatest Fireman," the companion mug said.

The thoughtfulness of her gift definitely touched him.

"Thanks…a lot," he said a little shocked but flattered.

Just then Ginny came into the small home.

"Look Mom," Beth held the pendant on her hand, "Pete gave it to me."

"Nice," Ginny said with an approving smile.

"And look what I got," Pete intentionally spoke like a child showing off some new toy from under the tree.

"Also nice," Ginny responded.

"I'm going to run Pete home," Beth told Ginny, picking up her coat and purse. "His folks went on back after church."

"Okay. I'll see you in a bit," Ginny answered.

They got into Beth's tiny grey car and Pete reminded her of the way to LC as she went. They discussed what their families' plans would be for Christmas Eve and Christmas Day. He described the Community Christmas Eve Service in Colsonburg. Beth said she wished she could go; it sounded like a great service. Coming into the Archers' driveway Pete told her thanks and that he would see her at five to prepare for the Cantata.

"What's that you have?" John asked his son.

"Beth gave me these for Christmas," Pete said, happily displaying the open box.

"That was thoughtful," Joanie said, exchanging glances with her husband. They both wondered what *this* might indicate, if anything at all.

The family had Sunday dinner together and spent the afternoon resting and napping as usual. Pete's nap was short as he had to go to the farm to put hay down for the cows. Pete left at quarter until five for the final cantata rehearsal.

The Social

The Cantata went off without any problem and sounded beautiful. It took up the entire evening service. Jim Corbin gave the closing prayer and surprised everyone with an unexpected announcement.

"The District Superintendent called me this afternoon to inform me that Pastor Baker who candidated here a couple weeks ago *has* accepted the call to become our new pastor!"

The whole church broke out in applause—what a Christmas gift: a new pastor!

"He will start in about six or eight weeks," he finished after pausing for the church's enthusiastic response.

The Fellowship Hall was beautifully decorated for the social and almost everyone was there. There was ham, cheese and crackers, cut vegetables, cakes, and pies, not to mention lots of discussion about the new pastor. Fred Holt gave the thanks after everyone had gathered and been seated.

The Archers and the Mortons shared a table, along with Bea Tanner. Beth wore her new pendant on the outside of her blue knit turtleneck sweater. It dangled and twisted, catching the light so beautifully. Pete heard several people comment to her about it. He even overheard her saying to one lady, "A dear friend gave it to me."

After about forty-five minutes, Pete had to leave. He had an early start again in the morning. He had been making the rounds talking to several friends. Then he made his way back to where Beth was seated.

"Hey, I gotta go," he said, taking the seat across from her. "Have a safe trip and a Merry Christmas. I'll be praying for you."

"I'll try. You too," she reciprocated.

"Don't forget the New Year Party," he reminded her.

"I hope to be there," she promised cautiously.

"Well...I really need to go," Pete admitted and pushed himself up and away from the table.

"See ya," he said.

"See ya," she replied with a smile.

Pete made his way to the door that led to the hallway. Pushing the door partway open he stood in it for a moment and looked back over at Beth, noticing the pendant dangling and flashing in the light. Their eyes caught one another's for a second. She smiled and waved, holding her hand up and wiggling her fingers. Pete gave a grin and a wave with a slightly raised hand plus a nod of the head.

Someone said something that caused Beth to look away for only a split second. When she looked back, the door was closed and Pete was gone.

A Laingeville Center Christmas

The weather continued to be cold through Christmas Eve. A few comparatively warm days arrived on Christmas but then the bottom fell out from under the temperatures again by the New Year.

The mad rush to finish shopping and gather the ingredients for the families' feasts reached its height on December twenty third. Then the busyness of wrapping gifts and beginning the meals started on Christmas Eve morning.

For Pete's family, the celebration began with Christmas Eve supper which always featured seafood or fish. Its roots were in the Wilmors' New England ancestry. This year was a clam and crab boil. The five had this annual supper together at the house down in LC. Then Pete's grandparents joined them in attending the Colsonburg Community Christmas Eve Service—one of only two services that Jack and John's families attended together, the other being the Easter sunrise service.

All the protestant churches in Colsonburg joined together for this colossal Christmas celebration. One service was held at seven and the other at eleven. The Archers attended the earlier service, though both were identical. First there was a series of readings ranging from Genesis to Revelation, all telling various parts of Christ's coming including the Old Testament prophecies, birth, and still-future second coming. Each reading was matched to an appropriate Christmas carol or song. A brief candle lighting ceremony followed this and everyone sang "Silent Night" while the house lights were off and each one held a burning candle. The service concluded with a community choir singing the "Hallelujah Chorus" from Handel's *Messiah*. They would practice for weeks ahead of time. The congregation stood as they sang, in accordance with tradition. Pete enjoyed singing and often wanted to take part in this but it required a commitment to be at both services and the rehearsals for both the cantata and the Christmas Eve service were too much to take on at once.

This year the service was held at the Episcopal Church on the square. This church was much different than 3C but Pete still looked to the left and two rows ahead, hoping to see Beth seated there. Instead, the Andrews children sat in that spot, fighting with each other while their parents did nothing but threaten that if they did not stop, Santa would give all their toys to some good children instead. Pete wondered what the parents did when the kids fought during the summer or figured out there was no such thing as Santa. Geoff also was not there, though the Light and Life folks were; he was with his grandparents in Wilkes-Barre.

At home later the wrapped gifts were arranged around the Christmas tree and everyone laid out an old wool sock for a stocking. During the various stages of the night the family members would wake up cramming candies and trinkets into one another's "stockings."

In the morning, everyone gathered in the living room and took the items from their stockings oohing and ahhing over each thing, saying thank you though everything was technically anonymous. A big breakfast, this year of sausage, fruit, and coffeecake, ensued. Being special, it was served in the dining room, not the kitchen. Then, coffee cups in hand, everyone returned to the living room to open their gifts. Pete drank from his new "World's Greatest Farmer" mug. Gifts for Grandpa and Grandma and the other Archers were set aside for later.

After a clean up of the torn paper, packaging and dirty dishes, the other gifts were loaded into the car. Everyone changed and headed over to Grandpa and Grandma's house. Pete had already left to tend to his chores in the barn.

It was no longer necessary to limit the celebration to Grandpa and Grandma's house since Grandpa had retired. But tradition prevailed over reason and it was done the same as always anyway.

Grandma baked a huge ham and the other women helped with the side dishes. The men set the table and arranged the chairs. Aunt Judy, Uncle Jerald, and Cousins Mike and Susan were there from Wellsboro and Uncle Jim from Centre Hall. At two o'clock the feast began with a prayer given by Pete's dad. The unwrapping of gifts followed, then dessert. It was well after dark when the other relatives began to leave.

Everyone had a wonderful time, as always. Uncle Jim caught Pete up on all the goings-on in Centre County. Uncle Jerald made jokes and pulled pranks as usual. Cousin Mike joined in, following his dad's unruly example. A few times Pete wondered about Beth—what she was doing, if she and Ginny were having any fun on this first Christmas without Pastor Dan.

After going to the barn again in the evening, he headed back home to meet his family there. Everyone was tired but very happy with the day. Pete headed upstairs to his room and speed dialed Beth's cell phone from his own.

"Hey, Pete," was her soft but happy greeting.

"How are you guys doing?" he asked.

"It's been okay—kind of up and down emotionally, but we're surviving it," she explained.

"I guess that's pretty good," he summed it up.

"Yeah, it could have been a lot worse."

Beth's family opened presents on Christmas Eve before church and just had dinner on Christmas Day. Beth had to again share a double bed with her mother in her grandmother's cramped townhouse. They all missed having Patty there but they did speak on the phone at least, telling about the gifts they each received and the ones they gave. Pete told her he had used the new coffee mugs and she said everyone commented on her beautiful necklace; she thanked him for it again.

"Well, it's late—I better go. I'll talk to you soon," he concluded.

"Merry Christmas, Pete," she wished him.

"Merry Christmas," he returned the sentiment.

"Bye."

"Bye."

Pete changed for bed and brushed his teeth. He read a couple of chapters from his Bible. He prayed for Beth and Ginny and for Beth's grandmother. After all Pastor Dan was her son and she herself was a widow. He prayed for Billy, wherever he was, and that he would soon be reconciled to his mother and sisters—that God would get through to him, *whatever* it took.

Pete was up early on the twenty-sixth; many chores had been skipped the day before and needed to be caught up. He worked alone in the cold barn.

Upstairs he retrieved bales of hay, cut the twine holding them together, and dropped the loose bales down into the mangers below. The cows knew their meal was coming and waited for him to drop it down to them.

The whole time he was turning thoughts about Beth over and over in his mind. Realizing that he was only *thinking* he stopped and spoke as if into the air but really to his Heavenly Father. His words were random and wandering.

"What am I supposed to do?" he started. "What does all of this mean? I'm excited, confused, thankful, scared—all at one time. I didn't expect this. I think about her so much. Are we just real good friends? Should we be more? Are we more already? How could this be happening? I wasn't supposed to deal with this stuff anymore. It was supposed to be just me from now on. I'm really worried, God. Every relationship I've had has been a train wreck. I lost those people from my life but how could I lose *her*—she's a friend like none before her. I'm already scared she'll want a 'relationship' and I won't dare and it will drive her away. Or, I'll want it and *that* will drive *her* away. She's so special." He sat down on a bale of hay. "But there's something different about this, God. It's not like the others. Does that mean… O, how can this be happening? I'm so scared, God. I'm so scared."

He began to get tears in the corners of his eyes and once he gave in to the tears he began to cry outright as he remembered the feeling of rejection and loneliness he felt when Lauren just plain dumped him with no explanation. It could happen again if he opened his heart up to Beth.

"Nevertheless not my will but Thine be done. But I am so scared."

He was calling out to God. He was still crying—so hard he slid from the bale to the floor. He hung his face between his knees, his hands folded in front of him, his shoulders and back heaving with the intense emotion coming over him. After a few minutes, though, he found the strength to regain his composure. Mostly under control again, he prayed once more.

"If You do want us to be together God, please show me. Give me some sign and make sure I don't miss it. If You give it, I will follow You the best I know how—just be speaking to her, too, *please.* But if You don't give it, I will leave well enough alone and simply enjoy the friendship we have right now."

He wiped his eyes and nose and headed outside again. Later, when he came around the end of the barn, there was a sight for sore eyes: Geoff walking up the lane towards him! They began to walk with purpose toward one another.

"Hey, brother," Pete greeted him.

"Good to see you, man," Geoff replied.

They gave one another a brief man-hug: not too close, not too long, but very sincere.

"It's almost lunchtime," Pete began. "How about a sub from down at the market?"

So they got in Geoff's car and drove the mile down to Holmes' Market. Ordering their sandwiches and sitting at one of the two small tables they began to eat and catch up with one another.

Geoff announced that he had started seeing someone; he had her pictures in his phone. He was very pleased and bragged about what a great Christian woman she was. She, too, was a student at the college. They didn't have any big plans right now, just living for the day. Geoff asked Pete about the farm. Pete spoke enthusiastically about his plans but also about how much work it was and how tight finances had been. But he also affirmed that he "wouldn't be doing anything else."

"I need you to pray for me about something, my friend," Pete requested.

"What's that," Geoff asked muffled, still pulling the sub back from his mouth.

"It's…about a relationship," Pete began to say.

"You? A *relationship*?" Geoff said in utter disbelief, his eyes popping wide open. "I thought you had taken the vow of bachelorhood!"

"Me too, but…I don't know maybe it's nothing."

"Okay, come clean with me," Geoff insisted, putting the sub down again.

So Pete started the tale from back almost a year ago when Pastor Dan died, all the way until yesterday when he called Beth down in Cumberland.

"I think you're gettin' bit by the *love bug*!" Geoff teased.

"I don't know. In one way I hope not but in another way, well, you know."

"Oh yes I do!" Geoff confirmed. "So what are you gonna do?"

"I guess we're going to have to have a talk when she gets back," Pete answered.

"Yeah, you need to get some things out in the open," Geoff affirmed that idea.

"Just pray it doesn't mess up what we already have. I couldn't take that," Pete worried out loud.

"Just trust the Lord, my friend. He'll give you the words," Geoff exhorted him, "If it's meant to be, it'll be. Just be sure to talk to her with an open mind so she doesn't feel like she's being pushed into something. Am I going to get to meet her?"

"Maybe. She's coming home on the thirty-first," Pete answered.

"It'll be close. We're all going to my other grandparents in Allentown for New Year's."

"You know, you sure get around," Pete observed.

"That's what happens when you're a transplant someplace. You live so far from family and it's always a big production to go see someone," Geoff said.

"That's how it is with Beth," Pete told him.

"There you go again, talking about 'Beth.' Beth this, Beth that," Geoff laughed. "But, keep me posted," he requested, pointing in Pete's direction.

Soon after that, Geoff took Pete back to the farm and he himself went back to Colsonburg. The lunch was a nice break and it felt so good to finally admit to another person what Pete was experiencing and struggling with about Beth.

* * * * * * *

Beth had no quiet spaces to think or pray as Pete had. One of the only exceptions was on the way to Cumberland. Beth drove. Though she and Ginny had spent some of the time talking, Ginny was eventually lulled off to sleep by the motion of the car. Beth used the time to pray quietly and try to listen to what God might be saying to her.

Janet's townhouse was crowded and the family stayed active the whole time. But she continued to think of Pete at some point or points each day. A couple of times she was asked if anyone special was in her life. She said no, but secretly she permitted the idea that perhaps Pete *could* become "him." She convinced Ginny to return to Colsonburg in time for the New Year party but Beth knew the real reason was to see Pete again.

One night as her mother slept next to her she made a decision, a decision made in light of all that had been going on, her prayers, and the things she was experiencing in her heart and mind. If there was to be anything between her and Pete he would need to take the first step (which was one of her rules anyway, based on her belief that God meant for the man to be the leader in a relationship). But if he *did* take that step she *would* truly pray about it and consider it. That night was the twenty-sixth. The next day she sent a text message to Pete.

Pete was in the loft again on that day, sending hay down to the hungry cattle below. His cell phone alerted him to a text. Retrieving it from inside his heavy, warm work clothes, he checked the messages. The sender was Beth. Selecting that message and then "read" he saw her words to him: "cant wait for dec 31 miss u."

Pete replied simply, "me 2."

Pete read it and looked up. "Is this it?" he asked the Lord, regarding his request for a sign. As he prayerfully pondered this he, too, made a decision. Unless Beth sent some signal that he should not do so, he would talk to her about a possible courtship as soon as practicable. He would finally do things right this time, taking the advice of his late mentor, Pastor Dan. But he also decided in advance that this would be the last time, the last chance for a relationship. He was convinced that too much was happening to the two of them to be ignored and that God must be turning their hearts toward one another, though he could hardly believe it was true, that he would even *remotely consider* that possibility. It would be a huge risk but he felt he had no choice; this had to be dealt with. So he would talk to her about it and if she was at all receptive he would have them each think about it for a while before forming a conclusion. If she was not receptive, saw things differently than he did, he would accept that but try to stay friends with her, even best friends. He prayed for God to stop him if he was wrong. He was at peace with this plan, though, and remained at peace the rest of the time Beth was away.

And would Beth be receptive? Pete knew she was no longer seriously considering the mission field. But the last he knew she was not planning on staying in Colsonburg for long either. Would she change her plans just for him?

* * * * * * *

Uncle Curt asked Beth about her plans. Was she going to stay in Colsonburg her whole life, move to the big city, or off to Zimbabwe?

"I don't know," she replied to him sincerely, "Whatever God shows me next will determine what the next steps will be." She had a plan, though. If Pete did not want her, she would move on with her life with no limitation as to where she might go, near or far. But if he demonstrated a desire to have that deeper relationship with her, she would stay in Colsonburg until she knew the outcome of this friendship. She would also be prepared to stay there permanently if God willed that they be together. Pete would not be going anywhere and so if her life was to be with him, her life would be in Colsonburg, actually Laingeville Center, and God would finally give her a purpose and a calling *there*. If His plan for her was somewhere else, even Zimbabwe, God would either call Pete there first, or He would not permit this relationship to easily move forward. Beth's mind was quiet and relaxed now; she would wait on the Lord and on her trusted friend, Pete.

The New Year

Finally the time had come for the New Year Party at the Holts'. Pete had been going ever since he entered the Senior High Sunday School Class and it had simply become a part of how he celebrated the holidays. The Holts started holding the party as an opportunity for the Senior High, Young Adult, and Couples Classes to have fellowship and good clean fun on New Year's Eve. They enjoyed sharing their home on the north end of the borough with the young people of the church. Many brought family and/or friends and several "alumni" of the party continued attending for years after.

Beth and Ginny were coming home that day but Pete did not know exactly when. He drove by the trailer on his way over to Holts'. The car was not there. At six o'clock he was one of the first to arrive at the party and the Mortons' car was not there yet either. Pete's heart sunk; maybe they would not be back in time, he worried. Hopefully nothing went wrong on the way back to Colsonburg. He tried to distract himself with the activities of the evening—talking and laughing with the other guests, games in the living room, food and drinks in the kitchen and dining room. Plus there was a movie showing in the rec room. He was treating it like any other New Year's Eve.

About eight o'clock, he heard two familiar voices—Ginny and Beth. Trying not to let his anxious anticipation show too much, Pete, swiftly crossed the room to meet them in front of that grand staircase. Their greetings were kept very casual though, things like: "Good to see you," and "How was the drive?" and so on.

The two of them spent a great deal of their time together. Pete was sitting with Beth at the dining room table talking with some other friends when Ginny came in the room. By then it was about eleven-thirty.

"I'm going to head home now, sweetie," she said.

It was expected. This was her first New Year without her husband and the sight of all the couples giving their New Year kisses to one another at midnight was just too much to face at that time.

"Are you gonna be okay?" Beth asked her mom with concern. "Do you want me to go home with you?"

Pete's heart sank again. He needed Beth to be able to focus on him for just a little longer; they needed to talk. If she left now it would only complicate his plans. He knew it was a little selfish but he just needed maybe up to another hour's time with Beth.

Ginny worked a little at producing a smile and replied, "No, hun, I think I would like to be alone for a little while."

Pete was torn. He felt for Ginny but he needed to get Beth alone for just even a few *minutes*. He could not wait much longer to have this talk with her. Just once he needed to be first. He was always putting others first. Could he be a priority for one short time tonight? He was afraid he might lose his nerve and ultimately fail to talk to her.

"Okay," Beth consented, "I'll see you a little later."

Pete was relieved then suddenly sick with fear almost at once.

"I'll bring her home," Pete offered, to Ginny's relief.

"Thanks, Pete," she acknowledged, "and have fun," she instructed her daughter.

Ginny left for home. It was going to be rough for her no matter what. She would cry before the New Year arrived. But no one could stop that and how could she help it? Being alone, however, is what she desired. At least during this past year God had given her the strength to make the most of her life as it now was. She would be all right again the next day.

In almost no time at all, it seemed, everyone was counting down and when they reached "zero," a loud cheer went up accompanied by the traditional New Year song. The couples greeted one another with a quick kiss, as expected.

Beth was seated on the living room ottoman in a cozy knit sweater with the image of a Christmas tree on the front. The pendant Pete had bought for her was hanging prominently from the collar. Pete stood next to her. He looked down at her and watched her for a moment. She was laughing with the rest, her smile wide and glowing. She looked up at him as she laughed and he smiled down at her. It was good to see her again and to see her so full of joy despite everything she had been through. In his mind he journeyed back to that horrid March day in Lewistown when she was so broken and lost. The contrast, what God had done, was so evident.

The experience of seeing her that way also reminded him of just how far he had come since that life-altering August afternoon almost four-and-a-half years ago. He had never been the same since.

He could easily have bent down and kissed her, even just on the cheek, right then and there, like the others, but he dare not. She might not accept it. It might embarrass or offend her. He now knew such a thing should never be done so impulsively, for any reason. Besides, he had a plan. He tried to remember and focus on the plan. He simply looked at her and smiled as he said, "Happy New Year!"

"Happy New Year to you, Pete," she reciprocated, smiling up at him.

Fred gathered everyone into the living room and he led in a brief prayer, thanking God for the evening and asking His blessing on the New Year. Everyone said, "Amen."

Shortly after that Beth indicated to Pete that she really should be getting home soon. She wanted to see how her mom was doing. The Holts understood her need to go and Pete's kindness in taking her back. Beth told them good night and Pete promised to be back to help with the clean up.

Stepping out the front door, they observed two things. First, it was snowing and it must have been doing so for a couple of hours or more, judging from the amount accumulated so far. Second, Pete's truck was blocked in and he would not be able to get out unless several others moved their vehicles first.

"It looks like we're walking," he said.

"That's fine," she responded adding, "We can see the Christmas lights better on foot."

"I had hoped to talk to you about something anyway," Pete told her, "so it's just as well I suppose." Now the plan had been sealed and was inescapable.

They started down the sidewalk toward downtown. The snow fell all around them. About half the houses were lit with a warm glow as the people inside observed the arrival of 2010. Christmas trees were lit in the windows and twinkling lights shown through the snow on hedges, from porch rails and eves, being reflected and magnified by the sparkling snow. A big yellow snowplow rumbled by, the orange warning lights flashing off the snow and the houses. The plow blades scraped loudly along the roadway. But it was soon still again as they walked along making plain, simple conversation, mostly about the party. They were in downtown now. Lit images of snowflakes hung on the sides of the light poles.

As they reached Susquehanna Street Beth asked, "So what did you want to talk about?"

"Well," he tactfully formulated his reply, "I have something I want you to pray about," mystifying Beth a little.

"Okay..." was her tentative-sounding response.

They were at the square now, right in front of the historic Colsonburg Inn with its tall, narrow porch pillars stretching up both stories from the sidewalk to the roof, Christmas lights winding up each one. The traffic signal was blinking yellow for Main Street and red for Susquehanna Street.

"Maybe we could sit down," Pete suggested, pointing across Main Street toward the gazebo in the center of the snow-blanketed square. They followed the snowy imprint of a previously cleared pathway leading to the small shelter. Walking up the steps and underneath the roof, they were shielded from the steadily dropping flakes but still surrounded by the holiday lights and glittering snow cover, street lights casting an additional glow. Pete sat on one of the benches and Beth followed his lead by sitting next to him, watching him as she did so, like the night he sat behind her in the almost-dark sanctuary after Missions Conference. Pete looked down, breathed a deep, cleansing breath and silently sought, one more time, Divine help.

"I'm glad you're home," he started, looking up at her, turning his head to the right to look straight at her.

Beth chimed right in, "Me too, I love my grandmother but—"

Pete intentionally interrupted her, saying, "No. I mean I missed you over Christmas."

"Oh," was her blushing reply. Taking her signal from him she dared to add, "I missed you, too."

Pete was relieved and encouraged to hear that again.

"I wish I could have seen you on Christmas Eve or Christmas Day, at least," he told her.

"Yeah," she agreed, smiling and nodding her head. "Me too."

He finally took the plunge: "Would you pray about something for me?"

She nodded.

"I suppose you've noticed," Pete began his speech both the speed and pitch of his voice eventually increasing, "that over the years our lives' pathways have kept crossing from time to time. But when I ran into you down in Lewistown that day in March it was like they were thrown together in a different sort of way—a way I would never have guessed." This was the point he starting speaking faster. "I hope you know, by the way, that I didn't put Fred up to giving you guys that trailer. I didn't even hint at it. I did ask if the Deacons could give your mom some money. He told me that God just laid it on his heart to let her have that place. Then slow, but sure, you were showing up more and more and then here all the time and we just started becoming friends."

Beth indicated by her nodding head that she could not disagree with anything he was saying. Pete continued. The words just seemed to appear in his mouth and flow out so smoothly. It was all an answer to prayer.

"When I realized how much I missed you at Thanksgiving it actually startled me. Then you called. It was such a blessing to me to hear you and talk with you. When you guys got back I just wanted to see you and be around you. Then you went away again for Christmas. The only relief I felt was in calling *you*."

Beth smiled approvingly, almost blushingly.

"I'm starting to ask God, literally, Beth," he stressed it, "whether He is trying to tell us something. You know what I mean? And if He is, *what* is He saying? Am I making *any* sense?" he begged to know.

"Yes," was all she could say but it was enough to keep him going.

"Does any of this apply to you, too, or is it just me?" he needed to know.

"It's...not just you," she stated quietly but very, very seriously. He had not realized this before. Beth was both relieved and at the same time terrified that Pete was finally starting to lead out in their relationship.

He resumed his speech: "I was hoping we could both pray and find out if God wants us to stay friends only or if He is trying to take us beyond that. I...I find myself wondering if He is leading us to something deeper and closer than friendship alone. But...I don't know...maybe you don't want to. Maybe you already know we're friends and *that's it* and if that's how you see it please say so. I would *never* ask you to be more to me than you feel you ought to be."

Beth interrupted him on purpose, partly to comfort him a little with her words.

"Look, I don't '*already know*' that," she clarified. "Pete, I *will* pray about it. If there is *anything* going on in either of our hearts we need to be clear about things so no one gets hurt."

"Yeah," Pete agreed, "we've both been through that before—*too* many times. And we have too much to lose, even just as friends. I couldn't lose you at even that level."

"Me, too," she harmonized with him.

"This is what I think we should pray about," Pete instructed her, taking the lead as he was taught he, the man, should and as Beth had hoped he would. "Courtship—just like your Dad taught about. I believe in that, and all the more in light of my experiences in college. I don't think we should just date, or call each other boyfriend and girlfriend, or just become affectionate—though all those are fine with me—"

Beth betrayed an agreeing smile, perhaps even a subtle nod.

"I know it's a big step but I also think that if we don't believe in what we are doing any more than that, then we should leave well enough alone. If we decide that God *is* leading us further in this friendship then I think we need to admit that—unless He directs otherwise—it would probably, naturally become permanent someday. I mean, if He's directing, well... *He's directing.* What else could we say? I don't want to date someone and just float along waiting for just 'whatever.' I also don't want a relationship that's just a temporary distraction. That's what courtship is, isn't it? You know, something more than dating or 'going out with.'"

He looked to her for confirmation. Her dad was, after all, the late, great exponent on courtship so surely she should know.

"You're right," she affirmed.

"I really, really care about you Beth," he was careful to avoid the "L word" until he would be certain it could be said mutually, though he was sure he was already there. "I care about you in a way that I thought I could never care about someone ever again. My heart has been closed and locked for awhile now so that's a pretty major thing to say. *But* if we are to remain just friends I am okay with that. I'm at peace with my life the way it is right now. It's not ideal but I've accepted it. But if there would be something more should we miss it?"

"No. We shouldn't," she said quietly, thoughtfully, looking out across the glittering snow cover.

"Will you also do this?" he continued to suggest to her, she turned to face him again. "Will you get at least one other person to pray with you and for you about this? I would too. That way it's not just emotions and we would get some outside perspective on this, too."

"I think that's a good idea," she agreed, "In fact Dad would be impressed that you thought of that."

Pete smiled at the thought of Pastor Dan and of his likely approval.

"You *do* realize," Pete examined her, "that if we would court, I would naturally start to include you in my dreams for the future—to even hope for the real possibility of a life with you. I mean...this is *serious*," he emphasized.

"I know. I'll remember that," she assured him.

"And if there is *any* hesitancy in you, *please* don't say 'yes' to a courtship with me. Starting something only to turn around and end it would ruin our friendship. It would be better to not court than to start only to stop again. I need you to be sure and sold out either way."

Pete was deliberately blunt but Beth understood. They both knew what the other had been through in the area of relationships so she understood automatically. She also knew that, of all the women on earth, she should be the last one to treat him wrong; as a man he felt likewise toward her.

"Good," Pete began to wrap up the discussion. "Could we talk about this again maybe after about a week, say...next Saturday? Is that long enough?" he checked with her.

"If I need more time, I'll tell you," she promised.

"Fair enough," he declared. "How about if we have brunch next Saturday at the Diner, around ten-thirty," he suggested. "If we're still talking to each other afterward," he teased, smiling, "we could go to a movie in Elmira or Williamsport, maybe. Until then I'll not say another word about it so there is no pressure on you."

"Okay," she cheerfully replied.

They quickly discussed what the newest movie releases were. Pete would check the show times. The snowplow groaned back through town, going the other way now. They must have been talking for longer than either one thought.

"I better go now," Beth stood up, "I want to be sure Mom is okay."

"How about you?" he looked up at her with genuine concern and interest, "Are *you* okay?"

"Yeah," she said believably. "It's hard, yes. But I'm doing okay with it all. At least now I know that we'll make it. I wasn't so sure back in March," referring to their lunch in Lewistown.

"Good," Pete affirmed. "And I *did* miss you and I *am* glad you're home," he said as he stood up from the bench.

"I missed you too, and I am glad to be home, and you are the main reason why," she said looking him in the eye. Pete blushed inside at the thought that he already meant so much to her.

He walked with her the rest of the way back to the trailer. She stood at the top of the steps, under the small porch and he was at the bottom of the steps, the snow accumulating on his head and on his shoulders.

"Happy New Year," he told her finally, with a smile.

"It is," she smiled back. "You too."

"It is."

"Bye."

"Bye."

Pete walked back across the ever-darkening town. His truck was no longer blocked in and after confirming that the Holts did not need any more help cleaning up, he headed for home, slowly navigating the snow-covered roads leading out of town, especially the steep, winding Narrows.

He was nervous again but glad it was done now. He was not sure if he would sleep at all. But he prayed, even as he drove, and gave it all over to the Lord. He slept well.

Christmas, Wilmor Style

It was a good thing Pete slept so well. The next day, New Year Day, was the traditional Wilmor Christmas. It had been observed ever since the death of Grandma Wilmor.

Joanie had four siblings in New York, all brothers, who also had families of their own: Uncle Harry in Cortland, Uncle Roy in Delphi Falls, Uncle Ralph in New Woodstock, and Uncle Ward in White Plains. Each of them had their own Christmas Day celebration but then the five siblings and their spouses and children gathered at one of the three upstate homes for a dinner together. Every third year everyone went to LC for the gathering. Only Uncle Ward was free from hosting; he and his family lived on the edges of New York City—too far for everyone else to go. There was also a picnic together in either May or June.

There was no time for sleeping in. Pete was back up to the farm at six AM to put hay down for the cattle. Grandpa would watch the farm for the remainder of the day. The family was on the road north at nine AM. The drive took them through Elmira, Ithaca, Dryden, and Cortland. At Ithaca, Cayuga Lake, one of the Finger Lakes, was prominent as they climbed the long hill out of town.

Initially Pete dozed off, tired from the long evening made longer by his talk with Beth. He awoke near downtown Ithaca. Pete's mind was preoccupied by his reflections on that discussion in the gazebo. He tried to think of reasons a courtship would *not* be the right thing to do. He then thought of reasons it *would* be the right thing to do. The latter list was significantly longer than the former, though he tried as hard as possible to be fair and impartial in his thinking. He tried to interpret the meanings in Beth's expressions and statements to him, things like, "You're not the only one," and "I don't 'already know' that." Her expressions were very serious and thoughtful. He knew whatever she decided it would not be a choice made lightly or on a superficial basis. Pete even tried to imagine a few scenes of him and Beth together in a courtship—what they might do, what it might be like, how it would feel. He even imagined what it would be like to kiss her for the first time (but then he scolded himself for thinking about that already). But Pete also imagined Beth turning him down and each scenario thereafter, still friends and no longer friends. The others spoke and listened to the radio but he looked out the window and remained quiet, and then suddenly they were leaving Cortland!

Uncle Harry's home was north of town. Compared to almost anywhere south of there, the snow was deep in Cortland and points north. This was compliments of Lake Ontario and her constant "lake effect" snows. Like

Laingeville Center, it had snowed the day and night before, only much more so, and snowplows had been at work everywhere.

Many of Pete's cousins were not at the dinner. Joanie was the youngest of her siblings so all the other "kids" were older than he was. They were grown and many were married and even had families of their own now. The gathering was now mostly for Joanie's family and her brothers and their wives.

Finally at one-thirty everyone gathered around the dining room table-turned-buffet. Uncle Ward gave thanks. Everyone filled their plates and found a seat in the living room or on the outer edges of the dining room to eat their meal.

Nosey Aunt Carrie asked Pete if he had a girlfriend. He was somewhat put out that the question even came up but tried not to let it show. But Pete's answer aroused the attention of the rest of the Archers. Instead of a simple "no" the reply was "not at this time," combined with a thinly veiled grin. He wanted to keep everything hush-hush but it was not necessarily so easy to do. He hoped no one would ask him anything more specific. He wanted his and Beth's conversation to be confidential, at least until a conclusion had been reached.

Uncle Ralph, thankfully, changed the subject, "So are you hosting in June, Ward?"

Pete was surprised by the question. He asked, "In White Plains?"

"Oh that's right," Ralph said to Pete. "You guys weren't here yet when Ward was showing off his newest purchase."

"I'll show you after dinner," Uncle Ward promised, pointing a forkful of stuffing in Pete's direction.

Pete was confused and mystified until Ward later stood and said, "Archers, come check this out."

John, Joanie, and Pete followed him to a laptop computer. Ward hit the mouse pad and a couple keys. On the screen appeared a rustic-looking cottage surrounded by a grove of trees and a lake or a pond in the background.

"I wanted a place closer to home—an escape from the city, a place to relax, and maybe go hunting or fishing," Ward explained.

"So where is it?" John inquired.

"It's on a small lake or large pond, whichever you please, west of a place called Guilford in Chenango County—the other side of Oxford from here," Ward answered, putting the address into the search engine and bringing up a map pinpointing the location.

He took them through a series of digital photographs showing each side, several interior shots, and a picture of the pond/lake.

"We can have the picnic there in May or June," he offered, "and if anyone needs a summer getaway, it's all yours, if we're not already there ourselves."

Later, everyone was reassembled in the dining room for pumpkin pie, carrot cake, and ice cream. After some conversation over coffee, it was time to leave for home. It was dark as they bundled up and said good bye, promising to see one another "at the lake."

It was still only early evening when the family arrived back at LC. Pete went out to the farm to say "hi" to his grandparents and to see that all was well out in the barn. He hurried home and was asleep by ten.

* * * * * * *

Sunday was odd for both Pete and Beth; the midnight conversation in the gazebo was still only a few days old. Though they greeted one another and sat together in Sunday School, each one knew what the other had on his or her mind, though neither one said a thing about it. They each took turns trying to interpret the other's mannerisms, expressions, and statements. But it was to no avail and it was too soon. Neither one had made a final decision yet but secretly wished the other one had.

Pete kept his word and never said or asked a thing about their discussion, but he sure wanted to! Beth was a blank page to him. He could not figure anything out from her.

On Wednesday, they were in different parts of the church as usual but Pete could not take it any longer. He had to say one thing but still not cross the boundary he himself had drawn for them both. At the end of the evening he approached Beth in the vestibule.

He asked only, "Is Saturday still going to be okay with you?"

"I think so," was her simple reply with no indication what she was thinking. Pete had to go, however. Jim Corbin was waiting for him on the other side of the vestibule.

Discernment

"This doesn't surprise me at all," Pete's mom observed as she, Pete, and John sat at the kitchen table after supper on Saturday, the day after the Wilmor Christmas. "We've both noticed how you two have been getting a lot closer over the past months and we're not the only ones. I have actually had a couple of folks ask me if you two were 'an item'."

"I never realized anyone was keeping track," Pete said, a little shocked and embarrassed.

"It looks like a perfectly natural step to me," she continued with a shrug mixed with a grin. She looked over at John.

"The fact is," John said, "you are a grown man now and the choice is up to you, not us. I'm sure you have our support one hundred percent whatever you two decide. But I personally see no reason why you shouldn't do it." He looked to his wife to confirm that she shared his feeling about it. She nodded, indicating complete harmony with her husband's thinking.

Pete's parents did not offer a lot of guidance but he knew they trusted his decision, which was a good feeling for Pete. It was also good for Pete to hear his dad again affirm him as a 'grown man'."

* * * * * * *

"It's been obvious to me, Beth," Ginny told her daughter as they sat in the living room, also on Saturday night (Beth had already summarized her talk with Pete from back on Thursday night) "that you two definitely need to clarify where this relationship is going. I almost spoke to you about it on a couple different occasions."

She continued, "When your father and I had a big decision to make one thing we always prayed was for God to 'close the doors' if it wasn't His will. That's risky but it also works. If you have to 'break down doors' to get someplace then it probably is not God's will, though there are rare exceptions to that rule. It seems to me, though, that the doors are wide open to you and Pete right now. With all that the Lord has been showing you about your life and your future, combined with what seems to be happening between you two, it seems to be a perhaps obvious and natural conclusion. Pete is a good man. Not perfect mind you, none of us are. I have no objections to him whatsoever but that doesn't make it God's will. It's also not my decision to make; it's yours."

"I prayed like you said already, Mom, for weeks now," Beth replied, "and I have thought about the way God seems to combining everything that's happening maybe into some inevitable conclusion. It looks like the doors keep opening wider and wider. But I'm so afraid that something will happen between us—that we'll break up and have nothing, maybe not even a friendship anymore."

"Remember, Pete is no Rob. But failure is always a risk," Ginny cautioned. "But it is just as risky, or more so, to miss the opportunity of a lifetime when it is right in front of you. What gives you more peace right now: picturing your life *with* Pete or *without* him?"

That almost settled the whole matter right then and there. Beth knew she wanted Pete in her life and had already lost the ability to see it without him. But the issue remained what *role* he would play in that life.

Ginny said forcefully, "If this is God's will and you don't follow Him in it, you likely won't get another chance at it. Be sure you're ready to live a lifetime with the decision you make this week, one way or the other."

"I know," Beth almost whispered.

"Keep praying," Ginny told her, "and I will too. If I think God is telling me something I will be sure to tell you and to keep 'Ginny' out of it."

"Thanks."

* * * * * * *

When Ginny and Beth returned home from Cumberland there was only one message on the answering machine. It was from Dr. Ramsey. He had called the day after Christmas and wanted Beth to return his call "as soon as possible."

The Monday following New Year's Day was the soonest possible from the day Beth received the message. Soon after waking, she called Dr. Ramsey's office. He was with patients, however, and would call her back at lunch time.

"Thanks for calling me back," Dr. Ramsey's voice was very deep and gravelly but had a friendly ring to it.

"I would have called sooner," Beth explained, "but we were out of town and I didn't get your message until New Year's Eve."

"That's fine. I assumed as much when I didn't hear back from you right away." He explained his reason for calling: "Almost a month ago you gave us a copy of your resume and filled out an employment application. Are you still interested in a position here?"

Momentarily reflecting again on Pete's words to her before Thanksgiving and the long talk in the square, she said she still was. Dr. Ramsey explained that he was welcoming a physician's assistant later in the month and a nurse practitioner sometime after that. He needed to hire at least two additional nurses, an LPN and an RN before spring and he was "very interested" in her application. The interview was set for Thursday afternoon.

* * * * * * *

"This is an interesting development," Jim Corbin said as he sat with Pete in the church library after the Wednesday night service, "I feel honored to be consulted by you. So how can I help?"

Pete had already told him about the talk in the gazebo. The friendship between Pete and Beth was already obvious to Jim.

"I want to be sure I'm in the Lord's will," Pete answered, "I know what I feel, what I think, but that's not enough to know it's right and best. I believe we need to get outside ourselves—me and Beth—to know we're being as objective as possible."

"I see," he replied with great interest, "that seems wise but what do you *believe* God's will is? What does faith tell you?"

"I believe He is leading in this way or I wouldn't have brought it up. All the evidence is pointing this way. I just want to be very sure. I've been wrong before and," Pete's voice cracked with emotion, "I don't think I'm up to another heartache."

"I understand," Jim affirmed and he did. He was there through the heartbreaks Pete had experienced. "There is a Biblical way to make a major decision. The Apostles used it in Acts Chapter 1. Do you know what I'm talking about?"

"I think so," Pete's reply was somewhat tentative, "the choosing of Matthias to take Judas' place?"

"Exactly. Let's look at that," Jim recommended, opening his Bible and flipping the pages to the Book of Acts.

"First there was an occasion or need to make a decision. Back then it was Judas' open spot among the Apostles but for you it's that you're at a point in life when people typically choose their mates and you have a person in your life that is becoming special or unique to you.

Second, the decision wasn't made in isolation. Too many people, too many Christians, do that—keep everything 'private.' Verse fifteen says their decision was made in 'the midst of the disciples'—the church. So you're doing the right thing being involved in the Body of Christ and looking to others for help with your decision.

Third, the Holy Spirit had been speaking and working even before the need became apparent. We see that in verse sixteen. It would appear that He has been at work here, too, to analyze the happenings between you two.

Next, they looked to the Scriptures for guidance in verse twenty. The Bible teaches us that marriage is the normal pattern for most people and dating or, in your case courtship, is, for most, the path to marriage.

Fifth, they determined ahead of time what the qualifications for a new Apostle had to be in verses twenty-one and twenty-two. Beth certainly meets all the criteria I know but only you know if she meets *your* unique criteria, in addition to the obvious things of Scripture.

Sixth in, verse twenty-three, they considered the possibilities, in their case Justus and Matthias, were the one who met the criteria. You have been considering the possibilities to some extent since you became a teenager and now you have Beth to consider. The obvious difference, though, is that you get to look at the candidates only one at a time.

Next in verses twenty-four and twenty-five they prayed about it. No doubt you've been doing that and I will too. God *does* answer prayer!

Then in verse twenty-six they sought to surrender control of the situation to the Lord by casting lots. You just need to be sure you are not manipulating or forcing this in either direction because of emotions or fear of living single or fear of failure.

Finally, in that same verse, it came down to one pick so they embraced the pick and moved forward from there. There is no indication they ever regretted the choice they made that day. You realize this is largely the process we used when we determined Pastor Baker was to be our next pastor. And we used it when we called Pastor Jackson, and, I might add, Pastor Morton."

Jim wrote the chapter and verse references and the major points on the back of a church bulletin as he spoke.

"Take some time to review whether you have satisfied these steps and if you have, then I think the answer will be right there in front of your face—maybe literally; *embrace it*!" he said, leaning forward a little with a grin and a wink.

* * * * * * *

"Oh this is so exciting, Beth!" Meredith Holt happily exclaimed, that hint of a southern accent still apparent after all these years.

"But why am I so nervous then?" Beth wondered out loud, as they drank tea at Meredith's kitchen table earlier on Wednesday.

"Well, it's a major decision and they are always nerve-wracking and the devil is always trying to get us to second guess God's will for us—just ask Eve about that. Trust me. You don't want the Enemy to prevail in this situation!" Meredith warned.

"That's what concerns me and I just don't want to make a shipwreck of this friendship either."

"I understand, dear," she assured Beth, putting her hand on top of Beth's. "It was a similar experience for me when I had to decide to choose Fred as my one and only."

"But how can I know for sure this is of God and not just wishful thinking or emotions," Beth begged to know.

Meredith began sharing with Beth from God's Word and from her own experience as a seasoned Christian woman:

> "There is a commonly used passage of Scripture that helps a lot, if we appreciate its meaning and application. It is Proverbs 3 verses five and six: 'Trust in the Lord with all your heart, and lean not on your own understanding; in all your ways acknowledge Him and He shall direct your paths.' Make sure you are fulfilling these statements: Trust Him. Allow Him to do something that surprises you, like falling in love with Peter Archer—something you *weren't* looking for. Give Him first place in everything. If you are doing those things then He promises to give direction to your life's pathway. But what I find is that God kind of rolls your pathway out just as you are ready to take the next step. What I see in your case is that God has been doing just that in yours and Pete's lives. Your pathway is emerging right before you and *already* blending with his. The question remains, in what way are they blending, exactly? Maybe the question you are really asking is not 'Which way do I go?' What you may really be asking is, 'Should I *stay* on the pathway God is already unveiling right before my eyes?' Think about that, and pray for a confirmation in your spirit that this is right. But I suspect that it probably is."

Beth observed to Meredith, "You know in 'my understanding' I would never have even given Pete a second look. He's a farmer and a fireman, settled in one place. I know nothing of that life. I could have seen myself with a pastor, a doctor, or a missionary. But now my heart is drawn in a way I might *never* have chosen."

"That's God, dear," Meredith said, "He's taking you beyond your expectations, beyond what you would have limited yourself to, like when I married a yank and moved north with him. Beth there is something else too. Have you thought what it would be like to have a family with Pete someday."

"Not really," she responded blushing, the very thought was taking her well past any ways she had ever thought of Pete before.

"Well, if you do this and it works out, you're likely going to have and raise children with Pete. It's not just about you two. I guarantee the subject will come up and you will have to talk about it and account for that in your dreams, in your plans."

"I'll think about that too, then," Beth agreed.

"You should but not *too* much," Meredith winked. Beth blushed.

That evening when Pete went over to Jim and began to talk to him Beth looked across the room at him. She studied him and thought, *what would our children look like?* But she also finally took note that he was handsome, strong, fit, godly, sensitive and thoughtful. The realization was that he was indeed *attractive* to her; she had never actually thought about it before.

She overheard Jim say, "I'll see you in the library, then, Pete."

Just before Pete followed Jim to the library he hesitated. He found he *wanted* to just *see* Beth for a moment. Saturday would take so long to arrive. She was speaking to one of the children from Clubs. She was so good with that child. She would be a wonderful mother one day. He noticed also how truly beautiful she was, her smile, her long red hair; there was nothing about her that was not beautiful to him. But he carefully minded what he thought. While they might choose a pathway that would lead them to look at each other in another new way, that was not what he should focus on now and so he did not. Beth stood up from speaking with the girl and noticed Pete. She smiled at him and he at her. Then he went to the library to meet Jim.

* * * * * * *

"Thanks for taking time to meet with me, Elizabeth," Dr. Ramsey greeted her in his office with a handshake on Thursday. "Is it all right if I call you by your first name?"

"Yes," she replied, "but I generally go by just 'Beth'."

"Beth it is then," he agreed as he walked behind his desk and motioned for her to take one of the chairs across from him. "And here comes the brains of the outfit," gesturing toward the open door, "Beth, this is Helen, my head nurse. She'll be joining us for this interview."

Beth stood and Helen reached her hand out to shake Beth's.

"Glad to meet you," Beth greeted Helen.

"Likewise," Helen replied with a smile.

This was the most sophisticated interview Beth had ever been to. There were questions about her experience and training, about her knowledge of privacy laws and some "what would you do if…" scenarios. Dr. Ramsey let Helen ask a few of the questions also. The job description was reviewed as well. It felt like the interview was nearing a conclusion. This was confirmed when Dr. Ramsey said, "very well, then."

A tingle went through Beth's stomach when Dr. Ramsey continued, "But let me be honest with you…" Beth knew this was not a positive sign. She had dared to hope in something becoming clear, about maybe getting this position but obviously it was just a set up for more disappointment. Dr. Ramsey continued talking, "Coming in to this interview today you were about the top contender for this particular position."

Were, Beth thought.

"And you still are, but you need to know a few things first."

"Okay," Beth said relieved but still concerned over what kinds of "things" she needed to know.

"First, you could make a lot more working some place else so if you want a lot of money, this is not where you belong." He wrote a dollar figure on a piece of paper and handed it to her.

"That's fine," she responded. It actually looked huge to a young nursing school graduate hoping to take her first fulltime position. But she also knew it was clearly below average and less than she would have made in Lewistown.

Dr. Ramsey added, "That does not include health plan, retirement, continuing education, vacation, and so on." Now it sounded even better to her.

He explained, "We care for a lot of economically disadvantaged folks here, folks on Medicare and Medicaid or with no insurance at all. Quite frankly I could pay more if I didn't consider their situations. An opportunity you would have here, too, if you chose it, is to participate in a once-a-year medical mission trip."

Beth almost cried on the spot: medical…mission!

"It is voluntary, of course, and does count against your vacation time and time off since not everybody wants to do that sort of thing."

Beth found a way to say, "I would be *very* interested in doing that."

"That's good to hear though I can't let it sway my hiring decision," he cautioned.

"I understand."

"You should also know that if you come to work here that I am looking for long-term commitment, not passers-through on the way to something bigger, though you're obviously free to do as you wish with your future."

"If I come here it will be for the foreseeable future. If I had any doubt about that I would not accept a position here."

"Okay," he concluded. "You were my last interview. The others were in last week. I'll call you as soon as I have decided. Thanks again for your time." Dr. Ramsey stood, came around his desk and shook hands with Beth.

* * * * * * *

When Beth came home from the Ericsons' on Friday a note on the door read: "Call Dr. Ramsey." The anticipation and uncertainty almost made her sick.

"He's with a patient," Helen said, "I'll have him call you after that appointment. He won't need to speak with you for long."

"Won't need to speak...long." What could that mean? It couldn't possibly be a positive sign. But Beth tried to keep an open mind. So she planned ahead for the potential answer of yes. Tomorrow she and Pete would meet and decide what they were going to do. If Dr. Ramsey wanted to hire her, she would take that as a further confirmation that she should say "yes" to Pete but even if Dr. Ramsey did not hire her she *still* knew her answer to Pete. But she would need to ask Dr. Ramsey for the weekend to answer him if he wanted to hire her; she hoped he would understand. If Pete had changed his mind, Beth would decline the position and move on.

The phone rang. Beth answered it instantly.

"Hi Beth, this is William Ramsey," the deep voice said, "How are you today?"

"Fine. Thanks."

"Good. I want to let you know that you are my first choice and the RN job is yours if you want it, so what do you think?"

"I hope you understand," she prepared him; "I am inclined to accept your offer but I need a couple days first. If I promise to say one way or the other first thing Monday morning, may I have the weekend? And it's not about another job; it's a personal matter."

"Okay," he conceded after a brief pause, "but be certain you call before lunch. I need to either hire the next in line or tell them the position is filled. They deserve to know as soon as possible."

"I promise. You will know by eight AM Monday."

"Very well, then, I'll be awaiting your call."

Any lingering doubt was completely erased from Beth's mind now. She would say yes to Pete. She just hoped that the intervening week or so had not caused him to change his mind. Beth longed for something to become clear. Within twenty-four hours things might be clearer than ever or the uncertainty would be renewed, intensified, and continue indefinitely.

The Decision, Part 1

Saturday finally came. At one and the same time it seemed it would never arrive but also that it arrived far too soon for Pete. Something would definitely change today but in what direction—for happiness or for heartache? Would Pete and Beth forever regret the week that had just passed or always be thankful for it? Was it all a set-up for devastation—a kind of self-inflicted injury? Would it signal just another transient season in life—that it would be just another relationship that would come and eventually go, like the others before it?

Pete could hardly sleep Friday night as the snow sifted down from the sky. While he felt a personal assurance that this step should be taken, he had also been hurt and disappointed so many times. He didn't see how he could weather another letdown or, even worse, another false start.

"Why," he wondered aloud to himself in his room, "did I even bring it up? I should have just played it safe and never said anything."

He knew if they chose courtship and it failed later on he might lose a great friend, one he needed, and be lonelier than ever. If they chose to remain friends, just the discussion they had in the gazebo will have changed their friendship in some way already. But what if they agreed together to a courtship...? What blessing might lie ahead that would have otherwise been left untapped?

But he knew what *he* needed to say; he had to be honest. He prayed (again) for strength, for the right words, and for grace for both of them and for their friendship should she not say the same thing he did.

Beth was having the same struggle as she awoke and prepared for the day. There had been too much pain in her life already. The life she knew just a year ago was a distant memory. Could she knowingly risk this dear friendship or should she just play it safe and remain with the familiar she now knew? But "the talk" was inevitable and necessary now; it was unavoidable. The boundaries of this relationship needed to be defined as either where they had been so far, or as much, much wider than ever before. Taking Pete's offer of a courtship would result in the complete exchange of her dream. But the old dream was dead already anyhow. Surely this must be the new one God was giving her.

When Pete came into the Diner, Beth was waiting near the register for him and greeted him with her usual "hi" and predictable smile. Both were bundled up against the cold and the overnight snow. The waitress took them to a booth at the south end; it was a good place for them. The north end was where it seemed their friendship began to stretch and grow that evening in November but it was also where that other pain-filled talk had been with Lauren—the most heartbreaking of all for Pete. The south end was free of memories—a "blank slate" for a new start.

They acted completely normal toward one another, like nothing unusual was going on that day. They greeted the waitress, ordered their drinks, looked over the menus, discussed their preferences, and ordered. They talked about just the usual things that any two friends might discuss. The orders came rather quickly. Pete gave thanks for both of their meals and they began to eat.

But Pete could not do it. He couldn't bring it up—not yet, but when? But he would have to. If he did not pursue the subject what would Beth think of him and how would he feel about himself afterward? That would only make things more awkward and confusing than ever. He forced himself to eat just to present a normal front. Beth, however, just picked at her food, too nervous to eat. Pete observed this and silently theorized as to all the dreadful things that it could signify. Maybe she could not find the words to say "no" to him. What if he did not follow through? Pete had no idea that she needed him to be clear because of the answer due to Dr. Ramsey come Monday morning.

The waitress took the plates, left the bills, and refilled the drinks. There was no easy way to do this so he might as well just jump in, strange though it may seem. Pete knew Beth would wait for him to take the initiative. That was her way, her belief; it was his too.

"So…" Pete started, "…have you thought about what we discussed on New Year's?" He felt like he was asking the doctor, "So is it cancer?" he had such a knot in his stomach.

"Yes I have," Beth said flatly, putting her drink down, not even looking him in the eye.

"Do you know your answer yet or do you need more time?" he examined her while inwardly he silently pleaded, *please say you need more time.*

"Yes, I know my answer. Do you know yours?" She looked at him. Her face betrayed no particular emotion.

"I do," he replied and continued, "So who goes first?"

She corrected him, "You mean who's going to stick their neck out first."

"I guess you could look at it that way," he admitted. Taking the coward's way out he invoked chivalry and said, "Well, ladies first."

"Thanks a lot," was her matter-of-fact reply, "but I suppose someone has to go first. Pete," she began, "you're a wonderful friend…"

Oh no, he thought, *here it comes—the "friend talk." Why did I do this? She's going to say 'no' and this whole relationship is going to come unraveled now.*

229

"Our friendship," she continued, "means so much to me. You've been such a comfort to me and to Mom. I would *never* want anything to ruin that."

"Beth…" Pete started but she said sharply, "please just hear me out, Pete."

"Okay," he resigned, sitting back. He could feel the tears getting ready to flow but he would not cry in front of her. That would not be right.

"I must admit," Beth restarted, "that I had already asked myself many of the same questions you asked me on New Year's Day. So I had already thought about it and prayed about it quite a bit. I had formed some tentative conclusions even before we spoke. This week I prayed. I talked to Mom and to Meredith and asked them to pray too. I mean everything is on the line here. In myself I don't know if I want safety or to take the risk. We have something special *right now*, Pete. I have been forced to ask like never before, 'what does God want?' That's what I've always been taught to ask and what you wanted me to ask—and I appreciate that about you Pete, your sensitivity to God's will in things, over anything else. I have done a lot of soul-searching for a month or so already. But no matter what, God's will is always the best, safest place to be, even if you don't understand it. So to make a long story short…" Pete felt sick for the thought of what he just knew was coming next. "…if your offer still stands," she began to light up a little and maybe blush a bit, "I *will* accept your invitation."

Pete carefully covered up his emotions. He wanted to jump up and dance a jig (whatever that was) right there in the middle of the Diner but he remained stoic, barely nodding his head. He took another sip of coffee. His heart pounded and he could hardly breathe; he wondered if she could tell.

Now it was Beth's turn to feel sick with anticipation mixed with fear. *What if he has had second thoughts?* She wondered to herself, *What if I got excited about this only to be crushed? Might I look like a fool now? What about Dr. Ramsey? What about the future now? What if he changed his mind and now says "yes" just to protect me?*

"Well," he began, "since I brought it up I have continued to pray about it. I talked with my folks and with Jim Corbin. I, too, have searched my soul and tried to trace God's hand in all of this. I don't want to make a decision based on emotion, good or bad, or fear, or wreck the relationship we have right now. I couldn't take another lost relationship. So I have concluded that…" he paused and tried to stay unanimated "…that it *is* God's will for us. And I am *excited* about it!"

They both smiled and laughed slightly; Beth wiped a tiny tear from one eye as Pete chided her, "Now don't do *that* or you'll have me going too."

"So it's official," she sought final confirmation. "We're courting now?"

He looked her right in the eye and said, "It's official. We're courting now." He was grinning from ear to ear.

"I'm glad," she affirmed through one of her big, bright smiles.

He looked at her seriously and said firmly but tenderly, "Me too."

He took her hand ever so gently in his—just his fingers holding hers actually. This was something that had never been done between them before this day. The waitress who was working the night the two of them closed down the Diner back in early November noticed and elbowed Ray, the owner, tilting her head toward Pete and Beth's booth. His eyes glittered and he nodded his head approvingly as he mumbled, "'bout time."

After a moment or two Beth spoke up, "So...when am I allowed to see this farm of yours up close?"

"No time like the present," Pete answered. "The movie starts at either one or four so we can go out there a spell and still be in Elmira by four o'clock."

They got up from their seats. He helped her with her coat and as she finished bundling up he took the two bills to the register and paid them, instructing the waitress that "the next time it would be just *one* bill."

The Decision, Part 2

It was very cold that day and since it had snowed the night before, the land was blanketed afresh with a blinding white cover. But it was only a couple of inches worth so people mostly just brushed it off their cars, walks, and driveways and went about their usual business. The tell-tale sound of snowplows scraping the blacktopped roads was short-lived that morning. The snow still lay almost completely undisturbed around the farm, except for Pete's tracks from earlier in the morning. The relatively few cows could be kept in the barn now so even the barnyard was pristine, pure, and white.

Grandpa was walking back from the mailbox when Pete and Beth pulled into the driveway. Pete's pickup truck was white, not with snow, but now with road salt splashed up during the drive over from Colsonburg.

Pulling up alongside the house and getting out of the truck, Pete called to Grandpa, "This is Beth. I'm just showing her around the farm."

"If you have time, come in for coffee after," was Grandpa's reply.

"Hopefully we'll have time," Pete answered cautiously.

Because of the snow, the driveway and the yard were almost indistinguishable from each other. Fortunately the ground was frozen solid so mud was not a problem. Both wore their heavy winter coats and gloves. Pete wore a cap with the earflaps extended down. Beth wore a dark ski hat, her long red hair flowing out from beneath its side and back edges and down over the matching scarf that was wrapped loosely around her throat.

Brown fence posts and lines of bare trees bordering the fields stood in contrast to the bright snow. Pete stood below the barn and pointed up the slowly rising hill, describing to Beth how he had been reorganizing the land to fit his model of farming. Beth did not understand most of it but listened and nodded with the occasional "okay" or "oh" to show she was trying to keep up with his enthusiasm for the farm.

Determining that he was at least close to done educating her about alfalfa, rotational grazing, and the pros and cons of grass-fed, grain-fed, and grain-finished beef, Beth asked him, "Do you have cows in the barn?"

"Sure do," was Pete's happy reply. "Wanna see 'em?"

"Yeah!" she sounded almost like a kid coming to a farm for the first time, she was so anxious to see them.

As they started toward the barn, Pete reached down with his right hand and, allowing it to "bump into" her left hand, he took it gently into his. She accepted this gesture very willingly. But even though it was new, it was so very natural—as if they had been doing it for years.

The handholding did not escape Grandma's attention. As she stood at the sink drying dishes she called to Grandpa, "Jack, come take a look at this!"

"At what?" was his curt reply. But after he made his way to the window over the sink he let the words, "Well, I'll be" just tumble out of his mouth.

"How about that..." Grandma said with pleasure in her almost singing voice, her face shining in its characteristic way.

Pete showed Beth the young heifers and calves. Some, the Holsteins, were the ones he had kept from Grandpa's herd and the younger ones he had purchased as calves when he had sold some of the older ones. The younger generation was all Polled Herefords. This led to a lecture about Holsteins versus Herefords versus Angus breeds and why Pete reckoned the Herefords the best for his purposes and how he did not want to hear anything about "one hundred percent pure Angus."

All the Holsteins, he explained, were destined for the auction or the butcher (Holsteins do make for good beef, by the way). The brown Herefords with their white faces were mostly to breed a new herd with most of the next generation going to the auction or butcher, too.

The cows watched them and many approached the gate that was across the doorway. Pete patted a couple of them on the snout and between the eyes. Beth tried to also but the cows startled and backed off, suspiciously watching this new person from a safe distance. Pete warned Beth not to get attached to them because many would be in someone's freezer sooner rather than later.

"Poor things," she mourned.

It was so cold they were ready to go inside for coffee when Beth asked, "Is that your rental house?"

"Sure is."

"Can we see it?" Beth wondered to him.

"If you want to but I have to warn you, it's a construction zone inside," he answered her.

"Is it safe?"

"Yeah, it's safe," Pete responded, "just not a pretty sight."

"That's okay with me," Beth shrugged.

So getting back in the truck, Pete took them down the lane that ran parallel to the fence line to the rear of the barn and the soon-to-be rental, almost ten acres' lengths to the south. The tires cut a fresh set of tracks in the shallow snow.

The rental was actually built relatively low to the ground and almost square in its dimensions. The upstairs windows were tucked in under the roof line on the gable ends and in a pair of low-pitched shed-roofed dormers, one facing toward the front and the other toward the rear. Most of the windows were in pairs, one double hung window set alongside another. The windows were six-on-ones—six small panes on the top half and one large pane on the bottom half. On the first floor the gable ends had one pair of windows in the front half of the wall and another pair in the back half with a chimney running up the center on the north end. On the south-facing side a door was set in the middle of the two pairs of windows. On the back side three pairs of windows were equally spaced along the wall between the foundation and the eve.

The front of the house was divided into thirds. There was one pair of windows in the left third and one pair in the right third. The middle third was a shallow porch that was set about four or five feet back from the rest of the front wall with the main roof extending all the way down to cover it so that the eve was one continuous line from left to right. The front-facing dormer was above and behind the porch with a pair of windows centered in it between its own eve and the main roof below. Whoever built that house could easily have had one continuous front wall but instead chose to have a well-sheltered porch nestled in the middle. On the recessed wall that was the back of the porch there was a door in the middle with just a single window centered on the wall on each side of it.

The north gable had two single windows each situated on one side of the chimney. The south gable had a double window centered under the peak. The rear dormer matched the one on the front.

Some of the snow had slid from the metal roof which was made of green corrugated steel. The old wooden Dutch lap siding was severely weathered to a grey-brown color with peeling white paint remaining only in the most sheltered areas. The windows, too, were the old wooden sashes, worn grey by the years of harsh weather; several panes were cracked or even broken.

Inside it was as cold as it was outside. All the walls were stripped of their lath and plaster; nothing but two-by-four wall frames with a door opening here and there were left. The diagonal board sheathing visible on the exterior walls showed the house to be sixty or seventy years old, maybe slightly more. The floors were hardwood but severely worn and scratched with other damage besides; one spot had a severe burn mark. The light, reflected off the snow, poured in through the windows from every direction.

The two of them walked through the first floor. Pete described where the kitchen, dining room, living room, and other rooms had been located. They did not go upstairs but he pointed up at the still intact ceiling to show where each of the bedrooms were located up there. But the building was just a shell now. Pete had even removed the wiring back to the circuit breaker panel that Grandpa had installed when he first bought the place, replacing the old fuse box. Beth commented on the hardwood floors and how much she had loved the hardwood floors in the house back in Compact.

"Did you ever consider living here?" Beth asked inquisitively.

"Not really," Pete replied flatly. A tinge of disappointment went through Beth when she heard that.

Pete continued, "I need the money from renting it and what does someone like me need with a house like this? I mean, there are nine rooms in this place."

They stepped out on the front porch for a minute or two and Beth noticed the view for the first time. It was calm and quiet. They were standing just above the rooftops of snow-blanketed Laingeville Center, only about a half mile or so away. Two white steeples poked up from the bare trees and the brick school stood on the opposite hill. State Road stretched out toward Colsonburg and Lainge's Creek meandered through the snow and among the homes. A mixture of farmland and forests made a quilt-like pattern of the rolling land. Smoke rose gently from most of the chimneys, giving a warm feeling to the cold January day. Beth tried to imagine what this view might look like in the other seasons of the year, especially fall. Pete pointed out his family's home on the further side of the village, as well as Holmes' Market, the Post Office, and the Fire House.

"It's beautiful," Beth whispered.

There was not much time to visit but Pete took Beth into the farmhouse made toasty warm by the coal-fueled fire in the furnace and introduced her to his grandparents who restrained themselves from saying or asking anything about their relationship. After a quick snack of homemade ginger snap cookies with coffee and cocoa, they were on their way back to Colsonburg, then north to Elmira.

* * * * * * *

In the truck on the way back to Colsonburg Beth finally told Pete, "I have some news I've been meaning to tell you about all day."

"What's that?"

"I took your advice about Dr. Ramsey and left an application there after Thanksgiving. I think I told you about that at the time. He called for an interview and it was on Thursday. I was the last one he met. He called yesterday to offer me the job!"

"Well you're a good one for secrets!" Pete said very surprised, "Did you accept it?"

"It all came together this week. All I have to do is call him on Monday to accept the position," she explained. "I didn't want to add any more topics to your mind this past week or else I would have said something."

"Wow! That's wonderful! What a surprise," Pete exclaimed.

"I didn't accept it the second he called because I wanted to be sure about us first—that you hadn't changed your mind about me. If you had I was going to say 'no,' but now I know that my place is here."

Pete was flattered beyond words. He could only say it again, "Wow." Beth's decision was a huge affirmation of her commitment to him and God's purpose in their lives.

"I wouldn't have changed my mind about you," he finally said, thoughtfully.

"I just wanted to hear you say it," she replied, setting her hand on his as it rested on the gear shift preparing for a downshift as they entered the Narrows.

"When will you start?" he asked.

Beth laughed at herself and admitted, "You know, I don't even know. I didn't even think to ask! But anytime is fine as long as I can give the Ericsons a fair notice."

* * * * * * *

It was almost ten o'clock when Pete and Beth pulled up to the trailer. After the movie they had gone for burgers and then walked around the mall for a time.

It was bitter cold now. As they spoke the steam from their mouths seemed to freeze in mid-air, one puff joining the one before, building up into a cloud. The thermometer on the porch post read something just slightly below zero. This time Pete walked with Beth up onto the porch where the light was on for her.

"May I walk you to church tomorrow?" he requested.

"That would be nice," was her quiet, soft reply.

"I'll see you at eight forty-five, then," Pete said.

"I'll be ready," she promised.

As he told her good night he bent toward her and kissed her softly on the cheek. Now many will view his kiss as weak or lame but Pete now knew that affection only grows, so best to start slow and simple lest things progress too quickly and lead to struggles and problems down the road. He hoped she appreciated it. A warm smile from her indicated Beth's approval and filled Pete with relief that it had neither been too much nor too little but just right for this first evening together on their first real date as a couple, but also in light of the weeks and months, even years, leading up to that moment. Beth did appreciate his restrained but genuine show of affection toward her. It felt good and safe and like a beginning, which it was indeed.

"Good night," she said with a blushing smile.

"Good night," he replied in kind.

She turned and went inside, finding her mom asleep in the recliner, under an afghan. Ginny quickly stirred awake and asked Beth about the day.

* * * * * * *

Pete was tired and needed to get some sleep. Tomorrow was going to be an early start in order to be ready for church and to spend time with Beth later. When his parents asked how his day had gone he only affirmed that it went "very well," and then excused himself to his room. John and Joanie were pleased and anxious to hear more but respected his need to get to bed.

Going upstairs to his room, Pete kneeled at the side of his bed and thanked God for it all—that day and all that had led him and Beth to this point. Changing into his sleep pants and brushing his teeth he crawled into bed and took up his Bible to read another chapter or two from Hebrews. He slept soundly this time.

* * * * * * *

It was eight forty-three when Pete drove right past the church. It was not unusual for him to drive to church by himself but to those who happened to see him go on by it was somewhat confusing.

By eight fifty Pete and Beth appeared on the sidewalk along Main Street, bundled up against the sub-zero cold, steam from their breath apparent as they talked. They were holding hands in the middle and each one carried their Bible in the available outer hand.

In the church kitchen Pete poured a coffee and Beth made herself a hot chocolate, much like usual. The handholding had stopped when they entered the door of the church—it was for them, not for others, not for display. Their relationship would not become a show for everyone to watch. But they had already been spotted by many and the word was spreading through the church faster than a wildfire.

"So what's up with you guys," Deanne prodded in her usual sneering tone, as they all took their seats for class.

"What do you *think*?" Beth asked back, grinning.

"Well it looks *to me* like a decision has been made," observed Jim Corbin, smiling with approval in Pete's direction.

"Yes, a decision *has* been made," Pete affirmed, smiling at Beth who smiled back at him.

The end of Part 2

Epilogue: Good Night

Pete had lunch with Beth and Ginny. Then Beth changed clothes and Pete drove them out to L.C. Beth visited with the rest of the Archers while Pete went upstairs and changed into his work clothes. The two went up to the farm to put hay down for the cows. It was a very new kind of experience for Beth but an important, if tiny, glimpse into Pete's life as a farmer.

With the exception of holding hands, the two were still somewhat reserved in their affection toward one another as they navigated this awkward but exciting transition from friendship to courtship. They simply enjoyed being around each other. In fact, up to that point, they had never enjoyed being around each other more than they did that day.

Back down in L.C. they each enjoyed a slice of one of Joanie's homemade apple pies. Then Pete was back upstairs changing. After the drive to Colsonburg there was just enough time for Beth to change before the evening service where Pete again joined Beth and Ginny in their usual pew.

* * * * * * *

It was freezing cold again as the two of them sat close to one another on the steps outside the trailer. They just wanted to be alone again for a few minutes before the busy week would begin tomorrow.

"It's really funny how things can work out isn't it?" Pete thought out loud.

"How do you mean?" Beth asked curiously, looking into his eyes.

"Well, there was a time when you totally hated me," he explained.

Smiling she retorted, "Well, you *deserved* it. You were so mean, calling me all those names."

"I know," he acknowledged. "I'm sorry for all that."

"Ancient history now," she assured him. Then she asked, "What was that you used to call me?'

"Ketchup head?"

"No, the other one."

Thinking for a moment he then said, "Spot?"

"Yeah," Beth affirmed, "Spot."

It was quiet a moment.

"Say it again?" she requested, leaning the side of her face on the top of his shoulder.

"Spot?"

"Yeah, but not like a question."

"Hi-ya, Spot," he teased softly, gently.

They both laughed.

"Good night, Pete," she said. Then she it was who shyly gave him a quick kiss on his cheek and it was he who smiled back at her.

Before Pete could respond any further she was standing and heading for the door. It was nice that she showed the initiative that time, even if it was again only a relatively small gesture. It was enough though. They had plenty of time to let it grow. They had their personal commitment to one another and that was all they needed right now. Each one knew what they now meant to the other.

"Good night," he affirmed back over his shoulder. "See you tomorrow evening," he thought to add.

"See you then," she agreed before shutting the door behind her.

After sitting on that step for a moment more, Pete stood up and walked over to his truck. Once again he thanked God for everything He was doing in all their lives.

Endnotes

[1]Reprinted from *The Pastor's Handbook (NIV Edition)*, copyright©2001 by Zur Ltd. Used by permission of WingSpread Publishers, a division of Zur Ltd., 800.233.4443. p. 167

[2]Ibid. p. 168

[3]Ibid. p. 167

[4]In recent years much has been written by various authors on the subject of courtship. I suppose the watershed volume (in my opinion) was *I Kissed Dating Goodbye* by Joshua Harris, written in 1997. As a pastor I would (and do) indeed recommend any of Harris' books or similar volumes to young persons, parents, pastors, or youth pastors. However most of my own views on courtship were already in place by January 1, 1992 when I first proposed such an arrangement with my dear friend Angela Miller (now my wife of almost twenty years) whom I originally met in late August of 1985. I no longer remember where all the input to those ideas came from. Folks like Mr. Harris definitely affirmed and solidified my views after the fact. I assure you the points made in this chapter are my own views, now updated for the twenty-first century. I actually referred to my own teaching outline (written for teens) called "Pure Romance" when I wrote this chapter, not to mention my (our) own experience. This subject of courtship will re-emerge later in the book and many chapters "press" toward it in either a positive or negative sense. Ultimately my goal is to promote courtship over the typical dating or "going out with" scenario. I do so not out of dogmatism or legalism but as an alternative presented out of genuine concern for the hearts of our young people which are so easily broken and scarred by the contemporary dating approach and its innumerable liabilities. You are obviously free to take it or leave it as you wish.

[5] Words and music 1908 by C. Austin Miles. Public Domain.

[6] Ibid.